HEART BOND

HEART BOND

AN ELVEN ALLIANCE COMPANION COLLECTION

TARA GRAYCE

HEART BOND

An Elven Alliance Companion Collection

Elven Alliance Book 8

Copyright © 2023 by Tara Grayce

Taragrayce.com

Published by Sword & Cross Publishing

Grand Rapids, MI

Sword & Cross Publishing and the Sword & Cross Publishing logo are trademarks. Absence of ™ in connection with Sword & Cross Publishing does not indicate an absence of trademark protection of those marks.

Cover Illustration by Sara Morello

www.deviantart.com/samo-art

Peril and Inventor artwork also by Sara Morello

Typography by Deranged Doctor Designs

Derangeddoctordesign.com

Map by Savannah Jezowski of Dragonpen Designs

Dragonpenpress.com

To God, my King and Father. Soli Deo Gloria

LCCN: 2023906537

ISBN: 978-1-943442-41-6

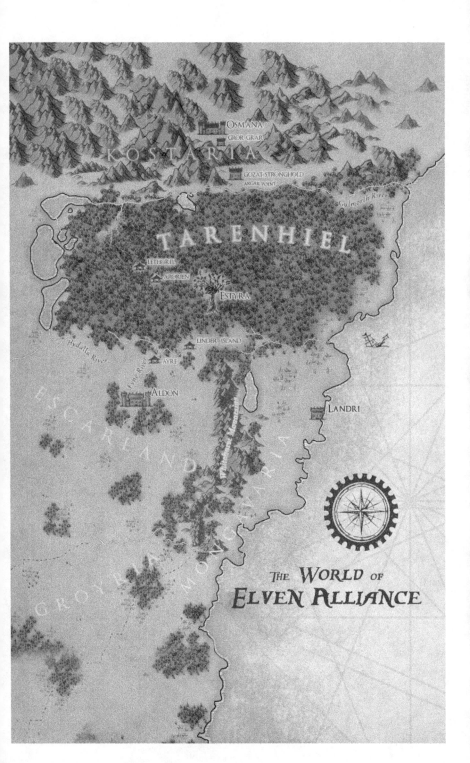

THE WORLD OF
ELVEN ALLIANCE

KING OF
ESCARLAND

" I won't be gone long." Averett's father gave him a hug, and Avie didn't pull away, even though he was twelve years old and starting to get a little old for hugs.

But his father was going to visit the battlefields of their stalled war with the elves, and if ever there was a time for hugs, this would be it.

Not that Avie was worried. His father would be fine. He wouldn't go anywhere near the fighting. He was, after all, the king of Escarland. His security team, the generals, and pretty much everyone would make sure he was kept well away from any active fighting.

His father straightened, resting his hands briefly on Avie's shoulders. "Look after your siblings while I'm gone."

Avie straightened his spine and nodded. He would be the man of the house—well, castle—while his father was away. "I will."

His father's dark brown eyes softened. His brown hair

curled slightly, even cut as short as it was, while his beard was close-cropped.

He turned to the rest of Avie's siblings, giving each of them hugs and ending with Essie who, at five, was crying and begging their father not to go.

Maybe Avie's throat was getting a bit choked too. But he wasn't going to admit it to anyone.

Father kissed Mother goodbye, glanced at them all one last time, and exchanged one last farewell. Then he climbed into the waiting carriage, which would take him to the train station at the far side of Aldon.

While construction had begun, the private train station inside the gates of Winstead Palace wasn't complete. Avie had spent many an afternoon with his siblings, hiding and watching the workers as they leveled the ground, spread the gravel, and carefully created a new gate in the outer wall.

Three weeks. His father was only going to be gone for three weeks. Everything was going to be fine.

NOTHING WAS FINE.

Avie sat at the end of Essie's bed, huddled close to Julien next to him. Their mother held Essie in her arms as Essie sobbed, while seven-year-old Edmund leaned into her other side.

Not that Essie was the only one crying. Avie was trying really hard not to cry. He was the oldest. He needed to be strong for his mother and siblings.

Look after your siblings. It was the last thing Avie had promised his father. His father was dead, but he would still keep that promise no matter what it took.

He was now king.

How was he supposed to be king? He was twelve years old.

He would have a regent, of course. He'd learned about such things from his tutors. He'd never thought he'd need one. He'd never thought...

No one had.

His father had been well-guarded. He'd been far enough from the Hydalla River that everyone had thought him safe.

But the elves had attacked the command tent. Father had been killed, along with several high-ranking generals.

Shouldn't Avie hate the elves? Right now, he was too numb. This didn't seem real. As if his father would just walk through that door at any moment.

But no. Father's body was on a train bound for Aldon. The next few days would hold funerals and processionals and standing in mourning. All eyes would be focused on Avie, judging their young king.

He clenched his jaw and his fists. He couldn't let them see just a boy. He'd have to appear a young man, worthy to inherit his father's throne.

A knock sounded on the outer door, the one that led from Essie's sitting room to the hallway, a moment before the voice of Father's head clerk echoed into the room. "I apologize for the interruption, ma'am. I wouldn't if it wasn't urgent."

Their mother's shoulders shook for a moment before her whole posture straightened. Her face was still wet with tears, but her expression smoothed. She gently set Essie onto the bed, extricated herself from Edmund, and stood. "I will be there in a moment, Algernon."

When she swung her gaze to Avie, something in her eyes said that he needed to go with her.

Avie hopped to his feet. Even though he was far too

old, a part of him wanted to hold his mother's hand as he used to do when he was little.

But he was twelve years old and king. A king didn't hold his mother's hand like a child.

His mother gave him a small nod, before she turned to Julien. He was already shifting over, hugging Essie and patting Edmund on the back.

As if assured that they would be all right for a few minutes, Mother marched from the room, Avie trotting to keep up.

When she stepped into the sitting room, she halted in front of the clerk. "What is it, Algernon?"

Algernon's brown hair was laced with gray, and he was older than Avie's mother, so that made him old. Really old. Not ancient, Avie supposed, but certainly old.

Algernon dipped into a bow, first to Avie, then to Mother. "Your Majesties."

Avie started, only then realizing the significance of the bow, the words. He was king. The staff would bow to him first, the way they always had his father.

His father. That choked feeling was back in his throat.

"Once again, I apologize, ma'am. I'm truly sorry to interrupt at a time like this." Algernon rocked back on his heels. "But I received word that Parliament is convening a special session tonight. It's about King Averett's regent. Word is that they intend to appoint one of their own instead of confirming you as his regent."

Mother's spine went even more straight. "Can they do that?"

"The law is clear that the next oldest sibling of the deceased king shall become regent for the heir, and on down the line if that sibling predeceased the king. However, the late king had no siblings. In this case, the law gives Parliament a bit more...discretion in the matter." Algernon gave a small cough. "I believe this may be an attempt by Parliament to wrest more power from the crown."

Avie only sort of understood all that. Politics were so confusing, and he was supposed to be good at it. He was king now, after all.

But he did know one thing. He wanted his mother as his regent, not some random lord selected by Parliament.

"Very well. Arrange for a carriage." Mother's tone held a note of ice.

"Yes, Your Majesty." Algernon bowed to Mother, then bowed to Avie, before leaving.

As soon as he was gone, Mother turned to Avie and rested her hands on his shoulders. "Avie, I'm going to need you to be strong right now. You're going to have to grow up fast. I wish you didn't, but you are king now."

"I know, Mama." Avie nodded and shoved aside the lump in his throat. He definitely couldn't cry right now.

"Get into your best black suit. I will fetch you in a few minutes." Mother gave him a gentle shove in front of her as they headed for the door.

In the hallway, Avie ran for his room while his mother disappeared into hers.

Avie blinked back tears as he dressed in the black suit he'd had hanging in his closet. He'd always had a black suit. He had never really put together why.

But of course. Everyone in the royal family always had something black on hand. Just in case of a death in the family. Just in case...

He blinked back tears, swallowed, and drew in a shaky breath. None of that now. He was king. Kings didn't cry.

He was just shrugging into his jacket when he heard raised voices just outside of his room. He peeked out the door and spotted his mother facing his grandmother. Grandmother lived in Buckmore Cottage, and she was in her customary black dress. She'd worn black for as long as Avie could remember since his grandfather—the king —had died when Avie was three.

But now Avie's mother also wore a black dress with a full, swishing skirt and a black veil over her bright red hair.

"The nerve of Parliament. They never would have dreamed of pulling something like this when my Edward was king." Grandmother pounded her cane on the floor, setting up a sharp rapping as the hardwood banged against the marble floor. It was almost as if she purposely avoided the carpet runner to hit the stone.

"I—" Mother opened her mouth.

"This is all a ploy to wrest the last bit of power from the crown. By the time Averett wears the crown, he will be nothing but Parliament's puppet, if they have their way." Grandmother sniffed, the sound and accompanying movement so sharp that her white hair shook where it was pinned into a bun.

"I was just—"

"It is disgraceful. Simply shameful. Our great country was founded on the principles of balance of powers. The crown plays a key role in ensuring that Parliament itself doesn't become too powerful and lord over the people of our fair kingdom."

Mother lifted her chin. "I quite agree. In fact, Averett and I are on our way to confront Parliament. Would you please excuse me?"

That was Avie's cue. He stepped from his room and hurried to his mother's side. She swept a glance over him, then nodded. Leaving Grandmother behind, Mother and Avie wound their way through the palace and exited onto the drive. There, the carriage waited, the horses stomping in the late afternoon sunlight.

They didn't speak in the carriage, and Avie spent most of the ride peeking past the black curtains to take in Aldon's streets.

Already, black swathed the shops and draped from the lampposts as the word spread that the king was dead. Crowds gathered in front of the main palace gates, leaving heaps of flowers beside the wall.

All too soon, they reached the grand sandstone building where Parliament met. As soon as Mother and Avie climbed down from the carriage, the crowd closed around them, held back by a cordon of guards. They were shouting out questions or expressing their sympathies. All of it just buzzed against Avie's ears, and it took all his courage to lift a hand in acknowledgement as he had been taught to do.

The coolness of the building closed around him, yet Avie's jacket clung hot over his shoulders while his neckcloth scratched far too warm and tight around his neck. He held his head high as he trotted at his mother's side.

She swept into the meeting room, ignoring the guards who were making noises in the backs of their throats, as if they weren't sure if they dared stop the queen—queen mother—especially when she had the king at her side, even if that king was a mere boy.

Not a mere boy. Avie kept his chin held high and tried to stand as tall as possible, which only brought him to just below his mother's shoulder.

Mother eyed the parliamentary leader, her eyes flashing. "May I be recognized to speak?"

The man quickly pounded his gavel. "Queen...Queen Mother Ariana is recognized."

"Thank you." Mother stepped onto the podium and faced the tiers of seats that rose on either side of the room.

Father had taken Avie to the convening of this year's Parliament, and he'd explained that the clusters of men on the various tiers often designated different factions, and those factions formed coalitions that eventually formed a party that had enough pull to vote in a bill. It all sounded confusing to Avie. How did they get anything done when the different factions were always jockeying among themselves?

Perhaps that was part of the point. The government only worked when it did as little as possible.

"Esteemed gentlemen, I am here to present my case why I should be recognized as my son's regent." Mother's voice rang crisp and clear across the large space. "Consider this, gentlemen. If you appoint one of your own, you will need to favor one party or another. Perhaps you will put the ruling party in such a position of power. Yet that goes against the ideal of balance of power that is so beloved to our kingdom and people. It would, instead, lead to a tyranny of one over the other."

A hushed thunder of voices filled the room as many of the men sitting on the benches leaned closer to murmur among themselves.

"The purpose of the crown is to remain neutral to such parties, providing a balancing force while the factions are given a voice here in these hallowed halls. To that end, my family, as is custom, has already absented themselves from Parliament so that no one party here has too close of ties to the crown and the crown does not exert undue influence in Parliament." Mother continued in a steady tone.

All Avie needed to do was stand there, looking as mature and kingly as possible.

"I provide that neutral balance as the regent for my son. I have ruled at my husband's side for the past ten years. I am well-equipped to rule as regent until King Averett is of age." Mother rested a hand on Averett's shoulder. "I don't wish for this position for power for myself. Ask yourselves, gentlemen. Can that be said of the men you would appoint to this position in my stead? Who do you wish to mold our king for the next nine years? Someone who has the best interests of the king and our kingdom in mind? Or someone who wishes to claim the position for the power he will gain at the expense of the king, our rule of law, and our beloved balance of power that protects our freedoms and keeps our kingdom from devolving into the tyranny that we have seen in the kingdoms around us?"

A nobleman on the left stood. When he was recognized by the chairman, he faced Mother. "Perhaps you are correct. However, we are concerned that you will be unable to perform both your duties as regent and as a mother to your four children. We would not, of course, wish to take you away from your primary duty of raising the future king. That is, in itself, a high calling."

Mother's eyes flashed, and her hand tightened on Avie's shoulder. But her tone remained that same, steady calm. "Raising my children is, of course, my primary concern. But how better can I raise the future king than as his regent? As his regent and his mother, I will train him in his duties with a focus that might be missing in another regent. As to my capabilities, I have balanced my duties quite capably as a queen, a wife, and a mother for the past ten years. I am no longer a wife. That leaves me even more time for fulfilling my duties as a queen regent and a mother."

Parliament debated for a while longer, but in the end, Avie's mother won out. She was confirmed as his regent.

And he had learned that his mother was likely the toughest, strongest woman in all of Escarland.

TWO

Twenty-one-year-old Averett strolled down the steps of Winstead Palace and waved to the crowd that pressed against the outer gates, trying to catch the first glimpse of their newly crowned king.

Sure, he had technically been king for the past nine years. But today he had been crowned. Today, the weight of the kingdom fully rested on his shoulders as surely as the heavy, ornate ceremonial crown now pressed into his skull.

He was as ready for this day as he possibly could be. From the very first day, his mother had discussed economics and politics and the state of the kingdom with him. When she'd ended the war with the elves only three weeks after Father had died, she'd told him all the details, including how reluctant most in Parliament were to admit defeat despite the death of their king and the fact that the Escarlish had never made it over the river into Tarenhiel no matter how hard they'd tried.

When he was sixteen, she began giving him more and

more paperwork to read. When he turned eighteen, she had given him every single piece of paperwork that crossed her desk to read over and discuss. It had been overwhelming, juggling all the paperwork of the kingdom along with taking classes at Hanford University.

His mother had been an exemplary regent. No one could have done better or worked harder to prepare him for this moment.

But now, she was stepping back and the burden was fully his. He had graduated from Hanford University, after taking extra classes so that he could finish his degree in only three years. Hopefully all those classes in economics, public relations, criminal justice, world affairs, and history would serve him well now.

As he descended the steps, the thick, crimson cloak dragged behind him, its weight causing his shoulder muscles to ache. But he kept his placid, regal expression in place. After so many years of practice, it was more automatic than struggle.

He climbed into a white, open carriage pulled by four white horses. Two guards climbed onto the rail on the back, standing alert and ready, while Captain Miller, the head of the royal guards, sat beside the driver.

Mother, Julien, Edmund, and Essie climbed into a second carriage, which would follow behind his.

Guards on horseback led the way out the gates and rode in rows on either side of his carriage.

Averett added a slight smile to his expression and waved at the people. All the streets were packed with people, smushed into the narrow walks so that the road was left clear. People even hung out of the upper story windows just to catch a glimpse of him.

Overwhelming. Humbling. All of this, and he wasn't anyone special. Not really. At heart, he was just a normal, twenty-one-year-old young man. Sure, one with a lot of training. But still just a young man.

The royal carriage took a circuitous route through Aldon to hit many of the nicest neighborhoods and to give the members of Parliament, who had been at the coronation, time to reach Ellory Hall, the Parliamentary building, before him.

When he finally arrived, the members of Parliament were arrayed on the steps of Ellory Hall. As the royal carriage stopped, a military band struck up the national anthem. Averett climbed down from the carriage. On cue, all the Parliament members bowed.

Averett strolled up the steps, subtly twitching the cumbersome royal cloak so that its train flowed down the steps behind him properly. Seriously, the hardest part of today was all the regalia he had to wear.

The vows, the oaths, the kingdom. The hard parts of those would start tomorrow when the euphoria of the coronation wore off and life returned to normal. Today would be a moment of national rejoicing and unity. Tomorrow, everyone would go back to arguing.

Mother, Julien, Edmund, and Essie all climbed out of their carriage, heading for their own spot to the side.

At the top of the steps beneath the columned porch at the front of the building, Averett halted, turned with a hidden kick to toss his cloak behind him, and faced the members of Parliament. With a wave of his hand, he gave permission for the men to straighten from their bows.

The parliamentary leader stepped forward, bowed again, then he shook Averett's hand. A sign that Averett received the approval of Parliament on top of the oaths of fealty these men had given—as noblemen of the kingdom —at the coronation.

The parliamentary leader faced the crowd and

launched into a speech. Averett only half-listened, just enough to make sure he nodded and smiled at the appropriate times. Any inattention in his expression would be noted and torn apart in the press.

But he kept most of his attention scanning the crowd, the Parliament members, his family, and just generally taking in the moment.

A few steps down and to the left, Edmund was frantically tugging at the sleeve of the nearest guard and pointing in a way that was far more obvious than was usually encouraged in public.

What was going on? Averett followed the direction of Edmund's pointing finger. He didn't see anything. Just a churning, cheering crowd. Nothing out of the ordinary there.

Until a man popped out of the mass of people. His movements had been so subtle, neither Averett nor the guards had spotted him earlier. The man's hand lifted, revealing the pistol he'd had tucked under his jacket.

Averett couldn't seem to make his feet move. The barrel pointed at him, the man's heated gaze focused on him with such hatred Avie couldn't breathe.

Julien leapt the last few steps—outpacing even the closest guards—and dove for Avie.

Then everything happened at once. The crack of the gunshot. The puff of smoke. Julien's tackle.

Something slammed into Avie's shoulder as he was falling. He hit the stone floor of the porch, his breath whooshing from his body. Pain lanced through him as the back of his skull smacked the ground. The heavy, ornamental crown clinked as it hit the stone and rolled a few feet away.

Then agony speared his left shoulder, so fiery that he

would have cried out if he'd had any breath left in his lungs.

Past the ringing in his ears, he could just hear the shouting. The screaming. Julien saying something.

Then Captain Miller was kneeling at Averett's side. His jaw tight, the captain brushed aside Averett's cloak and pressed his hands to the wound.

Avie groaned, then sucked in his first, deep breath. "I'm fine."

"No, Your Majesty. You've been shot." Captain Miller glanced up, his gaze taking in something farther down the steps, before he drew out a handkerchief from a pocket. "Lie still. We'll have a stretcher brought shortly and—"

"No." Avie forced his mind to think past the pain and the whirl of the last few seconds. "I'm not coughing on blood, and the wound isn't spurting, correct?"

"No, it appears to have missed your lung and artery. The bullet was likely slowed by the heavy gold chain holding the robe. But—"

"We can't let the people know he succeeded. We need to pretend I'm fine. I won't have my coronation stained with blood and the sight of the king hauled away on a stretcher." Avie gritted his teeth. "Now stuff that handkerchief in the wound and help me up."

"Your Majesty—" Captain Miller hesitated, a stubborn clench to his jaw.

"That's an order, Captain." Avie forced a commanding tone to his voice.

Captain Miller hesitated only a heartbeat longer before he nodded, paused only long enough for Avie to gather a single breath, and shoved the handkerchief into the bullet hole.

Only the knowledge that the entire kingdom would hear about it if he screamed kept Avie from wailing like a baby at the pain that shot through him. As it was, he groaned and black spots danced in front of his vision. For a few moments, he wasn't sure if he was going to puke or pass out.

Then he drew in another steadying breath and nodded to Captain Miller.

The captain stood and tugged Avie to his feet by his good, right hand.

As soon as he was upright, Avie's head swam, but he didn't pass out and he didn't puke.

Wordlessly, Julien fetched the crown and placed it back on Avie's head. It scratched against a tender spot on the back of Avie's head.

Captain Miller twitched the ceremonial robe. From farther away, it would look like he was simply straightening it. Instead, he was positioning it so that it covered the blood staining Avie's white shirt and jacket. Then, with a nod, Captain Miller stepped aside.

Avie forced his shaking legs to take a step forward as he faced the crowd, which had gone deathly silent. He forced a smile and lifted his right arm in a wave to his people.

A cheer broke out, as everyone realized that their fears of losing a second king in a decade were unfounded.

The Parliament members closest to him were gaping. They had, after all, been close enough to realize he had actually been shot. Julien, too, was still hovering a few feet away as if prepared to jump in to save him again.

A few steps down, Mother, Edmund, and Essie were no longer standing where they had been. He could just make out Mother's and Essie's bright red hair amid a cluster of guards as they were hustled into a carriage.

Good. They would be brought back to the palace and kept safe until this debacle could be figured out.

Avie forced himself to smile wider. If he could, he'd make sure that Essie never realized that he had actually been shot just now. She didn't need to fear that her brother would be taken away by violence the way their father had been.

Before the parliamentary leader had a chance to relaunch into his speech—Avie was holding it together, but he didn't know how long he could keep up the act before he keeled over—Avie stepped forward and spouted a shortened version of his own speech. He could only hope it turned out coherent.

Then he was striding down the steps and climbing back into the white carriage. The guards and Captain Miller claimed their places, and then they were moving.

Avie smiled and waved. Everything was fine. He was fine. Sure, his head was pounding as if a workman with a hammer was determined to break out through his temples. He didn't dare inspect his shoulder, and he only risked a brief glance down just to make sure the heavy robe covered the wound and any gushing blood. He could feel it, sticky and warm, as it trickled down his side.

Even though the driver must have taken the quickest route through Aldon, each jolt of the carriage over an uneven cobblestone sent a lance of pain through Avie. But he held his smile in place and his back straight.

Finally, they were through the gates of Winstead Palace. Captain Miller glanced back at Avie, sighed, and directed the driver to head for the front, gravel drive just as they would have if everything had gone smoothly, rather than one of the back doors, which would have been hidden from the crowd peering through the bars of the iron gates. Any deviation from the normal would be analyzed in the press.

As soon as the carriage stopped, it took a moment for Avie to gather his strength to push to his feet. Would the far-off crowd notice the way he kept a hand on the back of the carriage as he made his way to the door? Would they note his stumble as his feet hit the gravel of the path?

His head was going all whirly and fuzzy, strangely light while his limbs were so very, very heavy.

Had the stairs to the palace always been this steep? Had there always been so many of them? He dragged himself up at a slow but steady pace. At the top, he forced himself to pause, turn, and give one last wave to the crowd.

Two footmen opened the huge double doors, and Avie swept inside, halting just inside the entrance.

Would all his efforts be enough? What would the news stories look like in the morning?

Shots Fired: An Inauspicious Start to New King's Reign

Attempted Assassination Disrupts King Averett's Coronation

Crown Knocked Off the King's Head. Sign of the Times to Come?

At least that would be better than the alternative, if no one had been convinced by his acting.

King Shot on His First Day

New King's Reign Starts with Bloodshed

The doors whooshed shut, blocking out the sunlight and the stares of the crowd.

Boots rang on the marble floor behind him.

"The doors are shut?" Avie tugged aside the crimson cloak. Good thing the cloak was red. His shirt was now also red. So much red.

"Yes, Your Majesty." Captain Miller was at his elbow, steadying him.

"My family?"

"They've been secured in your mother's rooms."

"Good." Avie let his legs buckle as he gave in to the darkness consuming him.

CHAPTER

THREE

P aige Miller groaned as she set her books on the coffee table and sank into the plush chair in the sitting room of the multi-room suite that she and her father shared in Winstead Palace. As the captain in charge of the royal guards, her father was afforded a rather nice room. Sure, it was on the third floor—so, lots of stairs—but it was technically in the royal wing.

Watching the coronation had been fun, but now it was time to finish her homework before classes started up again next week after the holiday of the coronation festivities.

Ugh. She hated homework. Why had she decided that taking classes at Hanford University was a good idea?

Oh, right. Because she was eighteen years old with no marriage prospects and no idea what to do with her life.

If she had been a boy, it would have been easy. She would have joined the army and followed the Miller legacy.

Instead, she was a girl. Not that she minded. Joining the army didn't sound all that appealing.

Still, she was in a rather awkward social position. Her father's job as the head of the royal guards gained him entrance into the highest circles of society. Yet they were only distantly related to nobility—her grandmother's brother had been a lord, if she remembered correctly. That meant she wasn't actually eligible to marry any of the future lords who wandered in and out of the palace.

Perhaps her situation would have been better if Paige had a mother to take her out into society, introducing her to the correct wealthy-but-not-noble tier of eligible bachelors.

But Paige's mother had died giving birth to her. There weren't even any aunts beyond an elderly great-aunt who might—and that was a very big might—be willing to take on the job of bringing Paige out into society.

It hadn't even occurred to her father that this might be a problem. And Paige wasn't about to bring it up to him.

Instead, she'd asked to go to Hanford University. It had only started allowing female students in the past few decades, and students like her were still a rarity.

Her father hadn't questioned her—instead, he'd graciously funded her classes with the same indulgent, proud look he gave her whenever she asked to pursue something.

And if she was just taking a random smattering of classes as a way to meet eligible young men, well, that was her business. It had seemed a brilliant plan at the time. Take a few classes. Meet a few young men—who were all wealthy enough to afford to attend Hanford University. Find one of them who actually showed intelligence and an interest in learning—something that would weed out the wastrels. Fall in love. Get married. Start living the life of wife and mother that she longed for.

There was just one problem. She actually had to take the classes and do the homework.

Behind her, the door to the hall opened. Paige sprang to her feet, already talking as she turned. "Father, are you back already from—"

She froze. Standing in front of her father in the doorway was the fourteen-year-old Princess Elspeth, wearing a light green dress that was far simpler than the intricate ensemble she had worn at the coronation. Behind her, Father carried a carpet bag.

"Your Highness." Paige dropped into a curtsy. What was going on? What was the princess doing here of all places?

"Paige, I'd like you to make Princess Elspeth feel welcome. She's going to be staying in our suite of rooms for a few days." Father escorted the princess the rest of the way into the room before shutting the door behind them.

"There was an attempted assassination," Princess Elspeth stated with a mix of youthful exuberance and regal dignity that seemed odd in a fourteen-year-old. "Edmund realized what was happening, and he tried to warn the guards but they didn't listen to him because he is only sixteen but Julien listened and he tackled Avie and shoved him out of the way before the bullet hit him. It was all very heroic."

Had the princess taken a breath during that entire recitation of events? Paige glanced from Princess Elspeth to her father.

Her father had his mouth pressed into a tight line. When her gaze met his, he gave a small shake of his head.

More had gone on, but he wasn't going to talk about it in front of the young princess.

The attempted assassination would explain why the

princess would be staying with them for a few days. Someone in authority must have made the decision that it would be best if at least one of the royal family was in a secure, undisclosed location in case of more attempts. Sure, they weren't that far and a large bomb could still take them out along with the rest of the royal family. Father must suspect that it was likely someone who was working alone and not a part of a wider threat, otherwise more drastic measures would be taken to keep the royal family secure.

Although, they hadn't mentioned where Prince Julien and Prince Edmund were. While the king would likely need to stay here—both to continue to rule the kingdom and to avoid looking like the assassin had accomplished his goal—the younger two princes might be shuffled off to some more secure location. As the fourth child, Princess Elspeth was the least important of the royal children. Perhaps simply being moved to the rooms of the head of the royal guards and his daughter was good enough protection for her.

Before Paige had a chance to pull herself together, Princess Elspeth waltzed over to the coffee table, plopped onto the couch, and inspected the books there. "Ooh, old Escarlish literature! My tutor has had me read a bunch. Though doesn't it seem a bit advanced for a fourteen-year-old to have to read the *Lament of the Lonely Tree* in actual Old Escarlish? I don't mind the stuff that's been translated into modern Escarlish. But I can't make heads or tails of the originals. It doesn't even look like the same language."

Paige shared another glance with her father before she tiptoed around the couch, though she didn't sit. One didn't sit in the presence of royalty until invited. "The Old Escarlish is difficult."

"Glad someone agrees with me. Edmund doesn't complain about it nearly enough. I think he's actually taught himself to read and write in Old Escarlish." Princess Elspeth glanced up and a small frown puckered the center of her forehead. "Oh, sorry. You can sit. This is your home. Well, I guess technically it's my home too. Though it doesn't actually belong to me. It's more Averett's. Though it isn't his either, not really, even though he is king now. The palace just kind of belongs to "the crown," whatever that means. Does it mean that the palace belongs to Avie? Or to the kingdom as a whole? Does that mean just the people or just the government?"

Since the princess didn't seem to actually want an answer, Paige just nodded as she tentatively sat on the couch.

At least entertaining the princess wouldn't be that much of a challenge. As long as she smiled and nodded at the right times, the princess seemed perfectly happy talking non-stop and entertaining herself.

WHEN PRINCESS ELSPETH had retired for the night, Father motioned for Paige to follow him into the hallway. He had stepped out several times through the evening, though he didn't say a word about what he had been doing when he returned.

Once they were outside, with two sets of doors separating them from the princess, Paige crossed her arms and kept her voice low. "What really happened today?"

"It mostly went down as the princess believes, but the bullet didn't miss entirely. King Averett was shot in the shoulder." Father clasped his hands behind his back and spoke with a measured calm, although the lines in his face deepened.

Paige caught her breath. "Is he all right?"

"He's fine. The surgeon dug out the bullet, and the king is resting comfortably." Father sighed and shook his head. "But the king has given orders that he wishes the kingdom and his sister to believe that the bullet missed."

Understandable. King Averett and the entire kingdom had waited nine years for this day. Of course the king wouldn't want the national memory of his coronation to be forever linked with bloodshed. There would still be the assassination attempt, of course. No one would tell the story of the coronation without it. But at least it would be about how King Averett was saved by his brother and how the bullet missed and how lucky the king—and the kingdom—had been.

Still, keeping it from his sister seemed a bit overprotective. Sure, Princess Elspeth was only fourteen years old. But she was a princess. Surely she could handle knowing the truth.

That wasn't Paige's call. Instead, she would obey her king's command. "I won't breathe a word of the truth to the princess."

"I know you won't." Father gave a sharp nod, his proud smile creasing his face. "You'll need to keep her busy for the next few days. The king doesn't want her getting curious and seeing him before he's healed enough to pretend he was never injured."

"I think I can manage that." Paige had found the princess to be pleasant company. If the princess wasn't, well, the princess, she was someone Paige would like to have for a friend. She was a little young yet, but four years wouldn't be such a big age gap once they were both a few years older.

"Thank you." Father gave another of his stiff nods. He wasn't the most demonstrative, but his love was still there in his care.

"The assassin? Was he caught?" Paige rubbed her arms. She usually tried not to think about how much danger her father was in every day as he protected the royal family.

"Yes. He is a soldier disgruntled with the handling of the war nine years ago, and he decided to take out his frustrations on the new king." Father sighed and shook his head. "It appears that he was working alone, but the Intelligence Office is conducting a thorough investigation. We'll be on high alert for the next few days, but that will be it."

Paige nodded. This wasn't the first time the palace had gone on high alert. There had been a few threats made over the years while the queen mother ruled as regent. Although Paige had been only nine, she still vividly remembered those tense days after the late king had been killed.

Poor King Averett. King for less than a day and he'd been shot. He must be so worried that he'd die a premature death, just like his father.

She shook herself. Her pity didn't really matter one way or another. She was just Captain Miller's daughter. She would likely never even speak to the king, much less have an opportunity to express her opinions, should she dare do so.

FOUR

A vie groaned as he eased onto his bed. His whole body hurt, from the bruises on his back and head to the throbbing in his shoulder. His head pounded from a faint headache while his limbs shook with such weakness that he didn't shrug off Julien's helping hand as his brother steadied him.

When he was settled on the bed, Avie gingerly leaned back against the pillows that kept him propped up rather than flat on his back as he had been last night.

It had taken everything in him to get up this morning to go through the rigamarole of the opening of Parliament and ceremonial greeting of the ambassadors. He couldn't skip them, if he wanted to keep up the appearance that he hadn't been shot.

He wasn't sure how many people he was fooling, especially those in Parliament who had been close enough to see the blood. How long before some of them would try to leverage their knowledge into some kind of political move, well, only time would tell.

Until then, he was going to play up his "fine and

healthy" status in public as much as possible. The press stories had been as mixed as he'd feared. But mixed was still better than bad.

Julien stepped back, crossing his arms. "Perhaps I should see if I can postpone—"

"No." Avie shook his head. "If you use your rank to postpone basic training, the press will get wind of it, and they will start putting the pieces together. No, everything must go forward as normal. You've enlisted, so you'll go to basic training as planned."

Instead of going to Hanford University at eighteen, Julien had enlisted in the army. Avie had tried to talk him out of it, but Julien had been firm. He planned to go into the army and work his way toward a position guarding Avie. That had been Julien's plan even before the attempted assassination, but he had become even more set on it since. Although he was, apparently, debating if he should stay at Winstead until Avie was healed.

While Avie didn't want to ask his brother to sacrifice himself like this, he was still honored. And he couldn't help but be grateful at the thought of having his brother guarding his back someday.

Julien nodded, a frown creasing the stubble on his chin. Even at eighteen, Julien could grow a full beard. A beard he'd have to shave starting tomorrow to follow army regulations. Only those with the rank of captain and above were allowed to wear beards.

Julien sighed, his jaw working. "I still don't like leaving after what happened. I know Captain Miller said it was just a lone gunman, but if something were to happen while I was gone..."

"I'll be fine." Avie waved, then wished he hadn't when pain shot through his body. He hadn't even waved with his bad arm.

Julien just eyed him, as if unconvinced. He, after all, knew the truth of how badly Avie had been wounded. It wasn't life-threatening, as long as Avie didn't get an infection. But Julien had stayed while the surgeon dug out the bullet and fished out the shreds of royal regalia and white shirt from Avie's shoulder.

Avie had, thankfully, been under chloroform at the time and had no memories of the whole experience. The last thing he remembered, before being put under, was the head clerk shoving paperwork at him, asking him to sign the document that would re-confirm that Julien was his heir with Mother as regent until Julien became of age, if the worst should happen.

For those long minutes while Avie had been out of it, the authority of the kingdom had once again rested on Mother's shoulders as regent and Julien as heir apparent. If Avie had died under the surgeon's knife—if that bullet had been higher and nicked the artery or farther to the right and hit his heart or lung—then Julien would be king today.

Julien finally nodded and headed for the door. "I'll stop in again before I leave."

Avie swallowed, hoping his voice didn't sound scratchy. For the past nine years, he and Julien had been a pair, looking after Edmund and Essie together. Now Avie would be on his own, just when the whole kingdom landed on his shoulders alone. "Thanks." Avie paused. "How is Essie?"

"Happy and chatting up a storm, as always." For the first time, a smile crossed Julien's face. "She and Captain Miller's daughter are getting on well."

Of course they were. Essie could make a friend out of the grumpiest person in a few minutes.

What was Captain Miller's daughter's name again?

Avie had seen her a few times, at a distance, but he'd never spoken with her. Something that started with a *p*. Penelope? Prudence?

Paige, that was it.

Perhaps Avie would send for her and ask her how Essie was doing. Sure, Avie could ask Captain Miller. But the captain was far from verbose, and he was busy making sure there were no other threats against the royal family.

But Paige was the one actually spending time with Essie. She would know how Essie was holding up better than anyone.

PAIGE HEFTED her bag of books higher on her aching shoulder and stepped through the back, servants' entrance to Winstead Palace.

Classes today had been interesting, to say the least. The attempted assassination had been the topic of every conversation, including the professors'. Her Government and Politics class—a required course for every student—had spent the entire class period discussing the corona-tion, the assassination attempt, and the political ramifi-cations.

Everyone kept looking at Paige, asking her questions that she couldn't answer. Not because she didn't know. But because she did know the answers and knew better than to give them.

It turned out that keeping her head down and her mouth shut under the constant pressure was exhausting. It was such a relief to step back into the safety of Winstead's walls, knowing that here, no one would ask such questions. They, too, knew better.

"Miss Miller?" The guard next to the door stepped into her path.

She started, blinked, and nearly dropped her bag of books. "Yes?"

"The king has asked to see you as soon as you returned from your classes." The guard's tone and expression never wavered from stiff and official.

Paige swallowed. Why would the king want to see her? That he wanted to see her right away sounded ominous. "Thank you. Where would he like to see me?"

"His sitting room."

Paige nodded, then hurried through the corridors. Should she be worried? Was this about Princess Elspeth? Had Paige crossed a line she wasn't supposed to? Princess Elspeth had been the first one to claim that Paige was her friend. Paige hadn't presumed to claim such herself.

At the entrance to the royal wing, she was briefly stopped by the four guards on duty. The king's suite of rooms was just inside the royal wing, across the way from the queen mother's apartments.

The king's door was open, though it was also guarded by four guards. A steady stream of clerks hurried in and out, and Paige had to jump out of the way as a clerk barreled through, head down, a stack of paperwork in his arms.

Algernon, the head clerk, stood just outside of the door, directing traffic. He nodded to Paige, then stepped into the sitting room. "King Averett, Miss Paige Miller is here as you requested."

King Averett's voice rang from inside the room. "Thank you, Algernon. Everyone, please step out for a moment. But leave the door open."

Two clerks darted from the room, piles of papers and

file folders in their arms. They halted just down the hall, as if to make sure they were out of earshot of the door.

Algernon gestured to Paige, nodding for her to enter the room.

Heart pounding like a thunderstorm in her ears, Paige straightened her shoulders and stepped into the king's sitting room.

King Averett sat in a plush chair, the coffee table pulled close and piled with paperwork and a lap desk balanced on his knees. His left arm rested in a sling while his pallor had a gray, unhealthy cast.

But he was sitting up, industriously going through the stacks of paperwork that landed on a king's desk every day. An impressive feat, considering he had been shot a mere day and a half before.

"Your Majesty." Paige dipped into a curtsy, holding it.

"Rise and have a seat." King Averett gestured to the two floral-patterned couches facing each other.

Where should she sit? If she took a seat as far away from him as possible, would she appear rude? But would it be presumptuous to sit in the seat closest to him? If only she could just remain standing, the better to bolt as soon as the king said his piece.

The middle seat then. Not too far, but not too close. Paige scurried forward and lowered herself into the seat as gracefully as she could manage.

King Averett set aside his pen, then set the lap desk on the end of the coffee table. It wobbled on the uneven stacks of paperwork, but when it didn't fall over, King Averett leaned back in his chair. He met Paige's gaze. "Thank you for looking after my sister. How is she?"

His eyes were a chocolate brown. Not a dark chocolate. But more a warm, mellow chocolate mixed with a hint of caramel.

Wait, why was she staring into the king's eyes?

Her heart lurched. She was meeting the king's gaze. Surely that was a big no-no.

Paige dropped her gaze to her hands in her lap. What had he asked her? His sister. The princess. "She's fine. Very talkative." Paige could've kicked herself. That sounded like she was denigrating the princess. "Not that being talkative is a bad thing. I mean that in the best way possible."

"Essie *is* very talkative. That's just a fact." King Averett gave a small laugh, warm with love for his little sister.

The warmth settled on Paige, if just for a moment. Was that what it felt like, to have siblings? A big brother to look after his sister? She'd never had that, much as she'd missed it over the years. But her father had never been interested in marrying again. He was the type of man who only fell in love once in his life, and now that it was done and his wife gone, he was content to go on alone.

After another moment, the smile dropped from King Averett's face—something Paige only saw from the corner of her eye when she peeked at the king, lifting her gaze no higher than his nose. But when he spoke, his voice had gone guarded again. "Has she been sleeping all right? No...no signs that the attempted assassination has been weighing on her?"

Paige froze as she quickly sorted through the memories of the past few nights. "No, not that I noticed."

"Good." King Averett heaved a sigh.

"She's stronger than you think." As soon as the words popped out, Paige snapped her mouth shut. Had she really said that out loud? To the king? She quickly added, "Your Majesty."

Instead of getting mad or telling her to hold her

tongue, King Averett stilled, his brows lowering slightly. "I know that."

"But then why…" Paige managed to cut herself off this time. She was a commoner. It was not her place to speak up.

"Go ahead, Miss Miller. I'm not going to order your execution or throw your family out of Winstead Palace if you speak your mind."

Easy for him to say. Even if he didn't do either of those things, speaking her mind and angering the king could still have consequences. He could still make things difficult for Paige's father or snub her family in public, which would cause all of the most influential people in Escarland to snub them as well. And that would seriously interfere with Paige's plan to find a nice young man, fall in love, get married, and start a family of her own.

But Princess Elspeth was a sweet girl who was quickly becoming a friend, despite the difference in their social standing. She'd even spent last evening helping Paige with her homework.

Paige needed to say something, if just to appease the guilt that had been bitter on her tongue all day as she tried not to give away the truth to the princess.

Raising her chin, Paige forced herself to meet the king's gaze. "Why would you keep the truth from your sister? She might be talkative, but she wouldn't spill the truth to the press or to anyone else. She's strong enough to handle it, if she knew you had actually been shot. I think…I think it is rather heavy-handed of you to decide for her what you think she can and can't handle."

There. She'd said it.

Whatever burst of courage she'd felt fled, and she dropped her gaze back to her lap. She'd said it, and now she'd suffer the consequences.

Silence fell in the wake of her words, and it lingered, painful and tight.

Finally, Paige dared to peek up at the king to check just how thunderous his expression was to gauge how much trouble she was in.

Instead of thunder and red-faced anger, King Averett's face was drawn in tired lines, his eyes sad rather than sparking. He released a long breath that had a hint of a shudder. "Perhaps she can handle it. But what if *I* can't?"

Was he looking for her to answer? This seemed rather personal, and yet his tone almost begged for the opportunity to share a bit of the weight he carried on his shoulders.

Gathering her courage yet again, Paige forced her gaze to stay fixed on his face, though she focused on his chin rather than his eyes. "What do you mean, Your Majesty?"

"When our father died, Essie was only five. I saw the way it shattered her. She had nightmares for several days, and she'd wake up begging for our father to come save her as he always used to." King Averett's hands clenched over his knees, and it was his turn to look away. "I couldn't stand it if she started looking at me that way. As if I am a king who might be snatched away from her at any moment, the way our father was, instead of the big brother who always has—and always will—protect her. I couldn't bear it if I had to watch her living in fear. I'd rather see her living confidently with the image of Julien and Edmund heroically saving me. Which they did, if not as completely as Essie believes."

Paige still wasn't sure she agreed with the king's determination to keep something so important from his sister. But her heart still ached for the pain evident in the tight, agonized lines of his posture and the aching look in his eyes.

This wasn't about what Essie could handle. Not really. It was about what King Averett could. Right now, he had the burden of the whole kingdom on his shoulders. Adding the weight of his sister's fear was one burden too many for him.

"So please"—King Averett's voice softened further—"don't tell my sister the truth."

Paige swallowed. "I won't."

How could she tell the king anything else? In the end, it was his family's business what they wanted to keep from Essie or not. Paige might not agree, but she would follow her king's wishes.

"Thank you." King Averett held her gaze for another moment, before he seemed to shake himself. His gaze shuttered again, and he straightened into a posture that was once again formal. "That will be all, Miss Miller. Thank you for your time."

She recognized a dismissal when she heard it. Paige hopped to her feet, bobbed a curtsy, and mumbled something unintelligible even to herself. Then she hurried from the room, her school books clutched to her side.

AVIE STARED at the door long after Miss Miller had fled.

At first, she had seemed as polite and closed off as everyone was in his presence. But then, for a few minutes, her blue eyes had sparked with courage as she spoke up for Essie.

Intriguing. So intriguing. And beautiful. If she'd been a noblewoman, he probably would have asked to court her right on the spot.

But she was a commoner. A barrier, but not for the reasons the rest of the kingdom would make it out to be.

No, the problem was the fact that their differences in station made it difficult for him to even ask. Would she feel uncomfortable saying no, simply because he was king? The power disparity would make a healthy relationship difficult.

He suppressed a sigh. He was king. No matter who he courted, there would be a power disparity, unless he wanted to wait around until Mongalia's thirteen-year-old princess grew up a little. Or reached out to one of the smaller kingdoms that bordered Escarland to see if they were interested in a marriage of alliance.

Perhaps he should arrange such an alliance for himself. But he wasn't sure he wanted to give another kingdom that much power in the Escarlish monarchy. He didn't think he even wanted to marry off his siblings to such marriages, no matter how expected it was.

No, he wanted a true partner who could rule at his side, the way his mother had ruled at his father's side. He wanted a wife who could do what his mother had done in becoming regent, ruling the kingdom, and raising all four of them.

That left him with his original problem. Courting an Escarlish young woman and hoping their differences in station didn't make her feel pressured.

Though, there would be plenty who wouldn't care, since it was that very power—and the wealth and status that came with it—that would attract them. He'd been fending them off for years already.

He needed to marry sooner rather than later. He didn't dare wait until one of the more desperate and devious young ladies managed to trap him into marriage.

More than that, the assassination attempt just proved that he needed an heir. Sure, he had three younger siblings. There wouldn't be a succession crisis if he were killed off young.

But he knew none of his siblings wanted to wear the crown. Nor was the kingdom ready to go through another period of regency rule. Not to mention that he did not want to put his mother through that again.

Thus, his lack of an heir put the kingdom into a precarious position. The people needed to feel secure, knowing their king had an heir.

As his clerk re-entered the room, Avie shook himself and tried to concentrate on his paperwork once again, although he knew that he wouldn't be able to get Miss Paige Miller out of his head any time soon.

The matter of his future wife and heir would have to wait. Right now, he needed to concentrate on all the things that had been set aside for the past nine years during the regency, waiting for a king in his full power to once again ascend to the throne.

Establish himself on the throne first. Get married second.

CHAPTER
FIVE

A LITTLE OVER TWO YEARS LATER...

Paige resisted the urge to scrub her sweaty palms on her skirt. The last thing she wanted was to walk down the aisle in front of all the most important people in the kingdom with sweat stains smeared down the front of her dress.

Even where she stood, in an anteroom just outside of the throne room of Winstead Palace, the roar of the gathered people still filtered through the thick wooden doors. She'd made the mistake of peering out of one of the windows of her third-story bedroom that morning. The streets around Winstead Palace were packed with people, as if the entire city of Aldon had turned out to witness the wedding of their king to a girl who was a commoner like themselves.

Paige's breathing hitched, and she clasped her shaking hands in front of her. The common people loved her, but the nobles? The important people?

They *loathed* her. She was taking a place meant for one of their own, and they intensely resented it.

All those eyes on her as she walked down the aisle. Angry eyes attached to the claws of political clout and wealth, just waiting to tear her apart—and Avie along with her.

She couldn't do this. She just couldn't. All those people hating her. The focus of the entire nation on her. Not just today, but every day for the rest of her life. Every choice she made—from her clothes to how she raised any children they might someday have—would be scrutinized and viciously torn apart.

She'd thought she could handle it. She'd told herself that being married to Avie would be worth it.

But now, when this moment came…

She was shaking, her breathing coming in and out sharp and hard, vision narrowing.

The door opened and shut, then warm arms wrapped around her. "It's all right. Just breathe."

Avie's mother.

Paige rested her face against her soon-to-be mother-in-law's shoulder, soaking up her warmth and steadiness. "I can't do this."

"I know." Avie's mother didn't try to talk her out of it or give empty comforts. Just understanding.

"All those people. And they hate me. Will keep hating me." Paige couldn't stop her shudder.

"Yes, they will." His mother rubbed her back soothingly in a way Paige had never received from a mother before.

"If Avie was just a man, then I wouldn't hesitate. But he's not. He's king. I thought I could handle it, but standing here now…" Paige's throat closed. She wanted to marry Avie so badly her chest ached at the thought of walking away.

But she didn't want to marry King Averett of Escarland.

"I know." Avie's mother hugged her tighter. "I made the decision to walk down the aisle. But I won't judge if you make a different choice."

Would she really be so understanding, if Paige walked away now and broke her son's heart in front of the entire kingdom?

Paige forced herself to straighten and push away from the hug. "How did you do it?"

"At the time, he was just the crown prince. Yes, I knew he would be king, but I believed I would have a bit of time to ease into the role before becoming queen." Avie's mother's eyes grew distant as she focused on the wall more than Paige. "Little did I know I would be queen within four years."

"Not just that." Though, that was part of it. How had this woman before her conquered the panic that was now clawing up Paige's throat at the thought of walking down that aisle in front of all those judging, hateful gazes? "How did you do it, when he was killed? You were left alone, with four children to raise and an entire kingdom on your shoulders."

Paige had met Avie because of an assassination attempt. Unlike Essie and most of the rest of the kingdom, she knew the truth. The bullet hadn't missed.

How many other attempts had there been over the years? How many more would there be? How long would it be until one of them found their mark and Avie was killed? He was king. Assassination attempts were part of the job.

If she was queen, she would become a target as well.

She didn't necessarily fear for her own life. But what about any children they might have? She wouldn't survive it if her children were targeted.

Avie's mother gripped Paige's shoulders and waited until Paige met her gaze. The look in the woman's green eyes was warm, understanding, and filled with memories of the pain she had lived through. "The thing about trials in life is that we aren't given the strength to endure them until that strength is needed. Right now, you don't have the strength to endure whatever might come. But you'll find that, if the worst happens, the strength will be there when you need it."

Perhaps she would. But that wasn't comforting now, staring down a future where she might find herself widowed and alone like her future mother-in-law. Right now, she wasn't sure she even had the strength to walk down an aisle.

"Do you regret it?" Paige swallowed, her throat tight and aching. "Marrying the late king, knowing what you do now?"

"No." The answer was quick yet filled with the heaviness of grief. Unlike many queen mothers, Avie's mother didn't dress in black. She wore a dark green dress that set off her red hair and matched her green eyes. But the bright clothing did nothing to hide the edges of grief around her eyes and mouth. "I miss my husband each and every day so much it hurts. But I could never regret marrying him. I had fourteen years with him, and I wouldn't trade those years for anything, even knowing the pain that would follow."

Paige nodded, blinking, but she couldn't seem to make her throat work enough to speak.

"And I have my children." A soft smile banished some of the sorrow from her face. "How could I regret marrying him when I see Avie, standing tall and strong with his father's crown on his head? When I see Julien in his uniform, Edmund thriving in his classes at Hanford University, and Essie bright and happy no matter what she endured in her childhood? I might have lost my husband, but I see him in our children. So, no, I don't regret marrying him even for a moment."

Paige drew in a deep breath, then released it slowly. What would she regret more? Walking away from Avie—the love of her life—and spending the rest of her life wondering what could have been? Or walking toward Avie down that aisle and facing whatever came, no matter how tragic?

The woman before her had made the latter choice and didn't regret it. Even though her husband had been killed and her son had been shot on his coronation day.

Walking away now would be the coward's way out. Who walked away from love just because of what-ifs, which might not even come about?

Yes, she needed to face the possibilities. She couldn't walk into this with a rosy ignorance about the dangers. But she shouldn't dwell on them to the point that the fear ruled her life and dictated her decisions.

Avie was worth it. The year that they had been courting had shown her that.

All she had ever wanted was to be a wife and mother.

But it turned out she would be a queen as well. Far more than she had ever asked for or wanted. Yet she could do it. Because she would have Avie at her side and she would be at his.

When she released yet another long exhale, her shaking stopped, her breathing steady. "All right. I'm ready."

Avie tried not to shift as he waited on the dais at the far end of the throne room. Rows upon rows of benches filled the space, leaving only that center aisle with its red carpet.

Behind him, Julien stood, straight and unshifting, in his lieutenant's uniform. Edmund stood on the next step down, his hands clasped behind his back as he mirrored Julien's stance, even while his eyes were darting about, taking in everything. Avie's brothers had his back today, just as they had the day the crown was placed on his head.

Essie stood across the way, bouncing a bit on her toes, her smile just a hint too big to fully hide behind the practiced one they all knew to wear in public.

A squad of little girls—chosen from among the noble families—walked down the aisle, scattering white flowers over the red of the carpet.

Then the music changed, and everyone stood. Footmen opened the double doors.

And there she was. The most beautiful woman in the world, dressed in a flowing white dress of lace and silk with her blonde hair piled on her head in a way that would accommodate a crown when he placed it on her head. The only woman he wanted at his side as his queen.

But more than that, she was the woman he wanted at his side as his wife. When he was with her, he was just Avie and she was just Paige.

He only vaguely noted her father where he walked at his daughter's side with the same military bearing and stoic expression he used when on patrol around the palace. Yet a wet gleam to his eyes gave away that he wasn't quite as unmoved as he appeared.

Then Paige lifted her gaze from the red runner and met Avie's gaze.

His breath caught, lodged in his chest with something that felt like pain and delight and euphoria all in one. Was he floating on air? Or about to pass out?

His knees wobbled as he stepped forward. Captain Miller shook Avie's hand, then Paige's hand slipped into Avie's.

Together, they walked up the stairs of the dais, hand-in-hand, to begin the rest of their lives.

BIRTHDAYS

This story takes place between Troll Queen *and* Pretense.

CHAPTER
ONE

ESSIE'S BIRTHDAY

Farrendel trailed after Averett, Julien, and Edmund as they walked the muddy paths between Winstead Palace and Buckmore Cottage, six inches of snow covering the ground except for the shoveled walks. He skirted an icy puddle, adjusting his grip on the box he carried, which was filled with what looked like gaudy streamers, ribbons, and bows. "Is all of this necessary?"

He could not imagine that Essie would *enjoy* coming back from her shopping trip with Paige to find their parlor covered in an explosion of tacky decorations.

"Very necessary." Averett grinned, hoisting his own box of decorations higher.

"Twenty-one is an important age for humans." Julien's own grin crossed his face, and he shot a glance at Averett. "After all, Avie became king at twenty-one. It's a big deal, being old enough to legally inherit anything."

"But the decorations? And the surprise party?"

Farrendel balanced the box on one arm and opened the door to the cottage.

"Yes, it is *entirely* necessary." Edmund pushed past Farrendel and headed for the parlor. "She likely already knows Paige is keeping her distracted from something, so I doubt it will be much of a surprise. But the amount of effort we're going to put into this definitely *will* be a surprise. We have done elaborate birthdays before, but not since her eighteenth birthday."

"That was only three years ago." Three years did not seem like a long time between celebrations. Elves rarely made a big deal about birthdays, celebrating only the hundred year marks if they ever bothered to even do that much. When one lived nearly a thousand years, one did not mark the passing of each year so carefully.

Julien and Averett walked inside, then Farrendel followed after them. Savory smells filled the cottage while the sounds of sizzling food, bustling people, and murmuring voices came from the kitchen, where Miss Merrick, the chef from Winstead Palace, and a whole horde of cooking staff prepared the birthday feast and cake.

Definitely a room Farrendel was going to avoid until this was all over. Too many people in what was usually his quiet cottage retreat in Escarland.

Instead, he hurried into the parlor after his brothers-in-law. There, Averett had already dumped his box of decorations out in a jumbled heap on the floor.

Resisting the itchiness from such chaos, Farrendel set his own box on a chair and started sorting through it, making neat piles of each item. Julien joined him, and together they sorted through everything from their two boxes.

By the time they finished, Edmund and Averett had

already started on the decorating, haphazardly looping garlands and affixing bows to every imaginable surface. It did not look particularly pretty, but what did Farrendel know of the human custom of surprise birthday parties?

Essie's mother bustled into the room. "I thought I would check..." She stopped short, taking in the room, her hands on her hips. "This is a disaster. I knew I shouldn't have put the four of you in charge of decorating."

Farrendel grimaced, taking in the explosion of mismatching streamers and ribbons. This was awful.

Edmund grinned, raising an eyebrow. "Would you rather we helped with the cake?"

"No, of course not." Essie's macha turned in a circle as if taking in the chaos again. Then, she shrugged. "Oh, well. If this is the look you're going for, then let's embrace it. Avie, drape that garland over the lamp. Edmund, that chair only has one bow tied to it. Tie a few more on, and make sure they are as lopsided as possible. Farrendel, drape a few garlands from the chandelier. I think you'll be able to reach if Julien gives you a boost."

Farrendel stared up at the fancy chandelier hanging from the ten-foot-high ceiling. The candles had been replaced with gas lighting at some point. "Will not the garlands catch on fire?"

Macha waved away his concern. "Just make sure you keep the garlands well away from the flames."

It still did not seem very safe to him. But as an elf, he was particularly conscientious when it came to fire. What he would not give for a few enchanted elven lights instead of the gas lighting.

Farrendel picked up one of the garlands and turned to Julien. "Ready?"

Julien grinned and knelt on one knee. "Just like practice."

Farrendel stepped onto Julien's knee, then onto his shoulders. Julien gripped Farrendel's feet—a gesture that was unnecessary for Farrendel to keep his balance, but Julien did not know that—and slowly stood. Farrendel had to sway back to avoid getting a face-full of chandelier, and he crouched to avoid hitting his head on the ceiling when Julien straightened to his full height.

"It's a good thing you're such a lightweight." Julien stood steady underneath Farrendel's feet, though he smirked at Averett. "This would be a lot harder with Avie on my shoulders."

Averett straightened from where he had been affixing a ridiculous bow to one of the pillows. He puffed out his stomach. "Are you saying I'm getting fat?"

"Sitting behind a desk all day isn't doing you any favors. You should cut down on the snacks."

"You would snack too if you had to read through as much paperwork as I do in a day."

Farrendel ignored Averett and Julien as he looped the garland over the lowest tier of the chandelier, careful to keep the sparkling garland well away from the flicking gas flames. The last thing he wanted to do was burn down his and Essie's home here in Escarland. Especially now that they both loved it so much.

When he was finished, he did not wait for Julien to lower him. Instead, he jumped off Julien's shoulders, performed a front flip, and landed lightly on the carpet.

Not even Essie's mother commented on his elven acrobatics. Perhaps they were too engrossed in over-decorating the room. Or, maybe, they were so used to him that his agility no longer surprised them.

"There." Averett tied a bow in the ribbon he'd

fastened around one of the legs on the settee, then he stood, dusting off his hands. "I think that's the last of it."

It had better be. Farrendel took in the room. Every surface, piece of furniture, and wall hanging was draped in garlands, festooned with bows and ribbons, and overflowing with fake paper flowers, often paired in clashing colors. It was absolutely hideous...and Essie would probably love it. She had a thing for quirky, and she would likely find the awful decorating hilarious.

As Averett faced Farrendel, his gaze searched his face, his brows lowering. "We usually hide behind the couches, then jump out and yell *surprise* when Essie walks into the room. Will that be a problem for you?"

Loud, sudden noise created by people jumping out of hiding. Farrendel shuddered. Yes, it would definitely have been a problem if he had been in Essie's place, walking in on something like that.

But now that he was forewarned and would be one of those doing the hiding and surprising, he thought he could handle it. Probably.

Not meeting Averett's gaze, Farrendel shrugged. "I will be fine. But I appreciate the warning ahead of time." He finally managed to glance up. "Essie will like it?"

He could not imagine anyone *liking* such a surprise. But this was Essie. She'd found the surprise of getting married in two days an adventure rather than panicworthy.

"Yes." Averett gave him a single, firm nod.

"Like I said before, she's probably half-expecting it already, given the way Paige is currently keeping her distracted in Aldon." Edmund shrugged, flicking a stray piece of one of the garlands from his shoulder. "We've done this before, after all. Surprise parties are a common human custom."

Macha stepped closer to Farrendel, her eyes soft. "But my sons *will* curtail their exuberance if needed."

Averett, Julien, and Edmund shifted a bit, and Julien's murmured, "Yes, Mother," was not sarcastic but genuine.

Farrendel drew in a deep breath, hating that the breath still held a hint of a shudder from his tension.

He wanted to experience the full human custom, and he did not want his panic to hold Essie back from any enjoyment of this birthday. Since she and Farrendel would live so much longer than the rest of her family, she would only have a relatively few birthdays to celebrate with them.

That could be the reason her family was going so overboard with the excessive decorations, the massive cake, and the surprise party. They, too, felt the shortness of the time they had left with Essie before she would live the rest of her rather long life—by human standards—without them.

"I will be fine." Farrendel put as much firmness into those words as he could to convince Essie's family of the truth of them.

Still, he made a note to fetch the moss earplugs that he wore on the noisy Escarlish train as soon as he could so that he would have them ready when the time for the surprise came.

This was Essie's first birthday since she and Farrendel had married. He did not want to ruin it for her.

ESSIE WAS GOING to lose her voice from so much talking and laughing with Paige. It had been pleasant, spending time with her sister-in-law, even though she could see right past Paige's attempts at distraction.

Now, as they strolled toward Buckmore Cottage, Essie struggled to keep the tense anticipation from breaking across her face.

Paige glanced at her, then shook her head. "At least try to act surprised at your surprise party."

"That won't be hard. I always jump when the entire family leaps out of hiding." Essie grinned and reached for the door handle. After taking a moment to school her expression, she opened the door and stepped inside.

The main floor of Buckmore Cottage remained gloomy and dark. Suspiciously so. The gas lighting had been turned down as low as the flickering flames would go without turning them off entirely.

It was unlikely they would hold the party in the kitchen or upstairs. Essie turned and headed into the parlor.

She stopped short. Gaudy garlands, lacy ribbons, and lopsided bows embellished every surface, including the chandelier overhead.

No sooner had she taken in the decorations than Averett, Julien, Edmund, Mother, and the nephews Bertie and Finn leapt out from behind the couches and chairs, yelling "Surprise!"

Essie jumped, unable to help herself even though she had been expecting it. Then she laughed, shaking her head. "Look at this room. It looks like the decoration boxes threw up in here."

Across the room, Farrendel peeked over the back of one of the couches with the sheepish look of someone who had missed his cue and wasn't sure how to remedy the situation in a dignified manner.

Bertie and Finn raced forward, slamming into Essie's legs. "Auntie Essie!"

She hugged them, still laughing. Out of the corner of

her eye, she could see Farrendel slowly straighten, brushing himself off, before he tiptoed around the couch as if hoping no one would notice he hadn't jumped out with everyone else. At least he didn't seem panicked.

The rest of the evening passed in a blur of laughter and talking with her family. They ate a sumptuous meal and stuffed themselves with cake. Her family gave her a whole bunch of small gifts with their large gift being a painting of the family for her and Farrendel to hang in Estyra.

It was late by the time her family packed up and returned to Winstead Palace, though they left all the decorations in place. Except for the garland on the chandelier that Farrendel insisted on taking down before Julien left.

As the door closed behind her family, Essie sank onto the couch, shoving a beribboned pillow out of the way. "Whew. What an evening."

Farrendel flopped onto the seat next to her, resting his head on the back of the couch. He pulled the moss from his ears. "Your family is even louder when they are celebrating."

"I don't think that should surprise you." Essie took his hand, but she was too tired to move more than that.

"No." Farrendel tilted his head toward her. "Are you awake enough for one more surprise? I have yet to give you my gift."

She had noticed he hadn't given her anything, but he wasn't the type to make a big production out of giving a gift in front of her family. "Of course I'm awake enough for that."

Farrendel shifted, but he did not fully straighten from his slumped position on the couch. "Well, I cannot actually give you my gift since it is back in Estyra."

"Oh, really?" Essie smiled at Farrendel, wondering

what he had gotten her that he would leave it back in Estyra.

"Yes. It is rather...attached to our rooms there." Farrendel's smile twitched, a hint of mischief twinkling in his eyes.

"Do you want me to try to guess?" Essie fake-frowned at him. "I'm too tired for guessing games."

"It is something you mentioned you wanted in Estyra."

Essie rubbed her aching eyes. What had she wanted in Estyra? She tried to sort through her memories, but given the way Farrendel latched onto even the smallest details, it could have been a throwaway comment that she said, then promptly forgot.

Farrendel's smile took on even more of a smirk. He pushed slightly upright, twisting to face her. "I got you a bathtub."

That woke her up. "What? Really?"

"Yes. I ordered a copper tub from here in Escarland and left instructions for installing it in our rooms in Ellonahshinel." Farrendel was full-on grinning now. "And they are adding handrails on the branch up to our rooms and all the staircases in our suite."

"Really?" Her voice went up an octave with her excitement. She flung her arms around him and hugged him.

Handrails *and* a bathtub? He was spoiling her. Best birthday ever.

CHAPTER
TWO

FARRENDEL'S BIRTHDAY

"A 106th birthday is a ridiculous birthday to celebrate."

Essie grinned at Farrendel where he sat cross-legged on a cushion on the floor in the center of their main room in Estyra. The morning sunlight dappled the floor around him since, of course, elves would hold a birthday party in the morning rather than evening. "You didn't complain over the festivities for my birthday."

"But that was your birthday." Farrendel shrugged, staring at the floor. "And it was a culturally significant birthday. I would understand celebrating my hundredth birthday. We did that. Sort of. But celebrating a 106th birthday is just…excessive."

He was just nervous about being the center of attention. That was where this was coming from.

Essie sat on the floor across from him and touched his cheek, waiting until he met her gaze. "I know. And I'm sure your family won't go all out every year. But I think they need to celebrate. You came so close to never seeing this birthday. That's what they're celebrating—what I'm celebrating."

Farrendel took her hand, some of his tension easing. "Linshi, my shynafir."

He wasn't completely beyond his anxiety, but he was getting there.

Essie grinned and squeezed his hand. "Just be glad I convinced Weylind not to go a full surprise party route. Who knew he would find our stories about my surprise party so fascinating?"

Weylind had been enraptured by her descriptions of a human surprise party. Thankfully, he had seen the sense in having a not-surprise party for Farrendel instead. He wasn't going to take everyone jumping out and yelling "surprise" all that well, nor were elves really inclined toward the whole hiding and shouting thing.

When she glanced up, a branch outside their window was waving frantically back and forth. As she watched, a second branch joined it, dancing wildly to get her attention.

Essie laughed and pushed to her feet. "Your non-surprise party is ready. Come on. Just don't look down, all right?"

They had one rather large surprise for Farrendel, but hopefully it was the kind of surprise he would like. A non-loud, non-startling one.

Farrendel pushed to his feet, still looking more wary than excited. But he took her hand, and she didn't catch him peeking down as they left their main room.

Essie trailed her fingers along the new, safe handrails on either side of the stairs to their treetop bedroom. Instead of entering, they walked around the porch with its added spindles in the railing making it seem more secure, before they took the smaller branch to the lift.

The lift was shaped like a gazebo, dangling from a very sturdy elven rope. Over the past months, Farrendel had upgraded it with a hand crank to raise and lower it instead of the simple rope and pulley mechanism, making it easier for Essie to take the lift to go into Estyra.

Essie gestured to the crank in the center. "If you would, please."

After they stepped inside, Farrendel gripped the handle of the crank and started lowering them. It took a few minutes for the lift to descend. Then it clunked into something wooden, settling onto a platform.

Farrendel's forehead scrunched, and he had likely heard the minute difference in the sound compared to the old platform.

Essie held out her hand again. "Will you be all right if I ask you to close your eyes for this next part?"

He hesitated a moment, his gaze searching her face. After a moment, he nodded and squeezed his eyes shut.

It was an act of supreme trust in her. She wasn't going to let him down.

"No peeking." She tried to keep her voice light. Gently, she tugged him forward, stepping off the lift onto the platform built into the roof of the new building grown onto the forest floor. "There's a set of stairs in front of us. Here." She guided his hand to the handrail.

Some of the apprehension lifted as a smile curved the corners of his mouth. "Handrails."

"Of course." Essie led the way down the stairs, both of them running their hands over the handrail.

When they reached the forest floor, Essie tugged Farrendel into position in front of the new building. His family stood clustered in front of the building, grinning.

Weylind was downright beaming, and even Jalissa seemed to have pushed through the malaise that had plagued her for months.

"Your family is here. I don't want their presence to startle you." Essie still held his hand in the human way, their fingers clasped.

"I can sense them." Farrendel kept his eyes shut, and some of his tension eased.

"Of course he can." Weylind was as close to bouncing on his toes in excitement as a dignified elf king ever got.

"All right. Open your eyes." Essie held her breath. She knew Farrendel would like it, but somehow she was nervous all the same.

Farrendel opened his eyes and blinked. Then, he went rigid, his eyes widening. "What is this?"

"Your new workshop." Weylind gestured to it. "For doing your—what did you call it?—magical engineering. Machasheni, Jalissa, and I built it."

The workshop was grown out of saplings, their twigs dotted with the early spring buds that would turn into leaves. Like all elven buildings, it was airy and elegant, beautiful in the way it created walls and a roof out of living trees.

Weylind was still grinning in a way Essie had rarely seen. "Go ahead. Go inside."

Farrendel remained silent as he walked forward and opened the door.

Essie kept her grip on his hand, just as curious. She had yet to see inside, since she had been tasked with keeping Farrendel distracted while his family worked.

Inside, the building held only one room. At the moment, it was empty of cabinets or furniture. Only a few crates sat in the center.

Farrendel let go of her hand and turned in a slow circle, still silent.

Behind Essie, Farrendel's family filed into the workshop. Jalissa bit her lower lip, hiding in the corner. Ryfon and Brina glanced between Weylind and Farrendel, as if not sure what to do.

Weylind gestured to the crates, then the walls. "We did not furnish it yet. We figured that you would want a say in the layout."

Farrendel had yet to say a word.

Essie approached him and rested a hand on his arm. "Do you like it?"

When he finally turned to her, a slow grin spread across his face. "This is perfect."

That was all it took for the floodgates of his chatter to open. Farrendel started talking nonstop. Weylind and Jalissa set to work building a workbench across the back wall beneath the window, flanked by storage cupboards above and storage beneath. More cabinets filled the left-hand wall, including the cold cupboard that Rharreth and Melantha had sent.

Once the storage cupboards were built, Essie pitched in with the others, unpacking the crates of gears, mechanical parts, and tools she had ordered from Escarland, as per Lance Marion's instructions.

Partway through the day, elven servants provided lunch while Miss Merrick delivered a cake. They all paused for munching. Ryfon and Brina seemed especially enamored with the Escarlish dessert, though none of the others said no to a piece. Essie had to school her features so she didn't laugh at seeing Farrendel's dignified family sporting blue tongues thanks to the coloring in the icing.

It turned out even better than she had imagined while planning this.

BY THE TIME Farrendel's family left, the sun glowed golden orange through the trees.

Farrendel sat cross-legged on the workbench, sorting the boxes of nuts and bolts into the dividers grown into the drawer he had pulled out below him.

So many drawers and pegs and shelves where he could perfectly organize everything. It made something inside him giddy to see all those tools neatly lined up in the drawers.

Essie leaned against the workbench, smiling. "So was it worth celebrating your 106th birthday?"

He glanced up, grinning so broadly his face hurt. "Yes. Linshi." A worry stabbed into him. "Did I remember to thank my family before they left?"

He could not remember. Everything had been a blur of activity after the first surprise.

"Yes. Several times." Essie planted her hands on the workbench, bounced on her toes, then boosted herself onto the workbench, sitting next to him. "I'm never going to see you anymore, am I?"

"You will know where to find me." Farrendel touched her cheek before he leaned forward and kissed her.

He was not sure he could express how much this new workshop meant to him. By building it, his family had shown their support for his new pursuit of mechanical engineering. Essie had showered him with love by tracking down all the items to stock the workshop.

But, most of all, it was a new sanctuary for him. His rooms had become just as much Essie's space as his. And while he did not mind sharing with Essie, he had lost a space where he could be alone when needed.

This workshop gave that back to him.

Essie kissed him, making him thankful his family had, finally, left.

When he drew back, he searched Essie's gaze. The understanding in her eyes made him think that, perhaps, she knew just how much he had needed this sanctuary to call his own.

THE GUARD AND THE MAID

Chapters 1 and 2 of this story take place during Troll Queen. Chapter 3 occurs between Troll Queen and Pretense. The rest of the story takes place during Pretense. The epilogue takes place shortly after the end of Shield Band.

Iyrinder, elf warrior and guard to King Weylind, hefted his bag over his shoulder as he took in the sight of the human palace, its gardens, walls, forested parkland, and paths that led to Buckmore Cottage. This was going to be Iyrinder's home for the next number of months while he served on a temporary assignment to Prince Farrendel's guard detail.

It would be an interesting challenge, learning to work so closely with humans while guarding Prince Farrendel. But if Iyrinder wanted to eventually earn a spot as a captain of his own squad of royal guards, then this assignment would be a good stepping branch upward.

Iyrinder followed Prince Julien around the side of the square, wooden mansion that was crawling with vines and branches in a strange amalgamation of human design and elven magic.

He glanced over his shoulder as Prince Farrendel and Princess Elspetha hurried into the mansion. He would have felt better if he could have done a search of the place first, to ensure it was safe.

Prince Julien glanced at him and nodded gravely. "Don't worry. Captain Merrick and his guards have already swept the place this morning, and Buckmore Cottage is within the Winstead Palace complex. It's personally guarded by me and the palace guards, and we've made some structural changes after what happened three weeks ago. It's the most secure place in all of Aldon."

Iyrinder would have been more comforted if Prince Farrendel and Princess Elspetha had not been kidnapped from a hallway of Winstead Palace a mere three weeks ago.

When they reached the front of the mansion, they strolled along the short stretch of graveled drive that led from the manor's front door to the gate in the palace wall that gave a view into the city streets of Aldon.

To one side of the gate, a squat, stone building sat, its windows barred and its door made of solid, thick oak. Just looking at it made Iyrinder itchy. Surely he would not be expected to sleep inside, would he?

If he was, then he would have to deal with it. This was the assignment. Guard Prince Farrendel—and Princess Elspetha too, though the prince seemed to be more of a target—and learn how to integrate into a human guard squad, whatever it took.

Prince Julien rapped on the door.

It swung open, revealing a human male with sandy brown hair and wearing a leather vest. His stance had the confidence of someone who had faced a lot of trouble and come out on top. Iyrinder was no judge of human ages, but he did not appear old, though he seemed older than Iyrinder.

His face was familiar, and Iyrinder vaguely remembered that this human had been a part of King Averett's guard detail. They had crossed paths several times during the war, though Iyrinder had never directly spoken with him.

Prince Julien gestured to the man. "Iyrinder, this is Captain Eugene Merrick. He will be your commanding officer while you are here in Escarland. Merrick, this is Iyrinder. You might remember him from the war. Although he's under your command while he's here, listen to him. He's a respected member of King Weylind's guards."

"I look forward to working together." Captain Merrick stuck out his hand.

Iyrinder stared down at it.

Prince Julien gestured down at Captain Merrick's hand. "You shake it. If you want. You don't have to. But it is a standard human custom."

Right. Iyrinder had seen it several times during the war, but he was not sure exactly what it meant.

It meant something to the humans. So he needed to put aside his discomfort and just do it.

Iyrinder took Captain Merrick's hand as he had seen the humans do. Captain Merrick gave their hands a firm shake, then let go.

"I'll leave you to get settled." Prince Julien nodded to each of them. "See you in the morning at the crack of dawn."

As Prince Julien started to turn away, Iyrinder hesitated. Should he say something? He was used to working on King Weylind's guard squad, where his job was to keep his counsel to himself for the most part.

But this was different. How much would he be allowed to speak up? Should he?

He cleared his throat. "This is Farrendel Laesornysh.

You should plan to be here before the crack of dawn, if you indeed wish to join his morning practice."

Prince Julien grinned and nodded. "I'll plan on that."

There was something about the way he said it, almost as if he had already known that. Was that some kind of test? Of whom? Iyrinder? Captain Merrick?

Perhaps Iyrinder was imagining things.

As Prince Julien strolled away, Captain Merrick turned to Iyrinder. "Come inside. I'll show you around and introduce you to the guards assigned to the squad."

Iyrinder nodded and trailed behind the captain into the building. The stone pressed around him, eliciting a faint ache at his temples. Nothing severe, but bad enough that he did not relish the amount of time he would have to spend inside this building.

No matter. This was part of his training. He would have to learn to push through such discomfort to properly guard Prince Farrendel in this place of stone palaces and cobbled streets.

The entry hall to the place was spacious, more a staging area than a foyer. Captain Merrick gestured to a door on the right. "This room is the weapons room. Across the way is the kitchen. We're responsible for making our own food. If we're lucky, my sister will send food our way for lunch or supper, but we'll definitely be on our own for breakfast. The barracks for the rest of the squad is through here."

Captain Merrick opened a door on the left next to the kitchens. Inside, rows of stacked beds—bunks, if Iyrinder remembered correctly—lined each side of the room. A few men loitered inside or lay on the beds, though those who were awake snapped to attention at the sight of Captain Merrick.

Was this where Iyrinder was going to have to sleep? In

this barracks with all the other guards? In this stone guardhouse that was slowly, inevitably giving him a headache?

Captain Merrick gestured to Iyrinder. "Men, this is Iyrinder, a trained member of King Weylind's guard squad. While he is here, he is my second-in-command. Follow his orders as you would follow mine."

Really? That was unexpected. Iyrinder had thought Captain Merrick would treat him as just another member of the squad, not promote him to second-in-command.

Iyrinder swept a glance over the assembled humans. Would they take his orders, if he gave them? Or would they hesitate, since he was an elf?

The three men who were awake saluted Captain Merrick. "Yes, sir."

Nothing in their expressions or stances indicated that they were uncomfortable with the orders. Hopefully it was the case. If Captain Merrick had done his job when picking men for his squad, he would have ensured that he had men who had no problems with elves.

"Pass the word along to the others." Captain Merrick returned the salute, then turned and left the room.

Iyrinder followed him. Did that mean that Iyrinder was not going to have to sleep here? If not, where would he be assigned to sleep?

Captain Merrick strode across the way and into another hallway. "My room is here. There are a few other rooms here, and I figure we can use one of them as a strategy room if needed. The water closet is through here. The hot water can be temperamental, so I hope you don't mind a cold shower or two."

Great. That sounded…pleasant. Oh, well. Any shower was better than the utter lack of bathing opportunities they had experienced while fighting across Kostaria.

The short hallway between the rooms ended in another thick, oak door.

Captain Merrick turned and held out a large key. "Here's your key so you'll be able to come and go as needed. If I remember from the war, you elves are uncomfortable with stone, correct?"

Iyrinder nodded, not sure how much to say. The elves' weakness for stone was not exactly a secret anymore, but he was not sure how much he should say. In the end, he settled on, "Yes."

"Verbose as most elves, I see." Captain Merrick grinned at him, then pushed the door open. "It isn't much, but I trust that you'll be able to spruce it up to your satisfaction."

Captain Merrick strode through the door, then off to the side, giving Iyrinder a view of the outside.

A grove of trees grew a few yards away from the back door. In the center of the trees, a small wooden structure crouched, looking like one of the Escarlish tents, except that it was made of wood instead of canvas. A layer of canvas had been spread over it, probably to make it fully waterproof. The structure was big enough that it could probably house four elven guards comfortably enough, maybe more if they did not mind tight quarters. For just Iyrinder, it would be plenty spacious.

"Feel free to make any updates necessary and speak up if you have any suggestions. We would like to make a permanent place to stay for the elven guards who are here on rotation." Captain Merrick gestured toward the triangle-shaped structure perched a foot off the ground on a platform. "It will need more insulation and perhaps a wood stove installed before winter. It isn't the warmest shelter right now."

"I will be fine." Iyrinder shrugged against the weight of his pack. It would be warmer than Kostaria.

"Well, don't hesitate to speak up if you find yourself freezing out here." Captain Merrick eyed Iyrinder, as if he thought he would lie about being cold. "You and I will be on duty during the day so that we can escort Prince Farrendel and Princess Elspeth when necessary."

Iyrinder nodded. He had seen the state that Prince Farrendel was currently in. Keeping limited, friendly faces around him would lessen his anxiety as much as possible.

Captain Merrick continued without missing a beat. "The rest of the guards will rotate through night shifts, but with you out here, you will wake if you hear a disturbance at Buckmore Cottage."

A wise solution. Iyrinder studied the surrounding parkland. With the structure tucked into the trees at the back of the guardhouse, it was somewhat sheltered from the noise of the Aldon streets, and it was only a short walk through the parkland from Buckmore Cottage.

And he did not have to sleep in the stone building. He would even have a roof over his head. That was better than the bedroll under the stars that he had been hoping for as his best case scenario.

"Get settled in. Breakfast will be in the mess first thing in the morning." Captain Merrick saluted, turned, and strode back into the guardhouse.

Iyrinder strode toward the structure. It had nothing but thick canvas for the door, and it had clearly been put together in haste. Gaps remained between the boards and a few of the nails were not even pounded in all the way.

But the effort was appreciated. The Escarlish had not had much notice that they were on their way. This would have been built hastily in the hours between getting the telegram that Prince Farrendel and Princess Elspeth were on their way with an elf guard in tow and their arrival.

Iyrinder would just have to improve it a little at a time while he was here. He did not have the strength of magic to completely renovate it in a single night, the way someone like King Weylind could. But he could use some of his limited magic to close up one, maybe two gaps between the boards per night. He did not dare drain his magic too far in case it was needed to protect his prince or princess. But using a bit each night would make this more habitable within a week or two.

Setting down his gear, he created hooks in the walls on each side, then hung his hammock. While elves slept in beds at home, it was standard practice in the army to sleep in hammocks in treetop shelters, since they were quick to move and hang.

He settled in and stared up at the gaps in the boards, though all he could see was the canvas covering.

Hopefully this trip would work as King Weylind hoped. Peace and healing for Prince Farrendel. Training in working with humans for Iyrinder.

CHAPTER
TWO

Patience Merrick scrubbed the breakfast dishes, setting the clean dishes in a rack to drip dry while she finished with the rest in the basin.

In the month she had been working as combined cook, maid, and housekeeper for Prince Farrendel and Princess Elspeth, the new job had turned out to be just what Patience had hoped it would be. Now if only she could convince the prince and princess that she was so indispensable that they needed to take her along when they returned to Estyra. That was the only way to ensure that Patience would not be separated from her brother Eugene, the only family member she had left.

A knock sounded on the back kitchen door a moment before Eugene stuck his head inside. His light brown hair was a darker than Patience's blonde, though their blue eyes were nearly the same color. "Do you have a moment?"

"Yes, what do you need?" Patience dried her hands, then hung the towel from the bar.

"Have you come across any spare clothes in the

servants' quarters by chance?" Eugene stepped all the way inside the room. "Prince Farrendel would like to go into Aldon, and we'd like to keep it on the down-low. I need to track down workers' garb for Prince Farrendel, his elven guard, and myself."

"I think I saw a trunk in the storage room." Patience had taken a turn around the room when she arrived, just to familiarize herself with what was there, but she hadn't stepped foot in there since.

She led the way down the servants' hall and into the storage room. She shoved aside a few random boxes, tossed back the cloths draping the spare furniture, and located the trunk she'd seen. She pointed to it. Her brother was here. He might as well carry it. "Here it is. I think it might have been spare clothes for the gardeners at one point."

Eugene knelt, brushed off a layer of dust, and opened the lid. After a moment, he nodded, closed the lid, and hefted the trunk, standing as he did so. "Perfect. Do you have a moment to help? It might take a few pins and tucks to get these clothes to fit any of us."

"I'll grab my sewing kit and meet you in the guardhouse." Patience spun and hurried down the hall. She was a fair hand at mending. One had to be, when one's wardrobe and finances were limited.

It only took a moment to grab her sewing kit, then she hurried out the back door, around the side of Buckmore Cottage, and down the short drive to the guardhouse.

Perhaps her hurry was unnecessary, but it never paid to keep royalty waiting. If Prince Farrendel wanted to go into Aldon, then she wasn't going to be the reason he was delayed.

When she stepped into the entrance hall of the guardhouse, only Eugene was there, the trunk open as he sorted through the clothing. He held up a shirt. "I think this one should work. Could you mend this tear?"

She took the shirt, sat on the floor, and opened her sewing case. Within moments, she found a matching thread and set to work stitching the fabric. There would be a pucker. The threads around the tear were too frayed for her to make this mend invisible. But that would be just as well. If Prince Farrendel wanted to appear the down-on-his-luck gardener while strolling around Aldon, a few hasty mends would only help the façade.

As she finished, the prince's elf guard strode out of one of the doorways on the far side of the room. His chestnut hair—too brown to truly be red, but too red to be called brown—lay slightly damp against his elven-style tunic.

Patience had seen him around, of course. But she'd never spoken with him. She wasn't even sure what his name was. He seemed as shy and reticent as his prince.

Eugene took the shirt she had been mending from her, then tossed it to the elf guard. "Here. This one is yours. As is that pile, if you want to try them on."

The elf wore a flat look as he caught the shirt. As he bent and scooped up the pile Eugene had tossed on the floor, the elf's mouth might have twitched with a curl for a heartbeat before smoothing once again.

Patience ducked her head and tried to smother her grin. Apparently used gardeners' clothes weren't exactly this elf's cup of tea.

The elf retreated back the way he had come.

Eugene picked out a few outfits for himself, then also disappeared into his room to change.

Patience took a moment to look through the rest of the trunk. Her brother had set aside the nicest, best-smelling set of items, and she assumed those were saved for the prince.

The clothes her brother tossed to the elf guard would be way too big. Was he a belt kind of person or would he rather use pins to tuck in the waist?

Or...she pulled out suspenders. That might work. It would fit the persona her brother was going for.

She stood and glanced up, starting when she found the elf guard standing there, a hand gripping his trousers to keep them up. Far too big, as she had suspected. Those elves were rail-thin even when they hadn't been half-starved like the prince. She smoothed a hand over her apron, then held out the suspenders. "Here, these will help."

The elf stared down at the suspenders, then swung his gaze back up to her. The slight pinch to his brows was the only thing that gave away his puzzlement.

"They hold up your trousers. Do you..." She wasn't quite sure how to go about offering this. "Do you want help getting them on?"

The tips of the elf's ears turned pink. "I am sure I can figure them out."

She handed over the suspenders and slid her hands into her apron pockets, waiting.

The elf studied the suspenders, dangling them from one hand while his other hand still clutched his trousers so they didn't end up down at his knees. He tried to buckle the back clip to the front of his trousers' band with one hand, then held it out from his body as if he was trying to figure out what to do now.

Eugene's laugh rang out from the doorway before he strolled into the room, looking every inch the grubby factory worker.

It was enough for Patience's breath to catch on a lump

in her throat. Dressed in a grungy off-white shirt, suspenders, and a blandly brown set of trousers, Eugene looked so much like their father. Sure, their father's face had been more lined, his hair fully gray, his back more stooped. But it was like seeing their father walk into her life again.

Oblivious to her reaction—or perhaps ignoring it —Eugene slapped the elf guard on the back. "Need a little help?"

"He says he can figure it out." Patience pressed her mouth into a tight line to stop both her smile and her laughter.

"I see that." Eugene crossed his arms, a grin playing around his mouth.

The elf guard's gaze darted from Patience to Eugene, then his shoulders slumped. "I believe I could use help."

Eugene grinned, then stepped forward. "Just keep a hold of your trousers, and I'll set this to rights. This part goes in the back, and these clip to the front."

Within a few moments, Eugene had the suspenders situated the right way, and the elf tentatively released his death grip on his trousers. When they didn't immediately drop to his knees, his shoulders gave a slight wiggle, as if he was breathing a sigh of relief.

It was a strangely adorable gesture, especially with his pointed ears and that long, chestnut-verging-on-auburn hair of his.

Eugene waved to him. "Prince Farrendel has short hair, but Iyrinder here doesn't. Any ideas on how best to hide his hair? You have more experience with long hair than I do."

Patience shook herself. Right. Focus on helping her brother disguise the prince and his guard. "It's chilly out today. You'll be wearing coats. If you put the coat on over your hair, then wear a hat, that will hide most of your hair. Maybe turn the collar up. That wouldn't seem odd, given the chilly breeze. That should hide his hair well enough. It wouldn't hurt to tie it back first. That should keep it from straggling into view at an inopportune moment."

Eugene nodded, then picked up one of the ratty coats found in the trunks. "Good call. Iyrinder, are you all right with tying your hair back?"

The elf—Iyrinder—gave something like a grimace, but he nodded after a moment. He patted his pockets, as if looking for something to use.

Patience fished in her pockets and pulled out a black ribbon—black to match her servants' uniform—and stepped forward. "Let me help. No way either of you will get it right."

Iyrinder's shoulders stiffened, but he turned his back to her. Clear permission to go ahead.

She gathered up his slightly damp hair, the strands sliding silken and soft through her fingers. Her heart beat harder, rising in a flutter in her throat. This close to him, she caught a whiff of a minty, forest scent from his hair, and she was acutely aware of his tall, muscular frame and the tense set to his shoulders.

The door opened and closed behind her, and Prince Farrendel stepped inside. His hair, too, was damp, and he flicked a glance around the room as if he was thinking about bolting.

Patience kept her head down and concentrated on tying Iyrinder's hair without pulling it and without giving away how her fingers were trembling.

Eugene handed the stack of clothes to the prince, and Prince Farrendel disappeared into the water closet.

She tied off the ribbon with a simple knot rather than

a bow, then stepped away from Iyrinder, hoping her voice remained steady. "That should work. I'd better get back to the Cottage. I have bread rising that will need to go into the oven soon."

"Of course. Thanks for your help." Eugene nodded, then turned to Iyrinder. Probably to go over their plans for the day.

Patience hurried toward the door, stepping out into a chilly fall breeze that slapped against her heated face. She gasped in a few steadying breaths, trying to banish the memories of soft hair and hard muscles.

He was a guard. He had likely not even noticed her as anything more than the maid. And, truthfully, that was how she preferred it, no matter the draw.

Besides, she did have bread dough that would be the size of a pumpkin if she didn't attend to it soon.

CHAPTER
THREE

THREE AND A HALF MONTHS LATER...

Iyrinder stood to the side of the magic-powered heating coil that Prince Farrendel had designed with that human inventor friend of his. The heating device was one of three that the amir had gotten working before this sledding and boarding event organized by Princess Elspetha and Illyna.

A few yards away, fires with kettles heated water, and most of the older and stodgier elf nobles clustered there, their mouths curling as they sipped tea and took in the scene.

Iyrinder shifted, stomping his feet to keep his toes warm in his fur-lined boots. He tugged his wool cloak tighter over the coat he wore underneath, the thick mittens making his fingers clumsy.

Princess Elspetha stood behind the table, dispensing hot chocolate and talking cheerily with the line of elves waiting to get their cup of the beverage. A box sat next to the heating coil where the elves could stuff a donation.

All the proceeds of this event would go to the foundation Princess Elspeth and Prince Farrendel had started to support elven warriors wounded in the war.

An elf woman glanced down the line of tables and fires before she cautiously tiptoed up to the table. She dug into her pocket, coming up with only a couple of coins.

Princess Elspetha reached out a staying hand. "Don't worry about it. It's donate what you can. This one is on me." With her other hand, she pulled coins from her pocket and dumped them into the box.

"Are you sure, Amirah?" The woman blinked, glancing from the princess to the donation box to the few coins in her palm.

"Of course." Princess Elspetha smiled, then set to work preparing a cup of hot chocolate.

Iyrinder suppressed his own smile and tore his gaze away to scan their surroundings again, looking for threats to the princess.

No one was crowding close. No one was sticking their hands in their pocket in a suspicious way.

Prince Farrendel and Eugene were at the top of the hill, distributing sleds and boards to those waiting at the top for their turn. A rig of roots and pulleys, powered by elven magic, towed sleds, boards, and those who could not walk up the hill by themselves, up the hill. While most elves chose to go down on boards, there were those like Fingol who had permanent injuries to their legs or feet, who chose the Escarlish sleds instead.

"Enjoy your hot chocolate." Princess Elspetha handed the mug of hot chocolate to the elf.

For a moment, there were no more elves lining up in front of their table, and Iyrinder glanced at the princess, knowing she would probably want to fill the silence with chatter rather than let it remain quiet.

She met his gaze, grinning. "This has been a success, don't you think?"

"Yes, Amirah. Everyone seems to be enjoying themselves." Iyrinder glanced around, his gaze landing on the clusters of stuffy nobles once again.

It was a testament to the force of King Weylind's disapproval that the nobles had deigned to show up at all. Hopefully at least some of them would get into the spirit of the day and donate to the foundation.

"Almost everyone, anyway." Princess Elspetha sent a glance in the direction of the nobles as well. "At least my family is having a good time."

King Averett, Queen Paige, and their two sons piled onto a sled. Prince Julien gave them a push, then they whooped and hollered all the way down the hill at a pitch that no elf would ever willingly make in public. A third of their security team stood on top of the hill while a third waited at the bottom. But it was the third that piled into another sled and shadowed their king and queen, going down the hill with stoic expressions, that brought a smile.

Prince Julien remained at the top of the hill, lending a hand where he could. Only Prince Edmund was missing, and he must have been the token royal left behind in Aldon to ensure that the entire Escarlish royal family could not be killed off in one fell swoop.

It was the sight of King Weylind lining up on a board next to Ryfon, as if they were preparing to race each other down the hill, that threatened to break through Iyrinder's on-duty mask. It was not just Prince Farrendel who seemed to be more lighthearted now that the war was over.

Iyrinder's chest ached, as if something grated inside him. He was content with his work as a guard, and now that the war was over, it was a much more peaceful job.

But was *he* more at peace? Should he not feel more at peace in some way?

Instead, he felt more empty than ever. As if the peace just shone a light on how much his life was missing. His goal to become a captain with his own guard squad seemed far more hollow a dream than it used to be.

He had his macha and isciena. But he wanted...more. A wife. Children.

Why did Patience Merrick's face come to mind? Why could he not banish her from his thoughts?

But two big things still stood between them: the cultural divide and the fact that she was his commanding officer's younger sister.

This was not something he could simply pursue and move on if it did not work out. There would be consequences.

Perhaps when he returned to Escarland, he would simply attempt to talk to her more. Let things develop naturally, if they did. No formal courtship. Not until both of them were absolutely sure they were willing to overcome the things between them.

"Iyrinder?"

He blinked at the sound of Princess Elspetha's voice. When he turned to her, she was grinning.

She placed her hands on her hips. "I don't think guards are supposed to be distracted."

"Pardon, Amirah." Iyrinder straightened his shoulders. He was not about to admit what he had been thinking about, but he needed to say something before the princess drew her own—probably right—conclusions. He tipped his head toward the device. "I was contemplating the wonder of elven magic and human invention."

As he had known it would, the comment distracted

Princess Elspetha. "It is pretty amazing, isn't it? I'm so proud of Farrendel for applying to Hanford University."

"It is an unusual pursuit." Iyrinder still was not sure what he thought about an elven prince going to the humans for training in how to better use his magic. But his work with the human inventor had shown good results so far. It would be interesting to see where the prince took his magic from there.

"He will change both of our kingdoms, I think." Princess Elspetha's gaze strayed past Iyrinder, and her grin widened.

"That is an exaggeration." Prince Farrendel stomped toward them through the snow, then drew his wife into a hug.

Princess Elspetha laughed, then patted Farrendel's coat. "I don't think so. Back me up on this one, Iyrinder."

Iyrinder held up his hands and backed a step away. "No comment."

Princess Elspetha laughed, shook her head at him, then turned back to Prince Farrendel. "You've come to take me boarding?"

"I keep my promises." Prince Farrendel grinned, grabbed his wife's hand, and tugged her away from the table.

"But..." Princess Elspetha glanced toward the table she had been manning.

"I will take over." Queen Rheva glided into Princess Elspetha's spot behind the table.

"Linshi." Elspetha waved, then she was the one dragging Prince Farrendel toward the top of the hill. Prince Farrendel claimed a board as they passed Prince Julien.

Eugene joined Iyrinder, his coat covered in snow from the times he had gone down the hill. "Go on. I'll take up the station here for a while. I wouldn't mind the chance to warm up my fingers, and I'm sure you'd like the chance to go down the hill a few times."

"Linshi." Iyrinder was not going to argue.

As Eugene claimed a mug of hot chocolate from Queen Rheva, cradling it in his hands as he scanned the hillside for threats, Iyrinder located a board and took up a position next to Prince Farrendel and Princess Elspetha.

The two of them were still trying to get situated on the board. Prince Farrendel had his hands on the princess's waist. She was giggling as she tried to get on the board, but every time she did, the board started slipping down the hill, and she would stagger off. "You elves make this look so easy!"

Prince Farrendel, too, was laughing, his eyes squinted with the force of his laughter. "It is easy. I have you. Do not step back, and I will hop on."

"All right. On three." Princess Elspetha gathered herself through her giggles, drew in a deep breath, and braced herself. "One. Two."

Iyrinder bent his knees, poised to drop his own board to the snow the moment the prince and princess managed to get on their own board.

"Three." Elspetha hopped onto the board, then wobbled, nearly taking a step back.

Before she could, Farrendel jumped onto the board with his feet braced on either side of hers. He wrapped one arm around her waist, holding her close, while he held out his other arm to keep both of them balanced as the board glided down the hill.

Iyrinder dropped his board and lightly leapt onto it as it slid across the snow, packed hard and slick after the morning of boarding and sledding.

With two of them on their board, the prince and princess flew down the hill. Only the princess's wobbling and the prince's leaning into the turns to keep them from falling slowed them down.

Iyrinder bent his knees, keeping low to minimize his wind resistance and maximize his speed. He kept his gaze moving between the hill ahead, his prince and princess, and their surroundings.

Farrendel and Elspetha veered from the main track into the side where the snow was not as hard packed. Puffs of snow flared from under their board a moment before they tipped over and fell in an explosion of snow.

Iyrinder swerved across the hill, dodging around a sled coming down filled with four elves piled onto each other and whooping in a manner that was barely dignified. He pulled up, sending up a spray of snow, and hopped off the board.

Only then could he hear the way both Elspetha and Farrendel were laughing—her giggling, him chuckling.

"We're fine, Iyrinder. Thank you for rushing over here all worried." Elspetha spoke through her giggles, and she waved to herself and Farrendel where they sprawled in the snow. "It seems even Farrendel's athleticism can't entirely overcome my inability to balance on a board."

"You just need more practice." Farrendel sat up, brushing snow from his coat and cloak.

Elspetha grimaced. "Perhaps in a few minutes. But first, let's round up our brothers. I want to all pile onto a sled like we used to as kids. Oh, look. The big sled is nearly all the way up the hill. We'd better hurry if we want to snag it."

She popped to her feet, halfway to the base of the hill by the time Farrendel glided to his feet, calling after her, "I do not think that sled is designed to hold five adults."

"No, it isn't, but that's part of the fun." Elspetha

waved to catch Prince Julien's attention. "Julien, grab the big sled!"

After collecting both boards, Iyrinder tromped after them, keeping his thoughts to himself. It was his job to protect them from outside threats. But if they wanted to get themselves hurt while sledding, that was their own problem.

At the top of the hill, Iyrinder passed one of the boards to a waiting elf, but he kept the other. He waited in the background while Elspetha rounded up the largest sled, King Averett, Prince Julien, and a rather reluctant King Weylind. Queen Paige stood off to the side with Queen Rheva, both of them shaking their heads and laughing. The two young Escarlish princes were giggling, and their mother assured them that their father and uncles would go with them on the next trip.

Even Iyrinder had to fight a grin as he watched Prince Farrendel, Princess Elspetha, Princess Brina, Prince Ryfon, King Weylind, King Averett, and Prince Julien all piled onto the sled in a tangle of limbs and no personal space whatsoever.

King Weylind was squished between Prince Julien at the back of the sled and King Averett in front of him. His feet were somewhere on Princess Brina's lap, piled under everyone else's legs. Prince Farrendel had ended up at the very front of the sled, and he had his knees tucked up to his chin to fit everyone else behind him while he had to hug Princess Elspetha's feet to keep them from falling off the front of the sled.

"This is ridiculous." King Weylind squirmed, as if he intended to bail out of there, but he could barely move.

"It'll be fun!" Elspetha twisted as much as she could. "Iyrinder, give us a push!"

With so much weight on the sled, it had sunk into the snow instead of sliding.

Iyrinder stabbed the board into the snow and stepped forward past the huddle of kings' guards, who were watching with semi-horrified, semi-bewildered looks for the elves and grins for the humans.

Iyrinder hesitated for a moment, then he placed his hands on Prince Julien's back and pushed. He only managed to shift the sled a few inches before it ground to a halt.

He braced himself, dug deep, and pushed harder. This time, he got the sled over the crest of the hill, and it started down, gliding slowly at first, then picking up speed.

Elspetha's shrieking laugh mingled with her brothers' whooping cheers. Brina and Ryfon gave a few experimental whoops of their own, but King Weylind sat there stoically. Probably gritting his teeth, if Iyrinder were to guess. Julien kept turning his head to the side, spitting out King Weylind's hair as it lashed his face.

Before the sled could get too far away, some of the guards piled into their own sled while Iyrinder hopped on his board.

As the heavily laden sled careened down the hill, it picked up even more speed until it was leaving the guards and Iyrinder well behind. It flew past several other sleds and boards that had left before them and kept right on going, blowing by the end of the hill where most sleds and boards had been halting. Snow puffed, hitting Farrendel in the face.

Iyrinder crouched lower on the board. Could those in the sled even see the tree that they were headed for with all the snow they were getting pelted with? There was no way Iyrinder could get there in time to stop them.

At the last moment, everyone in the sled leaned. The sled swerved, its path curving. It missed the tree, but it tipped over as it crashed into a snow drift in a burst of white.

This time, Iyrinder did not rush over. The guards had it covered as they converged on their kings.

When Iyrinder got there, everyone—except for King Weylind—was laughing as they disentangled limbs. He might not have been laughing, but he was smiling. Coming from Iyrinder's king, that was quite the display of mirth.

Iyrinder simply stood back and faced the encroaching forest to watch for threats.

Months ago when he sat through Prince Farrendel's rushed wedding to a human princess, none of them could have guessed the joy that Princess Elspetha would bring not only to Prince Farrendel but to the whole royal family.

Maybe they would bring a new kind of life to all of Tarenhiel. Too long, Tarenhiel had languished in a haze of tradition even as the greatness of the elves seemed to be fading. It might look different, but Prince Farrendel and Princess Elspetha seemed determined to bring the greatness back, one way or another.

If one human could do all of that, then what could a human do in Iyrinder's life, if he was brave enough to take the leap?

FOUR

FOUR MONTHS LATER...

Patience whisked the eggs, then poured into a pan. She waited a moment to let the eggs get a nice, cooked bottom before she flipped the flat, round cooked eggs over. Once that was cooked, she piled chopped ham and veggies onto one half. Then she folded the other half of the eggs over, forming an omelet.

The kitchen door whooshed open, and the elf guard Iyrinder stepped inside, giving her a warm smile. In the predawn gray, his chestnut hair appeared more brown without the sunlight to turn the strands red. "Good morning, Miss Merrick."

She scooped the omelet onto a plate, then crossed the room to hold it out to him. "Morning."

Iyrinder leaned against the wall, eating the omelet standing rather than taking a seat at the table. Guarding the door even while eating his breakfast.

He could have eaten his breakfast with Patience's brother Eugene and the other guards in the guardhouse, but somewhere along the way Iyrinder had started coming by the kitchen in the mornings.

Patience looked forward to their early morning chats far more than she should, whether it was in the kitchen here at Buckmore Cottage or in the small kitchen attached to the elven cottage Patience shared with Eugene on the forest floor below Ellonahshinel.

She probably should not encourage him like this. While she enjoyed their chats and spending time with him, she could not let a relationship develop more than this. She could not risk giving her heart to anyone.

Yet she was too weak to push Iyrinder away. Instead she let things continue as they were. Pleasant. Platonic. All while desperately hoping Iyrinder never asked for more.

"What's the plan for today?" Patience returned to the stove, cracking more eggs into the pan. Prince Farrendel would be awake any minute, and she wanted to have his breakfast ready when he wandered down to the kitchen.

"The prince asked to go into Aldon this morning." Iyrinder sliced off another chunk of omelet, though he didn't yet eat it.

Patience shot him a look, taking in his very elven guard uniform, from the leather tunic embossed with the Tarenhieli tree insignia to the elven bow strapped to his back.

Iyrinder stared down at his bite of omelet. "He wishes to go as himself this time."

No disguise. It must be part of the prince and princess's plan to curry the favor of the Escarlish people before the news broke that Prince Farrendel was illegitimate.

But that would explain why Iyrinder's posture had that tense, wary look to it this morning. Keeping Prince

Farrendel safe while he walked the streets of Aldon was much easier when he was dressed as an Escarlish peasant than as an elven prince.

Patience swallowed as she dumped more meat and veggies into the pan. If there was trouble, both Eugene and Iyrinder could get hurt. That was their job. To get hurt so that Prince Farrendel wouldn't be.

She couldn't think about how easily she could lose them. If she did, something dark would twist up from her heart into her throat, boiling with all the memories of the family members she had already lost. Surely, they would be fine. They were well trained, and they would take plenty of guards.

"I'll whip up a batch of chocolate chip cookies. They'll be ready by the time you return." She had been planning to bake cookies the next day to have on hand after the prince and princess's planned tour of Hanford University, but moving her baking up by a day wouldn't hurt. "How you elves stay in shape while eating so many cookies is beyond me."

"Lots of sword practice." Iyrinder smiled and popped more omelet into his mouth.

And all that sword practice paid off, though she wouldn't say that out loud. Even thinking it made her face burn.

Trying to stuff back her thoughts, she flipped the eggs to form the omelet, then she crossed the room and took Iyrinder's plate as he chewed his last bite. From their many morning chats, she knew he wouldn't budge from his spot next to the door and he'd want his hands free as soon as possible.

"While we are in Aldon, I would like to get another book for my sister. She enjoyed the last book you recommended." Iyrinder leaned against the wall.

"I think that author just released a new book, if you can find it. It has been flying off the shelves." Patience reached for a plate. The omelet was about done.

Right on cue, the door from the hallway opened, and Prince Farrendel strode inside. His long, silver-blond hair lay across the Escarlish clothing he wore. Not workers' clothes, but the clothing of a gentleman, complete with a waistcoat and jacket. Though the jacket had been modified so that his twin swords lay sheathed across his back.

Iyrinder straightened. "Good morning, amir."

Patience checked that the omelet was done, then she slid it onto the plate. She held it out to Prince Farrendel. "Your breakfast, Your Highness."

"Linshi, Miss Merrick," Prince Farrendel murmured, ducking his head as he retreated to the kitchen table.

The fact that he was actually speaking to her and eating at the table instead of bolting was a rather large step. Her chocolate chip cookies had gone a long way in earning the prince's trust.

And his politeness had gone a long way to earning hers.

Prince Farrendel picked at his food, his posture nearly as tense as Iyrinder's.

Patience returned to chopping more veggies and ham. Princess Jalissa would be up shortly, then Patience would have an hour or two until Princess Elspeth awoke. If Patience prepped the omelets, she could then turn her attention to the cookies in the meantime.

As Prince Farrendel finished, Eugene strode into the kitchen, wearing his Escarlish guard uniform of leather vest, white shirt, and brown trousers.

Patience nodded to her brother, then headed for the pantry to start gathering the supplies for cookies. By the time she returned, Eugene, Iyrinder, and Prince Farrendel were gone, off for their trip into Aldon.

Hopefully Iyrinder could track down that book for his sister. A sister that Patience had yet to meet, even though she had been in Estyra a few times now.

Not that she needed to meet Iyrinder's family. They weren't courting. They didn't have an understanding. After all, she didn't *want* anything more. So of course she shouldn't actually want to meet his family either.

She wasn't sure what they had or when it had happened, whatever *it* was. Slowly, ever so slowly, Iyrinder had started hanging around her kitchen more often. And she had started joining him out on the back step while he guarded the kitchen door when Prince Farrendel was inside. They chatted about anything and everything. Everything, that is, except for their future.

What future was there for them? He was an elf. She was human. Such a pairing worked for Prince Farrendel and Princess Elspeth.

But for them? They didn't have the advantages to help them get over the hurdles of different cultures.

Besides, Patience couldn't lose her brother, not even by marrying an elf, forming a heart bond, and staying young while Eugene grew old and died well before her.

Her brother Eugene was all she had. They had been orphaned when he was fifteen and she'd been five. He'd practically raised her, while working a variety of nasty jobs until he finally joined the army at eighteen.

She and Eugene had never had jobs that kept them together as much as working for Prince Farrendel and Princess Essie did, and she couldn't ruin that, not even to marry someone as wonderful as Iyrinder.

Nor did she dare actually give her heart to anyone. It

was bad enough loving Eugene. But to love anyone else, knowing how easily they could be snatched away?

No. She would rather keep herself safe by loving as few people as possible.

Yet where did that leave her and Iyrinder? Dancing around this growing attraction, but neither of them making a move to make this something more.

She did not want more.

And yet from the moment her brother had asked for her help to disguise Prince Farrendel and his elf guard as humans and she'd helped Iyrinder tie back his hair, there had been a spark between her and Iyrinder. A spark she couldn't deny, no matter how much she had tried.

IYRINDER STROLLED the streets of Aldon at Prince Farrendel's side. The other elven and human guards spread out, forming a diamond that protected them on all sides and kept the bustle from getting too close.

Contrary to his fears, the Escarlish people had been polite, so far. Some had waved. Most had simply gotten out of their way without too much fuss.

That would likely change, once the Escarlish press broke the story about the amir's birth. But until then, Iyrinder was thankful the crowd's mood seemed genial today.

Prince Farrendel halted so abruptly that Iyrinder stumbled trying to stop, nearly stepping in one of the mounds of refuse that had yet to be cleaned from the walk.

"Your Highness?" Captain Merrick stopped and turned toward Farrendel, though his eyes kept scanning the shops and people around them. "Is there a problem?"

Iyrinder glanced at Prince Farrendel long enough to catch the slight shake of his head and the way his shoulders hunched, a sure sign of discomfort. "I would like to find a present for my wife. Something for our anniversary."

That would explain it. Elves—and especially Farrendel—were not big on discussing personal matters.

Iyrinder turned back to scan the crowd parting around them. He would let Captain Merrick handle this.

Captain Merrick nodded, then gestured. "Do you wish to proceed to the Aldon Market, then?"

The Aldon Market was one of two places where Prince Farrendel was most comfortable here in Aldon. The other was Lance Marion's workshop. The market, while noisy and enclosed, was self-contained and familiar enough to make security doable. Same for the workshop.

But Prince Farrendel shook his head, his expression twisting as if he tasted something sour. "No. I wish to visit the larger shops on the main streets."

That would make for better press, presumably. But it would make security more of a hassle.

But it was not Iyrinder's place to protest. It was his job to make it safe for Prince Farrendel to go wherever he wished.

"Very well. This way." Captain Merrick turned down a new street, this one with brick shops designated with freshly-painted signs. A few even had edging of gilt. Definitely a wealthier shopping district. "Is there something in particular you are looking for?"

"Something small." Prince Farrendel gestured vaguely, as if even he was not sure if that meant he was supposed to get something small in price or small in physical form. His shoulders hunched even more. "Do you have any suggestions?"

Iyrinder shot a glance at Captain Merrick. Prince Farrendel had become a friend, but this was something more personal than Iyrinder wanted to get involved with.

Captain Merrick gave a tiny shrug in return. It seemed they would have to get involved.

Iyrinder suppressed a sigh. From the beginning when King Weylind had ordered him to keep an eye on the newly married Prince Farrendel and Princess Elspetha, he had been crossing the line from impersonal guard to more personal friend.

Finally, Captain Merrick shrugged and turned back to Prince Farrendel. "I have heard jewelry is always appreciated."

"Is that what Escarlish women appreciate?" Iyrinder mentally clapped a hand over his mouth as soon as the words popped out. Sure, his attraction to Patience was not a secret from Captain Merrick. But they had never actually discussed it, since Iyrinder had never pursued Patience beyond very casual talking.

The look Captain Merrick shot him was sharp and searching. He held Iyrinder's gaze as he said, "They do. Something small and tasteful, I should think."

Was that Captain Merrick's blessing to Iyrinder to pursue Patience? Or was he simply replying to Prince Farrendel?

This was the reason—more than the fact that Patience was human and the complications that came with that— why Iyrinder had yet to press for more of a relationship. Patience was Captain Merrick's younger sister. As someone with a younger sister, Iyrinder knew exactly what that meant for protective instincts.

Not to mention, Captain Merrick was Iyrinder's superior officer as the overall commander of Prince Farrendel's guard detail. And Patience worked for Prince

Farrendel and Princess Elspetha, making her part of Iyrinder's responsibility. All reasons Iyrinder should stay away from her.

Yet logic did nothing to quell the spark that had flared the moment she had run gentle fingers through his hair to tie it back for his first Escarlish disguise months ago.

Prince Farrendel glanced between Captain Merrick and Iyrinder, then nodded. "Very well. We will start with the jewelers."

Captain Merrick nodded and led the way two doors down before stepping inside a brick building with decorative bars over the windows and a sign proclaiming some kind of jewelry. A very upscale place, but the kind of shop where a prince could find a piece of jewelry worthy of a princess.

The man behind the glass countertop stood as soon as they entered. He gave a half-bow. "Prince Farrendel, how may I help you today? Looking for something for Princess Elspeth? We just received a fine shipment of diamonds."

Prince Farrendel froze just inside the doorway, that rigid, panicked look widening his eyes.

Iyrinder stationed himself next to the door where he could keep an eye on those outside and the proprietor.

Captain Merrick rested a reassuring hand on Farrendel's shoulder for a moment before he stepped forward. "Thank you, but we'd like to speak with your father, if he's in. Tell him Eugene Merrick is here."

The man's eyebrows scrunched, but he nodded and opened the door to the back room. He didn't fully step inside, instead calling for someone, presumably his father.

Captain Merrick leaned closer to Prince Farrendel. "I

worked here as a night guard for a year. I saved the shop from robbery more than once."

An older man with gray hair and lines deeply etched into his face stumped from the back room, his back hunched and his eyes squinting through the thick-lensed glasses. As soon as his gaze swung to Captain Merrick, a broad smile added even more creases to his face. "Eugene! My favorite night guard!"

Captain Merrick stepped forward and shook the man's hand. "I have fond memories of working here. I'm working for Prince Farrendel now, and he's looking for something special for his wife. Do you have any new designs that might be a good fit for Princess Elspeth?"

As the man, his son, and Captain Merrick fell into a conversation about jewels and cuts and designs—with a few pauses while Captain Merrick waited for Farrendel's input—Iyrinder mostly tuned them out and kept watch.

All this jewelry discussion was...overwhelming. Even if Iyrinder wished to buy a gift for Patience—which he did not—he would get her something simple and much cheaper than what was found in this shop. Perhaps something of elven design from one of the shops in Estyra.

He shook himself. He should not be thinking about buying jewelry for Patience. Miss Merrick.

Eventually, a decision was made about jewelry that seemed to satisfy Prince Farrendel enough that he left the shop with a hint of a smile.

As they stepped back onto the street, Prince Farrendel released a long breath, a weary sag to his shoulders. "Is it too early to return to Winstead Palace?"

Captain Merrick grimaced. "Going into Aldon is good optics, but you should be seen stopping at a few more shops if you want it to make any kind of difference, I'm afraid."

Prince Farrendel sucked in a deep, slightly shuddery breath.

He was not up for more. Time for a distraction.

"My sister has discovered a love for Escarlish novels, and her favorite author just released a new book." Iyrinder glanced between Captain Merrick and Prince Farrendel. "Perhaps we could search the shops to find a copy?"

Prince Farrendel nodded almost too eagerly, as Iyrinder had guessed he would. This way, Iyrinder could get that book for his sister, and Prince Farrendel could catch a few quiet moments in a subdued bookshop or two.

And they would get the optics the prince needed for good press before all the bad press hit in a few days.

FIVE

I yrinder trailed behind Prince Farrendel and Princess Elspetha as they toured Hanford University. The more he saw, the more something started itching at the back of his mind.

It was a crazy idea. A far more permanent, life-altering idea than what he should be considering since he had yet to speak to Patience. He had yet to decide if he was willing to risk speaking to her about whatever was between them.

At the end of the tour, Professor Harrington led the prince and princess into one of the buildings and halted before an oak door. A voice reverberated from beyond the door.

The professor faced Captain Merrick and Iyrinder. "I will have to ask the guards to wait outside. It is university policy that any personal guards must wait outside the room to avoid any disruption of class or distraction to the other students."

Iyrinder stiffened. This was a complication he had not foreseen.

Prince Farrendel's eyes widened, his face paling as he glanced between Captain Merrick and Iyrinder as if begging them to do something so that he and the princess would not be left unguarded.

Princess Elspetha winced and stepped closer to Prince Farrendel. "I'm afraid he is correct. The Escarlish royalty has always complied, and there has never been an incident."

Prince Farrendel rocked back on his heels, as if about to bolt.

This was not going well. Iyrinder could not let his prince run out on this opportunity. Not when he had seen how excited he was about this.

"What if I were a prospective student thinking about enrolling?" For the second time in as many days, Iyrinder found himself blurting out something before fully thinking it through.

No, that was not quite true. He had been thinking about this. He just had not wanted to acknowledge that he had been contemplating it.

As everyone turned to look at him, he shifted. Yet, strangely, he found himself even more sure as the decision settled deep inside him. "Would I be able to sit in the class today?"

The professor shrugged. "You would have to leave your weapons behind, as is required of all students, but it is allowed for prospective students to sit in on classes with approval."

Not as good as Iyrinder was hoping, but it would be enough. He could sit in the class and watch the prince's back. Not just today, but when Prince Farrendel began his in-person classes in the fall. "And if I wished to attend the classes with the amir in the fall?"

"There is no rule against guards taking classes, but

you would have to be officially enrolled yourself, going for the same degree." Professor Harrington smiled broadly. "We would welcome you, of course. Any elves who wish to attend are very welcome to do so."

"Iyrinder?" Prince Farrendel turned to him, his posture stiff, a scrunch between his brows. "Is this what you wish?"

"It would be better if one of us were in the room with you to watch your back." Iyrinder glanced at Captain Merrick. Would the captain back him up on this one?

"I will appear less conspicuous standing outside the door since I am Escarlish." Captain Merrick's expression was somewhere between a wry smile and a grimace. "And I certainly don't want to get a degree in magical engineering. I became a guard because I didn't want to spend my days sitting in a classroom." His gaze sharpened, his words holding extra weight, as he focused on Iyrinder. "But if Iyrinder wants to do it, I'm not going to stand in his way."

Was that a tacit permission to move things forward with Patience? Iyrinder really needed to have that talk with Captain Merrick to make sure the man was good with him courting his sister. Iyrinder held Captain Merrick's gaze. "I am glad to hear it."

After a moment, Captain Merrick gave a slight nod. Not an acquiescence. More an agreement that they would have that long-delayed chat once the prince and princess were safely secured at home.

Princess Elspetha beamed, chattering even faster than usual. "If you wish to get a degree, Farrendel and I will definitely support you any way we can. We can help pay your tuition, since you'll be taking classes as part of your job to keep Farrendel safe."

Behind her eager excitement, Iyrinder could read her

relief that Farrendel would have someone with him when he took classes.

This was exactly what King Weylind would order Iyrinder to do, if his king had been here. Do whatever it took to stay by Prince Farrendel's side and ensure that the prince remained safe.

Yet this time, Iyrinder was doing it partially for himself. Yes, he wanted to be there to protect his prince. Not just physically, but his presence would help protect Prince Farrendel from the panic and anxiety as well.

But more than that, Iyrinder was choosing this for himself, just as he had chosen to stay on the prince's guard detail long after he could have rotated off of it.

Because he was choosing this for himself, he would pay for it himself. "Linshi, Amirah, but you already pay me well enough that I can afford my own tuition. I am also thinking of my future. In a hundred years, you will no longer be in line for the Escarlish throne. You will be so far down the Tarenhieli line of succession that you will no longer require such tight security. Unless I want to return to guarding Weylind Daresheni, it seems prudent to create more options for myself in the future."

He had enjoyed his time guarding the king. But if he wanted a life with Patience, then he would need to think about her, too. She would be more comfortable if they spent lots of time in Escarland rather than being stuck in the middle of Tarenhieli politics all the time.

Princess Elspetha's beaming grin took on a pleased-as-a-cat-with-a-bowl-of-fresh-fish look to it.

But Prince Farrendel breathed a long exhale, the tension leaving his shoulders. "Linshi. I would appreciate having someone guarding my back."

No going back now. Well, he could, but Iyrinder would not disappoint his prince like that.

Nor did he want to. In truth, he had been gathering his courage for this for months. Maybe not taking classes at Hanford University in particular.

But to take hold of a new life now that the war was over. It was time to stop being the perfect, unattached guard and start putting down roots for himself.

As the professor gestured for the prince and princess to enter the room, Iyrinder took off his sword, quiver, bow, and spare knives and handed them all to Captain Merrick.

Captain Merrick gave him one last, pointed look before he took up a station next to the door.

Iyrinder drew in a deep breath and stepped into the classroom.

A professor stood at the front of the room while rows of wooden desks filled the room, nearly all of them filled with young humans, who gaped as Prince Farrendel, Princess Elspetha, and Iyrinder entered.

Princess Elspetha picked a desk in the back row, and after a moment, Prince Farrendel chose a desk in the back row as well that put his back to the wall.

Since the seat in front of Prince Farrendel was open, Iyrinder claimed it. He resisted the urge to wrinkle his nose at the slightly sticky feeling of the wooden top. It was doodled all over with pen and...was that something stuck to the underside? When was the last time this desk was cleaned? Perhaps the greatest threat to his prince in this room was not the other people but the unsanitary conditions.

Iyrinder swept his gaze around the room, assessing each of the students. None of them seemed like much of a threat. Half of them appeared bleary-eyed and barely functional. They were more a threat to themselves than to the prince.

The professor at the front went back to lecturing, and Iyrinder attempted to split his attention between listening to the lecture and staying alert for threats.

This whole taking classes thing might be more challenging than he expected. It was going to be difficult, attempting to keep up with the homework and notes while guarding his prince. But he would manage.

This was a life he was choosing. If he wanted to pursue Patience romantically, then he would need to find a way to build a life in both Tarenhiel and Escarland, the way Prince Farrendel had.

But Patience was worth it. She was lovely. Both in appearance and in the beauty of her quiet smile as she saw to the needs of others. She worked so hard without complaint. She was thoughtful in the way she got up during the night to make sure the prince and princess had hot chocolate after Prince Farrendel had nightmares. Even when she had to wake before dawn, she had breakfast waiting for Prince Farrendel and Iyrinder before their morning practices. What was there not to love about someone who was so caring about everyone else around her?

He felt drawn to care for her in return. He had fought it for months, but no longer.

Once they arrived back at Winstead Palace, Prince Farrendel and Princess Elspetha promptly retreated into Buckmore Cottage, and Iyrinder caught a brief glimpse of Patience handing out chocolate chip cookies.

But Iyrinder halted just inside the tree line, turned, and faced Captain Merrick. This was it. After months of dancing around this topic, it was time he and his commanding officer had a frank discussion.

Captain Merrick halted in front of him and crossed his arms. "You've liked my sister for months."

"Yes." Iyrinder braced himself. Back there in the university, he had decided on his future. Now it was time to take a stand for it. "I know you are my commanding officer, and she is your sister. But I do not believe I have to prove to you that I can take care of her and make her happy."

Captain Merrick exhaled a long breath, a slightly wry twist to his mouth. "No. After so many months of working closely together, I know you're a good man. But it isn't me who will stand in your way. It's Patience."

"Patience?" Iyrinder resisted the urge to rock back on his heels. Had he misread the situation? He had thought she returned his affection. Surely all the warm smiles and plates of bacon she had been giving him had to mean something, right?

"Look. Just…give me a few days. I'll find a way to talk to her." Captain Merrick rubbed at the side of his jaw. "It's a long story. Perhaps she'll tell it to you someday. Don't worry, I'll be subtle. Well, mostly subtle. There are just a few things she's going to need to hear from me before she'll be ready to hear what you want to say. I should've talked to her a while ago, once I saw where things were progressing between the two of you. But I didn't want to pressure either of you."

Iyrinder's shoulders sagged, but he nodded. He had been ready to march right over there on the force of his realization and talk to Patience right now.

But if Captain Merrick—Eugene—thought this was the best course, then Iyrinder was going to take his advice and wait just a little bit longer.

CHAPTER
SIX

Patience kneaded the bread dough, leaning into the effort. The story had broken about Prince Farrendel's illegitimate birth, and it was just as bad as everyone had feared.

The prince and princess didn't deserve to be dragged through the mud like this, and Patience would tell anyone who asked just that.

Not that she had any intention of going anywhere near a reporter. If she did, she would stick to the palace policy of "no comment." But she would wish she could give them a piece of her mind.

Boots stomped on the stoop outside a moment before the door opened, and Eugene stepped inside. "Do you have a moment?"

"Yes. Just let me get this rising." She gave the dough a few more good thumps, then she put it in a bowl. She draped the bowl with a towel, then she placed the bowl on the stove where the radiant heat from the low coals inside would provide warmth for the rise.

Once done, she washed her hands, then turned to face her brother. "What did you want to speak to me about?"

Prince Farrendel and Princess Elspeth were up at the main palace, and Princess Jalissa was out somewhere with Prince Edmund, so Patience and Eugene had Buckmore Cottage to themselves at the moment.

Eugene strolled across the room, then leaned against the worktable in the center of the room. "Iyrinder."

Something like a sword stabbed down her back, stiffening her spine. "What about him?"

"You like him. He likes you. Don't think I haven't noticed." Eugene crossed his arms, giving her that *look*. The one he'd given her often when she'd been growing up. Part big brother, part parent. She knew better than to try to evade the truth when he gave her that look.

That didn't mean she wanted to talk about this with her brother. Especially since he had become so close to Iyrinder after working together for months.

She turned back to the countertop, grabbed a rag, and started wiping up the mess of flour she'd left behind after kneading the bread dough. "There's nothing between us. Sure, I find him attractive. He's an elf. He's better than good-looking. But that's just it. He's an elf. Nothing's going to happen between us."

"Patience." Eugene dragged her name out, pausing as if waiting for her to turn to look at him.

She tried to wait him out, but the silence stretched and tightened, twisting something inside her until she couldn't help it. She sighed and turned around.

Eugene held her gaze with that unbudging, big brother look he'd perfected. "I want you to be happy. Don't hold yourself back on my account."

She rested her hands on the worktable across from him. "We've always stuck together. That was the promise we made to each other years ago. And if I..." She couldn't manage to say it out loud. It sounded ludicrously presumptuous to even dream about Iyrinder marrying her and forming a heart bond with her. "I won't do anything that would take me away."

"This wouldn't take you away." Eugene shook his head. "Sure, there's a good chance that you would live a lot longer than I will. But you'll still be there for the rest of my life. And I won't miss a moment of the time I'll have with you, and I'll have the peace of knowing you're happy and well-cared for."

She blinked, her throat tightening. "But I'd still lose you. I'd have to live for hundreds of years alone."

"You wouldn't be alone. You'd have a husband. Maybe children. Your own family." Eugene's voice lowered and softened. "I know you've always wanted that."

She had to drop her gaze to the worn, scarred wooden surface of the table. Yes, she had wanted that. Of course she did. But she'd stuffed that dream down for so long that she wasn't sure she could grasp hold of it again.

The hired help in most noble houses were forbidden to marry. Especially forbidden to have children that would take them away from their duties.

Princess Elspeth might be more willing to keep Patience on, even if she were married and had children. But Patience wasn't sure she wanted to risk this job to find out.

If she were honest with herself, the worries about the job were just an excuse. Her hesitation wasn't about the job. It wasn't about Iyrinder or the fact that he was an elf and she a human.

Eugene's gaze remained fixed on her. Steady. Far too knowing.

It was too much. She couldn't think. Not with him giving her that searching, big brother look of his. She turned away, blinking, a choked feeling building in her throat. "I...I can't."

Eugene stepped around the worktable, then wrapped her in a hug. "Yes, you can."

"No, I can't." She buried her face against her brother's shoulder, her voice coming out on a sob. "I can't lose you. I can't..."

She couldn't let herself love anyone else. It was dangerous enough loving Eugene. But he was her brother. She wasn't going to cut him out when he was the last family member she had left.

But everyone else left.

No, not just left. But it was easier thinking of it that way than remembering the truth.

They had died. They'd all died. The sister who had succumbed to cholera. The brother she barely remembered who had been taken by a fever when she was three years old. Her parents, who had both been killed in a factory accident so infamous that laws now existed to prevent such tragedies again.

She swallowed back her sobs. This grief was too deep. Too much a part of her. She did not dare give in to the sorrow or it would consume her.

Eugene patted her back. "Our childhood was less than ideal. But don't let that stand in the way of your happiness. If you like Iyrinder, then you should see where this goes. Even if it doesn't work out with him, you should be open to finding happiness, even if it takes you away from me."

"But our pact..." The words came out weakly.

"I would never want to stand in the way of your happiness." Eugene stepped back, though he still gripped her shoulders as he held her gaze. "Don't let your fears stand in the way of your happiness either."

"I'll think about it, all right?" She wouldn't, but she had to say something to get Eugene off her case.

"That's all I can ask." Eugene released her, but his gaze remained assessing, as if he could read the equivocation in her tone. "I know you just want to look after me, but I'm the big brother. I'm the one who is supposed to look after you."

Patience nodded, not trusting her voice. Yes, he was ten years older than her, and he'd basically raised her after their parents died. All the more reason why she should be the one looking after him now. He had no one else to do so. Just as she had no one else but him.

And Iyrinder, if she let him.

But she couldn't let him. She couldn't marry an elf, even if he was a handsome, honorable, caring elf warrior who made her heart beat harder and who hung out in her kitchen every morning. She couldn't marry anyone and risk losing him.

PATIENCE SCRUBBED the pan she'd used to cook the eggs that morning while Princess Elspeth finished eating her eggs and pancakes.

The princess finished chewing her bite of pancake, then she speared her next bite, swiping it through the pools of maple syrup on her plate. "We agreed we would keep our anniversary gifts small. We both went a tad overboard on our birthday gifts for each other."

Patience made a non-committal noise and kept scrubbing. It wasn't her place to judge. They were a prince and a princess. They could afford extravagant gifts.

"But the problem is that we didn't specify how small. And knowing Farrendel, he's taken small as literally small, not monetarily small." Princess Elspeth sighed and popped her bite of pancake into her mouth. She chewed and swallowed before she spoke again. "Not that it matters. It's the thought that counts, and Farrendel won't care if my gift to him is objectively worth less than his. But it would be nice to know what direction he went with his gift."

Patience set the pan in the other side of the sink basin to dry, then dried her hands. She turned to face the princess. "I'm sure my brother likely knows. Would you like me to find out for you, Your Highness?"

The princess laughed and shook her head. "No, but thank you for offering that level of loyalty. But I'm not looking to turn my servants into spies on my husband. I'd much rather be surprised."

Patience released a breath, though she tried to disguise her relief. For a moment there, she'd started to get worried. Things never went well when she was asked to spill secrets.

The princess had just been chatting, not really looking for feedback. Patience had thought that was where their princess-servant friendship had progressed, but she'd learned long ago that it was better to be cautious.

"I was thinking about getting him a new set of protective goggles Lance recommended. He will love it, but it seems unromantic to get him something so practical. But it is what he really wants, and I want to support him in his magical engineering endeavors." The princess swiped the last bite of pancake from her plate.

Princess Jalissa peeked into the kitchen, her black hair flowing gracefully down the back of the gauzy blue-and-white dress that floated around her. "Are you ready to go, isciena?"

"Yes, just finished." Princess Elspeth hopped to her feet and held out her empty plate to Patience. "Don't expect us for lunch. Edmund is taking Jalissa to one of our favorite tea shops in Aldon, and I'm tagging along. Farrendel plans to spend most of the morning practicing with your brother and Iyrinder. He might make an appearance for lunch. Or he might not. You know how he is."

Patience did. She nodded and gestured to the pantry. "There's a loaf of fresh bread and some leftovers from last night."

"Perfect." Princess Elspeth waved, then followed Princess Jalissa from the room.

Patience returned to cleaning up the kitchen. The maids from Winstead Palace would be over shortly for their weekly cleaning. She should get a start on changing the sheets so she could send the dirty sheets back with them to be laundered at the palace.

She wasn't sure how much time passed as she stripped sheets, then remade the beds.

After straightening the room, she smoothed the blanket on the bed on the first floor that Princess Jalissa had claimed for herself.

A popping sound split the air.

Patience froze. What was that? Was that a gunshot? It had sounded far too close to the palace.

CHAPTER
SEVEN

Iyrinder spun as Prince Farrendel parried his swing, then side-stepped as one of the other guards lunged forward.

Prince Farrendel fought back-to-back with Prince Julien, the two of them taking on Iyrinder, the two other elven guards who had come along on this trip to Aldon, and a handful of Escarlish guards, just to make things interesting. Even with the odds stacked against them, Prince Farrendel and Prince Julien held their own.

As Iyrinder lunged into a smooth thrust, Farrendel's eyes widened, the blood draining from his face. As an echoing crack rose above the background noise of Aldon, the prince dropped his swords and collapsed to his knees.

A gunshot. That was a gunshot. Iyrinder had become familiar enough with the sound over the course of the war.

Had Prince Farrendel been shot? Iyrinder rushed to him, but he did not see any blood. Despite the lack of blood, Prince Farrendel gasped raggedly, his face twisted as if he were in pain. "Farrendel Amir, are you all right? What is wrong?"

Prince Julien gripped Prince Farrendel's shoulder, crouching. "Farrendel? What is it?"

Prince Farrendel shook his head, his eyes glassy and distant. He staggered to his feet, shoved past Iyrinder and Prince Julien, then broke into a run, headed for the palace's main gate as if his life depended on it.

Not his life. Iyrinder had seen this before. This was the work of an elishina.

If Farrendel was uninjured, that meant the princess had been hurt. The gunshot?

Iyrinder shared a glance with Prince Julien, and just that look was enough to know that Prince Julien understood the situation as well. Together, the two of them sprinted after Prince Farrendel, the rest of the guards hard on their heels.

Prince Farrendel reached the gate and grabbed the black iron bars, as if prepared to throw himself up and over rather than take the time to fumble with opening the gates. The Escarlish gate guards gaped at the elf prince climbing the gate, too stunned to move.

The gunshot. The elishina. The iron gate with open bars, leaving Prince Farrendel a perfect target.

There was no time to be polite or circumspect about this. Iyrinder had to get his prince behind the safety of the palace's outer stone wall as soon as possible.

Iyrinder lunged and grabbed Prince Farrendel by the shoulders, yanking him down from the gate. The surprise was enough to break Prince Farrendel's grip, and he tumbled back to the ground.

Before he could regain his balance, Iyrinder swung Prince Farrendel toward safety, then gave him a shove. "Amir, get down."

A crack rang out as something slammed into Iyrinder's middle.

He was on the ground, blinking up at the sky, as pain burst through him. Agony stabbed his stomach, and he pressed a hand to the spot. Something red and warm pooled against his palm, turning his shirt sticky.

He forced himself to turn his head, trying to focus.

Prince Julien gripped Prince Farrendel now. The amir was fighting him, but Prince Julien held on grimly, keeping Farrendel safe behind the protection of the wall.

Ducking, one of his fellow elf guards grabbed Iyrinder's arm, then dragged him over the gravel.

Agony tore through him, and Iyrinder ground his teeth on his cry of pain. By the time he could gather enough strength to gasp in a breath, he found himself lying on the ground in the shadow of the wall while the guard pressed his hands to Iyrinder's wound.

After another moment, the overwhelming power of Prince Farrendel's magic flared, and blue bolts climbed over the gate.

Iyrinder squeezed his eyes shut and concentrated on breathing. He had done his duty and kept his prince safe. Now, that duty would have to rest on someone else.

PATIENCE HURRIED through the back gardens of Winstead Palace, heading for the main gate. Perhaps it was foolish, heading toward the sound of gunshots. But it had been a few minutes since the second shot, and she needed to see what was going on. A sick, churning feeling filled her stomach, and she wouldn't be able to banish it until she found out what was going on.

Was Eugene all right? He was guarding Princess

Elspeth on her outing with Prince Edmund and Princess Jalissa. Had those gunshots been aimed at her—and thus, at Eugene?

She pressed her back to the wall of Winstead Palace and peeked around the corner.

A white carriage stood in the drive, the horses pawing and snorting. People ran to and fro with the frenetic pace of those dealing with a crisis.

A person lay sprawled across one of the carriage benches, her red hair the only indication of her identity. Prince Farrendel knelt in the footwell, his face pale.

Patience twisted her hands in her apron. What could she do? So many people already huddled over and around the princess that she would only get in the way.

Where was Eugene? Surely he wasn't...but if the princess was hurt...

There. She found him, kneeling beside another figure lying on the ground, his chestnut hair splayed across the gravel.

Iyrinder.

She raced across the drive and crashed to her knees beside him, nearly knocking into the elf guard who pressed a wad of cloth against a growing red spot across Iyrinder's stomach.

But he was alive. Gasping in pain, his eyes squeezed shut. But alive.

"We need more—Patience, your apron." Eugene held out his hand, not even glancing up at her.

She hastily untied her apron and held it out. "Here."

Instead of taking it, Eugene gripped Iyrinder's shoulder. "When I roll him, I need you to press your apron to the exit wound."

She nodded, wadded up her apron, then readied herself.

Eugene rolled Iyrinder, eliciting a groan. The other elf guard kept his hand pressed to the entry wound.

Patience pressed the apron to Iyrinder's wound and kept it there as Eugene laid him back down. When she pulled her hand free, her fingers were streaked with blood.

One of the human guards rushed up, a leather bag in his hand. "Captain, I brought the med kit."

Eugene pushed to his feet, making room for the guard. "Tend to Iyrinder. I'm going to check on the princess."

The two guards set to work cutting Iyrinder's shirt, replacing the apron and rags with gauze, and wrapping bandages around Iyrinder's middle.

While they worked, Patience rested a hand on Iyrinder's shoulder. She wasn't sure if her presence was helping or reassuring, but she couldn't make herself move away.

As they finished, Eugene returned. Two more guards followed, carrying a stretcher.

Eugene crouched across from Patience and met her gaze briefly before he glanced down at Iyrinder. "Princess Elspeth is badly wounded. They're rounding up a train now, then they're sending her north to meet elf healers at the border. We'll be sending you north as well, Iyrinder."

Iyrinder gave a slight nod, though he didn't open his eyes.

Patience scrubbed her bloody fingers on a semi-clean section of her ruined apron and pushed to her feet to give the guards with the stretcher room. Of course they would send the princess and Iyrinder north. While Iyrinder's wound might be survivable without elven healing magic, Princess Elspeth's wounds must be much worse, given the frantic movements of those tending her.

As the guards shifted Iyrinder onto the stretcher, then

picked it up, Patience dug her fingers into her apron, fighting the squeezing panic inside her chest.

Eugene briefly rested his hand on her shoulder. "I'm going along. They need their guards more than ever."

She straightened, pulling herself together. "I'm going too. The princess will need me."

Eugene held her gaze with a knowing look of his own before nodding. "The train is leaving in mere minutes."

In other words, there would be no time to pack or even change.

No matter. She was getting on that train.

Yet she found herself trailing, not after the princess's carriage, but after Iyrinder's stretcher instead.

Right now, the princess had plenty of people surrounding her. Patience would just get in the way.

But Iyrinder was alone.

A train screeched to a halt at the small platform to the side of Winstead Palace. It contained only an engine and two cars. No coal car, and no steam puffed from the train's stack. This must be one of the newfangled trains, which had been converted to run on magical power.

The guards carried Iyrinder's stretcher to the second train car, and they struggled to maneuver it up the stairs and through the narrow door.

Patience climbed into the car after them. It appeared to be a sleeper car for guards, with tiers of bunks— stacked three high—down each side of the train car. A single bunk was built into the front of the car next to the door to the front train car, possibly for a commanding officer, and the guards eased Iyrinder onto it.

Iyrinder groaned and pressed his hands to the bandage over his middle. The bandage was stained red, already soaked through.

How much blood could Iyrinder lose?

She scanned the car, but she didn't see any glasses or water. It was just a spartan, sleeper car.

A few more guards filed inside, though when she peeked through the window, more guards piled into the cab of the train's engine, including Eugene.

Prince Farrendel, cradling Princess Elspeth in his arms, climbed into the first train car, followed by the queen mother and the palace's surgeon.

Within seconds, the train shuddered into motion. Patience braced herself against Iyrinder's bunk, then glanced around. There weren't any chairs for her to pull up next to his bunk, and the next set of bunks was too far away for her to sit and still be near him.

Swallowing, she perched on the bunk next to Iyrinder and took his hand. "We're leaving for the border now. The elven healers will get you fixed up in no time."

Well, that wasn't exactly true. It was a twelve-hour trip to the border. Eight hours, perhaps, with this magically powered train.

Still, eight hours was a long time to be in pain.

He squeezed her fingers, his face tipping toward her even though he didn't open his eyes. "The amirah?"

"She's fine." Patience wrapped his hand in both of hers, hoping he couldn't hear the lie in her voice. Princess Elspeth looked far from fine when she had been carried onto the train.

Iyrinder's eyes snapped open, and he struggled, as if trying to push to his feet, even if he didn't even make it onto his elbows. "What happened? The amir? The amirah? I should—"

Patience rested a hand on his shoulder and pushed him back down. "Lie still. There's nothing you can do for them. Just rest. The others are looking after them."

With a whoosh and the increased noise of the clacking

of the wheels, the door opened, and the palace surgeon stepped into the car. He leaned into the door to close it. After a quick glance around, he set his black bag on the edge of the bunk and opened it. "I'm the palace's surgeon."

Patience eased aside but kept a hold of Iyrinder's hand as the surgeon unwrapped the bandage and examined the wound.

After a moment, the surgeon gave a nod. "It's a bad wound, but I think we can keep you stable until the elf healers can work their magic. I'm going to give you a shot of morphine to keep you comfortable, then I'll do what I can for you."

Iyrinder shook his head, struggling once again. "No, I cannot...I need to..."

"You need to rest." Patience pressed a firm hand to his shoulder once again. "You're wounded. You'll be a distraction. My brother is guarding the prince and princess. Your job now is to let the doctor work and survive until we reach the border."

After a moment, Iyrinder grimaced and slumped back onto the bed.

The physician rolled up Iyrinder's sleeve, prepared a hypodermic needle with the morphine, then administered the dose. Within a minute, Iyrinder's muscles relaxed beneath Patience's hand. He didn't seem asleep, but he wasn't fully awake either.

Patience kept her gaze focused on Iyrinder's face. When she glanced at the doctor, her stomach churned at the sight of the wound, and she quickly turned away.

As the physician finished rebandaging the wound and stood, Patience reached out and caught his arm. Now that Iyrinder was tended, she dared ask the question that had been building. "How bad off is he, really?"

"He is stable. For now." The physician's mouth pressed into a tight, thin line. "If he were a human, I would recommend surgery to repair some of the internal damage. But I believe he will remain stable enough for the elf healers. There is a possibility that he will take a turn for the worse so I will continue to monitor him."

Patience nodded, but she didn't let go of the doctor's sleeve. "And the princess?"

The physician hesitated, likely thinking through how much he could say, then sighed. "The elven heart bond is an amazing thing. We can be thankful that Prince Farrendel appears quite strong."

In other words, Princess Elspeth would already be dead, if not for her heart bond with Prince Farrendel.

Patience let go of the physician's sleeve. The man packed up his things, then headed back through the connecting doors, likely to check on Princess Elspeth once again. Keeping the princess alive was the priority, after all.

Patience picked up Iyrinder's hand once again. His eyes were closed, his face smoothed from pain thanks to the drug. He was still far too pale beneath his normal, silvery skin tone, and it made the strands of hair that straggled across his face stand out even more starkly.

Feeling daring with Iyrinder so unaware, she tentatively reached out and brushed a strand of his chestnut hair from his face. It was just as silken as she remembered from the one time she had touched his hair all those months ago to tie it back for his peasant disguise.

What would it be like, if she let herself dream? If she and Iyrinder stepped past this friendship they had formed to grow their relationship into something more?

She let her hand drop. She couldn't let herself dream. This just proved her hesitation was valid.

Iyrinder was a guard. He'd throw himself into the line of fire to protect his prince or princess both because it was his duty and because that was the kind of loyal, unselfish elf he was.

She couldn't marry someone she was so sure to lose. She just couldn't.

Still, she couldn't make herself move from Iyrinder's side as the train raced north toward the Escarlish-Tarenhieli border.

EIGHT

I yrinder sucked in a breath as those carrying his stretcher jostled it going through the door of the train car. The stretcher steadied as the elves reached the platform at the outskirts of Estyra. He pressed a hand to his healing wound. "I can walk."

Nylian, the elf healer who had met them at the border, halted next to him. "Perhaps. But I do not advise it for another few hours. The magic needs to finish the healing."

Iyrinder gritted his teeth and slumped back onto the stretcher. How he hated being stuck healing.

Patience climbed down from the train, her brother at her side. As Eugene followed Prince Farrendel and Princess Elspetha, Patience glanced between them and Iyrinder.

Iyrinder gestured in the direction Eugene had gone. "Go with them. I will be fine. The amir and amirah will need you."

Patience sent him one last, searching glance before she nodded and followed her brother toward the cottage they had on the forest floor beneath Prince Farrendel and Princess Elspetha's rooms.

Before the bearers could carry him from the platform, King Weylind halted next to Iyrinder's stretcher and gave him a nod. "Linshi, Iyrinder Loiatir, for protecting my brother."

"It was my duty and my honor, Daresheni." Iyrinder could not bow while lying on a stretcher, but he nodded with as much dignity as he could.

"You have my gratitude," King Weylind stated it firmly, as if to make sure Iyrinder did not miss his meaning.

Iyrinder's stomach twisted, sending a lance of pain through his wound. The gratitude of a king was no light thing. "I was just doing my duty, Daresheni. There is no need for gratitude."

"Perhaps. But if you wished, I would grant you any position." King Weylind tipped his head. "You could become a captain on my guard detail. Or on that of one of my children."

Iyrinder's breath caught. Any of those positions would be a promotion from being a secondary captain on the guard detail for the king's younger brother—a prince so far down the line of succession that he was unlikely to ever become king.

It was everything Iyrinder had wanted when he had accepted the position on Prince Farrendel's guard detail.

Now, though, things had changed. Prince Farrendel had become a friend. Iyrinder enjoyed working for him and with him.

Then there was Patience. If Iyrinder took a new position, he would lose her. Even if she was willing to take their relationship to something more, he did not think she would want to move to Estyra if he took a position guarding King Weylind, Prince Ryfon, or Princess Brina.

Strangely, a higher guard position was no longer the dream he wanted. Even without Patience, he had begun to formulate a new dream. One where he eventually stepped back from such intense guard duties and instead explored his options with magical engineering. Perhaps he would never be able to do what Prince Farrendel could, but he could find ways to contribute. He, too, could figure out how to live a life in both Escarland and Tarenhiel, if given the chance.

Would Patience give him the chance?

He would never find out if he accepted King Weylind's offer.

He dragged his gaze from Patience's retreating back— he had not even realized that his gaze had strayed in her direction—and met his king's eyes. "Linshi, Daresheni. But I wish to remain on the amir and amirah's guard detail."

A hint of a smile crossed King Weylind's face, as if he had seen right through Iyrinder's real reasons, and he nodded. "I suspected you would say that. In that case, you have my double gratitude for being so willing to continue guarding my shashon and isciena so dutifully."

King Weylind stepped back, and the two elves carrying Iyrinder's stretcher nodded to their king before they continued on their way.

Iyrinder tried to relax as he was carried through the back streets of Estyra. When they reached the tree where his family lived, they had to carry him up hundreds of stairs since this tree had yet to have a lift installed.

Each branch they passed had several homes in meandering rows. The magical protections around each home prevented all but the loudest of noise from bothering the neighbors, and most of the homes had their windows darkened so that he couldn't see inside.

Still, the tree felt crowded with people bustling across the branches and sitting on their porches. It was not as dirty and dingy as the tenement housing he had seen in Aldon, but it was as close as the elves got to such things.

Iyrinder had to grip the stretcher as it tilted with the steepness of the stairs, and he hunched as the neighbors stepped onto their porches to stare. He was going to have to answer a lot of questions about how he had been injured. Either that, or his macha and isciena would. The neighbors tended to be nosy, even if they pretended to be above such things.

Finally, they reached the rooms where his family lived. The elf in front juggled the stretcher so that he could knock on the door.

After a moment, the door opened, and Iyrinder's macha peeked out. As soon as her gaze latched on him, her eyes widened, her face paling. She flung the door open. "Iyrinder, sason!"

"I am fine, Macha." Iyrinder pushed onto one elbow, ignoring the pain that shot through his healing wound.

His words did not seem to reassure her. She stepped aside and motioned for the guards to enter. "Take him in."

The guards carried him inside their small kitchen and sitting area. They had to navigate around the table that stood in the center of the room.

Fayetha, Iyrinder's sister, stood to the side, her hand pressed over her mouth at the sight of him.

He gritted his teeth to hold back a groan. He had come through the whole war without a scratch. At least, no scratches that had not been healed by the time he returned home to his family.

But now that Tarenhiel was finally at peace, he took a bullet and worried his family.

"I am fine, isciena." He kept his tone soft. This would be too much like the moment they had been notified that their dacha had been killed, fighting at the late king's side.

Fayetha blinked, as if she did not find his words reassuring.

Macha opened the door to the room he shared with Fayetha. A curtain down the center of the room gave a semblance of privacy. Since he rarely stayed here anymore, Fayetha mostly had the room to herself.

Macha hurriedly tossed a few of Fayetha's things back to her side of the room, then smoothed the blanket on Iyrinder's bed. "Lay him here."

Iyrinder pushed to his elbows. "I can get myself in bed."

The guards shared a glance, but they held the stretcher steady as Iyrinder swung his legs to the side, then to the ground. His head swam a bit—he had lost a lot of blood over the last day—but he only had to stumble one step before he lowered himself onto his bed. He attempted to turn his groan into a sigh as he lay down on the soft warmth of his bed.

By the way his macha hurried over to fluff his pillow and spread his blanket over him, he was not fooling anyone.

The two guards rolled up the stretcher, then ducked out of his room.

"Is there anything I can get you?" His macha continued to fuss with his blanket, as if she had to make sure it was perfectly positioned over him.

He caught her arm, then reached up and squeezed her

shoulder. "I am truly all right, Macha. After a day of rest, my injury will be fully healed."

"I know. I just…" Her hand shook as she smoothed the blanket yet again. Weary lines dug across her face, making her appear older than she was.

His macha was young enough that she could have remarried after Dacha died. Yet she never had, and she did not seem to wish to do so. Even all these years later, the grief for their dacha weighed heavily on her.

There was no reassurance that Iyrinder could give her. Sure, he had come back this time. The wound was a mere through and through. The bullet had nicked a few internal organs, which, while painful, was nothing the elven healers could not fix easily enough.

Next time, he might not be so fortunate. He might be wounded worse—as Princess Elspetha had been—but he had no elishina to keep him alive as Prince Farrendel had kept Princess Elspetha alive. Or he might be killed outright. That was the risk he took every day as a guard.

Since there was nothing he could say that would take away the grief in his macha's eyes, Iyrinder dropped his hand and gestured toward the door. "I would appreciate a drink of water."

"Of course." Macha hurried from the room, bustling about as she fetched his water.

Fayetha stepped into the room, standing in the doorway as she glanced from him, to her feet, and back. "Are you truly all right?"

"Of course I am. I was healed by the queen herself." He forced himself to grin.

Sure, he had only been healed by Queen Rheva because she had come along as moral support, and she graciously provided her healing magic since Nylian, the head healer, had been busy tending Princess Elspetha. But he would still claim the distinction.

Fayetha sank onto her bed across the way. The curtain had yet to be pulled to provide privacy, so she could see him from where she sat. "You were still shot."

"Yes. But I saved Laesornysh's life. And I am fine." Iyrinder needed to distract his sister from her focus on his wound. "I had a book for you. That Escarlish author you like released a new book. But I am afraid it got left behind in the scramble to head here as quickly as possible."

"I do not care about the book." Fayetha swung her legs, gripping the edge of her bed. Her chestnut hair was nearly the same color as his—a color they had inherited from their dacha. She was fifty years younger than Iyrinder, and she worked in Ellonahshinel's library. "Well, I do care about the book. But not while you are hurt. You are more important."

"I am glad you consider me more important than a new book by your favorite author. I have sometimes wondered."

Fayetha grabbed one of her pillows and tossed it at him. While the room was not large, the pillow still landed short.

It did, however, nearly hit their macha as she stepped into the room, carrying a tray with both his requested glass of water and a bowl of fruit.

Their macha sighed, then set the tray on the table beside Iyrinder's bed. "I will make some of your favorite venison stew for supper tonight."

"Linshi, Macha." It was no light offer. Because of the risk of fire, none of the individual homes in this tree had fireplaces. There was a communal kitchen a little way from the base of the tree, but it was a hassle to share the space with everyone else attempting to cook hot food for the evening meal. Needless to say, they had often eaten cold meals growing up.

Perhaps one day, he could purchase one of those heating coils from Prince Farrendel. Once he and Lance perfected the design. Right now, the risk of it burning out or blowing up was still a little too high for Iyrinder to give one to his family.

Iyrinder pushed onto an elbow and took the glass of water, sipping it.

A day of rest, then he could return to his post guarding Prince Farrendel and Princess Elspetha.

And he could return to Patience. While his memories from the train ride from Aldon to the outpost were hazy, he had vague memories of her holding his hand the entire way.

She certainly had stuck close during the trip from the outpost to Estyra.

It felt like something had shifted between them. That tug he always felt around her had gotten stronger, deeper.

He had come close to dying. He did not want to keep waiting.

No, when he saw her again, he was going to ask to court her. He wanted to make what they had real.

PATIENCE POUNDED the bread dough with an extra vehemence. She already had a batch of chocolate cookies cooling on the countertops. A pot of broth simmered on the stove. Leftovers of yesterday's potato and cheese soup were in the ice box.

What else could she cook or bake? She needed to do something to keep her hands busy and her mind as occupied as possible. If she stopped moving, then she'd think.

And if she started thinking, then she would think about Iyrinder and his blood soaking into the gravel of Winstead Palace's drive.

And if she thought about that, then she'd think about how she'd have to break his heart the next time she saw him. Because it was either break his heart now or break her heart later, and she was selfish enough to choose to protect her own heart over his.

And that was why she was furiously pounding the bread dough, wishing she wasn't like this. Wishing she didn't have to hurt a good man—an honorable elf warrior. All because she was too scared to risk losing him later on.

It was messed up, and she knew it was messed up. But a panicked clawing filled her throat any time she thought about going forward with a future with him, only to lose him to some assassin, some war, some crazy person with a gun, as he tried to protect his prince.

"Miss Merrick?"

She whooshed out a breath, squeezed her eyes shut, and clenched her fists in the bread dough. Not now. Surely not now. She wasn't ready for this conversation.

But when she dragged her hands from the dough and turned around, there he was. Whole and standing tall, with his bow and quiver on his back, his sword at his side, and his long chestnut hair flowing free over his green tunic.

"You shouldn't be here. You should be resting. Surely you aren't back on duty already." She whirled back to the sink and took her time washing her hands rather than face him.

"I rested yesterday while my wound finished healing. But I am cleared for duty today."

Of course he was. Wonderful, annoying elf healing magic.

She dried her shaking hands on a towel and turned. Only to find herself nearly face-to-face with Iyrinder. She hadn't heard him cross the room.

"Miss Merrick. I wanted to thank you for the way you cared for me when I was injured." Iyrinder reached, as if he was going to take her hand. But he dropped his arm short of touching her.

No, no, no. He was going to ask if he could court her. She could tell in the expectant way his eyes focused on her, the lean to his posture as if he was drawn to her. She'd seen this before, when footmen or the young men at the factories tried to ask her.

She hated turning them down. They always got this sad, kicked puppy look when she turned them away.

But this would be worse. Much worse. Because Iyrinder wasn't just a sweet puppy who had tried to ask out a girl who wasn't interested.

No, Iyrinder was so much more than that. And she was interested. Even if she didn't dare accept what he would offer. He would offer her everything, if she let him.

But she couldn't let him. She just couldn't.

"Iyrinder, I…" Her throat closed as she tried to work up the courage to say what needed to be said.

"Miss Merrick. Patience." Iyrinder swallowed, his voice dropping a little as he said her name. "If I may…I would like…"

No, no. She couldn't bear it if he finished.

She stepped closer and pressed a finger to his mouth. "Iyrinder. I…I like you. But I can't. We can't. I lost my parents. Two of my siblings. It is bad enough that Eugene risks his life every day as a guard. I can handle that since he is my brother. But I couldn't marry a guard. I couldn't do that to any children we might have. I just couldn't. There's too much risk that I would lose you."

"Then I will—" he started to say around her finger.

"No, don't say that you will quit being a guard. It is too much a part of you. I couldn't ask that of you any more than I could ask Eugene to stop." Patience dropped her hand, a shudder shivering down her back as she stuffed back her tears, her pain. Not now. Not yet. "You are too honorable. Too faithful. Too loyal. Even if you stopped being a guard and simply worked in magical engineering with Prince Farrendel, your instincts are still there. The moment someone attacked him or Princess Elspeth, you would jump in to save them."

That warm look in his eyes died before being locked away behind a shuttered, blank expression. He took a step back, then bowed to her. "I see. Then I will bid you good day, Miss Merrick."

That flat, formal tone tore through her, but she refused to relent. This was for the best. For both of them.

She turned back to her bread, though she didn't dig her hands in.

The door clicked shut behind her. Even when hurting, Iyrinder was far too polite to slam the door.

She waited a heartbeat more before she braced herself against the countertop. Her sobs came hard and fast, too painful to choke back a second longer.

S omeone was pounding on her door. Patience blinked, shoving her way out of sleep. Deep night cloaked the forest outside of her window. It must be the middle of the night. "Who is it?"

"Eugene. Get up and get dressed." Her brother's voice rang through the wood. There was an edge to his words. A sharpness she had only heard when something really bad was going down.

Patience rolled out of bed and quickly changed into her dress. Instinct told her that she had better pack. Not that she had much to pack, since she'd left Escarland with nothing. All she had here were a few things she'd left since it had become more efficient to leave some items here rather than hauling everything back and forth when the prince and princess chose to travel.

Within ten minutes, she slung her bag over her shoulder and stepped from her room. She found Eugene in the kitchen, pacing back and forth in front of the cupboards. He, too, carried a pack. As she entered, he nodded and headed for the door. "Come on."

"What's going on?" She trotted to keep up as Eugene held the door for her.

"Not sure. But King Weylind sent an order through Iyrinder." Eugene shut the door behind her, then gestured to where Iyrinder was waiting, a pack over his shoulder as well.

His gaze slid over her, skipping as quickly as hers skated away from him. They'd been more or less success-fully ignoring each other since she'd turned him down.

It was an awkward situation to be in, given how closely they worked together. Perhaps she should have thought of that before she gave in to the temptation to let their friendship develop this far. Now the two of them were stuck seeing each other every day with this painful tension stretching between them, and there was no avoiding the situation unless one of them wanted to give up what had been their dream job.

Iyrinder spun on his heel and led the way through the nighttime forest. Patience stuck to Eugene's side, and they soon reached Prince Farrendel's magical engineering workshop on the forest floor.

She continued to hang back, hiding at her brother's side, as King Weylind arrived and explained the situation.

Mongavarian assassins were on their way to Tarenhiel, and they would likely want to finish what they had started with the bullets that had injured Princess Elspeth and Iyrinder. King Weylind had decided to send all of them to the elven summer palace of Lethorel for protec-tion until the assassins were caught.

Assassins. Suddenly, her romance troubles with Iyrinder didn't seem like the worst thing after all.

PATIENCE BUSTLED around the kitchen at the base of Lethorel, familiarizing herself with the layout and the food contained in the cupboards. Due to the haste, she had ended up pretty much the only servant here.

That left her in charge of feeding everyone with whatever happened to be in these cupboards.

The flour was still good. The wooden container seemed to have some kind of preservation magic on it that kept bugs from getting into it.

She could make another loaf of fresh bread. She had scrounged together a stew from the dried meat and vegetables the previous evening, and she could come up with various combinations of that. Hopefully one of the guards—possibly Iyrinder—could be persuaded to hunt so they would have some fresh meat.

The kitchen was, at least, decently stocked. Probably in case Lethorel needed to be used as a refuge for the elven royal family, as it was now. The food wouldn't be interesting or varied, but she could make this work.

"Miss Merrick?"

She jumped and nearly dropped the container of flour on her foot. Elves and their light-footed ways.

She turned to find Prince Farrendel standing there, shifting from foot to foot. She bobbed into a curtsy. "Was there something you needed, Your Highness? I'm afraid there isn't a hot breakfast this morning."

"No, I do not need anything. But my wife...she..." His words trailed off, and he gestured vaguely, as if he was struggling to put his thoughts into words. The tips of his ears turned pink in a sure sign that he was uncomfortable.

"She's suffering from morning sickness." That much had been rather obvious even before Princess Elspeth had been forced to confess to all of them on the train that she was expecting.

Patience waved to the stove, where a kettle was already heating. "I have water heating for ginger tea, and I'll bring up toast, now that she's awake."

"Linshi." Prince Farrendel hesitated another moment, rocking back and forth on his heels. "Tell Essie...tell her that if she needs anything sooner than two hours to send for me right away."

With that puzzling statement, the prince ducked out of the kitchen and all but ran into the surrounding forest.

The water in the kettle started bubbling and rattling against the metal. Patience poured the water over the ginger tea, then set it aside to steep while she toasted the bread, then spread it with butter. By the time that was done, the tea was done steeping.

She piled everything on the tray, then made her way to the rooms belonging to Prince Farrendel and Princess Elspeth. She had never been here in Lethorel, but Iyrinder had given both her and Eugene a quick tour shortly after they arrived. During the whole tour, Iyrinder had only addressed Eugene, as if she wasn't even there.

She only had herself to blame. She had told him she didn't want to move forward. Could she blame him if he was following her wishes and turning their relationship into something professional and cold?

At the door to the prince and princess's rooms, she knocked, then stepped inside. "Your Highness? I've brought ginger tea."

"Thank you." Princess Elspeth's voice held a depth of gratitude. She stepped from the bedroom, still wearing a nightdress beneath a flowing dressing gown. She sank into a chair by the table.

Patience set the tray on the far side of the table, then

placed the teacup and the plate with toast in front of Princess Elspeth. "The tea is sweetened with raspberry and honey to help cut the sharpness of the ginger."

Princess Elspeth took a sip and sighed. "This is perfect. Thank you. You're a lifesaver."

Patience picked up the tray, then stood back. She'd served more than a few pregnant noble ladies over the years. "Prince Farrendel said to tell you that if you need him before two hours are up to send for him."

Princess Elspeth laughed around the rim of the teacup. "Still hovering. I knew he was going to be like this, but the assassination attempt just made everything worse. He wasn't even going to leave my side long enough for his morning exercise if I didn't all but order him to stay away for the next two hours. And he needs that exercise."

Prince Farrendel had been particularly jittery when Patience had seen him a few minutes ago. Lack of his daily exercise would explain it. Patience had seen how much the prince needed the exercise to stay healthy mentally.

Nearly losing his wife and unborn child to an assassin would play with anyone's mind. But someone who had the anxieties and struggles that Prince Farrendel had? That only made it all the more intense for him.

"I am sure King Weylind, my brother Eugene, and Iyrinder will look after him." Patience hoped the princess didn't notice the hitch in her voice on Iyrinder's name.

No such luck. Princess Elspeth's eyes shot up. With deliberate grace, the princess set down her teacup and leaned against the back of her chair. "About Iyrinder... forgive me if I'm prying, but what happened between the two of you? You seemed to be growing quite close."

Patience opened her mouth, closed it, and clutched the

tray tighter. How much did she want to confide to Princess Elspeth?

Who else was there to confide in? Princess Elspeth had trusted Patience with confidences and secrets over the time she'd worked for her and the prince. The princess would keep Patience's trust just as Patience kept hers.

Though, Patience still wasn't sure how much she wanted to say.

Instead, she gathered herself and met Princess Elspeth's gaze. "How can you bear it? Loving Prince Farrendel when he's…"

She wasn't sure how to put it delicately. So far in her marriage, Princess Elspeth had nearly lost her husband several times to capture, torture, a war, a troll duel to the death, and now she had been shot in an attempt to kill him. If there was anyone who had reason to worry that her husband would be taken from her by a sudden death, it was Princess Elspeth.

"When he's an elf warrior with a target on his back?" Princess Elspeth shook her head and sighed.

Because Prince Farrendel had a target on his back, Eugene and Iyrinder were in the line of fire, prepared to take a bullet for the prince.

"Yes." Patience hugged the tray to her, as if it were a wall to shield her heart. "How can you love him, knowing he could be killed?"

Princess Elspeth picked up her toast, though she didn't take a bite. Instead, she tapped it against her plate, as if she needed to keep her fingers busy. Her gaze dropped to her toast for a long moment.

When she once again met Patience's gaze, her green eyes showed far too much of the truth of her emotions, a truth Patience wasn't sure she wanted to see. "I love him because each day I have with him is worth it. And, yes, it's made a bit easier, knowing that if he is in danger, I have a hope of keeping him alive with the heart bond. But even then, if he's killed tomorrow by these assassins, it would be tough. Beyond tough. But I wouldn't regret that I married him and loved him. Instead, I would treasure every moment I had with him, knowing that I lived and loved with no regrets."

Patience nodded, dropping her gaze when she couldn't hold the princess's any longer.

"I can't make your decision about Iyrinder for you. But ask yourself. If he were killed tomorrow, what would you regret more? The fact that you didn't let yourself love him? Or the fact that you did?"

Princess Elspeth was hitting a little too close to home, prodding things that Patience didn't want to examine.

"Thank you, Your Highness. You have given me much to think about." Patience curtsied without looking up, still gripping the tray. "Unless you need me, I should get back to the kitchens."

"No, go on. I understand you have a great deal to do, being the only servant attempting to cook for all of us." Princess Elspeth's voice remained warm, and it took on a hint of a laugh. "And if Farrendel wanders by, tell him I'm fine and I'll be down shortly. I'm pregnant, not dying."

Patience wasn't sure she'd quote the princess on that exactly, if Prince Farrendel asked. But she nodded anyway. "Yes, Your Highness."

Before the princess could say anything else, Patience ducked out of the room and hurried across the branches as quickly as she dared.

As she crossed one of the branches, movement below caught her gaze and halted her in her tracks.

Far below, Prince Farrendel, Iyrinder, and Eugene

sparred, the two elves moving so impossibly fast that it was amazing her brother was keeping up as well as he was.

Iyrinder spun backwards, his chestnut hair flying in a graceful arc. He lunged, even as he ducked Prince Farrendel's swing.

Her breath caught in her throat, and she couldn't seem to make herself look away.

He was a warrior. Powerful. Faithful. Gentle. Kind.

And she'd ripped his heart out. Even if she wanted to take the princess's advice and take a chance on love, would Iyrinder give her another chance?

CHAPTER
TEN

P atience huddled on one of the cushioned benches in Lethorel's main room, her knees drawn up to her chest in a very undignified manner. But she didn't care.

The assassin was here.

Somewhere out there, beyond the crackling shield of blue magic Princess Elspeth held in place around them, Prince Farrendel was facing the assassin.

What if he lost? What if he was shot? What if the assassin came for Princess Elspeth next, and Eugene or Iyrinder was killed trying to protect her?

Eugene sat next to her and wrapped an arm around her shoulders. "It will be all right. Prince Farrendel can take out one assassin easily enough."

Patience forced herself to nod. Prince Farrendel was formidable.

But Princess Elspeth had still been shot. Iyrinder had still been shot protecting Prince Farrendel. The same could happen yet again.

To one side of the room, the elven heirs Prince Ryfon

and Princess Brina sheltered behind a cordon of elven guards.

Princess Elspeth stood just to the side of one of the windows while Queen Melantha held station next to her, her fingers glowing with green magic. The troll guards took up a station near their queen.

Then there was Iyrinder, standing just a few feet away from Princess Elspeth as if prepared to pull her away from the window at a moment's notice. He rested a hand on his sword while his bow and quiver of arrows lay across his back.

So alert. So much the warrior.

A shot rang out.

Patience flinched, making a small squeak.

Eugene's grip tightened around her shoulders. "I am sure Prince Farrendel is fine."

He must be, for Princess Elspeth's face remained set in determined lines, no hint of pain as there would be if the prince were hurt.

Princess Elspeth had said that love was worth it. Even now, the princess showed no signs of regret. Just love for her prince.

Patience's gaze strayed to Iyrinder yet again. Would it be worth loving him? If he were shot while protecting them, what would Patience regret more?

Right now, she already regretted breaking his heart. What if that was the last thing she had said to him? What if he died with a broken heart because of her?

If he died today, she would regret how she had hurt him for the rest of her life. The look in his eyes would haunt her.

She had to fix this. She could not live with an aching heart filled with nothing but regret.

Princess Elspeth released a breath, and she started to lower her hands. Then she stiffened.

A second gunshot blasted through the morning, sharp and slicing.

Patience gasped, her gaze darting about. Had anyone in here been shot?

Princess Elspeth turned, her jaw hardening. Part of the magical shield around Lethorel lashed out into the forest to the side of Lethorel. "Got him." She paused, then a hint of a dangerously cold smile crossed her face. "Scratch that. Got her."

Princess Elspeth held the magic for another moment before she nodded and dropped the shield. She turned to the rest of them. "Guards, please secure the prisoners. They're going to need medical attention."

And just like that, it was over.

Patience sagged against Eugene, pressing her forehead against his shoulder for a moment.

They had not even been in that much danger, protected by Prince Farrendel's magic as they were.

Could she do it? Could she tell Iyrinder that she had made a mistake?

She had learned one thing in the past few minutes. Going into danger with an empty, aching heart was far, far worse than a full heart and chance of loss that she had so feared.

Iyrinder stayed close to Princess Elspetha as two of the elven guards re-grew the stairs before they headed toward the forest floor.

Princess Elspetha darted down the stairs, and Iyrinder hurried to catch up with her. He did not manage to reach her before she hopped from the still growing stairs to land on the forest floor. She rushed into Prince Farrendel's arms, wrapping her arms around his neck a moment before she kissed him.

Iyrinder halted at the base of the stairs and scanned the forest to look for threats instead of watching his prince and princess.

The rest of the elven guards hurried into the forest, taking custody of the two groaning assassins.

"Iyrinder?" Patience stepped from the stairs and met his gaze. Before he had done more than turn to her, she took another step and wrapped her arms around him in a hug.

What...Iyrinder's breath caught as her arms came around him, too frozen to wrap his arms around her in return.

The last time they had spoken, she had told him that she did not want more. And now she was hugging him? It was far too confusing. Too hard on his broken heart to take.

He gripped her shoulders and gently pushed her away. "I need to check on the amir."

A handy excuse, even if it was not true. The prince was clearly fine.

Right now, Iyrinder just had to get away. He could not deal with whatever this was or was not between him and Patience right now.

If Iyrinder had known how long it would be before he had a chance to talk with Patience, he might have taken the time then. As soon as the assassins were taken into custody, they had hurried back to Estyra and from there to the Escarlish-Mongavarian border. Only once the Mongavarian threat was dealt with did all of them troop back to Aldon just in time for the celebrations for the one year anniversary of the first treaty between Escarland and Tarenhiel, the one that had resulted in Prince Farrendel and Princess Elspetha's marriage.

Now, Iyrinder leaned against a tree in the parkland of Winstead Palace, cloaked in the darkness outside of the circle of light cast by the fire.

Around the fire at the campsite, most of the elven and Escarlish royal families gathered as they talked, laughed, roasted marshmallows, and drank hot chocolate.

To give them the semblance of privacy, Iyrinder lurked far enough back in the trees that he could not pick out individual words, just the overall murmur and laughter. From where he stood, he occasionally caught glimpses of the other guards—troll, elf, and human—who also hid among the trees.

Footsteps crunched on the loam behind him a moment before Patience appeared out of the darkness, casting about as if looking for someone.

Iyrinder drew in a breath and stepped forward into her path. "Miss Merrick."

She gave a squeak as she jumped. "Oh, there you are. I was just..." She trailed off, glanced away from him as if looking for the words, then gestured toward the fire. "I was just going to check if they needed anything."

"It does not appear so." Iyrinder was not sure he was ready for this conversation, especially if he was about to get his heart ripped out a second time. But he had spent the last few days turning that hug over in his mind, torturing himself with hope.

Patience released a breath, her hands twisting in her apron. "I talked with Princess Elspeth at Lethorel. Some of the things she said, well, it made me think about fear and regrets and the cost of love. Seeing the way she and Prince Farrendel deeply love each other even when in danger and at risk of losing each other..." She trailed off, staring off into the nighttime forest instead of at him. "I think I was wrong. And I'm sorry."

Iyrinder found himself stepping forward, leaning toward her. Drawn by something deeper than his rational will, which told him that giving in to the temptation of her was a great way to get his heart broken again when she rejected him.

"I can't say that I'm not still terrified. I've lost so much already. My parents. Two of my siblings. I'm still so afraid of losing you too." She rubbed her upper arms, as if cold. But after a long moment, her gaze, filled with pain and hope sparkling together in the moonlight, finally lifted to his. "But do you think—if I haven't totally messed this up —that you could be patient with me? Until I'm not so afraid?"

How could he resist when she was looking at him like that? The look in her eyes tugged on something so deep inside him that he had no words to put a name to the thoughts and feelings she worked in him.

Iyrinder eased another step forward and tentatively reached a hand to rest it on her shoulder. "Yes, I—"

Before he had even finished, she crossed the last few inches of space between them and wrapped her arms around him. This time, she leaned her head against his shoulder, as if making herself perfectly comfortable to stay there for as long as he would let her.

He froze, his breath catching, his mind screeching to a halt. This was...nice. Very nice. And even if his brain was paralyzed, his arms somehow found their way around her of their own accord, his fingers tangling in her soft, thick blonde hair. After another moment, he lowered his chin to lean his cheek against the top of her head.

Patience breathed a long breath and snuggled even closer.

"May I court you? I will be patient and give you the time you need. But I would like to be more than what we have been." Iyrinder held his breath, waiting for her reaction. The last time he had started to ask her this, she had rejected him and run.

Patience lifted her head, peeking up at him as she gave a tiny nod against the hand he still had buried in her hair. "Yes. I would like that."

With her looking at him like that, her face only inches from his, it was all he could do not to give in to the urge to kiss her.

But that would be moving far too fast. And he was an elf. He had plenty of time to spend courting her as slowly as she needed.

Instead, he simply held her as she snuggled against him again and savored the privilege she was giving him to hold her like this.

After several minutes, a few of those around the campfire started standing up, the murmurs holding a hint of farewells and goodnights.

Iyrinder sighed against Patience's hair and gently extricated himself from their embrace. "I am needed."

She jumped back, letting him go. "I'm so sorry. I've been distracting you from your duty."

He kept his mouth shut on that. If he said he was not distracted enough to be a danger, then it would seem an insult to her. But if he said he was distracted, then she would feel even worse. "Prince Farrendel and Princess Elspetha have ordered all of us to remain scarce tomorrow. Would you take a stroll with me after breakfast?"

Patience nodded, smiled, then glanced toward where Prince Farrendel and Princess Elspetha were slowly making their way through the trees toward Buckmore Cottage. "Yes. I'd like that."

With that, she hurried into the forest, going in a wide circle to avoid crossing paths with the prince and princess. By the way the two of them were leaning on each other, they did not want to be disturbed at the moment.

Iyrinder hung back, keeping his gaze on the forest rather than on his prince and princess to give them privacy.

The night remained quiet. No signs of assassins or threats. And he let his mind wander a bit, thinking of Patience. The future.

It would be a future filled with love. Family. Friends. As long as he was patient enough to wait for it.

PATIENCE PANTED, her calves burning, as she and Iyrinder climbed the seemingly never-ending steps up the tree where his mother and sister lived. Yet it was the churning in her stomach, the tightness in her chest that had nothing to do with her lack of breath, that had her wanting to turn around and run the way they had come.

What would his mother and sister think of her? She was a human. A maid. No one special.

It was slightly reassuring, seeing where they lived. With the small homes lined up on the branches, this was clearly the elf equivalent of lower-class housing. It was neat, clean, and far more airy than the tenements where Patience had grown up, but there was something almost familiar about the community life bustling around her.

To one side, an elf woman was hanging laundry on a line. A group of children tossed a ball back and forth, racing over the branches as easily as the groups of children used to run over the refuse-covered cobbles of the back alleys when Patience was growing up. Another group of elf women were clustered on a porch, stitching and talking.

As they ascended yet another layer of branches, Iyrinder lightly touched her back and steered her from the stairs onto one of the branches.

Finally. Patience had been about to beg for a rest if they did not reach their destination soon.

And yet, the churn in her stomach worsened. They were almost there. She was about to meet his family. This was really happening.

Iyrinder halted before one of the small tree houses growing from the branch, then knocked on the door.

The door swung open, revealing a lovely elf woman with brown hair standing there. She smiled, speaking in elvish and reaching to clasp Iyrinder's shoulders.

Was this his sister? Or his mother? Elves looked so ageless, Patience couldn't be sure.

Another elf female shoved her way past the other, gripping Iyrinder's shoulders.

Now that must be Iyrinder's sister. Fayetha, if Patience was remembering right. Fayetha had the same chestnut hair, and her exuberance spoke of youth while the other elf woman remained serene even in her excitement.

Patience really should have spent more time learning elvish. She had picked up a few words here and there. One couldn't work for and alongside as many elves as she had in the past months without learning a few basic words. But she didn't know enough to follow the conversation.

Iyrinder gestured to Patience, saying something in elvish that contained Patience's name.

The chestnut-haired elf female all but threw Iyrinder out of the way in her hurry to reach Patience. She gripped Patience's shoulders, then spoke in Escarlish, "I am so excited to finally meet you! Iyrinder could not stop talking about you last time he was home."

The tips of Iyrinder's ears turned a hint pink, and his smile held a sheepish tint. "I did not think I was that verbose."

"You did not have to be. You were clearly smitten." Fayetha grinned, her light brown eyes sparkling.

Iyrinder's mother stepped forward, nudging Fayetha out of the way, and gently gripped Patience's shoulders, speaking in elvish.

"She says that you are welcome any time, and that you clearly have made Iyrinder very happy." Fayetha translated, then added, "Macha does not know Escarlish. Iyrinder and I learned because I wanted to work in Ellonahshinel's library and Iyrinder wanted to earn a spot on the king's guard. You need to know the human languages for both of those positions."

"I see." Patience smiled back at Iyrinder's mother. "Tell her that Iyrinder makes me very happy."

Fayetha translated into elvish this time, and Iyrinder's mother smiled, flicking a glance at her son.

Iyrinder's ears were verging on red now, and he had ducked his head.

"Well, I am glad you both make each other happy." Fayetha leaned closer to Patience. "You already made *me* very happy with your taste in novels. I have loved all of your recommendations. I cannot imagine anyone better for an isciena than someone who shares my taste in reading."

Patience laughed and did not resist as she was steered into the small, cozy room. A small table with three chairs sat next to a small section of cupboards while a sitting area took up the rest of the space. Three doors cut into the far wall, likely leading to the bedrooms and the water closet.

She soon found herself at the table, a plate of some kind of elven pastry in front of her, Iyrinder's mother and sister taking turns talking. Iyrinder sat at her side, and Patience tentatively reached her hand out for his under the table, not sure if he would take it with his mother and sister there in the room.

After a moment, his warm fingers enfolded hers and rested their clasped hands on his knee.

She had been so afraid of reaching for this. But why hadn't it occurred to her that with Iyrinder, she also gained a sister and a mother? It had been so many years since Patience had a mother and sister to call her own. The ache of grief was still there, but the love of Iyrinder's family embracing her as one of their own, even though she and Iyrinder had only just started courting, soothed some of that aching emptiness inside of Patience's heart.

EPILOGUE

TEN MONTHS LATER...

"Are they ready yet, do you think?" Princess Essie leaned over the countertop, coming just short of poking one of the cooling chocolate chip cookies.

Prince Fieran—the squishy, red-haired baby—slept peacefully in a cradle in the corner of the kitchen where both of them could keep an eye on him.

Patience picked up one of the cookies. It was still warm but it wasn't so gooey that it flopped over. Perfectly cooled. "Yes, they're ready."

Princess Essie grinned, grabbed a plate, and quickly piled two cookies on it. Patience followed her lead and also put two cookies on a plate. As if the two elves studying in the parlor needed any more sugar at this point. They were going to be so jittery.

Though, a break from studying to exercise for a while would do both of them good. Fresh air did wonders for keeping a clear head, and all that.

Once both Patience and Princess Essie had plates loaded with cookies, they strode from the kitchen, down the hallways, and stepped into the parlor.

Prince Farrendel lay on the couch with his legs on the back against the wall and his head hanging off the cushion where his knees should have been. He held a stack of papers over his head while the fluffy orange cat Princess Essie had gotten him for their anniversary curled up on his stomach.

An explosion of papers and books covered the sofa, floor, and coffee table within arm's reach of the prince. It was surprisingly chaotic, given the meticulously neat way Prince Farrendel normally organized everything from his clothes to his workbench in both his workshop in Estyra and his corner of Lance Marion's place in Aldon.

Across the room, Iyrinder sat cross-legged on the floor with his back to one of the overstuffed chairs. He, too, had stacks of papers and books around him, along with an overwhelmed, rumpled air to him, from his loose shirt to the few strands of chestnut hair that straggled out of place to stick to the chair behind him.

Princess Essie held up her plate of cookies and marched into the room like a conquering general. "I brought cookies!"

"Linshi." Prince Farrendel breathed out the word and dropped the papers onto one of the stacks on the floor. "Exams are awful."

"Yes." Iyrinder set aside his own papers, squeezed his eyes shut, and rested his head against the seat cushion behind him.

"I'm sure both of you will do great tomorrow. A little cookie break will help, I'm sure." Princess Essie navigated around the papers and books without stepping on any of them.

Prince Farrendel nudged the cat off him, then swung his legs around until his feet were on the ground and his head upright as it ought to be.

The cat huffily stalked along the length of the couch, jumped down, then marched over to one of the open books. He plopped himself down on it, curling his tail around his paws as he gave Prince Farrendel a glare.

Princess Essie sat on the same cushion as Prince Farrendel, squeezing next to him since it was the only space free of papers and books, and held out the plate to him. "I made them myself."

Prince Farrendel's eager grab for the plate halted, and he glanced from the princess to the cookies as if he wasn't sure if they would be edible.

"Don't worry. I had a lot of supervision from Patience. She wouldn't let me serve them if they hadn't turned out just fine." Princess Essie shot a look at Patience, grinning. "A few more practice batches, and I'll be able to make them all by myself."

"Are you trying to leave me without a job?" Patience smiled as she crossed the room, headed for Iyrinder's corner.

Over the past few months as she had been courting Iyrinder, Patience had grown closer with the princess. There was something about being one of the few humans courting or married to an elf warrior that bound them together in a way that few others could understand. While Patience felt more free to joke with her princess, she had yet to be able to call her just "Essie," and they had compromised on "Princess Essie," which was the same thing Lance Marion called her.

Who knew? Perhaps in a hundred years, Patience would feel free enough to call the princess by her nickname with no title attached.

Maybe she was getting a little ahead of herself. She and Iyrinder were taking their time courting. They weren't even betrothed yet, much less married and forming a heart bond.

But as she sat next to Iyrinder and handed him the plate of cookies, she leaned into him and knew that was the direction their relationship would go. Someday, when they were both ready.

Iyrinder smiled back and took the plate. With his free hand, he clasped her hand, holding it even when it made it more difficult for him to balance the plate on his leg and eat his cookies with his other hand.

Patience leaned her head on his shoulder. He had been so steady, so gentle with her the past few months. Never pushing her to move faster than she wanted to go. Never asking more of her than she wanted to give. Carefully helping her work through her fears about someday losing him.

Princess Essie was right. Loving Iyrinder was worth the risk of losing him. She wouldn't trade the time she'd had with him already for anything.

She glanced across the room, but Princess Essie and Prince Farrendel were huddled together, laughing about something. Too distracted to pay any attention to Patience and Iyrinder.

Patience squeezed Iyrinder's fingers, not looking at him as she kept her head on his shoulder. "I love you."

Iyrinder stilled. He even stopped chewing his bite of chocolate chip cookie for a moment. Then he swallowed and coughed, as if he'd swallowed wrong.

Oops. Confessing her feelings while he was eating a cookie probably hadn't been the best timing.

Patience straightened, then patted his back. "Are you all right? Do you need a glass of water?"

Iyrinder shook his head, still coughing. After a moment, he pressed a hand to his chest, gave one last cough, and sucked in a breath. "No, I am fine." He set the plate aside, then turned to better face her. He traced his fingers lightly over her cheek. "I was just surprised. I did not think you would say it this soon."

"Soon?" She leaned into his hand. "I've been falling in love with you since the first day I met you."

"Then *this* is long overdue." Iyrinder smiled, leaned closer, and kissed her.

She leaned into him, her fingers somehow finding their way to gripping the softness of his shirt, then tangling in the sleek strands of his hair.

By the time he pulled away, her brain had gone hazy and mushy.

A laugh came from the other side of the room, then Princess Essie's voice. "It might be just me, but I'm not sure that is the most effective way to study. It seems a tad distracting."

Patience's face heated, and she peeked at Princess Essie and Prince Farrendel across the room. She had completely forgotten they were there. Oops.

"I would be up for trying it." Prince Farrendel's voice was low, almost shy, even as he attempted something that must have been a flirtatious smile as he tugged Princess Essie closer.

Princess Essie lightly poked him in the ribs, causing him to squirm. "I thought you didn't like it when I kissed you in front of everyone."

"I do not think they count. Not if Iyrinder is kissing Patience in front of us." Prince Farrendel gestured to them.

Patience sighed and smoothed Iyrinder's shirt where she'd wrinkled it. "You're a bad influence."

"Or a good one." Iyrinder's smile held his own flirtatious note.

"Exams must really be turning your brains to mush if mere chocolate chip cookies are making both of you so flirtatious." Patience shook her head and patted her hair, finding that it, too, had gotten a bit rumpled with all the kissing.

"Anything is better than studying." Prince Farrendel flopped against the back of the sofa.

Princess Essie laughed, then patted his arm. "I'm so glad that kissing me rates above studying. That isn't a high bar to get over."

"That is not what I meant." Prince Farrendel eyed her, and something passed between the two of them that seemed even more flirtatious than before.

"All right, that's it. Come on, Iyrinder. I think we'd better give them a moment." Patience gripped Iyrinder's hand and dragged him to his feet.

He resisted only as long as it took him to snag his plate with his second cookie from the floor. Then he let her tug him from the room and down the hallway. They didn't stop until they stepped outside onto the back patio, sheltered by the trees of the parkland.

Patience turned to Iyrinder. "Now. Where were we?"

He held up his plate between them. "I still have a second cookie to eat."

She planted her hands on her hips and fake-glared at him.

He grinned in that way that said he knew he had gotten under her skin. Then he set his plate on the metal patio table and took her hands in both of his. "I love you too."

"Also not what I meant, but I'm glad to hear it." She

stepped even closer and tipped her head up. "I was thinking of picking up where we left off."

She stood on her tiptoes and kissed him.

Why had she ever resisted falling in love with him? Because this was wonderful. She leaned into him, all but sagging in his arms as he deepened the kiss.

Abruptly, he pulled away from her, his gaze focused past her. "Hey! Shoo!"

She turned just in time to see a squirrel bound off the table, a piece of the cookie stuffed in its mouth. The rest of the cookie lay in pieces, chewed and crumbled.

"That squirrel ate my cookie." Iyrinder stared down at his plate, and even she couldn't tell if his disconsolate look was exaggerated or real.

She laughed and gripped his hand. "Come on. Let's get you another."

THE WAGER

This story overlaps with Troll Queen, Pretense, *and* Shield Band.

The Dulraith across the border in Kostaria was over. The celebration feast in the treetop shelter was winding to a close.

Averett stood off to the side with Weylind as Farrendel and Essie approached Melantha and Rharreth to express their goodbyes. Averett leaned closer to the elf king. "They are going to be expecting before their first anniversary."

"I beg your pardon?" Weylind turned to him with one dark, disapproving eyebrow raised.

"Essie and Farrendel." Averett tipped his head in their direction. "Just you wait. They'll announce they are expecting sooner rather than later."

Weylind snorted. "You are overly concerned with our siblings' business."

"You doubt my prediction?" Averett wasn't about to pry into Essie and Farrendel's business, but it was too much fun to needle Weylind about it. "Let's make a wager out of it."

Now that disapproving eyebrow was joined by Weylind's glower. "Elves do *not* gamble. Especially not over…this."

"We're not gambling, exactly. We aren't going to put money down or anything like that." Averett waved away Weylind's concern, trying to think of a proper wager on the fly. "It's more a dare than a wager, if you will. Let's say that if I win, then you will put one of those elf ear mugs on your desk for a month."

Some of the glower faded as Weylind turned more fully toward him, something almost like interest gleaming in his dark eyes. "And if I am correct?"

"Then you'll have to think of something suitably ugly that I will put on my desk for a month." Averett shrugged, unable to hide his grin.

Besides his family, he'd never had someone he could call a true friend the way he could Weylind. Sure, they still had the interests of their separate kingdoms to worry about. There would always be politics that lay between them.

But Weylind was still a fellow king. He understood the burdens Averett carried better than anyone else besides Paige.

As an elf, Weylind was also unfailingly honest in a way that few people were, especially when everyone was always clamoring for something and doing their best to disguise their intentions with flattery or pandering. When Weylind wanted something, he said so.

A wager like this was something done between friends. Averett had never been free to do something like this with anyone besides his brothers.

"That would be acceptable. I agree to this…wager."

Weylind met Averett's gaze for a moment before he glanced back to Rharreth and Melantha. "Looks like it is my turn."

Weylind strode off, gathering Rheva on his way toward his sister and her troll husband.

Averett watched them go, grinning. This was going to be fun.

Farrendel and Essie strode up, and Essie frowned at him. "What has you grinning like a cat that finally caught the mouse?"

"Nothing." Averett couldn't help it if his grin stretched even wider.

"WE'RE EXPECTING," Essie blurted out in a rush.

Averett blinked at her. Before he started internally celebrating, he needed confirmation. "Excuse me, did I hear that right?"

"Yes. Farrendel and I are expecting. It's early yet, but *someone* can't seem to keep it a secret." Essie gave Farrendel one of her fake-glares before she removed the hand from his mouth.

Averett had to resist pumping his fist and shouting. He glanced past Essie and Farrendel, meeting Weylind's gaze and mouthing *I was right*.

Weylind's shoulders fell in a sigh.

Now that gloating to Weylind was complete, Averett rushed forward and gave Farrendel a body-slam hug that he knew would ruffle Farrendel's feathers a bit. Not in a mean way. But in a gentle teasing way that Farrendel seemed to find annoying and yet didn't mind since it meant he was being included by his Escarlish brothers. "Congratulations!"

Averett was happy for Farrendel and Essie. They would make great parents.

And, selfishly, he was glad that he would be alive to see at least one of his half-elf, half-human nieces or nephews. Who knew? Depending on how this niece or nephew aged, he might even live to see them mature into adulthood.

ON THE TRAIN headed to Aldon now that the border was secure, Averett lounged in one of the plush, cushioned chairs in the sitting room.

Weylind plopped down in the cushioned chair across from him, setting a large canvas sack on the floor next to him. "I want another wager."

Averett raised his eyebrows. "One month of having an elf ear mug on your desk isn't enough? Don't think I've forgotten. I have a mug set aside for you, and I'll give it to you when we reach Aldon. You can't get out of this by giving the mug away, like you did with the one Essie and Farrendel gave you."

"I fully intend to keep my end of this wager." Weylind grimaced for a moment before his gaze fell back to the canvas sack. The grimace faded into something more... cunning. "Thus I propose another wager. I wager that Farrendel and Essie's child is a boy."

Averett eyed him, not taking the bait. "Can your elf healers find out if a baby is a boy or girl before the child is born? Did Rheva whisper a little tidbit in your ear? Is that why you are so certain?"

"Some elf healers are skilled enough to tell. But it is usually not done. Nor has Rheva given me any inside information that would affect this wager." Weylind stated it stiffly. "But that is why I wish to make the wager now. Before this information is shared, if it is at all."

"I see. Well then, I accept. If the baby is a girl, you will put the elf ear mug on your desk for a month yet again." Averett gestured toward the canvas sack. "I take it that is what I will be putting on my desk if the baby is a boy?"

"Yes." Weylind all but smirked as he reached for the sack. He held it out to Averett.

Averett took the sack and eased the canvas away from the item it contained.

As the canvas fell away, he saw the ugliest...was it a bust? A sculpture? He wasn't even sure what it was.

A human head had been grown out of tree branches, the face somewhat resembling Averett's, though only loosely. Twigs draped down from the scalp to form a wild version of hair. The eyes and open mouth were gaping, empty holes.

Averett grimaced at it, holding it out. "What is it?"

"It is a lamp, of course." Weylind uttered an elvish word.

Bright blue light flared inside the head, glowing through the eyes and mouth. As if the head had not been creepy enough already.

Averett sighed and shook his head. "I have to hand it to you. This is *ugly*."

"I think it is...quirky." Weylind's tone said he knew very well that it wasn't quirky but was just using that word since it was what Essie called the elf ear mugs. "I will, of course, teach you the elven words to turn it on and off. You will want to use it."

"Yes. Of course." Averett stared at the monstrosity in his hands. He was going to hold his breath for the next months until, hopefully, Essie and Farrendel announced they had been blessed with a baby girl.

AVERETT SAT AT HIS DESK, trying to work on paperwork. Essie was due any day now, according to the elf healers, and it was difficult to concentrate on work while knowing his first niece or nephew was soon to be born.

A knock came from the door a moment before his head clerk stepped inside. "A message from Tarenhiel for you, Your Majesty. It is marked for your eyes only."

Averett's stomach sank as he gestured the clerk forward. Had something happened? Weylind would wire Averett first, if that were the case.

His clerk crossed the room and held out the note. When Averett took it, he retreated back to the doorway to wait for a reply, if one was needed.

After a deep breath, Averett opened the telegram. It contained only a single line.

Put the lamp on your desk.

For a moment, Averett sagged against his leather chair, trying to absorb first the relief, then the growing excitement at the implication of the words.

Weylind would not wire about their wager if Essie and the baby were anything less than healthy.

A boy. Averett had a nephew.

Grinning, he pulled open one of the deep, bottom drawers of the desk and pulled out the ugly human head lamp, setting it in a prominent place on his large, oak desk. He did not even care that he would have to look at the thing for the next month.

The clerk made a noise in the back of his throat, his face twisting for a moment before he schooled his features.

"Please send a reply to King Weylind. Tell him *The*

lamp is front and center. Thank you." Averett carefully folded the telegram and placed it in a pocket.

With one last, wide-eyed glance at the lamp, the clerk bowed and left.

If Averett's grin remained in place for the entire day, no one commented on it. Not even when he didn't seem that surprised when the official word came from Essie and Farrendel that they had a son named Fieran and that both mother and baby were doing well.

With news like that, Averett might even consider leaving the lamp on his desk for two whole months.

Maybe.

Now he just needed to think of the next wager to make with Weylind. He was having too much fun to quit now, even if he had ended up with an ugly lamp on his desk.

THE PROPOSAL

This story takes place between chapters 40 and 41 of Pretense.
In Shield Band, *it occurs just between chapters 3 and 4.*

Edmund sorted through the stacks of paperwork strewn around his desk. The tax office had completed their audit of all the nobles who had donated to the *Sentinel*, a newspaper that had turned out to be a front for a Mongavarian spy ring. Now he was comparing the audits with all other government documents he could find, including trade applications and copies of log books from ships and dock masters.

In the months since the spy ring had been discovered, Edmund had been put in charge of tracking down any other Mongavarian spies still lingering in Escarland. It had been tedious work, involving a lot more paperwork than his previous job of undercover spying.

But Edmund no longer minded. This was important work, disentangling Mongavaria's claws from Escarland and Tarenhiel.

And he got to spend his lunch breaks and evenings

with a certain elf princess. He wouldn't trade time with Jalissa for anything.

Just the thought of Jalissa brought a smile, and he touched the pocket where the box—and its ring—rested. Today. He would ask her today.

"What has you grinning like a jester? Do you find tax reports amusing?"

Edmund glanced up as General Bloam—his superior in Escarland's Intelligence Office—halted next to his desk. While General Bloam's face remained blank, even forbidding, the twinkle in his eyes gave away that he was not chiding Edmund.

"No, sir." Edmund closed the report he had been reading.

"Ah. Your usual *distraction* then." General Bloam's expression turned even more dour, a sure sign he was teasing. "I suppose it's just as well that you have the afternoon off. You will accomplish little in your state."

Edmund let his grin linger for a moment longer before he turned back to business. He added the file to the *might be suspicious* pile. "I think I've narrowed down which of the nobles who donated to the *Sentinel* were simply duped and which ones warrant further investigation. There isn't much I can do here until after I've done a bit of investigating."

General Bloam's amusement fled, and his mouth pressed into a tighter line. "Be careful. Their connection to the *Sentinel* gives us cause to investigate them, but it wouldn't be a good look if a prince of Escarland were caught investigating his own people."

"I know." Edmund patted his pocket again, flashing another grin. "But haven't you heard? I've put all that spying stuff behind me, now that I have a lovely elf princess on my arm encouraging me to settle down. With her at my side, the nobles are going to welcome me into their homes freely and eagerly just to get a glimpse of the couple who is the toast of the town. If I happen to pick up a little gossip and fish out their political leanings while I'm at it, they can't blame me."

And if he could talk the noblemen into stepping into their study during the evenings for a nip of brandy and if he happened to catch a glimpse of incriminating evidence while he was at it, well, so much the better.

"Very well." General Bloam gave a sharp nod, then moved on to the section of desks dedicated to the analysts for Mongavaria.

Escarland's spying network in Mongavaria had been all but wiped out a few months ago. General Bloam and the others had been working feverishly to get a new network in place. But that took time, and they didn't dare move too fast, otherwise they might alert the already wary Mongavarians.

All the more reason for Edmund to put an end to whatever spying efforts Mongavaria still had in Escarland. If Escarland couldn't spy on Mongavaria, it was only fair that Mongavaria couldn't spy on Escarland.

After straightening the papers and placing them in locked drawers in his desk, Edmund nodded to the others as he wound his way through the maze of desks and left the room. He strode down the corridor that housed the Intelligence Office.

At the doors that connected this wing with the rest of Winstead Palace, he had to halt, show identification, and whisper that week's password to the four guards stationed there. It didn't matter that he was a prince and clearly recognizable. The Intelligence Office wasn't taking any chances with the new protocols after the embarrassment caused by the break-in several months ago.

Only then was Edmund free to wander through the corridors of Winstead Palace, headed for the door and the path to Buckmore Cottage.

As he strode past the open door to Averett's study, his brother glanced up. "Edmund. Anything to report?"

Edmund sighed, but he stepped inside Averett's office with a smile. As much as he wanted to rush off to spend the afternoon with Jalissa, reporting to his king about the spy situation came first.

After closing the door behind him, he took a seat in a chair across the desk from his brother. The oak surface overflowed with stacks of paperwork that made Edmund's files look piddling in comparison.

"Well? Any leads on additional spies?" Averett smoothed a hand over his face, dark circles underneath his eyes. His red-brown hair was mussed while his clothing was rumpled. All a testament to the long hours he had been pulling.

This situation with Mongavaria had to be weighing on Averett. If it came to war, they would be in for a long, bloody conflict.

But the price of peace was their brother Julien's marriage to King Rharreth's shield sister Vriska—unless she backed out the moment she met Julien and the next troll woman on the list took her place.

Edmund didn't envy either of his brothers for the position they were in. If he didn't love Jalissa so much, he would be tempted to feel guilty, falling in love when an arranged marriage should have been his duty as the third son instead of Julien's.

But he had Jalissa, and he wasn't about to give her up for duty and kingdom. Nor would either of his brothers ask that of him.

Edmund rested his elbows on the chair's armrests.

"We haven't received word yet from the investigators sent to the cities where the counterfeit money turned up, but I'm sure they'll report soon if they've found any more of the spy network there. It could be the whole network closed up shop or decided to lie low after word reached them about our raid on the *Sentinel*. It will make it that much harder to track them down."

"At least if they are in hiding, they aren't effectively spying. That's something." Averett sighed heavily and looked ready to rub his face again. "Please tell me I can at least be certain my nobles aren't about to turn on us the way Lord Bletchly did last year?"

"I've weeded out the ones I believe are fully innocent." Edmund grimaced, looking away from Averett to glance at the family portrait that hung on the wall. The one where their father was still alive, their mother's red hair hadn't faded, and Essie was a chubby-cheeked baby. "I'm going to dig deeper into the others. I don't believe any of them are truly spies or traitors—they just have a few illegal trade deals and stuff like that most likely—but I want to be thorough."

"Good. I've had enough surprises for one year." Averett's gaze also drifted to the portrait on the wall. "Escarland has been nearly at war or at war for the entire time I've been king, except for those few months this winter when we were blissfully ignorant about how much of a threat Mongavaria posed. Those were some wonderful months."

They would have been, if Edmund hadn't been pathetically pining for Jalissa. And he wasn't too proud to admit that, at least to himself.

"We'll get there again. Kostaria joining our alliance will make Mongavaria back off, we'll get a spying operation back up and running over there, we'll kick all their spies out of here, and we'll enjoy a golden age the likes of which Kostaria, Tarenhiel, and Escarland haven't seen in hundreds of years. You'll see." Edmund pushed to his feet. "If there isn't anything else…"

Averett waved him away. "No, no. Go on and see your elf princess."

Edmund grinned and strode to the door. He could mention the ring in his pocket and his plans for the afternoon, but he didn't. His family would find out soon enough when they saw the ring sparkling on Jalissa's finger at supper that evening.

JALISSA STROLLED through the Kingsley Gardens in the Escarlish capital of Aldon. At this time of summer, the outdoor gardens bloomed in a profusion. The rose garden was elegantly dressed in a bounty of blooms in all colors from delicate white to blushing pink to deepest, boldest red.

She trailed her fingers over a few of the struggling flowers, easing a hint of her magic into them.

"The gardeners always love it when you visit." Edmund's voice came from behind her a moment before his arms wrapped around her waist, tugging her back against him.

She leaned into him, enjoying the feel of his arms around her. This was her idea of a perfect afternoon. Edmund holding her. Gardens all around her. Butterflies dancing on the floral-scented breeze. "I am glad they do not mind if I help a few of the plants along."

"They are looking to hire a few elves to come and work here, if they can convince any to come." Edmund pressed a gentle kiss to her neck that had her knees buckling.

"I am sure some of those with weaker plant growing magic could be lured here." Jalissa's voice came out breathy. How was she supposed to concentrate on a conversation with Edmund trailing those gentle, tiny kisses down her neck until he kissed the base of her neck at her shoulder? "They are not as valued in Tarenhiel due to their weakness."

"Their magic is still a wonder." Edmund drew back just a little bit, though he did not let her go. "As is yours."

Jalissa closed her eyes, resting her arms over Edmund's around her. They had been officially courting for only three months, but they had been some of the best three months of her life. They had picked up right where their clandestine relationship had ended all those years ago.

Yet this was better. So much better. They were both more mature. More ready for something real and lasting than they had been while meeting in secret.

"The Gardens are also looking for a new patron. Lady Fiskre, their current patron, has decided to retire from her position on the board of directors." Edmund's voice took on a serious tone.

Jalissa turned in his arms and studied his face. Something inside her leapt at the thought of becoming personally involved with the running of these Gardens. "Could I become their patron?"

"You could...but you would have to be Escarlish." Edmund stepped back from her. "Or married to an Escarlish prince."

Before she had a chance to respond, he abruptly dropped onto one knee.

Jalissa gasped and reached for him. "Are you all right?

What is wrong?" She searched him, looking for a blossoming wound, although she had yet to hear a gunshot.

Edmund laughed and waved her hands away. "I'm fine. This is an Escarlish custom, so let me finish."

Finish what? Jalissa froze, staring down at him as he drew out a small box from a pocket.

He opened the box, revealing a delicate silver band formed of twining roses with a single, purple-colored stone set into a swirl of silver roses at the top. "Jalissa, my amirah, I know it has only been three months. But we've known each other much longer than that, and I know you'll tell me off if this is far too short of a courtship." He drew in a deep breath, then smiled up at her. "Will you marry me?"

Jalissa pressed her hands over her mouth, tears pricking in her eyes at his speech. "Yes! Yes, of course I will marry you."

She was not sure what to do first. Should she take the ring? Or kiss him? Yet he was still kneeling on the ground, and while she loved him, she was not about to get her dress dirty by flinging herself onto her knees in front of him.

He solved the problem by standing, plucking the ring from the box, and taking her hand. When he slid the ring on her finger, it fit perfectly.

Of course it did. Edmund would find out that detail about her before commissioning the ring.

"I love you, my amirah." Edmund kissed her, and her knees went so weak she had to cling to the front of his shirt to stay upright.

When the kiss ended, she tried to murmur that she loved him too. But she was not sure the words actually made it out of her mouth in an understandable manner. Her thoughts were not that coherent.

He brushed his fingers through her hair as he searched her face. "How long do you think it will take to plan the wedding? I don't want to rush you if you'd rather take longer, but is three months enough time?"

She raised her eyebrow, still trying to take in this moment, the ring on her finger, the *yes* she had given him without a moment's hesitation.

But even as she stood there, her sluggish, kiss-addled brain caught up. The engineers had just announced that they believed the new bridge over the Hydalla River would be finished in three months. "The new bridge?"

"We don't have to." Edmund's fingers tightened on hers, his forehead scrunching. "It was just a thought that getting married on the new bridge would be a good political statement. That was all. But if you don't like—"

Jalissa pressed her finger over his mouth. "I think it is a brilliant move. Three months is short notice, but we can pull it off. We have plenty of help." She removed her finger and eyed him. "Will it be soon enough that I can be the new patron for the Gardens?"

"I knew that was the reason you agreed to marry me. Your acceptance has nothing to do with being in love with me." Edmund finally pulled her back into his arms, grinning. "I believe being engaged to marry an Escarlish prince should be good enough for them to take you on as a patron. They will jump at the chance to have your help to facilitate hiring elves here. And it doesn't hurt that they like you."

"Good." Jalissa hugged him, though she was not ready to celebrate just yet. "And it will not be a problem that we will have duties in both kingdoms that will take us away?"

"The job of patron isn't too demanding. It will be flexible with us traveling between the two kingdoms."

Edmund pressed a kiss to her forehead. "And it does have its perks. Like the ability to host private parties at the Gardens when you wish."

As if she was not already excited enough as it was. The elven nobles would be much more likely to visit Escarland if the reception was held at the Kingsley Gardens instead of inside the stone walls of Winstead Palace. "Who do we approach so that I can apply to be their new patron? I wish to give my name to them as quickly as possible."

Edmund laughed and held up her hand, where her new ring glinted in the sunlight. "Shouldn't we tell our families before we start announcing our news to the directors of the Gardens?"

Jalissa waved his concerns away and started marching down the garden path. "Our families already know we will be getting married sooner rather than later. It is more important that I do not miss this opportunity."

Naming the Kitten

This story also takes place between chapters 40 and 41 of Pretense *and between chapters 3 and 4 of* Shield Band.

Edmund strode into the small garden that surrounded a brick patio outside of the back door of Buckmore Cottage. There, Farrendel sat on the bricks, trailing a short length of twine over the ground. A fluffball of orange fur pounced on the twine, trying to catch it between its paws.

Essie lounged on a bench, grinning as she watched Farrendel and the kitten. Wearing a loose shirt, any signs of her pregnancy were hidden.

"I see the kitten is old enough to go home with you." Edmund couldn't help but smile at the way his brother-in-law Farrendel was already wrapped around this little kitten's paw. It would be highly amusing to watch him fall head-over-heels for his son or daughter in a few months.

Essie glanced up. "Edmund. Help us decide. Which name do you think is better? Fluffy or Mustache?"

Edmund eyed the two of them, crossing his arms. "I think neither of you should be allowed to name your child."

Essie rolled her eyes and huffed. "Very funny. But really, which name is better?"

He resisted the urge to grimace. He would rather not get in the middle of this, thanks very much. He eyed the kitten for a long moment. It was a brilliant orange ball of fur with a tiny white line of fur below its nose, almost as if the kitten had a permanent milk mustache. "Mustache, if you go with a nickname like Stache or something like that."

"Ha!" Essie pointed at Farrendel. "Told you it was better."

Farrendel scowled, though the expression lacked any heat. "I do not see why *you* get to name *my* cat."

"Because the name Fluffy is too literal."

"But fluffy is exactly what he is." Farrendel picked up the floofball of a kitten, as if to demonstrate his point. When the kitten squirmed, he set it back on the patio, where it promptly raced off and attacked the toe of Edmund's boot.

Edmund wiggled his foot, causing the kitten to attack it even more energetically. Would Essie and Farrendel notice if Edmund slipped away quietly before he was pulled into this name discussion any further?

Farrendel's eyes narrowed and got that glint that said he was planning something. "If we go with your name for the kitten, then I get my first choice of name for our child."

"Hey, now that is playing dirty." Essie rested a hand on the tiny swell of her belly, her mouth moving like she was torn between scowling and smiling.

Farrendel did a better job of keeping a straight face. "How set on the name Mustache are you?"

After a moment, Essie sighed. "Our child is going to be named after his or her hair color, right?"

A smug grin crossed Farrendel's face. "Most likely."

"Fine. But I get a veto if the name is too terrible. And it has to be neutral enough to sound good in Escarland as well as Tarenhiel." Essie sprawled back in her chair.

"Are you saying my name is too long and elven?" Farrendel picked up the twine and sent it skittering across the patio again. The newly named Mustache raced after it.

Edmund took that as his cue to gracefully bow out. He backed away, then quietly slipped into the cottage.

Yet a hint of a smile tugged at his mouth. Would he and Jalissa someday have the same discussion over what to name their child?

Inside, Jalissa sat on the couch in the parlor, sorting through a pile of envelopes. She glanced up and smiled as he entered.

He leaned over and kissed her cheek. "Are those all invitations?"

"Yes. It seems the nobles of Escarland are rather delighted to have an elf princess engaged to their spy prince." Jalissa smiled and tossed the entire stack on the coffee table. "Do you have a preference as to which events we attend?"

In other words, which ones would aid in his investigation. It was the same thing they had done in Tarenhiel for the first month after they started courting. They schmoozed the elven court and the citizens of Estyra, searching for any indications of traitorous intentions. Once they were satisfied that Mongavaria hadn't managed to plant any spies in Tarenhiel, they returned to Escarland.

While he hadn't turned up any more Mongavarian spies among Escarland's nobility, several of them were up to some highly suspect importing practices—well, smuggling—that Edmund wanted to look into further.

Edmund joined her on the couch and began sifting through the invitations. This dinner party was hosted by one of the nobles on his list. He and Jalissa would definitely have to attend that one. This soiree would also have many of the nobles he was investigating in attendance. He set aside a few more of the invitations, making sure none of them conflicted with each other or the weeks he and Jalissa planned to spend at Lethorel with her family. "We'll need to attend these."

Jalissa's smile took on a hint of a smirk. "I see."

"Do any of the other invitations sound appealing to you?" Edmund spread them out on the table. "We might as well attend a few for enjoyment and not just for work. Besides, if we only attend parties for the investigation, someone might catch on."

Jalissa sorted through the invitations, then plucked one from the table. "Lord and Lady Fiskre invited us to attend an opera with them. I have heard of this human custom, and I would like to experience it at least once."

Lord and Lady Fiskre were elderly and loyal to the crown. Edmund wouldn't mind an evening spent in their box, though Lord Fiskre would likely snore his way through the opera. "Yes, let's accept that one. How about this one as well? It is at Lord and Lady Humberley's estate just outside of Aldon. They have extensive gardens that I think you would love to explore."

Jalissa's eyes lit up, and she all but snatched the invitation and slapped it onto the accept pile. "Yes, we must go to that one."

"We'll have to ask if Essie and Farrendel were invited

to that one as well. They might be willing to attend if we're there as well." While most of the furor over Farrendel's illegitimate birth had died down, it still wouldn't hurt if Farrendel and Essie made a public appearance or two while they were here in Escarland.

"Yes." Jalissa nodded, tapping the invitations they were going to accept into a neat stack.

Edmund looked through the remaining invitations and didn't see any others that looked even remotely appealing. Besides, they wouldn't want to overschedule themselves. They were sure to receive more invitations, and they would be leaving shortly for the vacation at Lethorel.

Not to mention, they had a wedding to plan. He'd heard those were complicated things, if one didn't hold it last minute like Essie and Farrendel had. And as much as simply eloping with Jalissa sounded like the better option, Edmund wasn't even going to suggest it. Sure, their wedding was likely going to be more for their kingdoms than for them. He and Jalissa were both politically minded enough that they would even play into that aspect.

But in the end, he would finally be married to Jalissa. And he'd do it as himself, not under disguise or hiding in the shadows. It was more than he had dared dream a year ago.

FAMILY VACATION

This story also takes place between chapters 40 and 41 of
Pretense, *and it occurs after chapter 5 of* Shield Band *(during
the time Julien is in Kostaria).*

E dmund was so incredibly bored. Sure, spending
time at Lethorel with Jalissa and her family had
been fun for the first few days. He'd challenged
Farrendel and Ryfon to a cannonball contest, and even
Weylind had joined them in swinging from the rope into
the lake, though Weylind performed a perfect dive rather
than attempt to make the biggest splash.

Edmund had talked Jalissa into teaching him archery,
and he might have taken advantage of her showing him
how to hold a bow to snuggle with her. He'd proven to be
rather terrible at archery, though he blamed his distraction. She rolled her eyes at him—a human gesture she'd
picked up and was becoming rather too adept at—and
lightly swatted his arm.

He was even running out of ways to annoy Weylind,

from slurping the soup at dinner to giving him brotherly backslaps at every opportunity.

But now they were a week into their two-week vacation, and he was about ready for an assassin to attack to break up the boredom. There was only so much rest and relaxation he could take before his mind went crazy craving a puzzle or danger or *something*.

Right now, Essie, Jalissa, Rheva, and Brina lounged near the lake. They laughed at something Essie said, and Jalissa's face lit with her smile. At least Jalissa was having a good time. Whatever he did, he couldn't let her see how bored he was. He didn't want to diminish this time with her family.

He'd just have to come up with another way to entertain himself.

He glanced at Farrendel, who was sprawled on the ground a few feet away. "Any ideas of what else we can do?"

Farrendel tilted his head enough to shoot a glance at Edmund. "You can join me for a run through the treetops." He spoke far too eagerly for someone who had already bounded through the treetops before the sun had even fully risen.

Edmund suppressed a shudder. While he was comfortable on the branch pathways the elves preferred, Farrendel ran along branches that were mere twigs. As bored as he was, Edmund wasn't bored enough to attempt that. "Thanks, but no thanks. What about a round of cards?"

"Cards?" Weylind lounged on the grass a few yards away. His mouth curled a bit. "As in, gambling?"

"There are plenty of card games that don't involve gambling. Or we can play those games for points or bragging rights." Edmund didn't think these elves would go for anything as uncouth as even small bets, but he was ready for something with stakes. Even if the stakes were bragging rights. A card game would at least make his brain feel like it was functioning again instead of rotting to mush with boredom.

Farrendel rolled into a sitting position. "Would this card game be something you would play with your brothers?"

"Yes." Edmund, Julien, and Averett enjoyed a good, just-for-fun game of cards. Essie, too. Edmund only played for money when in seedier taverns or the fancy drawing rooms of the elite, searching for information.

Weylind sighed and pushed to his feet. "I suppose one card game would be acceptable."

Finally. Something to do. Edmund shot to his feet and led the way toward the stairs up to Lethorel's main room. "I have cards in my room. I'll just fetch them. If you could clear a table in the main room, I'll be back in a moment."

He didn't wait to see the looks on Weylind's and Farrendel's faces. Instead, he navigated the branches as quickly as he dared. He had to traverse the branches to one of the farthest rooms in Lethorel to a room near Essie and Farrendel's. A room that also happened to be on the exact opposite side of Lethorel from Jalissa's. Not that Edmund would do anything dishonorable, but he suspected the placement of their rooms was Weylind's way of tweaking Edmund right back for all his teasing.

Reaching his room, Edmund found his pack and dug out a deck of cards. His good set of cards, not the whiskey-stained set that he trotted out when spying in disreputable taverns. As tempting as it was to show up with that deck of cards—smelling of liquor and slightly sticky—just to see the look of distaste on Weylind's and Farrendel's faces, he had already pushed them enough.

And this card game was going to provide plenty of opportunities as it was.

By the time he returned to the main room, he found Weylind and Farrendel sitting at a table, their postures perfectly straight and proper. Ryfon had joined them, and he was the only one of the three who grinned and leaned forward as if eager to learn an Escarlish card game. While Farrendel's tension betrayed the way he appeared torn between curiosity and trepidation, Weylind still had a slightly disgusted curl to his lip.

Edmund plopped into the open chair and casually shuffled the deck of cards. "Let's start with an easy game."

He wouldn't mention that it was a game often played by Escarlish children. Nor that he was exceptionally good at it, since it didn't take much to memorize which cards each of the players asked for and received.

He dealt the cards and explained the rules. The point of the game was to try to get the most sets of all four of the same denomination of card, such as all the threes or all the eights. The game ended when one player had no more cards. Once Edmund finished explaining the rules— this game would go especially smoothly with elves, who would not lie about the cards in their hand—they set to playing.

Weylind eyed his hand of cards, then glanced at Edmund. "Do you have any threes?"

Edmund smirked, then pointed at the draw pile. He could have told Weylind that Ryfon had a three. Weylind, presumably, had at least one, if not more. If Ryfon was paying attention, then he'd ask his father for threes on a future turn.

Weylind heaved a sigh and drew a card from the pile. The grim set to his mouth never wavered, giving away nothing about whether or not he was pleased with his new card. At least he had his poker face down pat.

Farrendel glanced at his cards once again, grimaced, and glanced at Weylind. "Do you have any kings?"

Weylind's expression only grew grimmer as he handed over one card.

Farrendel re-arranged his cards, then glanced at Ryfon. "Do you have any tens?"

"Nope." Ryfon prompted Farrendel to take a card.

Once Farrendel finished, Ryfon grinned and glanced across the table at Weylind. "Do you have any threes?"

Weylind sighed again and handed over two cards.

Ryfon took the cards, then turned to Edmund. "Do you have any queens?"

Edmund shook his head and pointed at the pile.

Finally, it was Edmund's turn. He eyed Weylind. "Do you have any twos?"

Weylind's jaw worked, and he held out a card.

Perfect. Edmund rearranged his cards, then he set four twos on the table. Then, smirking, he placed his final four cards on the table—four eights. "I believe that's the end of the game."

Farrendel had one set of four, as did Ryfon. But Weylind had none.

Gathering the cards, Edmund shuffled again. "Who's up for another round?"

Weylind gave the closest thing to a groan Edmund had ever heard from him. "Fine. One more round."

Edmund just grinned and shuffled the cards. Now to figure out a way to make the child's game even more interesting.

AN HOUR LATER, Edmund strode down the stairs from Lethorel. Jalissa stood to meet him, and he wrapped an arm around her waist. "Did you have a good afternoon?"

"It was lovely. Then again, it's always lovely here at Lethorel." Jalissa stood on her tiptoes, as if to kiss his cheek, but she halted as Weylind stalked by with an exceptionally dark glower. Jalissa raised her eyebrows at Edmund. "Why does my brother look like…"

"Like a bee stung his bottom?" Edmund couldn't help his grin. That final game had been *quite* interesting. Adding truth or dare to the child's card game had been just the thing. Juvenile, perhaps, but worth it. "Let's just say our card game got a little…interesting there at the end."

Farther around the lake, Essie tilted back her head and laughed. Farrendel must have been telling her about the card game. She, at least, would find the humor in the fact that they had been playing a child's card game, even if everyone else here didn't know it.

Jalissa shook her head, a hint of her grin tilting the corners of her mouth. "Do I want to know?"

"Probably not." Edmund was looking forward to dinner that evening. Between Weylind having to follow through on a dare to kiss Rheva in front of all of them and Farrendel having to recite a love poem to Essie that he would have to write himself, tonight, at least, was not going to be boring.

EDMUND PUSHED AWAY his empty plate and glanced around the oval-shaped dining table, which was held up by what looked like two tree trunks that branched into the tabletop itself. "So…"

At the head of the table, Weylind blanched before his face went too stiff and blank. "I do not think…"

"A dare is a dare." Edmund leaned back in his chair, crossing his arms. This was going to be quite entertaining.

"I have completed mine." Farrendel sounded supremely smug as a hint of something almost like a smirk played across his mouth. "You neglected to specify that my dare needed to be executed in public."

Edmund quickly stuffed down his own smirk before it could break free. Perfect. He'd hoped that Farrendel would figure out that loophole—a loophole that Edmund had purposely left in there, though he was never going to admit that to Farrendel. His brother-in-law's smug satisfaction at thinking he had gotten one over on Edmund was perfect.

If Farrendel hadn't noticed the loophole, then Edmund planned to stop him before he read his poem. Forcing him to do that in public would go past light teasing and into actual torment.

Edmund frowned and sighed as if he was disappointed. "I suppose I did."

Farrendel's smirk faded into something between a grin and a grimace. "I read my poem to Essie this afternoon."

Essie winced. "I can verify that he did."

The fact that she didn't even comment on the quality of the poem meant that it must have been terrible in the extreme.

She and Farrendel shared a look. Farrendel gave a little shudder, and Essie's mouth twitched as if she was trying to hide her laughter.

Good. That was what Edmund had been hoping for. They'd gotten an entertaining afternoon out of Edmund's dare.

Edmund turned to Weylind. "That still leaves you. And I know I specified that your dare had to be completed at dinner."

Rheva's eyebrows rose, and she glanced from Edmund to Weylind. "What is this *dare*?"

"He needs to kiss you in front of everyone." Now Edmund let himself smirk.

Rheva's eyebrows shot up even further. "Pardon?"

Weylind slouched just a hair in his seat, his frown so deep that furrows grooved his cheeks and his forehead. "That card game was ill-advised."

Edmund leaned slightly closer to Jalissa. "If you need a demonstration of how it is done, Jalissa and I would be happy to provide one."

Weylind straightened as if struck by lightning. "No."

Shaking her head, her ears pink, Jalissa elbowed Edmund in the ribs. "Do not even think about it."

Weylind gathered himself and sent Edmund one of his sternest, most forbidding glares. "I can still withdraw my blessing on your upcoming marriage. Do not try me."

"Fine, fine." Edmund slumped in his chair as if defeated. He wasn't going to press if Weylind—or Rheva —were truly uncomfortable. He had just thought it might be a good little nudge in the right direction for them.

But instead of glaring like Weylind was, Rheva had a hint of a smile on her face and a gleam in her dark brown eyes. She glided to her feet and rested a light hand on Weylind's shoulder. "Actually, I think this dare is a good idea."

"What—" Weylind turned to her, then froze as she leaned down and kissed him. Right on the lips.

Ryfon dropped his fork. Brina's mouth fell open. It was probably the first time the two of them had ever seen their parents kiss.

Edmund's job here was done. He'd orchestrated bonding experiences for Weylind, Rheva, Essie, and Farrendel. And if this all turned out as he hoped, everyone would be too distracted to notice if he and Jalissa slipped out of the room in a few minutes for a stroll along the lake in the starlight.

INVESTIGATING

This story also takes place between chapters 40 and 41 of Pretense, *and it occurs after chapter 5 of* Shield Band *(during the time Julien is in Kostaria) but before chapter 16.*

J
alissa kept her practiced smile in place as she surveyed the crowded ballroom of Lord Etchworth's townhouse. Escarlish ladies in shimmering skirts twirled on the dance floor in the arms of the suited and styled Escarlish gentlemen.

Across the way, Edmund was disappearing down a hallway in the company of a group of the noblemen. Good. It hadn't taken him long to talk his way into a private conversation over a brandy in the nobleman's study. It was doubtful Lord Etchworth would leave anything incriminating just lying around on his desk, but most people wouldn't anticipate the things Edmund could spot as clues.

Time for her to get to work.

She swept gracefully around the edge of the ballroom where she would not draw attention until she could quietly insert herself into a group of the older Escarlish ladies. The conversation paused as the ladies eyed her, but Jalissa plastered on her perfect, serene princess smile and that put the others at ease. Soon the conversation continued, and it only took a few discreet questions by Jalissa to steer it toward politics.

She observed as she listened, staying in the background as best she could so that the others would talk freely around her. Once she gleaned as much as she could from that group, she infiltrated another group of ladies and repeated the process.

A few more conversations. A few more observations. All hidden behind her mask. Just as she had done for every party she and Edmund had attended since returning from Lethorel.

As she glanced around to find another group, she found Edmund strolling toward her. The curls in his hair were combed as neatly as possible tonight while his jacket and waistcoat hugged his frame, somehow hiding the derringer and daggers that she knew he had stashed on his person.

He bowed and held out a hand. "May I have this next dance, my princess?"

Finally. Investigating was important, but the evening would be a failure if she did not get to dance with him. The one dance they had shared when they arrived had not been nearly enough.

Her smile genuine now, Jalissa took his hand and let him sweep her into the crowded center of the ballroom. As the first notes of the new song filled the air, she smirked. An Escarlish waltz. Edmund had impeccable timing, as always.

He pulled her as close as was proper and spoke in a

lowered voice, his elvish guaranteeing that no one but her would understand. "Did you learn anything?"

"It seems we have succeeded in making ourselves the most sought-after couple in society at the moment." Jalissa's smile twisted as she fought to keep it in place. "As for politics, any outcry against the alliance with Tarenhiel is fading. The reassurance of a second marriage of alliance between us has convinced the Escarlish nobility that Tarenhiel is indeed an ally at this point. They seem eager to turn it into a vacation destination."

Edmund shook his head. "Your brother will need to figure out how to handle that. Your elven society isn't designed to handle gawking tourists. But tourism would be a boon to Tarenhiel's economy, and if even a few Escarlish come away with a deeper appreciation of the elven people and culture, then it would be worth it."

Jalissa nodded, trying to picture the streets of Estyra packed with hustling, bustling, loud humans. It was definitely going to take a bit of an adjustment to open their borders to visitors.

She shook herself. That would be Weylind's worry, not hers. She had more to report to Edmund. "There remains skepticism about the new defense treaty with Kostaria. The rumor is already going around that Julien intends to marry a troll, due to his current visit there. The nobles do not seem to know that a marriage alliance is a part of the treaty. But the matrons with eligible daughters are especially put out that the one Escarlish prince they always assumed would be up for grabs might be married off to someone from a foreign kingdom."

"It probably was too much to hope that his marriage of alliance could be kept secret." Edmund did just as good a job of hiding his grimace behind a practiced smile. If anyone glanced their way, they would assume they were having an innocuous, romantic conversation rather than one about politics. "The noblemen, too, seem to think Julien would be better off looking elsewhere, if he were to seek a marriage of alliance. They think an arranged marriage with Mongavaria's princess would solve all our problems, and they're hoping her upcoming visit results in just that. We would end these new tensions with Mongavaria, Julien would eventually be the prince consort of Mongavaria's queen, and we wouldn't need an alliance with the trolls to do it."

Jalissa kept her expression smooth. "Better a human than another race, is that it?"

"Yes, that prejudice is definitely a big part of it." Edmund's distaste glinted in his eyes even if he did not allow it to color his expression. "But they would be right that a marriage alliance between Julien and the Mongavarian princess would be the normal way to go about ending these tensions. It worked for Escarland and Tarenhiel, after all, as well as Kostaria and Tarenhiel. But..."

"But Mongavaria's recent actions make you wary." Jalissa studied him, knowing that Edmund's instincts were rarely wrong when it came to these kinds of things.

"They executed our spies." Edmund's jaw clenched for a moment, a reaction too strong for even him to hide. "Escarland wasn't even given the chance to negotiate for their release. As a spy, you know that you're on your own if you're caught. But Escarland returned Mongavaria's spies—most of them, anyway—in a show of good faith. Any kingdom that was willing to negotiate and end tensions through a marriage alliance would have done the same. Rharreth did just that, after all, when he caught me."

"You are a prince of Escarland. Even if you were

caught spying, it would be an international incident if you were executed." Jalissa swallowed, working hard to keep her imagination from going there. Edmund had not been executed. There was no sense in torturing herself with what-ifs.

"Yes, but I'm not sure that would have stopped the Mongavarian king if he'd been in Rharreth's place." Edmund's jaw worked again, his eyes distant as he stared unseeingly past her. "I got the sense from the little time I spent in Mongavaria that their king would have made a big production of my execution, just to send a message to Averett. That's not a king with whom I want to make an alliance."

"I am thankful that your brothers are of the same mind." Jalissa resisted the urge to shudder. "Now that our kingdoms are so closely allied, Escarland's actions and alliances affect Tarenhiel. Strange as it sounds, I trust the trolls more than I trust Mongavaria."

With Melantha and Rharreth on the throne of Kostaria, the trolls were quickly redeeming their honor in the eyes of the elves. Perhaps their two peoples would someday be kin once again, as they had been thousands of years ago.

"So do I." Edmund blinked and turned back to her, the smile returning to his face. "But that is enough talk of politics. I'm simply going to enjoy dancing with the prettiest lady at the ball."

Jalissa raised her eyebrows, even as the tips of her ears heated. "Flattery. What scheme should I be worried about now?"

Edmund's smirk was twinkling in his eyes, which looked blue tonight in the candlelight and paired with his black coat and blue neckcloth. "Just my scheme to steal your heart. Is it working?"

"When you pull out inane lines like that, no." Jalissa

pressed her mouth into a line to suppress her laughter. "I expect better from Escarland's spy prince. Besides, your timing is terrible. This dance is almost over."

"That line was rather cliché, wasn't it?" Edmund bowed to her as the dance finished. Then he took her hand again, and they swept off the floor. Somehow, Edmund managed to tuck them into a shadowed corner before anyone caught them to draw them into a conversation or ask to dance. He leaned closer and whispered into her ear, "But that doesn't make it any less true. You are the prettiest lady here. Not to mention that you are intelligent, observant, poised, magical, and so much more."

It was a good thing they were in a sheltered corner where Jalissa could lean into him because her knees were going weak. It wasn't just because of his compliments or his nearness. But the look in his green-blue eyes said that he truly *saw* her.

Their wedding could not come soon enough.

Before things could get too romantic—they were still in a public setting, after all—Jalissa pulled back a step and tilted her head in the direction of the lord's study. "Do you have anything interesting to report?"

"While I think the tax office might want to take a deeper look into Lord Etchworth's finances because I don't believe his reported income is accurate, I don't think he's a traitor beyond simply wanting to make extra coin on some black market smuggling to get around the new tariffs with Mongavaria." Edmund's shrug was so subtle only an elf would notice it. "But some of his friends, Lord Farnley in particular, seemed a little shifty whenever Mongavaria came up."

"Hmm. Lord Farnley's wife was particularly quiet." Jalissa searched the ballroom. The lady in question had drifted into another group and did not appear to be participating in that conversation anymore than she had in the one with Jalissa.

"It is worth investigating further." Edmund's mask smile flickered a moment to let a hint of his real smirk come through. "But for tonight, I think we've done enough investigating. Let's step out into the garden and get a breath of fresh air."

"Yes, please." Jalissa fell into step with him as he headed for the nearby double doors. Of course, Edmund had positioned them close by, as if he had already been planning their escape outside from the moment the dance ended.

Footmen opened the doors for them, and the cool night air wrapped around them as they stepped onto a small brick patio surrounded by hedges and a small section of garden. A fountain bubbled in the center while a few other couples strolled among the plants, taking a respite from the noise and heat of the crowded ballroom.

Jalissa drew in a deep breath, the air laced with the damp scent of dew-covered greenery. While she did not fear crowded ballrooms the way Farrendel did, she was relieved to step away into the night-kissed garden. "This is better."

"Yes." Edmund sounded distracted, and when she glanced at him, his gaze was focused upward. "The light is back on in the study."

Jalissa glanced around the garden, then tugged Edmund into the shadows next to the townhouse wall. She knew that look. So much for no more investigating. "Do you want to eavesdrop? I can convince the ivy to get you up there."

Edmund's smirk was answer enough. He gripped the ivy as she pressed her fingers to the plants. She stood so that her body shielded the faint glow coming from her hands. The other couples in the gardens were too busy kissing or talking to look their way, but she did not want to draw their attention.

The vines wrapped around Edmund and lifted him into the air beside the wall. It must have been a strange sensation, but he did not make a sound.

She halted the vines just below the window, holding them in place.

Edmund peeked over the windowsill. The window must have already been cracked open because he nudged it slightly more open.

Jalissa held her breath and cocked her ear, trying to keep half her attention on the others in the garden in case someone spotted her or Edmund while also listening to the faint voices coming from the window high above. With her elven hearing, she could just make out the conversation that Edmund was listening to.

"...been sniffing around. He and that elf princess of his have been at every party I've been at in the past three weeks." Jalissa thought the voice might belong to Lord Farnley. She and Edmund had spoken to him several times over the past few parties they had attended.

"They are courting. It could be an attempt by the crown to court public opinion." Lord Etchworth's voice was slightly slurred as if the man had consumed too many glasses of the brandy that had been flowing freely that evening. "The royal family's reputation has taken a battering."

"Yes, but Prince Edmund never spent much time in the public eye. He rarely attended events before this."

"He could be taking a more active role now that Princess Elspeth has stepped back from being the face of the royal family. Don't worry about it."

"I still don't like it. The crown is likely to take a hard line on some things after Bletchly's bungling."

As if it was the crown's fault for punishing traitors instead of the fault of the traitors for betraying their kingdom.

A noise caught Jalissa's attention. A couple, the woman giggling as the man pulled her closer, were headed in Jalissa's direction. Likely looking for a dark corner.

Jalissa poured more of her magic into the ivy and yanked Edmund back down fast enough to earn her a muffled grunt of surprise. She slowed him just before his feet touched the ground.

"Jalissa, what—"

No time to explain. Jalissa banished the ivy back to its normal size with one hand and gripped the front of Edmund's shirt with the other. She pressed her lips to his, kissing him, just before the other couple stepped through the hedge into their shadowed corner.

The woman's giggling halted immediately. The man coughed. "My apologies, Your Highnesses."

The sounds of scrambling and rustling hedges came from behind her, but Jalissa forgot all about the other couple as Edmund's arms came around her and he drew her into a deeper kiss.

When he pulled back, he whispered, "I've always wanted to try the whole kiss-to-avoid-suspicion thing, but I never had anyone to kiss in those situations before."

Jalissa managed a laugh, but it came out as weak and lightheaded as she felt. She was not sure she could come up with a coherent response right now.

A creak from above caught her attention, and she glanced up to see Lord Etchworth swing the window open all the way and peek out.

Edmund's fingers gently cupped her face, and then he was kissing her again. Jalissa did not even care that it was for Lord Etchworth's benefit so he would not think they had been eavesdropping. Somehow, the edge of danger made the kiss all the sweeter.

She vaguely registered the slam of the window overhead. When she drew back this time, all she could think to murmur was, "Do you think he bought it?"

Edmund chuckled, still holding her against him. "I don't know about him, but I sure did. Careful, princess. I think your prim and proper reputation won't survive getting caught kissing me like that."

That helped shake the kissing haze from her mind. She swatted his chest and stepped out of his arms. "Everyone knows it is your terrible influence."

"True." Edmund straightened his neckcloth, then took her hand. "I believe we've worn out our welcome. Ready to return to the palace?"

Jalissa nodded, sending one last glance up at the study before she and Edmund made their way back toward the ballroom and the doors that would lead them to their waiting carriage.

Yes, both Lord Etchworth and Lord Farnley were worth investigating. Whatever they were up to, they didn't want Edmund and Jalissa to find out.

Which made it all the more important that they did.

EDMUND HELD Jalissa's two fingers in the elven style, the backs of their hands brushing, as they strolled up the steps of Winstead Palace after the carriage dropped them off in the front circle drive. The night closed around them, crickets and tree frogs setting up a chorus in the trees, while the lamps around the gravel drive lit the steps.

They would step inside to give a quick report to either Averett or General Bloam, depending on who was still awake. Then Edmund would walk Jalissa to the door of Buckmore Cottage before he returned to his own room in Winstead Palace.

A footman opened one of the large, double doors for them, bowing as they stepped through the doorway.

Inside, Averett paced across the entry hall, deep grooves in his forehead and around his mouth speaking to worry. General Bloam stood in the shadowed doorway to the corridor, staying out of his king's way at a respectful distance.

"What's wrong?" Edmund's fingers tightened around Jalissa's, and she stepped closer to him as if to lend support.

"I received a report from Julien while you were gone." Averett held out a piece of paper, astonishingly long for a telegram. "A deadly illness has spread across Kostaria, and King Rharreth has requested help in finding a cure."

Edmund's eyebrows shot up as he took the paper. King Rharreth wouldn't reach out to Escarland and Tarenhiel lightly. Quickly, Edmund scanned the paper, holding it so that Jalissa could read alongside him.

"I have already started composing messages to the doctors at the hospitals and the university professors to put together a team to send to Kostaria," Averett continued even as Edmund read. "While Escarland can't provide the aid of the elven healers, we can hopefully help them discover a cure for this illness. Based on the descriptions, we don't want it spreading to Escarland."

Edmund nodded, half-listening as he read. There was something about the description of the disease. He didn't know a lot about different illnesses, but he knew poisons. And if he didn't know better, the symptoms sounded rather similar to the effects of a poison. That rate of death seemed far too high for a mere disease.

He glanced at General Bloam where he still stood in the shadows, lifting an eyebrow.

General Bloam gave a slight nod, a dark look in his eyes.

The general had read the report and had similar suspicions.

Edmund and Jalissa's investigation here was important, but it could wait. Lives were on the line in Kostaria. That took precedence over a mere investigation into some illegal smuggling.

Edmund faced Averett again. "I'd like to go along with the scientists you send to Kostaria."

Jalissa's head shot up, her eyes flicking over his face for a moment before her jaw tightened. "*We* would like to go."

Her fingers squeezed his. She didn't even know his suspicions yet, but she knew it must be important if he wanted to go. She would be there at his side so they could face it together.

He would have asked her to go along, but she had beaten him to it and volunteered. Thanks to her training in detecting plant-based poisons in preparation for their upcoming trip to Mongavaria, she would provide more help to the trolls than he could, if his suspicions were correct.

He tugged her a little closer, hoping she understood how much her support meant.

Averett's gaze snapped to Edmund's. "Why? What is it?"

Edmund hesitated. He wasn't sure he was right, and

he wouldn't know that until he could see the situation for himself. And until Jalissa used her magic to look for poison.

Should he say something and worry Averett? Or should he keep this to himself for now?

Edmund sighed and shook his head. "I'm not sure I'm right. But there's something about the symptoms that seems more like a poison than a disease. But I won't know until Jalissa and I have a chance to see for ourselves."

Averett's jaw tightened, and he nodded. "I see. In that case, yes, you and Jalissa should go. And whoever else General Bloam deems necessary."

At Averett's glance, General Bloam bowed and nodded in silent agreement.

"This will change who we send. We'll want experts in diseases, but they will need to be flexible enough to change to researching a poison if needed." Averett ran a hand over his face. "If this is a poison…"

"Then someone has to be behind it." A chill settled into Edmund's chest. What were the odds that this was another plot by Mongavaria?

He and Jalissa would soon find out. Edmund glanced at Jalissa and lightly swung their clasped hands. "Ready for a trip to Kostaria?"

Jalissa gave a little shiver, perhaps remembering the last time they had all been in Kostaria. They had fought across the wintry landscape to rescue Farrendel from the previous troll king's torture. "Yes. It will be good to visit my sister." Jalissa's brow scrunched, and she glanced up at him. "Will Rharreth allow you to enter his kingdom?"

Edmund opened his mouth, then hesitated. Rharreth had *not* been amused to find Edmund spying in Kostaria. Perhaps he would not have been so affronted, except that

Edmund had approached Melantha while she had been sleeping to check that she was all right to send that information back to Tarenhiel—and thus reassure Jalissa that her sister was alive and well. Rharreth had taken Edmund's presence rather personally after that. "Um, probably not. We might need to enter incognito and hope Rharreth is desperate enough that he doesn't throw us out on our ears the moment he realizes who I am."

Averett grimaced. "Please don't cause an international incident. With Julien's upcoming marriage, things are beginning to thaw between Kostaria and Escarland. We don't need you messing that up."

"Don't worry about me." Edmund smirked and lifted his and Jalissa's clasped hands. "I'm rather good at international relations, after all."

Averett rolled his eyes. Jalissa huffed and lightly smacked him.

Totally worth it.

PERIL IN
MONGAVARIA

This novella occurs directly after Edmund and Jalissa's wedding (chapter 41 of Pretense; *chapter 21 of* Shield Band) *and overlaps chapters 22-31 of* Shield Band.

CHAPTER
ONE

E dmund leaned against the wooden railing of the balcony surrounding the cozy cabin in the treetops Jalissa constructed for their wedding trip.

Just him and Jalissa and the vast forest of Tarenhiel where they had disappeared for the past week. No duties. No lies. No spying. And no one even knew where they were. He couldn't remember the last time he'd relaxed this completely. Even now, wearing nothing but his loose trousers and his unbuttoned shirt, he didn't have the urge to reach for the arsenal of hidden weapons he'd left behind in the cabin. When was the last time he'd been this at peace?

He closed his eyes, savoring the tree-scented morning breeze as it brushed cool against his face and bare chest. The wooden floor was slick and a bit damp beneath his bare toes.

Jalissa's light footsteps brushed the floor a moment before her arms wrapped around him. "I wish this week did not have to end," she murmured against his back.

"I know." He rested his arms over hers for a moment

before he tugged her around to face him, pulling her into his arms as he did.

He still marveled at the privilege to do so. For so long, she'd been out of reach due to the secrets standing between them. Somehow, even after everything that had gone between them, she had still chosen him. Chosen to trust him.

And now she was his wife, and he was holding her. Seeing her in a light, flowing dressing gown with her dark brown hair tumbling with abandon over her shoulders and down her back. Everyone else saw the perfect elf princess. But he simply saw Jalissa.

She wrapped her arms around him, snuggling into his embrace. "It would not be so bad if we were going home. But…"

"But we have a mission in Mongavaria." He sighed into her hair.

Never had he regretted being called to a spying mission more.

All he wanted to do was return to either Escarland or Tarenhiel and start building a home together with Jalissa. He would have a place in Tarenhiel that he could truly claim as his. He wouldn't have to abandon it if things got too hot. He could keep personal mementos and tell others his real name. He'd have family there, and he could already see himself and Jalissa offering to babysit their new niece or nephew, whenever she or he was born.

And, most of all, it would be home because Jalissa was there.

Instead, settling into life together would have to wait. He and Jalissa were leaving for a dangerous mission to Mongavaria. They'd have to constantly be on guard. There would be little safety to relax, even behind closed doors. They'd be back to masks and pretending.

They didn't have a choice. Someone had to go, and there was no one else who could go in their place.

Nor did he want to send anyone else. He had seen the pain and death caused by the poisoned grain sent to Kostaria. He'd watched as the trolls mourned and buried their dead. He'd looked into the eyes of the orphaned children. He'd seen the hollow eyes of those who had survived the poisoning, only to realize that their loved ones had not.

An anger burned deep inside his chest every time he thought about it. After what he'd witnessed, he was determined to find answers. If the Mongavarian royalty were behind the poisoning, then he would find out. And if an Escarlish lord had aided in the poisoning by smuggling, then Edmund would discover that too.

He shook himself, realizing that his grip had tightened on Jalissa, giving away the tension inside him. He released a long breath that stirred her long, dark brown hair.

Beyond his worries and determination, there was the thrill of a mission. Strangely enough, he was looking forward to facing a spying mission with Jalissa at his side. He just wished it wasn't so soon after their wedding and wasn't going to cause them to miss being there when Essie and Farrendel's son or daughter was born. It was the timing, rather than the fact that they were going at all, that he had a problem with.

Even in that, they'd had no choice. At least Averett had negotiated so they could leave after their wedding rather than before.

After another moment, Edmund released Jalissa and forced himself to take a step back. "I suppose we should dress, finish packing, and leave. We wouldn't want to be late."

Jalissa's mouth got a coy little curve to it that he had seen often this past week. "Probably not. But I do not think our brothers would question us if we were late."

Edmund reached for her, smiling even as he drew her in for a kiss. No, they likely wouldn't.

JALISSA DIRECTED their small boat to the dock on the Tarenhieli shore. The small town beyond—normally a quiet port along the Hydalla River—bustled with the activity caused by the visit of not only their king but Escarland's king as well.

She secured the boat to the dock so it wouldn't rock, then waited for Edmund to hop out first and extend a hand to her. She didn't need the help in gracefully exiting the boat, but it was an excuse to hold Edmund's hand and linger just a moment longer before politics and peril came crashing down on them.

Her brother Weylind and Edmund's brother Averett waited at the end of the dock, supervising as servants loaded items onto the elven boat that would carry them to the meeting with the Mongavarians.

As Edmund hefted their bags out of the boat, Jalissa swept toward her brother. Well, brothers. King Averett of Escarland was her brother too, now that she had married Edmund.

Weylind stepped forward and gripped her shoulders. "You appear well, isciena."

"Linshi, shashon." Jalissa resisted the urge to give in to a dreamy smile.

Edmund sauntered down the dock, both of their travel bags slung over a shoulder. "We had an *excellent* week, thanks for asking."

Weylind shifted, going stiff. "I did not ask, and I do *not* want to know."

That just made Edmund grin wider as he halted next to Jalissa.

She gave him a nudge to the ribs. He got far too much pleasure out of teasing both of her brothers. Farrendel was becoming adept at teasing right back, but Weylind still had a ways to go.

"I see marriage agrees with you." Averett grinned, then nodded to Jalissa. "Both of you."

Now her ears were getting a little hot. Would anyone care if she ducked into her room on the boat to hide while she died of embarrassment?

Edmund grinned back at his brother, then adjusted the travel bags on his shoulder. "If we have a few minutes, I wouldn't mind sorting through our things to make sure we have everything."

Jalissa tensed, her stomach giving a lurch. Edmund seemed to think she was ready for this mission, but what if she was not? What if she made a mistake and it got Edmund hurt? Or killed?

She was a liability on this trip. Everyone else was either a soldier or a spy.

While she was a princess with mere months of training in spying.

Edmund reached for her hand and gently squeezed her fingers. Telling her without words that he believed in her.

She lifted her chin. She could not doubt herself. Not now. She was as ready as she possibly could be. Life as a princess had prepared her for masks and intrigue, even if the elven courtiers did not lie outright the way a human court would.

And she had her magic, small as it was. Hopefully it

would be adequate for the task. It had served her well in Kostaria, where she had gained a great deal of practice in detecting the poison ricin.

Weylind and Averett led the way onto the boat. While Edmund halted to talk to the two Escarlish spies who would double as their guards, Jalissa continued to her stateroom.

There she found Rheva sorting through a trunk. At Jalissa's entrance, she turned and smiled. "Welcome back, isciena. I wish we did not have to immediately bid you farewell."

Rheva gripped Jalissa's shoulders, and Jalissa returned the gesture, stifling the pang that speared her chest.

She was not ready to leave so soon either. She wanted to enjoy being married and spending time with Edmund, not hustle off to Mongavaria.

If all went as planned, they would likely still be in Mongavaria when Farrendel and Essie's baby was born. Her little brother was going to be a father for the first time, and she would not even be there. She likely would not even know the baby had been born until she and Edmund finally returned to Tarenhiel or Escarland, whenever that would be.

It hurt, but they had no choice. Who else could Tarenhiel and Escarland send to Mongavaria? Certainly not Farrendel and Essie, even if they were not about to be parents. Perhaps Edmund's brother Julien could have taken on the duty, but he was tied up with securing the alliance with Kostaria.

No, this was a duty for her and Edmund. It was why he had trained to become a spy, for situations just like this. She had known when she married him that setting off to dangerous missions as ambassadors to foreign kingdoms would likely be a part of her future.

She just had not expected it this soon after her wedding day.

She forced a smile onto her face and gestured to the stacks of trunks. "This is quite the collection of luggage you have procured. Is it not a tad excessive? We may end up abandoning it in Mongavaria if things go wrong."

Edmund had warned her not to pack anything that she would miss if they had to leave Mongavaria in a hurry with nothing but the clothes and weapons on their backs.

Rheva smiled, her eyes twinkling. "Perhaps. But you should arrive in Mongavaria in style. I believe Edmund requested that you appear the snooty, aloof elf princess?"

"Yes." It would be a part of their cover. She would wear the mask of the aloof elf while he would be a ridiculous, empty-headed human prince. They would appear an odd couple, but hopefully everyone would focus on that and dismiss them as relatively harmless.

"The appearance of a great deal of luggage will aid the image." Rheva returned to the trunk she had been sorting and pointed to it. "Besides, we had all the gear Edmund wished to smuggle into Mongavaria, and we could not do it in a single trunk without making it suspiciously heavy and too small inside. This way, we could spread the weight around."

Jalissa rested her hand on the nearest trunk. With her magic, she could sense the trunk's wood, and the hollow space at the bottom. When she opened the trunk, it was so skillfully constructed that she couldn't tell the inside was smaller than it should be, even when she lifted the dresses inside to peer at the bottom. "This is good work."

"Weylind built them himself." Rheva traced her hand over the trunk's lid.

Jalissa swallowed and blinked down at the silk dresses

filling the trunk before her. Her brother was looking out for her any way he could. "Linshi. I will have to thank Weylind. These will be perfect."

Jalissa shut the trunk and flipped the latch to keep it closed. Since these had been created by Weylind's magic, the secret compartment could only be opened by another elf with plant magic. Like Jalissa or her guard Sarya. There was no latch or button for the Mongavarians to find, even if they suspected those trunks had a false bottom. They would have to take an ax to them, and even then, Jalissa suspected they would be tough to break open.

Yet that would mean only Jalissa and Sarya could access the hidden items. Hopefully it would not be a problem that Edmund could not.

Though they were married now. The seed of a heart bond should be there, presumably. If Jalissa threaded a hint of her magic through these trunks, maybe she could convince her magic to open for him too?

She would have to experiment. While security from prying Mongavarians was nice, it seemed dangerous to bar Edmund from his supplies.

Then again, if they were in so much trouble that both Jalissa and Sarya were incapacitated, they likely had bigger problems than Edmund being unable to open the secret compartments.

Rheva tapped one of the smaller trunks on top of a stack. "This one holds my contribution. The hidden compartment is filled with vials of tea infused with the strongest dose of healing magic it would hold. It will not heal a mortal wound, but it will heal much."

"Linshi, isciena." This time, Jalissa embraced Rheva with a quick, human-style hug. The elven hug did not seem enough in this instance, and Jalissa was becoming increasingly comfortable with the human gesture.

Having healing magic along could mean the difference between life and death. Rheva must have been working on this from the moment this mission had been announced to have so many strong healing medicines to send. A sacrifice on her part, when the demands for healers had been so great due to all the healers who had been sent to Kostaria.

"It was the least I could do." Rheva stepped out of Jalissa's hug, but she was not tense as if the human gesture had been unwelcome. Perhaps she, too, was becoming used to human hugs after being around Essie so much. "We wish to ensure your safety."

No one could fully guarantee they would be safe. Not even Edmund, with all his skill.

But Rheva's healing magic and Weylind's hidden compartments would go a long way to ensuring that Edmund and Jalissa had the best chance possible.

TWO

E dmund leaned against the rail of the elven boat, the river breeze cool against his face. Ahead, a hint of a blue glow shimmered in the water of the Hydalla River, marking the border where the corners of Mongavaria and Escarland met along the river border with Tarenhiel.

At his side, Jalissa eased closer, her fingers tightening around his hand.

He squeezed her fingers in return. "You don't have to come. I can go alone."

Jalissa's spine straightened, her eyes flashing with determination mixed with a hint of anger. "Of course I will come. I am not going to let you walk into Mongavaria alone. We are in this together."

The sight of her determination twitched a smile onto his face and eased some of the tension in his chest. She was afraid, as she should be.

But as he'd known she would, she'd shown him her courage. Assuring him, but assuring herself as well. She was as ready as she could be for her first spy mission.

Ahem. Diplomatic mission.

Although, come to think of it, this wasn't her first *diplomatic* mission. She'd gone to Escarland a year ago to negotiate continued peace after Escarlish weapons had been used by the trolls. And she had been far more the diplomat than he had on their recent trip to Kostaria.

It was the added element of the danger of spying that worried both of them. This wouldn't be like her visit to Escarland, where Essie and Farrendel's marriage had already started a shaky peace between their kingdoms.

Right now, Mongavaria and Escarland were one wrong word away from war. The only thing stopping them was that neither side could be assured of victory. If a war started now, it would be long, grinding, and would likely lead to mutual destruction. Mongavaria had the bigger army and slightly more resources. Escarland had strong, magical allies in the elves and trolls.

Edmund and Jalissa's job was to find enough information to keep Mongavaria at bay and continue this uneasy but cold almost-war.

On the other side of the glow of the border magic, a Mongavarian ship waited. Its sides were covered in iron plating while masts and sails still jutted into the sky alongside the smoke stacks for the steam engine.

Edmund turned to put his back to the Mongavarian ship and pulled Jalissa into his arms. They only had a few more moments to just be themselves. Once they boarded that ship, they would have to pull on their masks. Even in private, it would be difficult to set aside the mask since they wouldn't dare fully relax.

Jalissa snuggled against him, her head against his chest. "I wish we had more time before…"

"I know." He rested his cheek against her hair. They'd been married for a mere week.

But at least they'd had their wedding. They'd had an amazing week. He would have to be thankful for the time they'd had rather than mourn that it had been cut short with this trip.

Edmund raised his head, then tipped Jalissa's face up so that she met his gaze. "I know you're nervous. I am too. But this will be fun, too."

Jalissa shook her head, giving a hint of an eyeroll. "Only you would call danger *fun*."

"Admit it. You secretly like a bit of danger in your life." Edmund gently brushed a strand of her dark brown hair behind her ear. "Otherwise you wouldn't have married me."

That earned him a hint of her smile. If she would have said anything in response, he didn't wait to find out. Instead, he kissed her, losing himself to the kiss as he wouldn't dare to do once they were in Mongavaria.

All too soon, a throat cleared. "Your Highnesses, we are nearing the border."

Edmund pulled away from Jalissa just enough to lean his forehead against hers for another long moment before he gathered the strength to step all the way back.

Sarya stood a few feet away, her arms crossed and a stern expression on her face. Edmund hoped the stern expression was exaggerated. He thought Sarya liked him well enough, but it was hard to tell sometimes with Jalissa's stoic guard.

At least there would be someone else looking after Jalissa in Mongavaria. Even if Edmund failed, he knew Sarya would see to it that Jalissa was safe.

Drawing his shoulders straighter, Edmund pressed another kiss to Jalissa's forehead, then stepped back. "Excuse me for a moment. I need to change into my disguise."

"Disguise?" Jalissa raised her eyebrows at him. "We're still going as ourselves."

"Sort of." Edmund flashed her a grin. "You'll see."

He strode away, letting himself strut just a little bit. He couldn't wait to see the look on Jalissa's face when he reappeared.

He stepped into the cabin assigned to him and Jalissa, opened one of the trunks Weylind had provided for them, and found the outfit he was looking for.

As he finished tying the lacy neckcloth into a complicated knot, Jalissa's footsteps sounded in the passageway a moment before the door behind him opened. "Edmund, we are—what are you wearing?"

He turned and gestured at himself with a flourish. "What? You don't think fuchsia is my color?"

"No." Jalissa grimaced, her gaze flicking up and down his outfit.

He wore ivory breeches with brightly polished black boots. His white shirt set off the bright purple jacket while his neckcloth was a slightly lighter purple and edged in ivory lace. Hints of lace also edged his sleeves and his collar.

Definitely not something he would normally wear. But one glance at him dressed in this, and the Mongavarians were sure to dismiss him as an indolent, younger prince. From what he'd heard, bright colors and elaborate fabrics were all the rage in Mongavaria.

Not to mention, he wouldn't be at all disappointed if he was forced to abandon this outfit in Mongavaria in the event that they had to make a quick getaway.

"But I look like a fop, right?" Edmund picked up the black bowler with its matching purple band.

"A foolish fop, yes." Jalissa sighed and shook her

head. "They are going to wonder why I would consent to marry you. I clearly could do better."

"True. Funny what we will do for our kingdoms." Edmund grinned and adjusted the angle of the bowler so that it sat slightly askew. "It's a good thing I'm too brainless to notice the disdain in your voice. You can freely insult me in elvish since I'm too unintelligent to understand your language."

Another of their precautions. As far as the Mongavarians were to know, Edmund didn't know elvish. Not only would it fit the picture of a foolish fop that he was presenting, but he also couldn't risk the Mongavarian king realizing that the spy who had threatened him six months ago was Edmund.

"Or perhaps there is no accounting for love." Jalissa straightened her shoulders and faced him with her most icy expression, though Edmund could see the hint of humor lurking just below the mask. After a moment, the iciness gave way to a hint of pain. "I am not sure I can pretend I do not love you."

Edmund reached for her, pulling her close. "I am still in wonder that you love me, even after everything I've done." He swept a strand of hair from her face and longed to kiss her again. As themselves, one last time.

But he could feel the ship gliding to a halt, the magic-powered paddles sloshing to keep the ship as stationary as possible against the current of the Hydalla River.

After a moment, he stepped back and offered her an arm, making sure his own masked expression was suitably charming and empty. "Yes, perhaps icy but indulgent spouse would be the correct role to play."

Jalissa rested her hand on his arm in the elven manner, and together they made their way back to the upper deck. There, the crews of the two ships were securing a rope-

and-wood bridge across the space dividing the two ships. The water below the swaying rope bridge churned with the effort it took to keep the two ships in place in the middle of the river, a remarkable display on the part of the helmsmen of both ships.

Deep below the frothing river between the ships, Farrendel's magic glowed blue, marking the border that neither ship had crossed.

At the far side of the bridge, a beautiful young woman, her blonde hair glowing in the late morning sunlight and set off to perfection against her cream complexion and her pale blue dress, stood waiting with two stoic guards at her back.

Edmund leaned in closer to Jalissa, keeping the placid expression on his face even as he whispered, "The others are going to have their hands full."

"Yes." Jalissa's expression edged a touch colder, and she tilted her chin upward just enough to give off that elegant snootiness that the elves had perfected.

Even with all her perfection of human loveliness, the Mongavarian princess facing them couldn't hold a candle to Jalissa's silvery elven skin tone, ethereal features, and air of otherworldliness. Though, Edmund was biased in that regard.

For a moment, they simply stared across at the Mongavarian princess as she studied them in return. The swaying rope bridge wasn't wide enough for them to cross at the same time. One party would have to go first, and he wasn't about to step across the safety of the border without the surety of the other princess on this side of the border first.

The princess met his gaze, something cool and calculating and a hint knowing in her clear blue eyes. With a twist to her mouth that disappeared after a moment into a blandly pleasant expression, Princess Bella of Mongavaria gestured to one of the guards next to her.

The guard drew in a deep breath and raised his voice. "Permission to come aboard?"

"Granted," the elven captain of the ship called back, his arms crossed as he eyed the visiting princess who would soon step foot on his ship.

A few yards away, a senior member of Escarland's Parliament waited to greet the princess and convey the good wishes of the Escarlish people. He would be her government escort until they joined Averett and Weylind at the Tarenhieli border town. There, Princess Bella would spend a few hours greeting the elven nobility before the ship conveyed her and Averett across the river, where they would catch the royal train to Aldon.

With one guard leading the way and the other following, Princess Bella minced her way across the swaying rope bridge, though her face didn't betray any fear.

As one actor to another, Edmund suspected the proper princess was just a façade. This princess was as cool a customer as he was.

And he didn't have any way to warn Averett of that fact. Perhaps he could whisper it to the captain, but Princess Bella was watching. She'd notice if he suddenly ducked away for a hurried, whispered conversation.

No, Edmund would just have to trust his brother. Averett wasn't a slouch when it came to judging someone's character. Not to mention that their mother and Paige would also be able to tell the act from genuine sincerity.

They would have things well in hand at home. Right now, Edmund's focus had to be on the mission ahead.

He kept a wary eye on the princess as she and her guards stepped across the border. In the water below, the blue of Farrendel's magic flared a bit brighter, but it didn't shoot up into a wall and incinerate the princess. As much as Edmund already distrusted her, he didn't want to think about the ramifications if that had happened.

It must mean that the princess and her guards weren't carrying any weapons. They'd been warned that weapons could cause an unpleasant reaction from the border protections.

Luckily Edmund and Jalissa didn't have such restrictions—at least, not from Farrendel's magic. They would be free to take any number of weapons across the border. Still, they didn't wear any now, and Edmund's sleeve felt oddly empty without his hidden derringer. It was safely tucked in one of the hidden compartments of their luggage, along with his knives and other items they might need for spying.

Princess Bella held out her hand, and one of her guards helped her step delicately from the bridge onto the deck of the Tarenhieli ship.

Edmund stepped forward, swept his hat off his head, and gave a gallant bow. "Welcome to Escarland, Princess Bella. I hope you enjoy your stay in my fair kingdom."

"As I hope you enjoy your stay in mine. Landri is particularly lovely this time of year." Princess Bella's smile flashed a row of perfectly straight, white teeth. Almost too perfect. Had she worked with some human magician to get her teeth that perfect?

"I look forward to seeing it." Edmund put on an even dopier smile as he turned to Jalissa. "Come, my muffin cake. We should step aboard."

Jalissa took his arm, wrapping her hand over his bicep in the human style this time. The better to give him a hard squeeze. Mild revenge for the nickname, probably. "Yes, dear. You are due for your mid-morning nap."

"Yes. We had to be up atrociously early. Abominable hour to rise and all that." Edmund steered her toward the swaying bridge, then hesitated to step onto the first, swaying section. "Is it truly safe, you think?"

"It is far safer than the bridges of my kingdom." Jalissa tugged him forward, her face twisted with a mix of elven aloofness and a frustrated fondness. Playing her role to perfection.

"Right you are, my flower blossom." Edmund squeezed his eyes shut. "I'll just keep my eyes closed and let you lead me across like you always do."

Jalissa's soft, frustrated huff seemed more real than exaggerated this time. But she obligingly steered him onto the bridge.

After the first few steps, Edmund cracked his eyes open, though he still kept up the pretense of staggering and wandering, as if needing constant guidance from Jalissa to keep him from taking a tumble.

Sarya followed closely behind them, all icy wariness. There would be no mistaking her for anything but a guard, and there was no reason for her to play a role.

Behind her, the two Escarlish guards filed onto the bridge in their matching uniforms. Well, they were posing as guards, at any rate. They were from the Intelligence Office. One of them, James, was a spy who had worked in Mongavaria and been forced to flee six months ago. He had bravely volunteered to return to Mongavaria to lend his expertise to Edmund and Jalissa. If all went well, he would quietly disappear during their departure to aid in rebuilding the new Escarlish spying network under a new false identity.

As they stepped onto the teak deck of the Mongavarian ironclad, a Mongavarian nobleman dressed in a neatly tailored black coat and white trousers approached and bobbed a half-bow to them. "Prince Edmund, Princess Jalissa, welcome to Mongavaria. I am Lord Crest, member of King Solan's Consular Prime."

Edmund nodded in return, keeping his empty and genial expression in place. "It is our pleasure to be here, Lord Crest."

In Mongavaria, the Consular Prime was a group of the ranking nobles in the land. For centuries, what had then been Mongalia had remained an absolute monarchy with the Consular Prime merely a group of advisors. In recent years, the Consular Prime had been trying to wrest some of the power from the king to become more like a Parliament than a mere council. Some of the nobles had done it out of an honorable concern for the direction of the kingdom. Others were simply power hungry.

Which one was Lord Crest? Honorable man concerned for his kingdom? Or a lord coveting the power of the king for himself?

Or perhaps a little bit of both?

Jalissa drew Edmund to the side as crews from both ships started hauling Princess Bella's luggage to the Tarenhieli ship and their luggage over to the Mongavarian ship. Compared to their mountain of luggage, Princess Bella had a mere three trunks.

Was she simply disciplined when packing? Did she plan to buy the things she'd need in Escarland?

Or...was she, like them, packing with the knowledge that whatever she took might get left behind?

Either way, Farrendel's magic didn't trigger as the trunks passed over, so they likely didn't contain any weapons, even if they had hidden compartments.

Lord Crest gestured toward a hatchway. "If you would follow me, Your Highnesses, I will show you to your quarters to settle in. Lunch will be served in the captain's quarters shortly."

"Linshi." Jalissa bobbed her head in a regal fashion.

Edmund leaned closer to Lord Crest and stage-whispered, "That means *thank-you*. It is one of the few words of elvish I know."

He said the last line with a smug note, as if it was a huge accomplishment to pick up a word or two while married to an elf.

"Ah, yes, Your Highness." Lord Crest coughed, then gestured again. "Please follow me."

He and Jalissa followed Lord Crest to a large cabin. As soon as Lord Crest stepped out and Edmund closed the door firmly behind him, Jalissa gave a sigh and leaned against the bank of windows that looked out the stern of the ship. "Muffin cake? Flower blossom? Really?"

"What? You don't like ridiculous nicknames?" Edmund smirked at her, crossing his arms. It felt good to let his real expression break through, his face aching as if it physically hurt to keep up the vague geniality.

"No." Jalissa pinched the bridge of her nose. "This is going to be harder than I thought."

Edmund pushed away from the door, crossed the cabin, and pulled her into his arms. "I know. Keeping up a pretense isn't easy."

They had done a mild version of this when interacting with their courts and investigating their nobles for signs of treachery or spying. But they were still mostly themselves.

This wasn't them. It was a shell.

"How did you keep up the act for so long while spying on Tarenhiel?" Jalissa shook her head against his chest. "You changed your voice, your stance, your manner, your accent. Everything. And kept it up for years."

Edmund cupped her chin and gently tipped her head up to face him. "Yes. But it was a struggle at times. Especially once I met a certain elf princess who made me want to be more myself than I should have been as a spy. I could change everything about myself but my heart. And that won't change, Jalissa, no matter how ridiculous and empty-headed I seem while in public the next few weeks. I'm still the man you love, underneath the mask."

Jalissa nodded, leaning into his hand and closing her eyes. "My ispamir."

Her spy prince. Edmund held her close for several more, long minutes. It felt so good to hold her as he'd longed to do for years.

And now she was his wife. It was his duty to cherish her, and that was going to be a little difficult to do as he ought over the next few weeks.

After a few more minutes, Edmund cradled Jalissa's face in both of his hands. "We promised each other that we would always help each other remember who we are beneath the masks. We're going to be tested over the next few weeks, but together we are strong enough."

Her mouth twisted with the smirk she was letting him see far more often now than she used to. "Yes. I suppose I will just have to be strong enough not to stomp on your foot every time you call me a ridiculous nickname."

He threw back his head and laughed. Now there was the Jalissa he had fallen in love with.

CHAPTER

THREE

J alissa braced herself against the rail at the bow of
the ship and breathed in the sea breeze that tossed
her hair. To her left, the ocean stretched out as far as
she could see, deep blue and so vast she could not
fathom it.

To her right, a distant smudge marked the shoreline.
When they had swung closer to the shore, she had caught
sight of long stretches of sandy beaches and grassy shore-
lines so unlike the rocky shores and high ocean cliffs
along Tarenhiel's coastline.

"Princess Jalissa, may I intrude?" Lord Crest stepped
to the rail to join her.

Jalissa schooled her features into the regal mask she
wore when around others. "Of course, Lord Crest."

"I have observed that you seem to be rather astute,
Princess Jalissa." Lord Crest leaned against the rail
glancing from her to where Edmund stood near the
captain, laughing as they discussed the ironclad's steam
engine. "It makes me wonder if the prince is not as empty
and charming as he seems."

Jalissa resisted the urge to stiffen. Had she and Edmund given themselves away even before they had reached the Mongavarian capital? She forced that indulgent smile onto her face. "He can have his moments."

"Perhaps." Lord Crest eyed Edmund with a piercing gaze that reminded Jalissa of Edmund's, when he was not pretending to be a brainless fop.

Could Lord Crest tell that Edmund's genial, schmoozing act was disguising the fact that he was gathering information on the Mongavarian ironclad ships from the captain and crew? Had he noticed that Jalissa, with all her staring out at the ocean, was taking notes on the number of both merchantmen and warships flying the Mongavarian flag that plied the waters up and down the coast?

"Was there something you wished to discuss?" Jalissa raised her eyebrows, tilting her head to stare down her nose at Lord Crest with her most aloof, elven expression.

"I'm sure you've heard of the...struggles Mongavaria has experienced between the king and the Consular Prime?" Lord Crest phrased it as a question, but his tone indicated that he already knew the answer.

Jalissa tilted her head into a slight nod. All the answer she would commit to giving him.

"While the king doesn't view Escarland and Tarenhiel in a favorable light, there are others in the government who could be persuaded to take a more peaceable stance toward your kingdoms, if you take my meaning." Lord Crest's eyes bored into her, making it clear that he was one of those.

Jalissa did not dare commit to anything. "I see. I shall keep that in mind, Lord Crest."

Was he truly implying that there were those among the Consular Prime who would back peace with the alliance, if they had the power to do so? What did he want out of the alliance in return? It could be rather messy—and dangerous—for Escarland and Tarenhiel to get mixed up in the politics of Mongavaria.

"That's all I ask." Lord Crest nodded, then stepped away from the rail. "If you will excuse me, Your Highness, I need to consult with the captain on our entrance into Landri Harbor."

With that, he strolled away, leaving Jalissa with her churning thoughts. Was Lord Crest an ally? Or a very dangerous enemy?

More smoke poured from the stacks as the ship shuddered into a turn, angling toward the coast.

Jalissa braced herself against the rail, focusing ahead as the coastline drew closer. The smudge turned into a long, sandy point. The sand changed to tall seagrass, then curved as the full extent of the bay came into view.

Even with the extra, affected saunter, Jalissa could still recognize Edmund's footsteps on the deck behind her a moment before his arms wrapped around her from behind. She leaned into him, savoring the feel of his arms around her.

"I think this is one moment we should take in together, my princess." His tone was low. Far more real than it had been when he had been laughing with the captain and crew. Even if he still used the Escarlish *princess* rather than his customary elvish *amirah*.

They lapsed into silence as the ship turned into the bay. A city spilled along one side of a huge river, which poured into the bay. On a bluff above the river and city, a tall castle speared its turrets into the clear blue sky far above. It was built entirely of white marble with red roof tiles. A glittering jewel set against the deep blue sea.

Landri and its castle were just as beautiful as

promised. The port in the bay bustled with trade ships from kingdoms all along the coast and across the ocean. It made even the city of Aldon appear like a small, backwater village compared to the economic might wielded by Mongavaria.

"It is beautiful. But I still prefer Estyra," Edmund murmured against her hair.

So did she. Due to their long lives, her people achieved a level of detail and craftsmanship rarely seen among the humans.

But the time when elves were a great power, ruling an empire of their own, was a long time in the past. Now, their struggle was to preserve their culture while squeezed on every side by the rising might of the human kingdoms.

Only their alliance with Escarland could help them achieve it. And their peace with Kostaria, who faced the same challenge. Without Escarland as a buffer, how long would it take before Mongavaria invaded both Tarenhiel and Kostaria?

Even with Escarland's help, Mongavaria was hungrily eyeing all three of their kingdoms. As if all this—the bay, the bustling city, the impressive castle—were not enough.

JALISSA KEPT HER BACK STRAIGHT, her posture poised as she picked at her salad during the royal banquet in Edmund and Jalissa's honor. They were seated to King Solan's right while Crown Prince Jimson sat on the king's left.

Her face still ached from holding the perfect princess smile. When they docked below the castle, they had been greeted by several more lords of the Consular Prime, then by King Solan and Crown Prince Jimson in the entry hall of Ventre Castle. The seventy-year-old king and his fifty-year-old son gave Jalissa the same slimy, shivering feeling as Princess Bella had.

The suite they had been given consisted of a bedroom with wide windows overlooking the bay, a spacious and lavishly appointed sitting room, and two sets of rooms that connected to the sitting room for Sarya and their other two guards.

A maid collected the dishes from the salad course moments before a footman set bowls of soup in front of them.

As subtly as she could, Jalissa brushed her fingers over her soup. No poison. At least, no plant-based poison that she could detect.

"My flower, I suspect the soup might be too hot." Edmund's slightly nasal tone grated against her nerves as he leaned close.

But she was pretending to be in love with this inane, annoying version of Edmund. So she let her smile go a touch more warm as she leaned into him.

"Oh, let me check for you, Eddie dearest." She purposely used the nickname, knowing he hated it. She dipped her pinky into his soup, letting her magic filter into the broth. Once again, no poison. "Perfect temperature."

"Thanks, muffin cake." Edmund gave her a tiny peck on the cheek.

The brush of his lips sent very real tingles through her. A reminder of the real him and the real her beneath this façade.

Across the table, King Solan did not try to hide the slight curl to his mouth. At least they were convincing someone that Edmund was empty-headed.

But Crown Prince Jimson eyed them, his gaze far too sharp for her liking.

Edmund dug into his soup, his manners utterly impeccable. Not even the slightest slurp. So strange from the relaxed meals with his family where he and Julien would start exaggerating their slurping noises just to see if their mother, Jalissa, or Farrendel would give them a stern look first.

Jalissa dipped her spoon into her own soup, unable to stop the slight smile that played across her face. Next time Edmund slurped his soup just to get a rise out of her family, she would remind him that she knew very well how perfect his manners could be when he wished.

"How are you enjoying our seaside palace so far?" King Solan gave them a smile over his soup.

"It is lovely." Jalissa sipped another bite of the creamy shrimp and potato soup. It was far too heavily seasoned for her taste. Far too much dill. Not to mention, seafood was not her favorite. While the elves living by the coast in Tarenhiel consumed great quantities of fish and lobster, she was a child of the forest. She preferred venison to fish.

But she kept her smile in place despite the overpowering taste.

"We haven't had a chance to explore it yet." Edmund smiled that empty smile at the king and the crown prince. "Is a tour of the city on our schedule?"

"We have a tour planned for the day after tomorrow." The king's face was so lined that his smile disappeared in the wrinkles. "And we have a welcome banquet in your honor planned in a week."

"Sounds splendid. Don't you agree, sugarcake?" Edmund wrapped his arm around her, tugging her close enough it was probably uncomfortable for everyone else watching.

"Yes." Jalissa was looking forward to seeing the seaside city. And walking along the beach in the moonlight with Edmund sounded romantic.

If only they were not here on a spying mission where they might get poisoned at any moment.

Finally, the soup course ended, and the main course of some kind of fish crusted in a bread crumb and herb layer with mixed vegetables on the side was set in front of them. Once again, Jalissa surreptitiously checked both meals with her magic. No poison, thankfully.

Jalissa nearly choked on her first bite of fish, her eyes watering, thanks to all the dill, chives, and pepper in the herbal crust. Still, the over-spiced food was preferable to the interminable small talk.

After supper, they all sat in the parlor and King Solan made some attempt at discussing politics. Mostly insinuations that Mongavaria was superior while Tarenhiel and Escarland should bow to their demands. Of course, it was not said in so many words.

Finally, Edmund and Jalissa could retreat to their room with Sarya and one of Edmund's spy-turned-guard-friends shadowing their every move until they reached their rooms.

Inside the rooms, Jalissa breathed a sigh of relief and tried to relax now that a door separated her from the pretense.

Their second guard-spy straightened from where he had been sprawled on the couch facing the door. A glint of something, perhaps a derringer, caught Jalissa's eye before the spy flicked it out of sight up his sleeve once again.

When Edmund turned to them, the blank look fell from his face as he glanced between them. "Sarya, Alvin, you'll stay with Jalissa tonight. James, you and I are going to sneak out and start scouting. See if you can find their records room or military planning room. I'll go through the king's study."

Jalissa's stomach churned. This was the mission, but she still did not like knowing exactly what Edmund was up to. If he were caught...

He would not be caught. This was Edmund.

"Until then, we should all get some rest." Edmund rested his hand on Jalissa's back and steered her toward their room.

They stepped into the lavishly appointed room, with its large, canopied bed and massive, velvet upholstered furniture.

Instead of pausing, Edmund threw open the double doors on the far side. The salty, cool night breeze washed over them, stirring Jalissa's hair. Below, the lights of the city glowed in the night, reflecting off the water of the river and the bay. Far above, the stars twinkled in the depth of the sky, reflecting in the deeper dark of the ocean.

She closed her eyes as she leaned against the railing, drinking in the peace of the night.

Edmund's fingers brushed the back of her neck, then his strong fingers massaged the tight muscles at her shoulders.

She relaxed against him. "That feels good."

"You're tense." Edmund spoke near her ear, and this time it sent shivers down her spine instead of grating against her nerves. This was the real him, not the annoying persona he had been wearing before.

"I know we are prepared, but this is more difficult than I expected." Jalissa reached up and rested a hand over one of Edmund's. Searching out possible traitors among the Escarlish court had been one thing. The secrecy had been kind of fun.

But this was not fun. It was deadly and dangerous and every moment she had to be hyper aware of everyone and everything.

"I know." Edmund wrapped his arms around her waist and held her close.

Jalissa turned in Edmund's arms and leaned into the strength of his embrace. As long as she had him, she could face whatever danger came their way.

WELL AFTER MIDNIGHT, Jalissa opened the secret compartments in many of the trunks. While Edmund changed into dark gray trousers, shirt, and gloves, she located his knives and his derringer. Once she had a pile of weapons for Edmund and for the other spies, she found the trunk that held the rope.

As she dragged the rope out of the trunk, Edmund reached her side and took it from her, kissing her cheek. "I should be back well before dawn. Get some sleep, if you can."

"You know I am not going to be able to sleep." Jalissa rested a hand on his arm. A goodbye kiss sounded good, but this probably was not the time for such distractions. "Stay safe."

"Always." Edmund pressed a kiss to her forehead, then tied the rope to one of the posts of the bed. He carried the rope to the balcony, then tossed it off. "James, you first."

The other spy—wearing identical dark clothing to Edmund's—gripped the rope and dropped over the balcony as if scrambling up and down castle walls was an everyday occurrence. Perhaps it was, for him.

Edmund paused, turning back to Jalissa. He tugged her close and kissed her one last time. "I'll be back."

Before she could think of something to say in return, Edmund dropped over the balcony and climbed down the rope.

Jalissa remained on the balcony for several minutes longer, staring off into the night, the darkness seeming deeper than it was before.

CHAPTER
FOUR

E dmund slipped down the deserted corridor, sticking to the side where the floor was less likely to creak.

At the corner, he knelt, then peered into the next hallway.

Two Mongavarian guards stood in front of the king's study. Fewer guards than he feared, but more than he was hoping. Then again, it had probably been too much to hope that the Mongavarian king would leave his study unguarded while an Escarlish delegation was staying in the castle.

Retreating a few steps, Edmund tried the nearest door. Unlocked. Hopefully that was a good sign.

Inside, the room was filled with desks. Castle clerks, perhaps? Edmund glanced at a few as he passed, taking in the paperwork left in the open. Apparently this room was for the clerks checking the tax reports of the entire kingdom. Perhaps a team could find something useful, but Edmund doubted the time would be worth it.

Instead, he tried the door at the back of the room. This

room was locked, meaning it probably held far more sensitive items than the other desks.

He withdrew a leather roll from its spot on his belt, unrolled it, and sorted through his picks until he found the ones he wanted.

Seconds later, he packed away his picks and stepped into the small office. A quick scan of the room confirmed it must belong to the supervisor in charge of the clerks. Edmund quickly glanced over the paperwork, but nothing stuck out to him. Just boring tax paperwork.

Locking the door behind him, he unlocked the window. A narrow ledge ran along the outside below the sets of windows. Not terribly wide, but wide enough.

He eased out of the window and shuffled along the outside of the building. Navigating the corner proved to be slightly precarious, but he survived. Counting the windows outside, he located the king's study.

Picking the window's lock proved to be a bit more difficult since he was balanced on the side of the castle while doing it. But he managed, and soon he slipped inside.

Mindful of the guards outside the door, Edmund eased the curtains open to let in as much outside light as possible.

The light wasn't very good, and it would have been nice to have elven eyesight right about then. He did not dare light a lamp or use the elven light he kept in his pocket since the guards outside would see it under the door.

He methodically searched through the items on the desk, then all the drawers. Next he went through the books on the shelves and the ledgers in the various other drawers.

Nothing stood out to him. All of this was the basic paperwork of running a kingdom.

Not that Edmund had too much cause to know what such paperwork should look like. It wasn't as if he had snooped through his brother's office more than once or twice. Or three times.

But even Averett had more interesting paperwork filed away in a corner of his study.

It was as if this study was purposely boring. All it had was the final tax reports, boring proposals for non-controversial laws, and meaningless communication.

As if this study was simply staged. A set piece where the king could do the boring stuff and meet with dignitaries.

Where was the real study, then? Was it connected to this room? That would make the most sense. The king would need to be able to move back and forth easily, stashing the more important paperwork there while being able to duck back in here when needed.

Edmund searched the walls, running his fingers over the woodwork, the furniture, the books on the shelves. He couldn't find any hidden switches or latches. That didn't mean there wasn't one. Edmund just couldn't find it.

Voices sounded outside the door. The changing of the guards. If they were thorough, they would search the study before taking up their posts.

He eased the curtains back into place, dropped outside the window onto the ledge, then swung the window closed.

A light flickered inside the room, casting light outside.

Edmund crouched as much as he could on the ledge, trying to stay out of the pool of light. He froze, breathing shallowly. Shadows flitted through the light before the light shut off.

He waited several more minutes before he shuffled along the ledge once again.

This time, he broke into the room next to the one he'd gone out of. Another room filled with desks and incredibly boring paperwork.

And he'd thought his paperwork in the Intelligence Office was boring. He was never going to transfer to the tax division. Ever. Even if he lived hundreds of years thanks to being married to Jalissa.

After searching through several more of the rooms near the king's study, it was time to return to his room.

While it was frustrating to spend a night with nothing to show for it, that was often the case for a spy. Often, it took many nights of searching before he found anything worthwhile.

He found his way to the balcony below his and Jalissa's and found the rope still waiting for him. It only took moments to climb it and roll to his feet on the balcony.

There, Jalissa perched in one of the wooden chairs on the balcony, wrapped in a blanket and a tendril of the ficus in the decorative pot next to her twined around her arm. A hint of a smile played across her face. "You are all right."

"Of course I am all right." He crossed the balcony and kissed her.

"You are my ispamir." Jalissa shook off the plant, then held out her hand to him.

He tugged her to her feet, but he didn't sweep her into his arms just yet. "Did James get back yet?"

"Yes, about half an hour ago." Jalissa gestured toward their suite of rooms. "He located a room with military records, but it is going to take some digging."

"That's about what I came up with too." Edmund

shrugged and turned back to the rope. They had to pack away the spy gear, then they could head for bed to get some sleep before another tense day.

EDMUND RESTED his hand over Jalissa's on his arm, keeping her tucked against him as they strolled the seaside market of Landri. The royal carriage had parked at the end of the street to wait for them while they enjoyed the market.

Crown Prince Jimson strolled in a pack of guards. More guards surrounded Edmund and Jalissa. A few of the minor lords and ladies had joined their excursion to the market, making it harder to enjoy the market since the lords and ladies kept trying to talk to them.

The gusts of the sea breeze ruffled his hair and snapped the flapping awnings over the market stalls. The seagulls squawked so loudly they could be heard over the haggling voices, yelling vendors, and tramping of hundreds of feet.

So many people. Even for him, the sprawling city and the vast numbers of people who lived here were staggering. It made Aldon look like a tiny, upstart town compared to this prosperous, bustling seaside city, which had already been a center of trade for the region when Aldon had been nothing but forest as part of the great elven empire.

Next to him, Jalissa's eyes were wide, even if she managed to keep her mouth from gaping. Edmund remembered how awed she'd been at seeing Aldon for the first time. Landri was just so much more.

Edmund and Jalissa politely looked at a variety of booths, taking in the colors and patterns that were foreign to Escarland or Tarenhiel. Many booths sold items decorated with seashells, something that wasn't the fashion in their kingdoms. Here, they could buy jewelry fashioned from shells, large shells by themselves, or any number of items covered with shells from jewelry boxes to bird baths to snuff boxes.

At another booth, Edmund held up a particularly shell-encrusted jewelry box. "Would you like something like this, my angel cake?"

He could see the way Jalissa gritted her teeth beneath her perfect princess smile. "Of course, darling."

Edmund purchased the jewelry box, even though he could tell Jalissa hated it. At least that would make it easier to leave behind if they had to flee for their lives.

But buying a few items in the market would endear them to the people and look good in the eyes of their host. After all, King Solan—through his steward—had graciously given them a wad of money that morning, a gift for them to use here in the market.

Edmund was being careful with how he spent the money. He tried to appear as if he was spending it profligately without actually spending that much. He'd need to keep as much as he could for the plan he had in mind.

As he finished purchasing the jewelry box and handed the wrapped package off to the footman trailing their group for this purpose, Edmund steered Jalissa toward the next booth.

Jalissa leaned in closer and whispered, "This would be more pleasant if we could be ourselves."

"Yes." Edmund squeezed her fingers on his arm. He agreed. If only he and Jalissa could have sneaked into Mongavaria on their own and walked this market in disguise as two normal people. Talking in this nasal tone was making his sinuses hurt.

Crown Prince Jimson was dropping back, half-turned as he waited for them with sharp eyes. There was something about the prince that set Edmund's instincts on edge.

Edmund checked that his charming smile was in place before he wrapped his arm around Jalissa's waist and tugged her closer. He gave her an exaggerated kiss on the temple in the flamboyant manner of his persona. "Isn't this romantic? Is there anything else you would like, my rosebud? I would buy you the world if you wished it."

Jalissa's smile tightened, the lines smoothing to that serene, aloof look of hers. Her gaze strayed, looking away from him. After a moment, her eyes lit up as she focused on something to their left and ahead of them.

Edmund lifted his gaze from her, quickly spotting what had drawn her attention.

A booth ahead was filled with plants with broad, dark leaves and vibrant flowers. He didn't know much about flowers, but he had visited the Kingsley Gardens in Aldon with Jalissa enough times to recognize the flowers as ones that were foreign to Escarland or Tarenhiel, the kinds that were grown in the large glass house of the Gardens.

Edmund steered her toward the booth. "Would you like to look at the flowers?"

"Would that not be too like ourselves?" Jalissa glanced between him and the plants, a longing in the depth of her eyes.

Edmund gave an elven shrug—a gesture too subtle to be noticed by the humans around them. "You are an elf. It would be unusual if you didn't want to see the flowers."

Jalissa's shoulders sagged in relief, then a real smile crossed her face.

Edmund flourished a wave in the direction of the

booth. "Come along, darling flower. I know how you love plants."

Jalissa was just about bouncing on her toes by the time they reached the booth. Once there, Edmund let her go to wander through the booth. She trailed her fingers over the plants, and each of them perked up a bit at her touch.

At the far corner, she halted by a small, white orchid, her fingers lingering on one of its leaves.

Edmund sauntered to the proprietor and pointed at the orchid. "How much for that one?"

When the man told him, Edmund handed over the bills, then strolled to Jalissa. He rested a hand on her lower back and leaned in close. "It's yours."

"Really?" Jalissa picked up the tiny orchid in the pot and cradled it to her.

If they had to flee, Edmund would make sure that orchid came along, no matter what it took. He wasn't going to ask her to leave it behind when he could see how much she had already bonded with it.

THAT EVENING AFTER SUPPER, Edmund left Jalissa in the drawing room with the other ladies. Most of the noblemen retired to the smoking room. A few stood around, sipping brandy and talking. But a group of them gathered around the table, and one started shuffling a deck of cards.

Edmund plopped into an open seat, reached inside his velvet, burgundy jacket, and tossed some of the bills he'd saved from the morning's jaunt onto the table. "Well, gentlemen, what are we playing for? Bragging rights, or real money?"

Several of the noblemen exchanged looks, before the

one shuffling cards grinned. "Real money, of course. If that doesn't go against your uptight Escarlish morals, Prince Edmund?"

"The rumors of Escarlish morals are greatly exaggerated." Edmund waved airily, then swept up the cards he was dealt.

He worked to keep his expression empty, even as he studied each of his opponents. As the hands progressed, he mentally counted the cards, picking which hands to win and which hands to lose.

By the end of the night, he had won enough to double the meager stash of money he'd started with. It was a decent amount, but not enough to raise eyebrows. Several of the men at that table had won far more—while others had lost amounts that would have been huge for anyone but these far-too-wealthy noblemen.

As the night grew later, Edmund finally bowed out and strolled toward the parlor to collect Jalissa to catch some sleep before he left for another night of spying.

A few more evenings of cards like this, and he'd grow his money into quite the sum. Hopefully it would be enough for his first choice of escape route out of Mongavaria if things went wrong here. He had alternate escape routes—and an alternate stash of money hidden away in one of his trunks—if this current plan didn't work out. But this first option was the quickest and safest. As long as he could amass enough money without the king or his son thinking anything of it.

As they left yet another luncheon, Edmund steered Jalissa down the hallway that led to the king's bedchamber. Sarya and Alvin trailed behind them.

Jalissa's eyebrows scrunched. "Where are we going?"

"I need to search the king's bedchamber while he's gone. I can't do that at night while he's sleeping in the room." Edmund glanced around as they hurried down the halls as quickly as he dared.

As he had hoped, the king's suite wasn't guarded during the day. Which likely meant that he didn't keep any incriminating paperwork here, but it was worth a look.

It was locked, but a few seconds and his lockpicks quickly fixed that problem.

"Keep a look out, will you, Sarya?" Edmund glanced at her as he slid his lockpicks back into the hidden pocket in his shirt.

Sarya nodded, then took up a station next to the door.

Alvin pointed at the next door down. "I'll check the crown prince's room."

Edmund nodded, then steered Jalissa inside the king's room. An opulent sitting room in light blues and golden yellows spread before them. "Could you search this room? Pay attention for any hidden levers or panels. I'll check the bedchamber."

Jalissa nodded, then set to work searching through the books on the small bookshelf to one side. It seemed to be more decorative than anything else, but it wouldn't hurt to check everything.

He stepped inside the bedchamber and started at one side of the room, checking the wall, the floor, and all the furniture as he made his way in a circle around the room.

He'd been in this room before, when he'd threatened the king six months ago. It had been dark then, and he hadn't taken the time to thoroughly search the place except to locate the king's weapons hidden near the bed.

He found even more weapons stashed around the bed now.

He stumbled across a few other things that he definitely didn't want to know about the Mongavarian king. He also found a secret cupboard behind the wardrobe that was some kind of hideaway; it was stocked with dried food and jugs of water. But other than that, he discovered no other hidden panels or passages.

As he stepped into the sitting room once again, voices sounded outside the door. Sarya's light, serene tones contrasted with the Mongavarian king's raised voice.

Jalissa's eyes widened as she glanced from the door to Edmund.

"Apologies for this." Edmund wrapped his arms around Jalissa and kissed her. Not just a gentle, light kiss that he would normally give her in public. Nope. This was the kind of kiss he normally would reserve only for in private.

Jalissa melted into him but stiffened in his arms as the door opened. But even if her posture went tense, she didn't end the kiss or try to pull away. All she did was dig her fingers tighter into his shirt as if to pull him closer.

"What is the meaning of this?" King Solan's voice thundered in the room.

Edmund forced himself to flinch and yank away from Jalissa as if startled, though he didn't let her go. He cleared his throat and gave one of those inane laughs. "Oh, I think that should be obvious, Your Majesty. I'm kissing my wife."

King Solan's face darkened in a glower. "What are you doing in my bedroom suite?"

"Oh, that." Edmund gave an empty grin and stepped a little farther away from Jalissa, though he kept an arm around her waist. "Uh, well, we ducked in here for a little privacy."

The king's mouth curled. "This is my bedchamber. Get out."

"Of course, sorry. We'll just pop over to our own room. Newlyweds, you know." Edmund gave another smarmy smile as he steered Jalissa toward the door. At this point, Jalissa's ears were red as strawberries, and she ducked her head against Edmund's chest.

Once they were out in the hallway, the king slammed the door behind them. His guards took up stations in front of the door. Hopefully the king would simply assume he'd forgotten to lock his doors, leaving them wide open for Edmund and Jalissa to stumble inside.

As they hurried down the hall, Jalissa muttered against Edmund's shirt, "That was embarrassing."

"I know. I'm sorry." Edmund still held her close as

they continued the ruse for the benefit of the guards. "But I'm glad that if I get to live the whole spy ruse of kissing my beautiful female spy partner, I'm glad she happens to be you. And I'm lucky enough to be married to you."

Jalissa snorted against his chest. "Flatterer."

"Is it working?"

"Maybe." Some of the tension eased from her shoulders. After a moment, her smile returned, her gaze warming a bit. "I am rather happy to be your beautiful spy partner for life. You are stuck with me."

"That I am." And he couldn't be happier about it.

EDMUND SNEAKED down the hallway yet again. He'd searched the king's study for the past three nights. Perhaps the fourth night would be the charm.

So far, James and Alvin had turned up some fascinating things about the Mongavarian spy network and some evidence of smuggling activities into and out of Escarland. So far, they didn't have anything to tie the king directly to the poisoning in Kostaria, but they at least could prove which lords in Escarland were involved in smuggling elven goods illegally into Mongavaria as well as Mongavarian goods into Escarland.

But there had to be more to find here in the king's study.

Slipping in through the window once again, Edmund landed in a crouch in the study. This time, he didn't bother searching the desk. Or the bookshelves.

No, he just stood there for several minutes, cataloging the room. When he'd inspected the hallway with Jalissa earlier in the day, he'd noticed that the space between the study and the next door over was longer than any of the others. The outside, too, had a larger space between windows. It wasn't a large space. Not enough to be immediately noticeable, but he could see it now that he was looking.

The wall on that side contained a large fireplace with a bookshelf on one side, an empty wall of wood paneling on the other.

After all his searching of this office, he knew the bookshelf was too tightly fitted to be a hinged door. That meant the empty wall likely held the door.

He took off his gloves and ran his fingers over every inch of the wall. Perhaps he could detect a faint line where the door might be, but the craftsmanship of the door was so well done that he couldn't be sure. And he couldn't find any kind of latch or keyhole.

Putting on his gloves once again, he stepped back and studied the wall again. This would have been so much easier if he could have risked a light.

He inspected the fireplace as best he could, but there were so many nooks and crannies in the stones that the keyhole or latch could be hiding anywhere. It would take him weeks of searching to find it in the dark. Even if he found it, it could be tucked so deep between the stones that only the special key—which King Solan no doubt kept on his person at all times—could open it. It would be nearly impossible to pick the lock.

But as he crouched in front of the fireplace, he felt a faint draft. Something about the draft seemed off in a way he couldn't define.

He reached into the fireplace and felt along the flue. Where there should have been solid stone, his hand met air.

Of course. This was a double fireplace. The king might want a hidden room, but he wouldn't want it to be an icebox in the winter if he planned to spend time working in there. A stone wall separated the two fireplaces, but they shared a single chimney.

It wouldn't be pretty, but he didn't need the door to get into the secret room.

Crawling into the fireplace, he slowly stood, tucking in his shoulders as much as he could. At least the king preferred a palatial fireplace. It was tight, but he wasn't in danger of getting stuck.

Once he was standing, the wall between the two fireplaces was at his waist. It took a lot of shimmying and wiggling to curl his body over the fake wall and into the fireplace on the other side.

He rolled onto the hearth on the other side and gently peeled his gloves off and left them by the hearth. He did the same with his boots. He didn't want to accidentally track ashes all around the room.

Without a window or door, this room was pitch black. At least the guards wouldn't be able to see a light if he lit one here.

He pulled a small wooden box out of a pocket, then flipped open the lid. He whispered the elven word to activate the light.

Blue-white light flared in the darkness, coming from the glass ball that was protected inside the box. Taking it out, he held it up and surveyed the room.

The wooden floor was covered in a plain, blue rug while the walls were bare of tapestries and other opulent decorations. A large desk dominated the center of the room, covered with papers. More cabinets held drawers of what was likely paperwork while shelves held ledgers.

This was the king's real office. If Edmund was going to find anything incriminating, it would be here.

He went through the desk first. In the bottom drawer, he found a stack of correspondence. Not from King Solan, as expected, but from Crown Prince Jimson.

King Solan must have confiscated them from his son. The drawer contained correspondence between Lord Farnley in Escarland and the crown prince, arranging for a cut of the smuggling profits. Underneath, Edmund found more letters, these to a dock worker to arrange for adding the poison to the grain that was loaded onto Lord Farnley's ships to be smuggled into Kostaria.

So the Escarlish smuggler was Lord Farnley. Edmund felt a grim smile tug his mouth as he folded that particular letter and tucked it into the inside pocket of his shirt. He looked forward to taking down the smug lord.

Apparently Crown Prince Jimson had been behind the poisoning. King Solan seemingly knew about it, but nothing here indicated whether he approved of it or not.

Not that it mattered. Either way, the Mongavarian royalty was involved.

Edmund took the most incriminating of the papers and stuffed them into his shirt.

Voices came from the other room. He whispered, and his light winked out. They shouldn't be able to see it, given the tight way the secret door fit into the wall and the height of the stone wall that divided the two fireplaces. But he wouldn't take the chance.

As before, the guards searched the outer office, then left without searching the secret room.

Likely, they didn't know about the secret room. The king wasn't about to trust this secret to random guards. Only a few trusted individuals would know about it.

Once he was sure the new guards had resumed their

post, Edmund continued searching the room. He found more information about the smuggling operation. Notes on which members of the Consular Prime the king thought he could trust and which ones he had put under surveillance since he was suspicious of them. And he had notes on the difficulties they were having trying to start a new spy ring in Escarland.

That made Edmund smile. Good. He, Jalissa, and the Escarlish Intelligence Office were doing their jobs.

He still memorized the names of those who were trying to infiltrate Escarland. The Intelligence Office would find that information helpful. There was also a mention of several of the telegraph lines being tapped. That was something that would need to be fixed as soon as he returned to Escarland.

He could feel the time ticking away. He was cutting it close toward dawn, but there was so much useful information here. He would push it just a little longer.

As quickly as he could, he searched through the rest of the drawers, then paged through the most recent ledgers on the shelves. He tried to memorize as much as he could, but he'd also tell James and Alvin about this place and how to get in through the fireplace. Even if he couldn't get all the information today, they might be able to come back and get the rest later.

Finally, he could push it no longer. It must be nearly dawn, and he had to get back into his room before darkness no longer hid his movements as he climbed the rope.

He stuffed the most important papers into a hidden pocket of his shirt, then checked that he had returned everything else to its rightful place. He brushed away a few of the ashes that he'd scattered, then he whispered the elven word to cut off the elven light. He closed its box, put on his boots and gloves, then stepped into the fireplace.

After listening for a moment to check that the guards weren't in the staged office, he wiggled up and over the dividing wall before rolling out on the other side.

Careful not to leave ashy footprints on the floor, he crossed to the window and once again exited onto the ledge. Moments later, he was back in the empty clerks' offices.

At this time of morning, the corridors had a subdued bustle as maids started their duties, kindling fires, cleaning the rooms before the nobles woke up, and returning clothes that had been washed the night before.

Edmund had to duck into several rooms and hide while he waited for the maids to pass. His heart pounded a little harder, and he clamped down on the reaction. This was fine. Sure, there were more people about, but he would just have to be extra careful.

As he reached the room where he would find the rope, a shout came from the other end of the corridor. Alvin raced across the end of the corridor, ducking out of sight in a nearby room.

Moments later, two Mongavarian guards raced after him, shouting and pointing. "He went this way! Search the rooms!"

Uh-oh. It wouldn't be good if one of them was caught snooping. Or if the Mongavarians found the rope.

Edmund stepped out of hiding and knocked over a nearby potted plant.

At the crash, the two guards snapped to attention and looked straight at him.

Hopefully the dimly lit corridor was dark enough that they wouldn't be able to tell who he was.

Spinning on his heel, he ran down the corridor, then

whirled around the nearest corner. He nearly bumped into a maid, and she stumbled, shrieking and dropping her pile of laundry.

The guards' footsteps pounded after him. Good, he'd provided enough distraction to lure the guards away from Alvin, but now what was he going to do? The only thing worse than having one of his guards get caught spying was to be caught spying himself.

He glanced over his shoulder, gauging how close the guards were. He'd put a little distance on them.

He whirled around another corner, then immediately tried the nearest door. Unlocked.

He ducked inside, the room smelling musty enough to tell him that it wasn't currently in use.

Quickly, he raced across the room, unlocked the window, and climbed onto the ledge. Shutting the window behind him, he eased along the ledge and halted when he was between two of the windows.

His body tensed, but he forced himself to stay still and wait, hugging the outside of the castle.

Far below, the formal gardens spread out, filling the space from the castle wall all the way to the edge of the cliff. Below the cliff, the ocean waves crashed against the rock in a steady, soothing rhythm.

At least on this side of the castle, there were no walls and thus no patrolling guards. A few guards wandered in the gardens in a circuit, but none of them seemed inclined to look up. Even if they did, they likely wouldn't be able to spot Edmund against the castle wall, dressed in dark clothing as he was.

At least, he would remain invisible until the sun started rising. Then he would be a very dark bug high-lighted against a bright white wall.

How long should he wait before he dared move? The

guards would quickly realize they'd lost him, then they'd start searching room by room. When that happened, hopefully they wouldn't think to peek out the windows. Only once they were finished would he dare move and return to Jalissa.

In the meantime, he might as well settle in as comfortably as possible and memorize the guard rotation below. It seemed like something that might come in handy to know in the future.

JALISSA STIRRED from her light doze. She must have drifted off while waiting for Edmund to return. Where was he? He was usually back by now.

Had something happened? Had he been caught snooping?

As she blinked and stared into the darkness, the voices outside her door grew louder.

Sarya. And…Crown Prince Jimson.

What was he doing here? At this time of morning? It was not yet light out.

"I am sorry, Your Highness. You cannot go in there." Sarya's voice held a tight, flustered quality that it normally did not.

"Are both of your ambassadors in that room? Are you sure?" Crown Prince Jimson's voice rose.

Sarya's voice called in elvish, "Has the amir returned?"

How should she react? What should she say?

How would she react if Edmund really was here and they had been woken up from a sound sleep?

She drew in a deep breath and attempted to make her tone sound angry as she replied, also in elvish, "No, not yet. Keep stalling."

"Now you have done it, sir. You have woken my princess," Sarya said in the language that Escarland and Mongavaria shared, though Sarya had a distinct elven accent.

"I demand to see the ambassadors." Crown Prince Jimson's voice sounded even closer. "They are here on my family's gracious invitation. I have the right to know where my visitors are at all times, and if they are abusing the hospitality my family has provided."

What was Jalissa supposed to do now?

She rolled off the bed and quickly stuffed pillows under the blankets on the far side. She left the rest of the blankets rumpled.

A glance around the room, and she quickly stuffed several spy items out of sight in the trunks. They weren't fully concealed, but hopefully the crown prince would not be rude enough to start searching their things.

Though, he might do that if he barged in and found Edmund missing.

She glanced toward the rope still tied to the bed and draped over the balcony. Neither Edmund nor his fellow spy Alvin were back yet. If she took in that rope, they might not be able to get back. But if she did not take in the rope and the crown prince came in, he would see it and know.

At that point, it would not matter, not with Edmund still missing. She simply had to make sure the crown prince did not step into this room.

Should she pretend that she and Edmund were...that they...after all, they were newlyweds...

Her ears burned just thinking about it. Nope, she was too much of an elf to pull that off.

Instead, she raced to the door and shoved a hint of her

magic into the door, growing tendrils of it to the door-frame. Now the crown prince could not get in without breaking the door down.

Just in time. There was a thump and a protest from Sarya. Then the door latch rattled. "Prince Edmund, Princess Jalissa, I demand to be allowed in."

Jalissa started shouting back in elvish. She was not even saying anything intelligible. She just needed to sound angry and as if she was cussing the prince out in elvish.

She quickly threw on a silk robe over her clothes and mussed her hair to look as if she had just rolled out of bed.

With a deep breath, she unbarred the door, slipped out into the main room, then shut the door and secured it again behind her before the crown prince had a chance to shove it open.

She pulled herself straight and gave Crown Prince Jimson the iciest, most aloof princess glare that she could. "What is the meaning of this? If you keep yelling like this, you will wake my husband."

Crown Prince Jimson snorted. "As if he wouldn't have woken already with all this shouting. Is he even there, Princess Jalissa, or are you covering for your husband sneaking around this castle at night? Is your visit just a cover for spying?"

She forced her expression to go icier to hide the way her heart thumped harder at the accusation. "How dare you! We are here as emissaries on an official diplomatic visit to your kingdom. I gave up my wedding trip to come here, and I find you barging in here at this hour highly offensive. We have every right to an expectation of privacy. My brother will hear about this. We came here to salvage relations between our kingdoms but you, sir, are not helping your kingdom's cause."

The door behind her opened, and Edmund rested a hand on her waist. His sleep-gravelly voice spoke near her ear. "What's going on here, dearest heart?"

She glanced over her shoulder and nearly gaped at him. He was bare-chested, clutching a blanket around his waist and his hair sticking up in all directions. She forced the icy anger back onto her face and in her voice. "The crown prince barged in here and demanded to see you. He seems to think you were wandering the castle or something."

Edmund raised his eyebrows and tugged her against him. "What would give you such an idea, Your Highness? I have been here the whole time with my wife." He pressed a kiss against Jalissa's neck, nuzzling her ear a bit. "We were married two weeks ago, you know."

Jalissa's ears burned, her skin going hot. She had gone from fear to relief to embarrassment in the span of a few short seconds.

Crown Prince Jimson swept his sharp gaze over Jalissa, giving a little smirk. "Yes, I can see how I should have known better. Of course you wouldn't be anywhere else when you have a wife like that."

That was an innuendo, right? Jalissa's ears burned even worse. The way Crown Prince Jimson was looking at her was far from appropriate.

Edmund's empty smile remained in place without even a flash in his eyes to betray any anger. "She is rather special."

"Before I go, I would like to see all your guards. Just to make sure they are accounted for." Crown Prince Jimson gave such a fake smile that Jalissa's skin crawled. "An intruder was spotted in the hallways of the palace.

He wasn't caught, but one of my guards seemed to think they had caught a glimpse of you. He was clearly mistaken, but perhaps one of your guards decided to wander?"

Edmund motioned to the door to one of the spare rooms. "Sarya, please wake the others."

Sarya gave him a look but headed to the door. She stepped inside. A few moments later, she stepped back into the main room, followed by both Alvin and James in states of sleepy befuddlement.

Crown Prince Jimson's jaw worked, his eyes sharp as he turned back to Prince Edmund. "I apologize for disturbing you. It seems my guard was mistaken."

He spun on his heel and marched from the room, the door shutting with slightly more force than necessary.

Jalissa held her breath for a few more minutes before she sagged against Edmund. "That was close. What happened?"

Alvin winced. "I was spotted. Prince Edmund was on his way back and caused a distraction to help me get away."

"And I wasn't fast enough ducking around a corner. One of the guards and a maid got a glimpse of me." Edmund shifted his grip on the blanket he was wearing.

"I see. And what are you wearing?" Jalissa raised her eyebrows at him. Not that she did not find him rather distracting shirtless, but he was definitely going all-out to sell the ruse.

"Don't you mean, what am I not wearing?" Edmund smirked.

She rolled her eyes and slapped him slightly on the arm. "Really?"

"I had to sell the I've-been-with-you-all-night story." Edmund shrugged. "Not to mention, my clothes were covered in ash, and I couldn't risk the prince catching a glimpse of them."

"Ah." Still did not make this less embarrassing.

Edmund glanced from her to his two spies. "We'll have to lie low for the next few days. I found some incriminating evidence in the king's study, so at least we have what we came for, even if we don't get a chance to search for anything else."

The two spies nodded, then retreated into the bedroom once again.

Edmund faced Jalissa's guard. "Sarya, could you secure the outer door with your magic? I would prefer there are no more interruptions for tonight."

"Yes, amir." Sarya hurried to the door to the hall. Green laced around her fingers a moment before she touched the door.

That reminded Jalissa. She turned to Edmund. "How did you open the door? I secured it with my magic behind me."

"I am not sure. It resisted for a moment, then it was like I could sense your magic. And it just kind of...gave for me. I can't explain it." Edmund opened the door again, as if to prove that he still could. "Your magic isn't tied to any heart bond we might be forming in the way Farrendel tied his magic to his heart bond with Essie. But is it possible it is starting to recognize me somehow? Perhaps I'm immune to your magic or something like that?"

"It is possible. Heart bonds are mysterious things and are especially mysterious when it comes to a marriage between a human and an elf." Jalissa held up her fingers, letting her magic twine around her hand. She held out her hand, palm up.

Edmund took her hand. Her magic twined around both of their hands, not reacting to Edmund.

Huh. She had not expected that. "Do you think this means we already have the beginnings of a heart bond?"

Edmund met her gaze, his eyes solemn and warm. "I hope so."

CHAPTER
SIX

Edmund leaned forward, gesturing animatedly as he spouted some nonsense about his favorite barber in Aldon. Even he wasn't sure what he was saying. He didn't have to sound intelligent.

What mattered was that he blocked both his plate and Jalissa's from the sight of King Solan and Crown Prince Jimson, giving Jalissa a chance to check for poisons.

Across the table, Lord Crest eyed them. If he looked closely, he probably could see the flicker of Jalissa's green magic.

But he was part of the faction that didn't seem to trust the king, so hopefully he would keep his mouth shut.

Even as a stranger here in this court, the division between those who supported the king and those who sided with various members of the Consular Prime was obvious. Lord Crest and some of the top members of the Consular Prime sat along one side of the table, looking at the king with thinly veiled disgust while the Crown Prince and the king's supporters lined the other side of the table. The least powerful gentry chatted with an almost desperate geniality, toadying up to both sides just to be safe.

The Escarlish court had its factions. Even the elven court did.

But at least in both of those places, if a noble disagreed with Averett or Weylind, they still respected their king. Averett and Weylind were both good, noble people. No one could argue with that.

Here, even Edmund could see that those who opposed the king didn't respect him, even if they hid it under a veneer of politeness. Granted, King Solan wasn't a good man, and his son Crown Prince Jimson was even more shifty.

Not that Edmund would characterize those opposing King Solan as good either. Lord Crest seemed all right—mostly—though he was still out for what power he could grab for himself. And he was on the list of those who were involved in smuggling with Escarland. The trade with Escarland could be why he was in favor of cooling tensions with Escarland. It would hurt his profits if Escarland kept cracking down on smuggling and strengthening the border.

"Eddie dearest, I doubt the king is interested in frequenting an Escarlish barber." Jalissa touched Edmund's arm, gently nudging him back.

That meant the food and drink in front of them were safe.

He resisted the urge to grimace at her use of a nickname for him. She was gently teasing him with it. But it fit the role they were playing.

King Solan looked down his nose at Edmund, a hint of disgust playing around his mouth. With a slight shake of his head, he turned back to his food.

Crown Prince Jimson narrowed his eyes at Edmund

before he too took another bite of his salmon.

Edmund pretended to be oblivious to how stilted the conversation was around them. Lord Crest and Crown Prince Jimson were basically stabbing each other with their gazes while King Solan glared at both of them.

Edmund just tried to remain pleasant to everyone. He didn't want to get caught in the crossfire.

As the supper finished, King Solan gestured to him. "Prince Edmund, would you please join me for a drink?"

Edmund's instincts crawled, but he nodded and pushed to his feet. He picked up Jalissa's hand and kissed her knuckles. "I'll be along shortly, my dearest sugarcake."

"Do not take too long." Jalissa's smile was warm, but her eyes had a sharp look. Her words might sound flirty, but Edmund could hear what she was really saying. *Stay safe.*

The other nobles started dispersing. Lord Crest gave first Edmund, then King Solan a studied look before he climbed to his feet and disappeared into a group of his cronies.

Edmund waited long enough to watch Jalissa stroll away, Sarya at her heels.

Crown Prince Jimson, too, was waiting, and he didn't start walking until after Edmund did. Edmund tried to pretend the back of his neck wasn't prickling as he followed King Solan toward his study.

Inside the study, Edmund glanced around, taking in the room in the daylight for the first time. The hidden door was truly clever. Even in the daylight, he couldn't spot the line of the secret door or the latch that he had yet to find in the dark.

King Solan strolled to the sideboard and took out three glasses and a bottle of brandy. "As my son reminded me, I haven't properly welcomed you to Mongavaria, Prince Edmund. I will admit, I was not in favor of this emissary exchange when my son initially suggested it. But I can see its advantages. I am looking forward to discussing the issues our kingdoms are facing."

Crown Prince Jimson was the one to suggest this emissary exchange? Now Edmund's instincts wound even tighter in his chest. The crown prince was the one who had been behind the poisoning in Kostaria. So what was he planning with this emissary exchange? An exchange that he had arranged even *before* he'd poisoned the trolls.

Had King Solan truly been behind the attempted assassination of Farrendel, Essie, and the whole elven royal family? Or had Edmund threatened the wrong royal six months ago?

Even if Crown Prince Jimson had truly been behind it, King Solan must have tacitly approved of his actions. After all, the order to execute the captured Escarlish spies could only have come from him. The crown prince didn't have the authority to execute anyone.

And the whole plan to take over Nevaria had begun over twenty years ago with Crown Prince Jimson's arranged marriage to Nevaria's princess. Even if Crown Prince Jimson had come up with the idea, King Solan had certainly gone along with it readily enough.

As Crown Prince Jimson shut the door behind him, King Solan poured the brandy into the three glasses. He turned and handed one glass to his son and the other to Edmund before taking the third glass for himself.

King Solan sipped, then turned to Edmund. "Your elven wife is...lovely. But does your brother truly believe that such close ties with the elves and trolls is in the best interest of your kingdom? Yes, the elves ruled an empire that nearly spanned the continent but that was millennia ago. The time of the elves is long over. The time of the humans is now. Can you imagine the world power we could be if Escarland and Mongavaria formed an alliance?"

What he really meant was what power he could wield if he subsumed Escarland into his growing empire. And King Solan wondered why Averett would choose to ally with the elves and trolls instead.

"I must beg to differ." Edmund forced his smile to remain friendly and empty. "Our alliance with the elves has many benefits."

Crown Prince Jimson snorted, swirling his brandy in his glass. "You would say that. I'm sure your wife provides plenty of benefits."

King Solan sent a glare at his son. "Don't be crude, Jimson."

Edmund scrunched his eyebrows, as if the innuendo had gone over his head, and tried not to let his fingers clench on his glass. Sure, he'd left himself open to something like that, knowing one of them would likely say it. It fit with his oblivious persona.

That didn't make it any easier to hear and take. If he'd been back in Escarland, he would have rebuked someone for saying something crass about any woman, much less Edmund's wife. But here, all he could do was smile like a ninny and take it.

"What I meant is that her magic must be useful." Crown Prince Jimson studied the glass of brandy in his hand, not quite a good enough actor to hide that this hadn't been what he meant at all. His gaze flicked up to Edmund. "She has plant growing magic, I believe?"

Edmund hesitated, not wanting to confirm anything about Jalissa's magic. But if Crown Prince Jimson had been paying attention, he would have seen how the plants in the market had reacted to her. And the spies who had been captured in Tarenhiel had seen her magic in action. Surely they would have reported that to their king before they were executed for their failures.

"Yes, she does. It is quite beneficial for maintaining lovely gardens around our home." Edmund lifted his glass of brandy to his mouth but hesitated before taking a sip. Jalissa wasn't here to check if the brandy was safe to drink. He lowered his glass without drinking.

"I'm sure the elven magic is useful. But it hardly compares to economic power." King Solan sipped his brandy, then faced Edmund. "You've toured Landri and seen the riches of trade that Mongavaria has to offer. For years, trade has flourished between our kingdoms. Both of our kingdoms are suffering under the trade restrictions your brother has imposed. Why would we continue these hostilities when loosening the trade restrictions would benefit both of our kingdoms so much?"

Maybe because Mongavaria was the one to start the hostilities. Better to ally themselves with honorable kings like Rharreth and Weylind than a tenuous alliance with a power-hungry empire like Mongavaria. Sure, trade was suffering now. But eventually, overseas trade would reroute through ports in Tarenhiel and Kostaria, then flow down into Escarland. As long as the Hydalla River remained open, riverboats from Escarland could traverse that seaway all the way to the coast to meet trade ships. In the long run, Escarland didn't need Mongavaria.

If Escarland joined with Mongavaria, how long would it be before Mongavaria wanted to unite to wipe out Tarenhiel and Kostaria? King Solan wanted an empire of humans. He would end the age of the elves, even if he had to do it through war and genocide. Crown Prince

Jimson had shown through his poisoning of Kostaria that he was willing to do just that.

Edmund shrugged and struggled with his placid expression. "I'm afraid my brother is set on this course. The fact that one of your assassins shot my sister might have something to do with that."

Crown Prince Jimson's gaze snapped to Edmund, his look sharpening.

Edmund kept his smile neutral. That probably had been a little too pointed. But even the most bland and empty-headed of men would hold a grudge over his sister getting shot.

"That was a little bit of a misunderstanding." King Solan sent a glare in Crown Prince Jimson's direction. "I can assure you that such aggression against Escarland won't happen again."

Another instance of Crown Prince Jimson taking initiative and King Solan approving of it as long as it pleased him to use his son's ambitions to expand his empire.

King Solan tossed back the rest of his brandy, then strolled over to the sideboard and refilled his glass. "Does anyone else need theirs topped off?"

"No, thank you." Edmund raised his glass, swirling it a bit to hide that he hadn't taken so much as a sip.

"I'm all set, Father." Crown Prince Jimson also raised his glass.

A cold sensation filled Edmund's chest, and it was all he could do not to let his smile slip.

Crown Prince Jimson hadn't drunk any of his brandy either.

The brandy was poisoned, and Crown Prince Jimson knew it. And that meant...he was the one who had poisoned it.

King Solan was already poisoned. He'd had a whole glass of the brandy and was starting on his second. He would be dead in a day or two, even if he didn't know it yet.

Crown Prince Jimson had done it with Edmund in the room. He was going to pin the blame on Edmund.

"Prince Edmund." Crown Prince Jimson met Edmund's gaze. "You haven't touched your brandy. Is it not to your liking?"

Edmund forced an easy grin, even as all his instincts screamed in his head. "I rarely drink. I get tipsy so easily. Sadly, I can't hold my alcohol."

"Hmm." Crown Prince Jimson gave him a thin smile. "You've had no problem drinking the wine at the meals all week."

Crown Prince Jimson suspected that Edmund was more than what he seemed, and now the crown prince was trying to poison Edmund. The story would probably be that Edmund poisoned King Solan but accidentally took a sip and poisoned himself along with his victim. Case closed, and Crown Prince Jimson would both cast the blame for the poisoning on Escarland and kill off Edmund in a manner that didn't appear to be Mongavaria's fault.

"Jimson, really, what has gotten into you?" King Solan shook his head. "I apologize, Prince Edmund. I raised him to be more polite than this."

"Think nothing of it. I'm sure this is excellent brandy. I would be impolite if I refused your hospitality." Edmund grinned and flourished his hand, accidentally-on-purpose sloshing half his brandy onto his sleeve. He jumped back, spilling even more brandy onto the floor. "Oh, I'm so sorry."

King Solan grimaced, then waved him away. "I'll have

one of the maids clean it up. Here, let me refill your glass. Perhaps there is something else that you would prefer more?"

There was nothing in that sideboard that he would dare drink. Perhaps the crown prince had only poisoned the brandy, knowing that it was his father's favorite. But he seemed like the type to be generous with his poisons. He had probably poisoned everything in there, and he'd swap it all out once his father went to bed. After all, he'd have a few hours before the king began to show symptoms. He would have plenty of time to cover his tracks and plant evidence that Edmund was behind it.

"If you'd like, the wine is also excellent." Crown Prince Jimson gestured toward the sideboard, that sharp look glittering in his gaze.

Yep, he'd poisoned all of it. Better to stick with the poison he knew—and had evidence of soaking into his sleeve—than risk the poison he didn't.

"The brandy is fine." Edmund handed over his glass. His skin crawled with the feeling of the brandy causing his sleeve to cling to his arm. But he tried to tell himself not to freak out. As long as he washed his hand and arm thoroughly, he wasn't likely to get poisoned simply from the skin contact.

King Solan poured more brandy into Edmund's glass, then held it out to him. "The brandy is made locally just south of Landri and shipped all over the kingdom."

As he took the glass, Edmund could feel the weight of Crown Prince Jimson's gaze on him. Edmund's stunt of spilling the brandy had only made the crown prince more suspicious. If Edmund didn't allay his suspicions in some way, then Crown Prince Jimson would never relax his guard enough to allow Edmund, Jalissa, and the guards to sneak out of the castle.

They had to flee. Tonight. Before King Solan showed symptoms of his poisoning.

Edmund raised his glass, his heart thumping harder. This brandy was poisoned. He knew it. Crown Prince Jimson knew it.

That left Edmund with only two choices. Either he could refuse the brandy and possibly tip his hand to his spying, or he could drink the brandy and gamble that he and Jalissa were really forming a heart bond.

He resisted the urge to touch the hidden pocket of his shirt where he kept the papers he'd stolen. This information was too crucial. He had to get it back to Escarland by the safest means possible. He couldn't risk that Crown Prince Jimson would set a watch on them or, worse, arrest them and throw them in the dungeon tower as spies.

Edmund had no choice. Not really.

He brought the glass to his mouth and sipped. The warm brandy sloshed over his tongue, and he had to draw in a breath to control his gag reflex before he swallowed it down. The liquor burned in his throat, and maybe it was his imagination, but it churned in his stomach. It took all his acting skills to salute King Solan, his smile still in place. "This is excellent brandy. I can see why you are so proud of it."

King Solan nodded, saluted with his glass, and drank again. "Brandy like this could be something my kingdom could trade with yours, if the restrictions were lifted."

Edmund had no choice but to salute the king with his glass and drink another mouthful.

Crown Prince Jimson's stance relaxed a fraction, and his gaze swung away from Edmund to focus once again on his father.

At least poisoning himself had been worth it. Even if the crown prince remained suspicious of Edmund, he was assured now that Edmund was going to die, poisoned and married to an elf with plant magic rather than healing magic. He didn't know about Edmund's hope for a heart bond or the healing magic Rheva had provided. Hopefully that assumption would gain them enough time to get out of this castle tonight.

JALISSA PACED ACROSS THE SUITE. What was taking Edmund so long? He had just gone to have a drink with the king. Perhaps discuss a little politics. How long could that take? It was not like either Escarland or Mongavaria was going to budge.

She had such a bad feeling in the pit of her stomach. She could not explain it, but it was there all the same and no amount of telling herself that everything was fine could banish it.

Sarya leaned against the wall, not commenting on Jalissa's restlessness. James was guarding the outer door while Alvin was in the guards' room, resting before another night of snooping.

Finally, the door opened, and Edmund stepped inside, followed by James. Edmund's face had a white, almost scared look to it that she had never seen before, not even when Edmund had been shot by the spy-assassins.

She raced to him. "What happened? What is wrong?"

He held up his sleeve, its end damp. "Could you examine this with your magic? Don't touch the damp spot."

That bad feeling in her stomach worsened. She gripped his sleeve above the damp spot and sent her magic into it. She could sense the cotton of the fabric, the apple of what was probably an apple brandy based on the smell, and…and…

Something she was all too familiar with after her time in Kostaria.

Castor beans. Ricin.

She lifted her gaze to meet Edmund's. "It is poisoned. Ricin."

Edmund nodded, his expression going even more taut, as if she had simply confirmed what he had already feared. "I thought so."

She drew in a deep breath and tried to force herself to calm. "Ricin is unlikely to be absorbed through skin contact. As long as you wash before eating anything, you will be fine. This is fine."

"Jalissa, amirah." Edmund's tone was gentle, though he did not reach out to touch her. "I didn't have a choice. I drank some of that brandy. I've been poisoned."

Her stomach lurched as it dropped into her toes. For a moment, it was all she could do to breathe through the tightness squeezing her chest.

She could not lose Edmund. She just could not. They had only been married a little over two weeks. They were supposed to have more time to enjoy their happy ending. This could not be happening.

"I'm going to be fine, Jalissa." Edmund's voice remained far too steady for someone who was dying. "We have the medicine from Rheva. Hopefully it will be enough to reach an elf healer."

Yes, yes, that was right. They had the medicine. Edmund would be fine. She was not going to lose him.

She drew in a deep breath and pulled herself together. This was not the time to panic. She was an elf princess. She could think about this logically.

She would not let Edmund die. That was all there was

to it. She would cling to Edmund in the heart bond—because they simply had to have a heart bond—and not let him go. Just like Essie with Farrendel. And Farrendel with Essie.

She took his hand and held up their linked fingers. "I guess we will find out if we have an elishina or not."

The tight look disappeared in a hint of Edmund's smile. "I guess we will." He withdrew his hand from hers. "But we have a while before that will become necessary. First, I need to wash, and we need to pack."

She nodded and took a step back. Right. She could handle this. Edmund was poisoned, but he would be fine. They would be fine.

Edmund turned to the rest of the room. One of the others must have fetched Alvin because he, James, and Sarya were standing there, waiting for an explanation. Edmund glanced over the three of them. "Crown Prince Jimson poisoned his father, and he plans to pin it on me. He poisoned me too. We need to leave tonight."

James and Alvin nodded, spun on their heels, and disappeared inside the guard room. Probably to pack their spy gear.

Jalissa touched Edmund's arm. "Go ahead and wash. Sarya and I can start packing."

"I love you." Edmund leaned in, then halted. "Right. I can't kiss you until I have thoroughly brushed my teeth and rinsed my mouth. Don't want to poison you too. Come to think of it, we probably shouldn't risk it for a few days, just to be safe."

Not unless they discovered they did not have a heart bond like Farrendel and Essie did and Edmund really was dying and there was no way Jalissa was letting him die without a kiss and…

And she was going to break down into sobs if she kept

thinking like that.

Swallowing back the choked tightness in her throat, Jalissa forced herself to smile and nod. It was all she could manage.

While Edmund disappeared into the water closet, Jalissa and Sarya opened all the hidden compartments in the trunks and sorted through the various items, placing them in five piles.

She hesitated as she divvied up the vials of elven medicine. Edmund might need every single one to get him to an elven healer.

But what if James or Alvin were hurt on their mission, whatever it was? It seemed selfish to keep all the medicine for Edmund.

James joined her and pushed the elven medicine back at her. "You keep them. The prince will need them more."

"Are you sure?" Jalissa was not sure why she was arguing. Those vials could be the difference between life and death for Edmund.

"Yes." James did not explain as he moved off and instead took one of the coils of rope.

By the time Edmund returned, scrubbed and dressed in his dark, charcoal-colored clothing, all of the gear was packed, and the empty, secret compartments were melded back into the trunks as if they had never existed, just in case the Mongavarians decided to take an ax to the trunks to see what they might have been hiding.

Jalissa changed into dark gray trousers, shirt, and tunic of her own. All the fancy dresses she had brought would be left behind, abandoned as expected, except for two dresses that Edmund told her and Sarya to pack. For what reason, he did not explain. But Jalissa would trust he already had a plan for them, since he folded one of his nicer suits of clothing into his pack as well.

At one of the end tables, Jalissa trailed her fingers over the orchid. It would probably be too much to take it along. She needed to concentrate on keeping Edmund alive, not thinking about a plant.

Edmund reached around her and picked up the plant. "It's small. Take it along."

"Are you sure?" Jalissa glanced between Edmund and the orchid.

"Yes." Edmund carried the orchid to their packs. He eased the plant into her pack, securing it snugly along one side. When he turned back toward her, he wrapped an arm around her waist. "We're going to get through this. The next few days might get a little rough, but we'll survive, all right?"

Jalissa nodded, trying not to betray how much her fingers were trembling.

She had to pull herself together. She had married Edmund and gone on this mission knowing something like this was likely in her future. She had spent months preparing for this possibility. She could handle this.

While she checked their items one last time, Edmund talked with James and Alvin in a low voice. After a few minutes, he shook their hands, and they slipped out the door.

Jalissa was not sure if she would ever see James and Alvin again. They were off to disappear into Mongavaria, helping to rebuild Escarland's spy network.

Edmund shouldered his pack, then gripped Jalissa's hand. His fingers were not clammy and his grip firm. No signs of his poisoning yet. "Ready?"

"Yes." Jalissa drew her shoulders straight underneath the weight of her pack. Time to go home, whatever it took.

CHAPTER
SEVEN

E dmund peeked out the door, then slipped into the corridor, tugging Jalissa after him. Sarya trailed after them, the largest pack of all on her back. Edmund might have argued, but it made the most sense for Sarya to carry the biggest burden. Edmund was poisoned and would soon weaken. Jalissa would be under a lot of strain keeping him alive. That left Sarya as the only one strong enough to carry the bulk of their items.

"Where are we going?" Jalissa trotted at his side, though she didn't complain about the pace he was setting. "Should we not be heading for a door or a window or something?"

"We will soon, but we need to make a stop first." Edmund glanced around before he took a corner and headed into another wing of the castle. "It's risky, but I think it will be worth it."

Jalissa's eyebrows scrunched, but she quickened her pace.

A few more turns, and Edmund halted and knocked

on a door. At this point, he really hoped this gamble would pay off. He didn't want to admit it to Jalissa yet, but he felt...off. Not in pain or sick just yet. But an off feeling spread through his stomach, though that could be his imagination playing tricks on him.

King Solan had consumed far more of the poison, and at over seventy years old, he would likely feel the effects more quickly. They didn't have much time to get out of the castle before it was locked down due to the king's "illness."

The door opened, and a guard stood there. He blinked, only a slight lift to his eyebrows betraying his surprise to see Edmund and Jalissa standing there at this hour. "Can I help you, Your Highnesses?"

"We need to speak with your lord immediately. It's urgent. May we step in?" Edmund resisted the urge to push his way into the room.

The guard hesitated for a moment before he nodded and stepped aside, letting them in.

Edmund, Jalissa, and Sarya stepped into the sitting room, and the guard closed the door after them. "If you will please have a seat, I will wake my lord."

With a nod, Edmund sank onto the couch, Jalissa at his side. Sarya took up a position at the door, ready to protect them from whatever came.

After a few minutes, the door to the bedchamber opened, and Lord Crest stepped into the sitting room, tying the belt of his dressing gown. "Your Highnesses, you wished to speak with me?"

"Were you sincere about your wish to improve relations with Escarland?" Edmund held Lord Crest's gaze.

"Yes." Lord Crest drew out the word as he sank into the chair across from them.

"I have information you might find interesting. In

exchange, I would like your promise that you will work with Escarland when I contact you once I return to my kingdom." Edmund relaxed against the couch as much as he could with his pack on his back, trying to pretend he was nonchalant instead of tense.

Lord Crest's eyebrows shot up, though the expression seemed more feigned than true surprise. The man was canny, that was for sure. "What is this information? And why would it be worth something that could possibly be considered treason?"

Edmund continued to hold Lord Crest's gaze. "My information could give you and the Consular Prime the means to wield power over the king, if you have the chance to be prepared."

Lord Crest studied him for yet another moment before he motioned to his guard. "Please, step outside."

The guard nodded, spun on his heel, and stepped outside, clicking the door shut behind him. Sarya took up her post in front of the door once again.

Edmund leaned his elbows on his knees. "Crown Prince Jimson poisoned his father with ricin tonight. In a few hours, your king will fall ill. Depending on his strength and how much poison was in the brandy, your king will be dead in a day or two."

Lord Crest's eyebrows shot up in genuine surprise this time. "That is...unexpected."

"I suspect that King Solan was attempting to rein in his son's schemes after the debacles of the assassination attempts and the mass poisoning in Kostaria, and the crown prince decided that is was simpler just to dispatch his father than continue to seek his permission." Edmund shrugged, his tone light as if he wasn't talking about murder and assassination.

"Do you have any proof?" Lord Crest crossed his

arms, his gaze steady. "It will be your word against the crown prince's that he poisoned his father."

"No, I don't have proof." He wasn't about to mention that he had been poisoned as well. He didn't trust Lord Crest that much. "But why would I poison your king? Escarland has defended herself, but we have not been the aggressors. If you will look at your kingdom's recent history, you will see that assassination and poisoning is more your thing than Escarland's."

Lord Crest hesitated, as if unwilling to admit that fact to an Escarlish prince. Finally, he gave a short nod. "Jimson will try to pin the poisoning on you. Running off in the middle of the night won't look good."

Then Lord Crest had guessed they were in the process of fleeing the castle. The packs and traveling clothes they were all wearing were a rather obvious giveaway, even if Edmund hadn't said anything about leaving.

"It can't be helped. We can't risk staying here. As you said, it is my word against his, and I've seen what your kingdom does to those it labels as Escarlish spies." Edmund couldn't help the angry note that crept into his voice.

Besides, even if he thought he could bluster his way out of the crown prince's allegations, there was the poison currently coursing through his blood. Unless he wanted to end up as dead as King Solan, he needed to get to an elven healer as soon as possible.

Lord Crest studied Edmund for another long moment. "This is, indeed, important information. But what you ask in return puts me at great risk. If I am caught conspiring with Escarland against my king, then I will be accused of treason. That would greatly impact my ability to capitalize on the changes in the kingdom."

"True." Edmund had known this would be the

sticking point. "Once I return home, I will send you a message to set up a meeting between your king and mine. At that time, I will provide the proof you will need to keep your new king's power in check. All I ask is that you aid with setting up that meeting on your end, nothing more."

Lord Crest eyed him, as if trying to decide if he could have Edmund searched and get the proof now, rather than later.

He could try, and he'd probably find the papers Edmund had stashed on his person to carry back to Escarland.

But Edmund was betting that Lord Crest would gamble in order to gain the support of Escarland for his faction in the Mongavarian government.

After a moment, Lord Crest nodded. "Very well, Prince Edmund. You have a deal."

Good. Lord Crest and the Consular Prime staging a little coup here in Mongavaria would hopefully turn Mongavaria's attention away from the alliance to deal with internal affairs. It would buy a few years of peace.

Now Edmund just had to figure a way out of this castle and back to Escarland without being caught or dying of poison first.

He pushed to his feet and held out his hand. "Thank you for your time, Lord Crest. I look forward to better relations between our kingdoms in the future."

Lord Crest also stood, and he gave Edmund a firm handshake. "So I do." He hesitated, then added, "A cargo train leaves from the station outside of Landri in a few hours."

That was more help than Edmund had expected to receive. Lord Crest wouldn't actively aid Edmund and Jalissa to leave the castle. That would be skirting too close to treason and interfere with his ambitions.

But sometimes information could be just as valuable as actual help.

With a final nod in Lord Crest's direction, Edmund headed for the door. Sarya peeked outside, then opened the door wider and motioned for Edmund and Jalissa to follow.

Together, the three of them tiptoed down the quiet corridors, ducking into rooms or alcoves whenever a servant or guard hustled past.

On the first floor, they crossed the ballroom, then exited the large doors into the private gardens. This side of the castle overlooked the bluff and the ocean beyond, so only a short railing separated them from the bluff rather than high walls that would have blocked the view of the sea. The steep cliffs and the harbor defenses out in the bay were enough to protect the king's palace without the need for strong walls.

All the better for Edmund, Jalissa, and Sarya. The cliffs would have been difficult to climb for anyone but someone very skilled or in possession of a very long rope.

Unless one had elven magic on their side.

Edmund gestured to the cliff. "Sarya, are there enough roots in the cliff that you and Jalissa can get us to the bottom?"

Sarya pressed her hand to the ground, and a hint of green spread from her fingers before disappearing into the soil. After a moment, she frowned and shook her head. "After a few yards down, the cliffs are solid rock. But I think that ivy over there is sturdy enough that we can lower ourselves down the cliffs with that." She pointed at a flowering vine that twined around a nearby arbor and onto part of the balustrade along the cliff edge.

"That will work." Edmund glanced around, checking that the garden was still deserted.

Sarya led the way over to that portion of railing. She wrapped a hand around a section of the vine. It glowed with her green magic as it twined up her arm, then wrapped around her torso to hold her securely. She climbed over the railing, then eased over the edge of the cliff.

Next to Edmund, Jalissa gripped the vine with her free hand, adding her magic as well. She glanced down at their clasped hands, as if reluctant to let him go.

Edmund released her hand to grip the vine with both hands. "The poison hasn't had time to fully get into my system yet. I'll be fine for the time it will take to climb down the cliff."

He had vomited up as much of the poisoned brandy as he could back in the water closet before he'd washed up. His body had likely still absorbed some of the poison before he'd purged as much as he could, but hopefully his efforts would buy him a little more time.

Jalissa nodded, then gestured to the cliff. "You go first, and I will climb down after you. That way, Sarya and I can more easily keep the vines twined around you."

It went against his instincts to go first while leaving Jalissa to take up the rear, but she had a point. He didn't have magic, so he would be a burden that Jalissa and Sarya would have to hold suspended between them.

Being a burden was something he was going to have to accept. Once the poison took hold of him, he was going to be a burden on Jalissa as she kept him alive and both of them would be a burden to Sarya.

Edmund climbed over the balustrade, waited until the vine had wrapped around his waist, then leaned backwards over the edge of the cliff. The vine tightened but held him securely as he took another step lower.

Once he was a few feet down, Jalissa climbed over the railing and started easing down the cliff, and Edmund breathed a little easier once all three of them were far enough down that a guard patrol was unlikely to see them unless they peeked over the cliff.

The vines slowly grew, lowering them foot-by-foot down the cliff. The *whump* of the ocean waves breaking on the cliff below grew louder as they neared, until spray misted over Edmund's face.

Sarya reached the bottom, her feet sinking into the wet sand at the base of the cliff. Another wave crashed in, breaking over the boulders scattered over the narrow strip of shoreline and washing all the way to the cliff, soaking Sarya to her knees.

After a few more seconds, Edmund dropped to the sand beside her. He reached up and steadied Jalissa as she descended the final feet just as a wave crashed into them, soaking through his boots and his trousers with a wet, cold slap.

Jalissa staggered against him with the force of the wave, her face pale in the moonlight. "That is cold."

Edmund opened his mouth to reply, only to get smacked with another, even larger wave. Splashes of salt water coated his tongue with an unpleasant, briny taste while the cold salt water made his clothes feel extra sticky and scratchy. "I agree. Let's get moving. I think we should leave the vines connecting us, in case one of us slips or is knocked over by a wave."

Sarya nodded, reached up, and sent a little of her magic up the vine, severing the vine partway up the cliff.

They left the rest of the vine trailing down the cliff face, its leaves curling and dying as the elven magic left it.

Jalissa glanced at the vine one last time, a hint of sadness in her eyes, before she reached for Edmund's hand, her jaw set.

He squeezed her fingers, the only comfort he could give her right then. Jalissa wouldn't like sacrificing the plant, even if it had been for their escape. Likely, the plant wouldn't die off entirely. Vines like that were extremely difficult to kill. Based on the way the vine had been taking over not just the arbor but also the nearby balustrade, the gardeners would likely be thankful that the vine was tamed for a while.

Sarya led the way south, hugging the strip of sand dotted with fallen boulders at the base of the cliffs. Their feet sank into the sloshing sand with each step while waves battered them every minute or two. Edmund didn't know enough about the ocean to tell if the tide was coming in or going out. Either way, he wanted to get out of there and reach safer ground as quickly as possible.

At least the crashing waves would quickly wash away their tracks. If the castle was searched thoroughly, someone might eventually connect the vines trailing down the cliff with them. And they would puzzle out that they would have gone south toward the river mouth and the town rather than north toward a shoreline that featured high cliffs for at least a mile before it spread out into grassy, sandy beaches.

But hopefully by that point, they would be long gone.

After a few more minutes of miserable trudging, the cliffs became less steep, and they eventually climbed out onto a small rise topped with seagrass and sand.

The dry sand provided another challenge as it slid beneath their feet with every step and coated their boots with a gritty layer.

By the time they reached the docks that jutted into the river mouth, all three of them were breathing hard.

Edmund called a halt for a moment so they could catch their breath. Neither Sarya nor Jalissa had the strength of magic of someone like Weylind. Growing the vine like they had would have tired them out, and they likely couldn't depend on either of them having much left for defense if it came to that. He wasn't sure how long his own strength would last before he'd start to feel the effects of the poison.

They needed to get on that train as soon as possible so they could all rest. But the cargo train would be at the station on the far side of the river, tucked amongst the docks and warehouses rather than the upscale district that crowded this side of the river next to the castle.

A few bridges spanned the river, but bridges meant guards and venturing deeper into the nicer part of the city.

Edmund scanned the docks below them, then pointed to where someone had pulled a small rowboat onto the shore. "I think we need to steal a boat."

Jalissa grimaced but nodded. He didn't really like it either, especially since the rowboat probably belonged to some fisherman who could little afford the loss. Hopefully the man would eventually get it back.

But right now, it was a matter of life and death.

They sneaked to the boat, and between the three of them, they quickly had it in the water. Edmund let the flow of the river and ocean catch them and pull them farther from shore before he dipped the oars in and started rowing.

The water kept trying to drag them farther out to sea. An outgoing tide, then. An incoming tide would have been easier, since it would have carried them into the river instead of trying to drag them out to the ocean, but the lower tide had probably saved them when it came to that trek along the cliffs.

After a few minutes of rowing, he was breathing hard and his arms ached. With a few silent gestures, Sarya took over rowing. Once she tired, Edmund took over once again.

Sarya was on her second turn when they finally fought free of the current and nudged the boat into the sprawling dock system on the far side.

Even at this late hour, dock workers, ship hands, stevedores, guards, and inspectors roamed the wharf. Lanterns sporadically placed along the docks provided some light but left enough shadows and darkness for Edmund to silently motion Sarya over to one of the deserted docks. In the shadows, they used the remnants of the vine to secure the rowboat to a pylon so that it wouldn't be swept out into the ocean. Then they all rolled onto the wooden dock and rose to their feet.

"Follow my lead." Edmund rested one arm around Jalissa's shoulders, the other arm around Sarya's shoulders, and set off at a staggering, swaying pace down the dock and into the bustle of the wharf district.

Despite his deceptively meandering pace, he stuck to the patches of shadows. If anyone looked closely at them, they'd notice that they weren't dressed like a ship hand and a pair of floozies. Not to mention their traveling packs and the fact that Jalissa and Sarya were elves.

But the point was to appear so normal that no one gave them a second glance to realize the things that were out of place.

It seemed to work. The dock workers didn't give them much of a glance, and they passed other meandering couples or groups of sozzled sailors staggering along the wharf.

As they entered the streets near the wharf, taverns and places of ill repute packed either side of the street while music, shouting, giggling, and rowdy laughter filled the air. Light spilled from the surrounding businesses even if most of the gas lamps were broken or only emitted a guttering flame. Plenty of people roamed these streets, even at this time of night, and Edmund simply joined the bustle as if he were one of them.

To make it even more convincing, he broke into a tavern song, slurring the words.

As they passed through the light cast by one of the nearby taverns, Jalissa ducked her head against his shoulder and even gave a little attempt at a giggle. It sounded forced, but at least she was trying to act the part.

Despite his staggering steps and casual, drunken singing, Edmund's back was tight, and he kept a wary eye out. While he was armed, he didn't want the delay caused by getting into a brawl. Nor did he want that much attention drawn to them.

Finally, the tangle of streets opened into an industrial train station with its weaving snakes of train tracks criss-crossing the area before the long, huge warehouses where the railcars and engines would be housed when not in use.

One train stretched out on the tracks, workers bustling around the engine as they filled the coal car and topped off the boiler with water. More workers carried crates into the train cars, working from the front toward the back, shutting the doors of the filled railcars as they went.

Letting go of Sarya and Jalissa, Edmund divested himself of his pack, then carried it on his shoulder, hunching as if he was carrying a heavy sack filled with flour or wheat or something like that. After waiting in the shadows for a moment, he joined the end of the line of workers, marching along toward the train car.

Sarya and Jalissa also carried their packs on their shoulders and fell into step behind him, using the hunched posture and the packs to hide the fact that they were both female elves.

At the train car, the worker before Edmund set down his crate inside, then turned and blinked when he found Edmund standing there, as if he wasn't expecting anyone to be behind him. But then he just grunted, shook his head, and ambled back down the ramp once again. Hopefully the man would be too busy thoughtlessly carrying crates back and forth that he wouldn't ask questions when the three unexpected workers suddenly weren't behind him anymore.

As soon as Jalissa and Sarya followed him inside, Edmund squeezed between the stacks of crates until he reached the back wall. The crates were stacked to just above his head, leaving no room to climb on top of them, with very little space around them for hiding.

But this far back in the crates, it was so dark no one would be able to see them in their dark clothing, even if they looked right at them.

He, Jalissa, and Sarya stood still as the workers returned, loading the next round of crates. It took one more trip before the workers deemed the railcar full and shut the sliding door.

Jalissa released a breath that brushed against Edmund's neck in the tight space.

He squeezed her fingers, which were icy in his grip. "We'll stay hidden here until the train gets moving, in case they do one last glance through each of the cars. Once the train is on its way, we can make ourselves more comfortable. There should be more room near the door."

There was a pause. Perhaps Jalissa had nodded, and then realized he couldn't see in the dark, for she finally said, "Good."

He waited, occasionally shifting from foot to foot. His feet squished in his wet boots while his cold, soggy trousers stuck to his skin. What he wouldn't give for dry clothes and a warm fire right about now.

Next to him, Jalissa shivered, and he tugged her closer to try to share some of his body heat.

After long minutes of waiting in the dark and cramped corner, the door to the train car slid open a foot, and someone held up a lamp, shining the orange light inside. They didn't give the railcar more than a cursory glance before shutting the door once again.

Minutes later, the train finally shuddered into motion, the chugging of the engine and the clacking of the wheels vibrating through the train car.

Jalissa breathed out a sigh of relief that gusted against his neck. "We made it."

"This far, anyway." Edmund could see the map sprawling ahead of them in his mind. They had to cross the width of Mongavaria, climb up and over the thickly forested Whitehurst Mountains, then travel across Escarland to Aldon.

Such a long way to go. He'd done it before, and it wouldn't have been so daunting normally.

But he was in a bit of a time crunch. How long would his strength hold out before the poison weakened him?

Perhaps it would have been quicker to reach a healer if they went north for Tarenhiel instead of heading west toward Escarland.

But Princess Bella of Mongavaria was in Aldon at this

very moment, and who knew what she might be up to? Crown Prince Jimson hadn't just poisoned his father on a whim. This had been cold and calculated, and that meant that the princess's presence in Escarland was just as much a part of this plot as everything else.

Edmund needed to get to Aldon as soon as possible and warn Averett. He didn't even dare send something like this over the telegraph lines once they reached Escarland, due to the evidence he'd found that Mongavaria had tapped the telegraph lines. He couldn't risk word reaching Crown Prince Jimson—or worse, Princess Bella—before he had a chance to get to Averett.

Edmund gently nudged Jalissa toward the middle of the car. "Let's make ourselves comfortable and try to get some rest."

After inching their way back to the space near the doorway, Sarya and Edmund rearranged some of the crates to make more space while Jalissa changed into dry clothes. Once Jalissa returned and helped Sarya spread out their bedrolls, Edmund took a turn fumbling through changing out of his sticky, wet clothes and putting on a set of dry clothes, all while in the pitch black and cramped in a far corner between piles of crates.

Once done, he spread his wet clothes on some of the crates to dry, then lay down on his bedroll next to Jalissa. She already curled on her side, wiggling as she tried to get comfortable on the hard floor.

He shifted closer, wrapped an arm around her waist, and settled her against his chest. "We'll get through this, my amirah."

She snuggled into his arms, heaving a deep breath. "I know."

He drew in the floral scent of her hair, relaxing into the warmth of holding her in his arms. He didn't know if they'd make it to the border or the toll the poison would take on him or what dangers their future held.

But right now, he held his wife in his arms. The cargo train clacked and vibrated into the night with a soothing rhythm, each moment taking them farther from danger and closer to safety.

CHAPTER
EIGHT

Asharp pain stabbed through her middle.
Jalissa woke with a gasp and curled into a tighter ball, trying to breathe through the pain. She pressed a hand to her middle. What was this? Her stomach twisted in agony, bile rising in her throat.

Behind her, Edmund groaned and rolled away from her, his arm sliding from around her waist and leaving her cold.

As soon as they lost contact, the stabbing pain vanished, replaced with only a vague sort of nausea and hazy pain.

The poison. Of course. She wasn't the one in pain. Edmund was.

Jalissa bolted upright and reached for him. "Edmund."

He curled around his stomach, sweat beading on his forehead. But he waved her away. "No, don't touch me. Not yet. The medicine. Please."

Right. Jalissa whirled, so frantic it took her a moment to even focus on the crates around them. Before she could scramble for the packs, Sarya was already there, opening a pack and digging out one of the vials. She handed the vial to Jalissa.

Jalissa drew in a deep breath, trying to steady her hands enough that she did not drop the medicine. She needed to be calm about this. No reason to panic. Not yet.

She uncorked the vial, then lifted Edmund's head. As soon as she touched him, the pain slammed into her once again. This time she was ready for it, and she gritted her teeth and shoved the agony aside. Her hands remained steady as she held the vial of medicine to his lips.

He drank it in a few swallows, wincing as he coughed. "Linshi."

She gently set his head down, handed the empty vial to Sarya, then picked up Edmund's fingers. Already, he was breathing easier, and the stabbing in her middle—and his, presumably—was lessening as the elven healing magic soothed the agony.

After a moment, Edmund pulled his hand free from hers. "No, save your strength. I'll be fine for a while yet."

Jalissa clasped her hands in her lap. Despite the pain, it seemed wrong to sit there, not holding his hand when he was hurting.

Edmund glanced past her toward the doorway. "It's getting light out. Once the train stops at a station to take on more coal and water, we need to get off."

She had been so frantic on waking that she had not noted the ring of light around the door, nor the fact that she could actually see in the gray half-light filling the railcar instead of the inky black it had been when she had fallen asleep.

Jalissa scrubbed her fingers over her dark trousers. "Should we not ride this train as far west as we can?"

"Lord Crest knows we are on this train. While he

might be on our side, somewhat, I don't trust him." Edmund sucked in a breath, his hand clenching over his stomach, before he exhaled slowly. "And if Jimson decides to hunt us down, he will wire to have this train searched. It was the only train leaving Landri during the night. I'd rather switch trains long before then."

She had not thought of that. Apparently she still had a lot to learn about being a spy, especially thinking like a spy on the run.

She had never been hunted before. Not like this, anyway. They had sneaked across Escarland in disguise, but back then they had been the hunters, not the hunted.

Sarya held out a piece of dried meat toward Jalissa. "You should eat, amirah."

Jalissa took the jerky and gnawed at the tough, though flavorful meat.

Edmund refused to eat anything. That was concerning since he normally never skipped breakfast. But she did not push him.

After she finished eating, Jalissa helped Sarya pack their things, including the still slightly damp clothing from the night before, and check the entire railcar to make sure they had not left any trace of their presence. No sense in making it easy for Crown Prince—soon King —Jimson to track them.

Edmund managed to roll into a sitting position, leaning his back against a stack of crates, so they could pack up his bedroll. Even with the elven medicine, his face had a white-gray cast to it, and he simply sat there, eyes shut, arms over his stomach, not a hint of a smile curving his mouth.

After picking up, they had nothing to do but wait. Jalissa sat with her back to the same crate as Edmund, but she did not touch him, as much as she wanted to hold his hand and reassure him—and herself—that he would be all right.

Finally, the train shuddered as it slowed. Sarya crept to the door on the right side of the train and peeked out. "It appears to be a station near a large town."

"Perfect." Edmund gestured toward the left side of the train. "And the other side?"

Sarya crossed the railcar, then peeked out once again. "Smaller huts and dirtier buildings."

Edmund nodded again, this time a hint of his usual smile flicking at the corners of his mouth. "Even better. Can you get that door open, or is it locked from the outside?"

Sarya tugged on the door, frowned, then pressed her hand to the wooden wall. A moment later, the door slid free. "It is not locked now."

Jalissa pushed to her feet and swung her pack onto her back, securing the buckles. She was not sure what kind of feats of athleticism they might have to perform to exit this train—whether jumping off while it was still moving or running from train workers. Perhaps as part of her preparation for this mission, she should have added stretching and exercise. She was naturally graceful as an elf but she had not inherited the fighting skills and agility that Weylind, Melantha, and Farrendel all possessed.

Grimacing, Edmund staggered to his feet, using the crates behind him for support. He reached for his pack, but Sarya snagged it and shouldered it alongside hers. Edmund gave her a sharp look but did not argue.

And that just added to the nausea in Jalissa's stomach. If Edmund had any energy left, he would have argued. He would have been smiling and joking even as they prepared to jump off this train.

Dragging in a breath, Edmund tottered toward the

door. "We'll need to jump out when the train is almost stopped. The engineers will be too busy stopping the train to glance back looking for anyone jumping off. That should give us the time we need to get into the shelter of the town."

Sarya took up a station by the door, peering out.

Jalissa tensed, waiting for the signal to jump. Her heart thudded in her ears, and she scrubbed her palms against her trousers. She could do this.

Beneath her feet, the train vibrated as it slowed. A piercing whistle stabbed into Jalissa's ears as the train announced it was pulling into the station.

With her ears still ringing, Jalissa barely heard the sliding of the door before Sarya leapt from the train.

Jalissa startled at Edmund's slight nudge to her back, then she stepped forward and jumped before giving herself time to think about it.

The drop was only about five feet, and she landed lightly, bending her knees and not even staggering. Apparently she did have a touch of athleticism after all.

Edmund landed next to her, though he fell all the way to his knees, steadying himself with a hand to the ground. He did not immediately push himself upright, his face going yet another shade of white.

They did not have the time for Edmund to rest here. Jalissa grabbed his arm and threw all her strength into hauling him to his feet. He managed to get his feet under him, then they ran, or stumbled as the case might be, toward the ramshackle buildings on the far side of the train tracks.

Sarya led the way, hopping over the rails, scrambling over the rail bed, then darting between the first two shacks on the far side.

Once they were out of sight in an alley between two of

the shacks, Edmund pulled free of Jalissa's grip. He staggered a few feet away, collapsed to his knees, and promptly vomited.

Jalissa squeezed her eyes shut, resisting the urge to plug her ears. Her stomach churned, and she did not think all the nausea was his. While she was not as bothered by vomit as Farrendel was, the sight still made her go queasy.

She shoved the sensation aside and tried to draw in a steadying breath. She could not just leave Edmund to suffer on his own. They were in this together.

Swallowing, she forced herself to cross the alley, take off her pack, and fish out another vial of the elven medicine.

Edmund remained hunched, gasping in breaths, but he seemed to be getting the vomiting under control. He took the medicine without looking at her, downed it in a single swig, then he dug a handkerchief out of his pocket and swiped it over his mouth. He glanced at the handkerchief before folding the dirty side inward and stuffing it back into his pocket. "No blood yet. That's good."

Jalissa swallowed back the lump in her throat. In what world was *No blood yet* considered looking on the bright side?

Oh, right. The world where her husband was poisoned and they were on the run in an enemy kingdom, most likely blamed for poisoning the king. Had King Solan died yet? Had Crown Prince Jimson blamed the poisoning on them?

Edmund used the side of the building to shakily push to his feet. "All right. Here's the plan."

THREE HOURS LATER, Jalissa strolled at Edmund's side, her hand tucked into the crook of his arm. She held on more tightly than was normal, but hopefully no one would realize that she was subtly steadying him.

She wore the dark green, velvet dress that Edmund had told her to pack. Her hair was coiled in a bun at the back of her head, her ears hidden while a hat and veil they had purchased during their stroll through town further obscured her face. She struggled to keep her stride steady as their packs bumped and shifted where they were tied around her hips, giving her skirt the volume that was in style in Mongavaria at the moment.

Edmund wore a green tailored suit—the first time he had worn green while in Mongavaria—and he had picked up a bowler hat from the haberdashers, making him the picture of an elegant Mongavarian gentleman. A monocle and a silver-topped cane completed the look.

Behind them, Sarya trailed in their wake with her head slightly down. Her dress was of good quality, though a touch more plain. A hat and veil obscured her features as well. She was the picture of a lady's companion.

Edmund strolled right past the lines waiting at the ticket counter, as would any pompous lord. The people waiting in line grumbled, but they made room, a sign that their disguise was convincing.

Jalissa kept her head high, her chin tilted in a haughty manner. All she had to do was appear the grand lady. Since Edmund was the only one who could mimic a Mongavarian accent, he had to do all the talking.

At the ticket window, Edmund pulled out a billfold and drew out a wad of Mongavarian currency. More than Jalissa realized he had. He plunked it down. "Three first-class tickets to the Woodlands. I will need two private compartments."

As Edmund had explained as they hid and waited for the passenger train's first departure time, the Woodlands was a luxury resort in the mountains that was a favorite gathering spot for Mongavaria's elite during the summer.

For their purposes, it was not that far from the border. Not to mention, those hunting them would be looking for a group of fugitives. They would not think to look among the Mongavarian nobility, at least not right away.

The man behind the ticket counter bobbed Edmund a polite nod, took his money, quickly punched three tickets, and handed over two brass keys. "You are all set, sir."

Edmund did not nod or thank the man but swept off toward the train, steering Jalissa along with him.

All she wanted to do was run to the train, but she forced herself to glide at Edmund's side. He kept up a steady but unhurried pace, even taking the time to stop and purchase a newspaper.

Finally, they boarded one of the first-class passenger cars. The first half of the train car was a shared parlor and dining area while the back half consisted of a narrow hallway with compartments on either side.

Edmund halted in front of the compartment indicated by the embossed leather tab attached to the key. He handed the other key to Sarya, the number indicating that it was for the next door down. "Get some rest while you can."

Sarya nodded, but she waited in the hall while Edmund unlocked the door and stepped inside his and Jalissa's compartment.

Jalissa followed him and closed the door behind her. The compartment was small, just big enough for a bed built into the wall and piled with velvet blankets, two chairs facing each other, and a small table.

Edmund crossed the room, keeping a hand on the wall or the furniture as if to steady himself, and opened a small door set into the wall. "As I thought. The water closet is shared with Sarya's room."

That would explain why he spent the money on two rooms when they could have squished into one. Though, it likely helped their cover as well. A gentleman would never squish but would instead secure a second room for his wife's traveling companion.

Jalissa sank onto the bed and dug out the hatpin, which had been digging into her scalp, then set the hat and pin aside. "Where did you get all that Mongavarian money?"

Edmund shifted a bit as he shed his hat, jacket, and waistcoat. "You know those times when you had tea with the Mongavarian ladies? It turns out their husbands enjoy a good card game or two. And I am rather excellent at cards."

Jalissa blinked at him, unable to hide the distaste in her tone. "You won it by gambling."

"Well, yes. I started with the small stipend King Solan gave us and grew it from there until I had the amount I estimated we would need for my planned escape route. But I made sure I didn't win too extravagantly and break my empty-headed persona." Edmund shrugged and started unbuttoning his white shirt. "I did bring along some counterfeit Mongavarian money that the Intelligence Office had whipped up. We had the printing press and supplies their spy ring left behind, after all. But I prefer real money instead of fake for our escape if I can help it. We already have enough risks without the risk of being caught passing phony money. The fake money at least pads my wallet so it looks like I have more than I actually do."

Jalissa sighed and shook her head. "You are rather morally shady when you are on one of your missions."

"Spying is a morally shady business." Edmund tossed his shirt onto the chair with his jacket and waistcoat, then kicked off his shoes. "It involves breaking and entering, pawing through someone's personal papers, stealing important documents, lying, and, yes, gambling with money or with my life."

The disguises, the masks, the gleaning of information were all things she could live with.

But the darker side of spying...she was not sure she was comfortable with that.

Jalissa dug her fingers into the thick blankets on the bed. She might not like it, but as long as there were morally shady kingdoms like Mongavaria who would not hesitate to spy on their neighbors and plot assassinations, then men like Edmund would be needed to defend Escarland, Tarenhiel, and Kostaria from them. It was not a pretty job. Not as laudable, perhaps. But it had to be done.

Edmund's face twisted and went white again. "Now, if you need me, I'll..."

He trailed off and raced for the water closet, shutting the door behind him.

The flimsy door did not entirely block the noises from inside, and Jalissa distracted herself by divesting herself of the packs hidden under her skirt and picking up Edmund's discarded clothes. Apparently, he had not been simply getting comfortable, but instead he had taken off his one set of nicer clothes to avoid getting them messy.

After some debate, she slipped into the hallway to

Sarya's room to pass along her pack. Sarya gave her a sympathetic look but did not comment.

Jalissa returned to the room she shared with Edmund and changed into her shirt and trousers once again. They would be on this train for seven hours before they would transfer to another train, which would take them into the mountains to the resort. She might as well be comfortable during that time.

After changing, she lay down on the bed, but she ended up staring at the ceiling. While she had not slept well on the cargo train, she was not yet tired enough to nap during daylight hours.

And Edmund still had not emerged from the water closet. The twisting in Jalissa's stomach was growing worse, even though she was not touching him.

After fetching another vial of elven healing medicine, Jalissa crossed the tiny room and knocked on the door to the water closet. "Edmund? Are you all right?"

"I'm fine." His words were short, clipped.

Clearly not fine.

She tried the handle, but the door was still locked with a sliding bolt.

"No, don't come in." Edmund's voice rose a bit, almost panicked. "This is not...pleasant."

But she could feel deep in her gut how much he was hurting. No way was she just going to ignore him and go away.

Sending her magic into the wood of the door, she moved the wood away from the nails holding the locking bolt in place. The door swung open easily.

Edmund hunched over the commode, just about hugging it. Sweat plastered his hair to his forehead, and his bare back was slick with sweat. A decidedly putrid stench filled the room.

Jalissa stepped inside anyway. She would not flinch away from him, no matter how unpleasant and disgusting this was.

At her entrance, his head hung lower. His mutter held a caustic tone he had never directed at her before. "What's the point of locks when you elves just ignore them?"

The sharpness of his tone hurt, but Jalissa knelt on the floor next to him anyway. Even though his face was mostly hidden from her, she could make out enough to see in his expression something she had never seen on him before.

Humiliation.

She had seen him charming. Nonchalant. Always in control behind that easy-going smile. She had even seen him contrite, back when he had confessed that he was also Elidyr, the elf she had fallen for and thought dead.

But she had never seen him embarrassed quite like this. This was a level of degradation that he did not want her to see.

She rested a hand on his arm, sucking in a breath at the pain that lanced through her. Not just her stomach, but her whole gut twisted as if shredding from the inside out. Still, she pushed it aside, keeping her voice steady. "Two and a half weeks ago, I promised in our Escarlish vows that I would stick by you, for better or worse, in sickness and in health. I am not going anywhere."

He gave a harsh laugh, which turned into a groan. "No man wants his wife to see him like this."

"Well, tough." Jalissa held out the vial of medicine. "Drink this. You need it."

Edmund shook his head, his mouth pressed tight for a long moment, before he spoke between his teeth. "We need to ration it."

"No. Right now, we need you to be functional." Jalissa tightened her grip on his arm, waiting until he half-peeked up at her before she continued. "You are the only one who can speak with a Mongavarian accent. We will use as much healing medicine as it takes to keep you going until the border. Once we are in Escarland, I can get you the rest of the way."

While it might be tempting to ration while they were on the train for the next seven hours, she suspected that it would be better to keep feeding him the healing magic and maintain his current level of pain rather than let him slip far worse and hope the magic was enough to pull him out of it.

"Jalissa..." Edmund drew in a deep breath, as if he was preparing to argue.

"Do you think I am weak?" She did not try to keep the bite from her voice.

"What?" His head snapped up, and he fully met her eyes for the first time since she had entered.

"Do you think I am weak? Do you believe I am less capable than your sister was when she kept Farrendel alive? Or Farrendel when he kept her alive?" Jalissa lifted her chin, holding his gaze.

Did he truly think so little of her? Had she not proven over and over again in the time he had known her how capable she could be? After all, he was the one who had encouraged her to see herself as capable. He had never let her doubt herself or the strength of her magic.

Perhaps that was why his doubt stung so much now.

"No. No. Of course not. I just..." Edmund hung his head again, his gaze swinging away from her. "I just wish it wasn't necessary."

"Well, it is." Jalissa uncorked the vial, then held it out to him again. "Drink."

With trembling fingers, Edmund took the vial and drank. Both of them sat still for long moments, letting the healing magic work.

Finally, Edmund's tension eased, and he breathed out a long sigh.

Since she still rested a hand on his arm, she could feel as the burning pain lessened, though it did not go away entirely as it had before.

He pushed away from the commode, though his shoulders and back remained hunched, his head hanging. "Jalissa, you are not weak." His voice was quieter, softer, than before. "But it seems I am."

She reached for him and pulled him to her, cradling his head against her shoulder. He sagged into her, and she simply held him, gross and sweaty as he was.

Finally, she pressed a light kiss to his hair. "We will get through this."

His nod was more felt than seen, and he did not attempt more of a reply than that.

CHAPTER

NINE

Edmund tried to hide his shakiness as he strolled through the Woodlands, the resort tucked high into the Mongavarian side of the Whitehurst Mountains. At his side, Jalissa kept a firm grip on his elbow, steadying him if he wobbled. He had to use the silver-topped cane more for support than show.

At least he was standing. That was something. It had taken two vials of the elven healing medicine this time to banish the pain and pallor enough that he could pass as a functional person.

The humiliation of that train ride was something he would gladly scrub from his memory—and Jalissa's too, for that matter. He'd spent most of it either napping on the bed or in the water closet.

The train had stopped for longer than usual at one of the towns. The conductor had gone down the hallway, assuring them that the stop was temporary. Edmund guessed that someone had wired ahead to have the cheap seats searched. But as he had hoped, no one bothered the first-class cars, and they had gone on their way.

Once they switched trains at the base of the mountains, their new compartments hadn't included a separate water closet. Instead, the seat of one of the chairs lifted to reveal the commode while its back flipped down into a sink. As if he hadn't been humiliated enough, he had then been unable to be sick in private.

At least Sarya had respectfully remained in the other compartment the whole time so only Jalissa had witnessed his embarrassment.

Now, he attempted to strut through the front lobby of the main lodge of the resort. It was built with massive logs, the décor the kind of rustic elegance that only upscale lodges like this achieved. Elk antlers, mounted deer heads, and bear skins decorated the walls while a massive stone fireplace dominated one wall, surrounded by a plush seating area.

Edmund halted in front of the desk and attempted to stare down his nose at the clerk behind it. Somehow, haughtiness was a lot harder to pull off after the debasement of that train ride. "I would like to secure lodging for myself, my wife, and her lady's maid."

"Do you have a reservation, sir?" The clerk reached for a ledger, fingers poised as if to flip to the correct page.

"I'm afraid not." Edmund leaned against the desk as subtly as he could. The churning was back in his stomach. How long did he have before he succumbed to another vomiting fit?

The clerk frowned, then pulled out another ledger and opened it to the last page. "I'm sorry, sir, but I'm afraid this is a very busy time of year. All our luxury cabins and suites of rooms here in the lodge are full or reserved. But if you would be willing to take two adjoining rooms in one of the lower floors, I can assure you that our staff will work to accommodate any requests you might have and ensure your stay is up to your usual standards of comfort."

If Edmund were truly some stuffy lord, he would probably argue. But right now, he didn't have the energy for the charade. Perhaps the clerk would chalk it up to Edmund being a very easy-going lord. Or that he was a lord down on his luck who was secretly relieved for the excuse to take a cheaper room instead of trying to keep up appearances.

"Yes, that would be acceptable." Edmund gave the clerk a false name, then scrawled a fake signature in the ledger, attempting to change his handwriting as much as possible while he was at it. The shakiness in his fingers helped with that.

Once done, the clerk handed over the keys, already turning away as if prepared to serve the next group in line.

Edmund lingered at the desk. "Would it be possible to arrange for a ride before supper?"

The clerk blinked up at him, and Edmund refused the urge to shift. Yes, Edmund probably looked like death warmed over, and a ride before supper was an unusual request. But surely the clerk wouldn't question him. The elite were known for their quirks.

With a slight shake of his head, the clerk's falsely genial smile returned. "Of course, sir. The stables are down the path to the left. The stablehands will be happy to accommodate you."

Edmund nodded, then steered Jalissa away from the desk. He made a show of climbing the stairs and finding their rooms before they left the lodge once again.

Outside, gravel paths wound from the main lodge to the various separate cabins and facilities. The path to the far left branched off into a forested mountain path, and it was even marked with a helpful wooden sign labeled "Stables" with an arrow.

With each step, his legs felt more numb while the gnawing in his gut grew.

Only a few more minutes, then he could collapse. He just had to secure them horses, and then they could ride away into the mountains. They were so close.

While the morning paper hadn't contained any news about the king's illness, everyone had been gossiping about it by the time they changed trains in the foothills. How long would King Solan hang on? It was closing in on a full day since he was poisoned. While ricin usually killed within two or three days, King Solan had consumed quite a bit of the brandy. If Edmund's symptoms were any indication, Crown Prince Jimson hadn't scrimped on the poison. Not to mention, King Solan was in his seventies. He was fit and healthy, but his age would be a factor.

Either way, they needed to get these horses and disappear into the mountains as soon as possible. If they could be in Escarland by the time King Solan died, all the better.

The pain was growing sharper in his gut. Where were these stables? Why was this path so long?

Of course it was tucked far back into the trees. This was a luxury resort. They couldn't risk the guests smelling the stables from their rooms.

Finally, the stables came into view. A small paddock branched out from it where several horses grazed on the short remnants of grass.

Edmund marched straight to the stables and entered, Jalissa still at his side.

A stablehand had been just inside, forking hay from a pile into a nearby stall. At Edmund's appearance, he straightened, then bobbed a bow. "How may I help you, sir?"

"We would like a ride before supper." Edmund stamped his cane imperiously on the floor.

"Oh, of course, sir." The stablehand hastily leaned his pitchfork against the wall. "I'll go fetch horses for you, if you would like to wait outside."

"No, no, I must pick out my horses myself. Never get the right ones, otherwise." Edmund strolled down the center aisle, staring down his nose at each of the horses. Horses at resorts like this were usually dull, plodding animals who were used to going on short, slow rides. He had to pick his own to ensure he found the three hardiest of the lot.

Three horses that he was planning to steal, since he, Jalissa, and Sarya would ride away into the mountains and not return.

Jalissa was right. This spying and escaping business was rather morally shady.

That dun gelding over there looked like it would do. And that shaggy, brown pony would be perfect. Ponies in general tended to be sturdy as well as have more spunk than horses. As for a third horse, the gray mare in the corner didn't look like much, but she would likely have grit.

Edmund pointed out his choices, ignoring the side-long looks the stablehand was giving him, before he steered Jalissa back outside to wait.

Finally, the stablehand reappeared, leading the dun and the gray mare. He disappeared back into the stables, returning a moment later with the pony.

If he found it odd that Edmund, Jalissa, and Sarya weren't dressed for riding, he didn't question them. That was the power of unquestioned authority that the nobility wore like a fine wool cloak.

The stablehand offered to go along as a guide, but Edmund waved him off, assuring him that they wouldn't be gone long. With one last nod, the stablehand returned to his work.

Edmund would have helped Jalissa mount and arrange her skirts, which hid their packs once again, but he was barely staying upright himself at this point. Sarya helped Jalissa, then him onto horses before she climbed onto the pony.

After a quick glance over the trails branching off from the stable, Edmund chose one that appeared to head deeper into the forest in the general direction they wanted to go. They would have to ride hard to outdistance any well-meaning search parties. When he, Jalissa, and Sarya didn't return as scheduled, the stablehand would raise the alarm, thinking that three wayward guests had gotten themselves lost.

Another stab of guilt accompanied the agony in his gut. A lot of well-meaning and concerned people would probably be out that night, searching for a lost nobleman, his wife, and her lady's maid. It was something he wouldn't have thought twice about before marrying Jalissa.

Morally shady, indeed.

About a half an hour into the ride, a stream crossed their path, flowing underneath a wooden bridge built over it for the guests to ride across.

Instead of going over the bridge, Edmund urged his horse around it. The horse balked at the edge of the stream and tried to veer back onto the bridge. He firmly pulled its head around, though he didn't yank harshly.

Snorting, the horse finally stepped into the stream, prancing a few steps before it settled.

Jalissa's mare plodded along behind Edmund's horse without so much as a pause at the stream. The horse was probably so well trained to follow the horse ahead of it that it would walk right off a cliff if Edmund's horse did it first.

Sarya's pony hesitated at the edge, but as Edmund's and Jalissa's horses strode farther upstream, the pony must have decided that its fear of being left behind was worse than its fear of the stream. It gave a lurching jump over the edge, splashing down and trotting a few steps before Sarya calmed it once again.

The stream meandered its way upward. It wasn't the straightest path to their destination, but the stream was at least free of the dense undergrowth that they would have to fight through if they tried to go in a straight line. Not to mention the rippling water would eventually wash away their tracks. The resort might employ a man who was skilled at tracking to lead the noblemen on hunting expeditions. Hopefully by the time the resort staff thought to get him involved, the stream would have done its work and erased their trail.

Each jolt of the horse's hooves sent waves of pain through Edmund. He hunched over the saddle, thankful when the horse seemed to decide to stick to the stream of its own accord since he barely had the energy left to hang on.

As he ducked under a low-hanging branch, agony lanced through his lower back. Blackness danced at the corners of his vision, and it was all he could do to breathe through it.

Next thing he knew, Jalissa was urging her horse next to his, reaching out and grabbing the reins from him. "We need to rest for a moment. You need more medicine, and Sarya and I would not mind changing into more suitable clothing."

He blinked at her, and it took him far too long to bring her and her long velvet dress into focus. Right. Those dresses would snag on undergrowth and lead trackers right to them. And it couldn't be comfortable for Jalissa, riding with all their packs tried around her waist underneath her voluminous skirt.

It was all he could do to hold on as Jalissa led his horse up the bank and into the forest once again.

When his horse halted, he tried to slide off and ended up falling to a heap on the forest floor.

No matter. It felt rather good just to curl there on the dead leaves and dirt. His head pounded while his tongue felt dry and sticky in his mouth. His internal organs burned, though the urge to vomit was gone for the moment.

"Edmund." Jalissa's light touch rested on his shoulder for a moment, then brushed his forehead.

Then she was pressing one of the cool vials of elven healing medicine to his mouth. He sipped it almost desperately, gladly sinking into the small but soothing relief it provided.

JALISSA GNAWED on a piece of hard bread and a wedge of cheese. A meager meal, but at this point she was grateful they had food.

Across their small camp, Edmund curled on a blanket, sleeping fitfully thanks to the elven medicine easing his pain. Tomorrow, if not tonight, she would need to hold his hand for the deep connection of the heart bond and not let go until they reached an elven healer.

She glanced at Sarya, who was hunched over a map, reading it by the glow of the small elven light she cupped in her hand. "How far are we from the border?"

Sarya gave a small shrug, then folded up the map. "I think we will cross the border early tomorrow afternoon. If my estimates are correct."

They probably were. Sarya was well trained in both her guard duties and the basics of scouting and forest navigation.

Sarya slipped the map into her pack, then met Jalissa's gaze. "You should rest, amirah. I will keep watch."

"All night?" Jalissa glanced between Sarya and Edmund. "You need your rest as well."

"I will set up a magical alert around our camp. It will not act as a shield, but it will wake me if someone or something comes close." As she spoke, Sarya's green magic played around her fingers before she pressed her hand to a nearby tree. "It will allow me to get some rest."

"Do you want my help to put it in place?" Jalissa drew on her own magic.

Sarya shook her head. "No, save your strength. I think you will need it."

Jalissa nodded, then lay down on her bedroll next to Edmund. She could feel the ache in his stomach, but it was not yet intense since she was not touching his skin. He was shivering, and she snuggled closer to him to try to keep him warm. While the nights had been warm in the lower elevations, here in the mountains the night breeze blew in crisp and cold.

If only they dared light a fire. But on a clear night like this, a fire would be seen for miles, drawing both the king's men and well-meaning searchers from the resort straight to them.

Jalissa took Edmund's hand and sucked in a breath at the pain that flowed into her.

But she did not let go. And she was not about to let go, no matter how long their journey took and how far they had to travel.

TEN

J alissa wrapped her arms around Edmund's waist as he swayed and lurched, not strong enough to keep himself upright in the saddle.

At least he was alert enough to grip the saddle and mostly hold himself on the horse. She would not have been strong enough to hold him if he were fully unconscious.

She tucked one hand inside his shirt, resting her fingers against the skin of his stomach to make sure they stayed in contact for the elishina.

They had given Edmund the last of the elven healing medicine a couple of hours ago, and now it was up to Jalissa to keep him alive.

Her body ached, her internal organs burned, and her muscles trembled. If she already felt this bad, how much worse would it get once the last of the elven healing magic wore off?

Sarya held up her hand, then quickly swung off her pony and led it and the gray mare into a thicker section of brush. She hurried to Jalissa and Edmund, grabbing their horse's reins. "Hurry. Stay quiet."

Jalissa gripped Edmund as twigs slapped their faces and clawed at their clothes.

As soon as they were off the semblance of cleared trail they had been following, Sarya pressed her hand to a nearby tree. The brush around them thickened further, completely obscuring them.

Jalissa held her breath, gripping Edmund tighter.

Moments passed, then the faint thudding of horse hooves on the loam echoed through the quiet forest. Clinking accompanied the thuds.

Jalissa peered out of a small gap between the leaves. A patrol of soldiers in leather vests, slim swords at their sides, and muskets in sheaths alongside their saddles, rode along the trail.

No wonder it had been clear. It was a patrol path for the Mongavarian army.

Would they notice the churned leaves left behind on the trail? How observant were these soldiers?

The leader reached the churned leaves and did not pause, leading his band of ten men onward. Perhaps he assumed the path had been disturbed by animals. Or maybe he was simply going through the motions and did not care to pay too close attention.

The riders kept going without a pause, disappearing deeper into the forest heading in the opposite direction.

Jalissa, Sarya, and Edmund waited for a good fifteen minutes before Sarya used her magic to withdraw the concealing thicket.

"We must be getting close to the border." Edmund rested his arm over Jalissa's hand, hunching over the horse's neck. His voice was rough, his words spoken through clenched teeth.

Sarya nodded. "It should only be a mile or so away."

Only a mile until safety.

Sarya took the lead again, and Jalissa gripped Edmund as he steered their horse to follow. She rested her forehead against his back and drew in his remnants of strength, even as she poured her strength into him.

The minutes ticked off in the clomping of the horses' hooves and the beating of Jalissa's heart in time with Edmund's.

"Jalissa, look." Edmund's voice rumbled in his chest beneath her ear.

She lifted her head, blinking before she could bring the tree-covered mountainside into focus.

Ahead, partway down the side of the ridge they were crossing, a blue glow cut through the ground and illuminated the large, six-foot-tall stone that must have been placed there long ago. This side of the rock had words etched into it, though Jalissa was not close enough to read what it said.

Edmund glanced over his shoulder at her, a smile creasing his tight mouth and easing some of the white look to his face. "Hold on."

He urged the horse into a trot, and Jalissa leaned into him as the horse scrambled down the mountainside.

Sarya's sure-footed pony broke into a trot, quickly overtaking, then passing them while the mare gamely kept up in the pony's wake.

Jalissa held her breath as they approached the blue line in the ground. Then, a tingly feeling washed over her, prickling her scalp like a static charge.

Then they were through, and the blue line was behind them.

Jalissa released a breath, and it came out as a choked

sound somewhere between a sob and a laugh. They were in Escarland. They were safe.

Well, safe from Mongavaria, anyway. Edmund was still dying of poison, and they had a long way to go until they reached Aldon and the nearest elf healer.

At the bottom of the ridge, Sarya halted her pony and glanced over her shoulder at them. "Where should we go from here, amir?"

Edmund halted his and Jalissa's horse as well. He attempted to straighten, but he did not manage to get his shoulders fully straight or unhunch his back. "I think there's an army outpost south of here. Or if we keep heading west out of the mountains, there should be a town with a rail line."

"Which one is closer?" Jalissa winced as another, deeper wave of agony flared in her stomach.

Edmund hunched lower over the horse's neck once again, giving a muffled groan. "Not sure. Not sure if the outpost has a rail line yet or not. It is a small one. And they would probably wire Averett, and I'm not sure we want to risk the news of our escape to get back to Mongavaria just yet. Either way, we will not reach the town or the outpost before nightfall."

"Then we will head for the town." Sarya turned the pony in that direction.

Edmund started to also nudge their horse that way, but he fumbled the reins, the leather slipping from his fingers as he groaned.

Agony flared through Jalissa, and she tightened her grip on Edmund's waist. She reached past him and picked up the reins herself. Thankfully, the horse followed Sarya's pony without much urging from Jalissa.

As the hours passed, Edmund grew worse. Jalissa held him tight and concentrated on breathing.

By the time they halted in the twilight of evening, Edmund was sweating and shivering, a constant agony flaring from him into Jalissa. When they halted, Jalissa swung down from the horse first, keeping a grip on his hand. He all but fell off the horse, and it took both Sarya and Jalissa to half-drag him to the bedroll that Sarya laid out.

Since Jalissa could not leave Edmund's side, Sarya was left to set up their camp. Now that they were safely in Escarland, Sarya gathered wood and started a fire. She boiled water from the nearby stream for their drinking water, then set to work creating a soup out of their meager supplies.

Once it was done, she filled a bowl and handed it to Jalissa.

Since she did not dare let go of Edmund's hand, Jalissa rested the bowl on her lap. She squeezed Edmund's fingers. "You should try to eat something."

Edmund curled on his side on his bedroll, his eyes squeezed shut. He gave a slight shake of his head.

Sarya approached and held out one of their tin cups. "This is some of the broth from the soup. Perhaps you can sip it, amir? The hot broth might feel good."

Edmund groaned, but he pushed onto an elbow, then upright, sagging against Jalissa's shoulder. His hand shook as he took the tin cup, and he rested it on his knee rather than bringing it to his mouth right away. "I'll try."

Jalissa attempted to eat her own soup. The hot meal warmed her fingers and toes, but the churning pain coming from Edmund twisted her stomach so much that she could barely choke down more than a few bites.

Edmund tried a sip, gagged, then set the mug aside, shaking his head. He leaned his forehead against Jalissa's shoulder, his weight heavy against her. "I'm sorry, my amirah."

Jalissa set aside her own, mostly uneaten bowl and wrapped both arms around him. "Tomorrow, we will ride out of these mountains, board a train for Aldon, and get you to the healer. Only one more day."

No need to remind either of them that it would be the hardest day. They were out of elven healing magic, and the poison was thoroughly at work in his system. Tomorrow would mark the third day of being poisoned. The day he would have died or already been dead, if not for the healing magic and their heart bond.

Sarya took the tin cup and the bowl without a word, going about cleaning up supper and picketing the horses in a nearby glade for the night.

Edmund sagged away from Jalissa's shoulder to curl onto the bedroll again.

Jalissa curled beside him, tucking her hands underneath his loose shirt against his skin to make sure she did not lose contact with him if she drifted off to sleep.

EDMUND WOKE FROM HIS LIGHT, pained doze and blinked into the darkness of the surrounding forest. Jalissa lay behind him, her arms clutched tight around him with a desperate determination even in sleep.

His whole body hurt in a way he'd never experienced before. Even getting shot hadn't hurt this badly. All his insides burned with a clawing agony.

But worse than his own pain was knowing that Jalissa felt every stab of pain right along with him. He'd seen the taut lines of her face, her pallor, the liquid sheen of pain in her eyes. Even now, she gave a small whimper of pain in her sleep.

And it was killing him just as much as the poison.

How could he keep doing this to her? He was draining the life out of her to stay alive.

He'd gambled that he and Jalissa would form a heart bond, but he hadn't expected it to be like...this. This was far more raw. Painful. Guilt-filled. She was giving so much of herself while he was taking.

And they still had a day to go. He was not sure he could watch Jalissa suffer for yet another day, knowing that he was the one causing her that pain.

What other choice did he have? His only other option was to disentangle himself from Jalissa's grip and crawl away into the forest to die before she or Sarya woke up.

A part of him toyed with the idea far longer than he should. It was not right. It would be giving up, and he knew Jalissa would far rather take the pain of keeping him alive than losing him altogether.

Do you think I am weak? Her accusation from the train speared his head once again.

By contemplating letting go instead of clinging to her in the heart bond, he was treating her as if she was weak. As if he thought she was not strong enough to bear his pain and sustain his life.

He knew better. She was far from weak, and she had proven that over and over on this journey.

No, he was the weak one. Too weak to cling to her when he should. Too weak for letting his mind drift to dark places it shouldn't go.

But knowing what tomorrow would bring still tore through him. How could he knowingly do this to Jalissa?

He'd chosen this, back when he'd calculated that it was

better to drink the poison than give away that he suspected the brandy was poisoned. He'd known the heart bond would take a toll on Jalissa. He'd known this would hurt her.

And he had done it anyway.

What kind of person did that make him? He'd thought he'd been changing. That he had walked away from the lies and deception to marry Jalissa.

But the moment he'd been sent on a mission, he'd gone right back to the lies, the shady morals, the gambles. And Jalissa was the one paying the price. Again.

He had to be done. For real this time. He could not continue to put Jalissa through this. When they returned, he would have to speak with Averett and General Bloam. Even if he ended up with a desk job for the rest of his elven-heart-bond-extended life, he'd do it because it was what was best for Jalissa.

If he survived.

Another stab of pain coiled in his gut, and he stifled his groan. He didn't want to wake Jalissa from the little bit of sleep she'd managed to snatch.

Jalissa stirred, her fingers sliding against his stomach. "Edmund?"

He rested his arm over hers. "Go back to sleep. You need your rest."

She pushed to an elbow and rested a hand on his forehead. "Have you gotten any sleep?"

"Some." He was not sure if what he'd gotten was sleep or slipping into unconsciousness. He laced his fingers with hers, the metal of her wedding ring warm against his finger. "I love you."

He hadn't said that nearly enough. And if he didn't survive tomorrow, he had to make sure she knew that tonight.

She leaned over and kissed his cheek. "I love you too."

He could not rest. Not yet. He rolled, wincing, to better face her. "I'm sorry, Jalissa."

"Shh, you said that already." She lightly ran her fingers through his hair. Even in the faint light of the stars above, her face was drawn in pained lines unlike her normal, ethereal elven beauty. "You should be resting."

Probably. But he needed to say this. Just in case. "I'm not just sorry for the past few days. And the poisoning. And everything you're enduring in the heart bond. But I'm sorry for how this mission turned out. For all the gambles and lies and…"

Jalissa pressed her finger to his lips. "I know, darling. I know." She settled on the bedroll with her head on his shoulder. "We will get through this."

It was becoming their mantra for this trip.

He just had to survive one more day, then he could start sorting out his life so he didn't do this to Jalissa ever again.

But until then, he would have to be smart. They had been so busy fleeing for their lives that they hadn't had much of a chance to talk. Nor had he shared everything he'd learned with Jalissa. Back in Mongavaria, he'd hoped to protect her in case they were caught and interrogated.

But now they were safe across the border in Escarland. And it was becoming clear that he would have to trust her with the information now.

He rested his hands over hers once again. "Jalissa, I need to tell you what I learned in Mongavaria, just in case—"

She shoved to her elbow again, pressing a hand over his mouth. "Do not talk like that. You are going to survive, got it?"

He reached up, hating the way his fingers trembled,

and clasped her hand, pulling it away from his mouth. "I was going to say in case I am unconscious when we reach Aldon."

"Oh." Jalissa eyed him, clearly not believing his lie.

Well, it was only half a lie. He had been about to say in case he died, but it was also important that she knew in case he was unconscious when they arrived.

He grimaced and sucked in a sharp breath at the pain lancing through him, especially in his gut. But the pain was worth it as he tugged Jalissa back down, holding her in his arms against his chest. "I've seen a heart bond in action before. When Essie kept Farrendel alive, she passed out doing it the first two times. But when Essie was shot, Farrendel was awake and alert as he kept her alive. There's a good chance I might not be very alert when we reach Aldon. But you're the elf. You will be, and it's vital that Averett is warned about Princess Bella and that General Bloam is given the information I discovered as soon as possible."

Jalissa tensed in his arms, but she nodded. "All right. I can see your logic, even if I do not like it."

"I know. I don't really like my logic at the moment either." He took her hand and guided it to his shirt. "I have a hidden pocket on the inside of my shirt where I've stashed the papers I took from the king's hidden study. They will need to be given to General Bloam."

Jalissa nodded in his arms once again, then she traced her fingers over the edge of the folded papers beneath the thin layer of fabric. "I will make sure he gets them. Anything else?"

Edmund picked up her hand and kissed her knuckles. "A few more things."

By the time they finished talking, he curled tighter around Jalissa, pain shuddering through his entire body.

Blackness that wasn't caused by the night danced at the edges of his vision, blocking out the light of the stars.

When his voice trailed off as he was forced to grit his teeth and breathe through another wave of pain, Jalissa's fingers rested on his cheek. "Is that all? If it is, you should rest. Morning will come soon enough."

He gave a nod, only then registering that his eyes had already fallen shut of their own accord.

CHAPTER
ELEVEN

J alissa gripped Edmund's hand and listened to the steady clacking of the train wheels as it carried them closer and closer to Aldon.

Edmund curled on the bench, his head on her lap. He trembled in his sleep—or perhaps he was unconscious. He had been slipping in and out of a restless kind of sleep throughout their train ride.

When they had ridden out of the mountains and seen the small town with its single train track ending at the station, Jalissa had nearly cried at the sight.

Sarya had sold the horses, and they had used the money to purchase second-class tickets on the train. It was not as opulent as a first-class ticket, but they at least had a private compartment with two benches facing each other rather than being stuck in the rows of the cheap seats.

Outside the windows, the sun sank lower until it was nothing but an orange glow on the horizon.

The sliding door to their compartment opened, and Sarya stepped inside with a tray of tea. She set the tray on the small, folding table. "You should attempt to drink something, amirah. This honey vanilla chamomile tea should be gentle on your stomach."

Jalissa reached for one of the cups, blew on it, and sipped the tea. Sweetened with honey, just as she preferred. The tea soothed her aching stomach and relaxed her tense muscles. "Linshi."

Sarya sank onto the bench across from her and Edmund. "We are thirty miles out of Aldon."

Thirty miles. So tantalizingly close, yet achingly far at the same time. There would likely be two, if not three more stops before they reached Aldon, and each stop would drag out as passengers disembarked, luggage was removed, and new passengers boarded.

Perhaps they should have made for an army post where they could have used Edmund's status as a prince to get them a train that would not stop except for coal and water all the way to Aldon. Maybe they would have been fortunate enough to get a magically powered train, which could make the trip without stopping.

But that would have risked word of their escape making it back to Mongavaria. Or tipping off Princess Bella in Aldon to step up her plan, whatever it might be.

No, right now Jalissa did not dare trust anyone. Not until she could speak with either Averett or Julien in person. Both of them should be in Aldon. Somehow she would just have to get to them, then everything would be all right.

Edmund shuddered, his breathing going even more ragged.

Keeping her grip on Edmund's fingers with one hand, Jalissa hastily set aside the teacup, then rested her other hand against Edmund's chest, over his heart. The papers he had stuffed into the pocket on the inside of his shirt rubbed against her knuckles. Beneath her fingers, his skin was clammy but his heart beat in a steady rhythm in time with her own. Still alive. Still strong.

Jalissa closed her eyes and rested her head against the back of the bench behind her. She concentrated on the simple acts of breathing in, breathing out, and clinging to Edmund both with her hands and that extra something deep in her chest where she could sense him.

The clacking of the wheels slowed, then the shriek of the train's whistle announced the stop.

One stop down. Only a handful more to go.

Jalissa let herself drift, lulled into a wakeful doze once the train started moving once again.

Another screech of the whistle. Another stop. Another shuddering vibration as the train eased into motion once again.

Finally, Sarya touched Jalissa's shoulder. "We are here, amirah."

Jalissa blinked and pushed upright, her head spinning a bit. Gathering her strength, she shook Edmund. "We are here, darling. Time to wake up."

Edmund's head lolled in her lap, his face a pasty gray-white. Only his heartbeat and the rise and fall of his chest under her fingers reassured her that he was still alive.

She shook him harder. "Edmund, ispamir. Wake up."

Could she and Sarya carry Edmund between them if he did not wake?

His eyes flickered open, his gaze lifting to her, his eyebrows scrunching.

"We have reached Aldon. It is time to get up." Jalissa kept her voice soft, soothing, as she tried to lift his head and upper body to prop him upright. She could barely shift him.

"Aldon?" The word came out so slurred that Jalissa

barely understood what he was saying. But he at least made a weak attempt at swinging his feet off the bench and woozily tipping upright.

As Jalissa steadied him, the train's whistle shrieked into the night while the city lights flashed outside the train window, a blur against the black of the night.

Sarya shouldered their one remaining pack. They had ditched anything that could be abandoned, leaving only a few essentials and Jalissa's orchid still in the pack.

As the train vibrated to a halt, steam whistling, Sarya and Jalissa each tugged one of Edmund's arms over their shoulders.

Jalissa stumbled under his weight, but she forced herself to straighten. She kept a grip on his hand, her insides churning and shredding with each breath.

The deep connection of the heart bond was well and truly in effect now. If she let go of his hand, he would die.

They stepped into the narrow corridor, joining the stream of people heading for the doors and the platform.

Edmund attempted to walk, stumbling as if drunk. He sagged heavily against Jalissa, and her legs shook under his weight.

How were they going to haul him across half of Aldon to the palace?

They did not have a choice. She and Sarya would simply have to grit their teeth and do it.

While a few of their fellow passengers gave them side-long looks, no one focused on them for long, usually looking away and shaking their heads in disgust. With their hair tied back in buns at the back of their heads and their ears hidden, Jalissa and Sarya simply looked like two young women helping a drunken man from the train.

Once they reached the platform, Sarya tugged Jalissa and Edmund across the platform, through the station, then into the dark streets beyond. A few gaslights provided some pools of orange light, but other than that the streets remained cloaked in black and relatively empty at this late hour.

With each step, Jalissa's knees shook under Edmund's weight. Sweat trickled between her shoulder blades, and her heart pounded painfully in her chest and thundered in her ears. Agony stabbed through her gut, growing with each street they walked.

She squeezed her eyes shut, concentrating on breathing and trusting Sarya to guide them.

It would be so easy to sink to her knees right there in the street. All she wanted to do was collapse into tears and beg for someone else just to take over.

Just one more step. She forced her aching leg to shuffle forward. Now another step. Yet another. She gritted her teeth and pushed forward.

In her arms, Edmund's breath caught, his body seizing.

Jalissa stumbled to a halt and frantically tugged at his shirt, pressing her hand to his chest over his heart. Her own breath caught in her chest, her stomach heaving.

Sarya gripped Edmund with one arm, reaching for Jalissa with her other hand. "Amirah?"

No, Jalissa would not give up, and she would not let Edmund go. She was just as strong as Essie or Farrendel or anyone else who had kept their loved one alive with a heart bond.

She would breathe. She would live. And so would Edmund.

With something almost like a scream building in her throat, she sucked in a breath. Then another. In her arms, Edmund's body shuddered as he dragged in another breath.

Jalissa glanced at Sarya and managed a nod, unable to waste the breath to speak.

Her mouth pressed into a tight line, Sarya set out once again.

Once they reached the nicer streets, some of those out and about at this time of night gave them longer, suspicious looks.

Jalissa kept her head down and hoped they could reach the castle before someone called the city guard to report drunks wandering the streets of the elite.

When the tall wall of Winstead Palace loomed before them, Jalissa could have cried. Perhaps a few tears even leaked out of the corners of her eyes as she all but collapsed against it.

While it would have been so much easier to walk to the nearest gate, Edmund had been adamant that they could not alert anyone to their presence. That had been the point of sneaking across the kingdom rather than going up to the nearest telegraph office and wiring his brother.

Jalissa gasped in a breath. "Sarya, can you get us over? I do not have the strength."

Sarya nodded, then pressed her hand to the stones. Her face taut, her magic crawled over the stones, seeking a plant to grow.

Finally, a tree on the other side of the wall bent and reached its branches toward them. The twigs wrapped around them, then lifted all three of them off their feet.

Jalissa clutched Edmund, making sure she did not lose contact with his hand, as the tree whipped them through the air, then set them down heavily on the inside of Winstead Palace's wall. She collapsed onto the ground, her arms clutching Edmund.

Sarya released her magic, falling to her knees with a

gasp. Sweat beaded on her forehead, her face white, a testament to the strain of that much magic had taken on her. Weylind would have been able to work such a feat easily. He could have sent his magic into the entire parkland of Winstead Palace without breaking a sweat.

But neither Sarya nor Jalissa had that much strength of magic. For Sarya, taking control of that one tree had drained her.

After another moment, Sarya pushed to her feet and approached Edmund and Jalissa. She tugged Edmund's arm over her shoulder again, hauling him to his feet, and Jalissa along with him.

Only a few more yards to go. Jalissa stumbled to her feet. They just had to walk through the parkland and somehow find Averett or Julien without alerting anyone else to their presence, especially not Princess Bella or her guards.

Perhaps they should go straight to the elven healer's cottage. Then she could get help for Edmund before sending Sarya to find Edmund's brothers.

Jalissa tottered through the forested parkland, trying to draw as much strength as she could from the trees around her. It took her a moment to place where they were on Winstead Palace's grounds.

They were approaching from the northeast, meaning they would have to more or less pass Winstead Palace to reach either Buckmore Cottage or the healer's cottage. As they neared the palace, music and light poured into the surrounding gardens. Dancing couples whirled past the tall windows of the ballroom.

This was a formal ball. The perfect event for Princess Bella to put her plan into action, whatever that plan happened to be.

Jalissa turned toward the back gardens of the palace,

headed for the private royal gardens where they were not likely to run into guests wandering the paths, as they would in the public gardens extending out from the ball-room. "We need to find Edmund's brothers right away."

Sarya nodded, and Jalissa led them deeper into the gardens. Perhaps she would wait there in the gardens and send Sarya into the palace to find Averett or Julien. It would be difficult to pull them away from the ball without being seen, but surely Sarya...

They turned a corner of the hedge, and Jalissa halted in her tracks.

Julien stood there with his betrothed, the troll warrior Vriska, in his arms. He was leaning toward her, as if about to kiss her.

Jalissa's knees wobbled as she nearly sagged at the sight. They had found one of Edmund's brothers. Even better, he was alone, except for Vriska, and thanks to Mongavaria's poisoning of Kostaria's grain, Vriska had little love for Mongavaria. She could be trusted.

Perhaps Jalissa should feel bad interrupting, but another lance of pain stabbed through her stomach. There was no time to waste. Not for her and Edmund, and not for whatever scheme Princess Bella might be enacting even now.

Jalissa dragged in a breath, trying to speak loud enough that Julien and Vriska would hear her over the noise coming from the ballroom. "Julien, shashon."

Julien started, then pulled away from Vriska. He whirled, his eyes widening, before he raced toward them.

Jalissa could not hold herself upright anymore. She sank to her knees, still gripping Edmund. They were safe now.

CHAPTER TWELVE

J alissa kept her grip on Edmund's hand as Julien carried him toward Buckmore Cottage. Vriska carried Jalissa as easily as a sack of flour, and Jalissa might have been more uncomfortable if she had not been so exhausted. Sarya hurried off to fetch the healer, despite her own exhaustion.

Finally, they entered Buckmore Cottage, reached their room, and Julien laid Edmund down on the bed.

As soon as Vriska set her down, Jalissa scooched closer to Edmund's side, never letting go of his hand. She needed him to wake. They had made it. Edmund should wake to witness it, and he should be the one to report to his brother.

Jalissa rested a hand on Edmund's chest, shoving the last scraps of her strength into him until her head spun with dizziness. "Wake up, darling. We made it, as you said we would."

Edmund groaned and curled tighter on the bed. His eyes fluttered open, more sweat beading on his forehead.

His head tilted toward her, his eyes mere slits as he slurred, "Jalissa...love..."

Tears heated her eyes, and she dabbed at the sweat on his forehead with her sleeve. She had come so close to never hearing his voice again. She leaned closer, whispering so Julien and Vriska would not hear, "And I love you, my ispamir."

That earned her a twitch of a smile, and she pressed a kiss to his clammy forehead.

His fingers squeezed hers, then he tilted his head, taking in the rest of the room. It was a sign of his illness that he had not glanced around in the first moments of waking.

When his gaze turned to Julien and Vriska, Julien rested a hand on Edmund's shoulder. "What happened?"

Edmund's shaky breath filled his chest beneath her hand, his voice weak as he said, "The Mongavarian king is dead. Poisoned by his son. Poisoned me too."

Actually, they did not know for sure if King Solan was dead yet. But given that Jalissa had been keeping Edmund alive through the heart bond for the last day, it was a good guess that he was dead.

"Warn Averett..." Edmund's eyes fluttered closed again, and she could feel him drifting away even as he whispered, "She might be in on it..."

Jalissa tightened her grip on Edmund's hand, her head spinning as she held tight to him in the heart bond. He was fading yet again.

It was as he had predicted. He was in no shape to report to his brother. It was up to her to pass at least some of the information on. She would tell the rest to General Bloam once Julien alerted him, as he surely would as soon as he left here. "We discovered that your Lord Farnley was the smuggler. But it seems he was ignorant of the poison. He has been illegally importing luxury goods from Mongavaria into Escarland ever since Averett introduced the higher tariffs. When merchants in Mongavaria approached him about smuggling grain into Kostaria, he jumped on the chance to double his profits by selling the Escarlish grain from his holdings to Kostaria legally and smuggling Mongavarian grain on the side."

Vriska's knuckles cracked, and Jalissa blinked up at them. She could not manage to focus.

Julien's blurry shape pushed to his feet from where he had been sitting next to the bed. "We need to talk to Averett. Jalissa?"

"Go. We will be fine until the healer arrives." Jalissa tipped her head in the vague direction of the door, the movement adding to the queasiness in her stomach. "There is nothing either of you can do."

They could not heal Edmund or lend her strength. All they could do now was complete Edmund's mission and warn Averett.

Julien's hazy shape gave something that might have been a nod, then he and Vriska jogged out of the room.

Jalissa turned to Edmund, one hand over his heart, the other gripping his hand. She just had to hang onto him for a few more minutes. Then the healer would arrive, and they would be fine.

Her heart thunked in her chest while pain seared through each of her internal organs. She drew in another breath, and Edmund's chest rose beneath her hand. She exhaled, and his chest fell.

The door swung open again, and two blurry shapes hurried inside.

The stuffy tones of the elf healer Nylian rang in the room. "Jalissa Amirah."

"Please heal him. He has been poisoned with ricin."

Jalissa did not budge from her spot beside Edmund.

"So I have been told." Nylian leaned over Edmund, then pressed a green-glowing hand to Edmund's chest next to Jalissa's hand.

Jalissa gasped as soothing relief spread through her, banishing the pain that had become so constant over the past few days.

Sarya sank into the chair beside the bed, her face falling in lines of exhaustion.

Jalissa blinked back her own weariness, black spots dancing at the edge of her vision. But she did not dare give in to sleep—or unconsciousness—until she knew Edmund would be all right.

Nylian continued to pour magic into Edmund, his face lined in concentration. How much magic was it taking to heal Edmund? Would Edmund be all right, or would he find himself permanently weakened as some of the trolls had been after their poisoning?

Finally, Nylian drew his hand away. "He should rest comfortably, for now. I will need to continue healing him as the poison works through his system."

Jalissa nodded, her head still swimming a bit even though she was no longer in pain.

Nylian gave a small bow. "I will return in a few hours."

"Linshi." Jalissa did not even glance up as Nylian left. Instead, she dared to lift her hand from Edmund's chest to sweep some of his sweaty hair from his forehead. With the elven healing magic doing its work inside him, his face had smoothed in peaceful sleep for the first time in days. His chest rose and fell steadily, though she still kept her grip on his hand. If lending her strength to him helped him heal, then she would do it.

A knock sounded on the door a moment before

Edmund's mother peeked into the doorway, a servant behind her. "May I come in?"

"Of course...Macha." The name still felt strange on Jalissa's tongue. She had not called anyone *macha* since her macha had died over a hundred years ago.

But when Edmund's mother had offered that she could call her macha or mother or mama if she wished, Jalissa had tried to make an effort to do just that. It felt good to have a mother again, and Jalissa would not take it for granted, especially since they would only have Edmund's mother with them for a short time, given her human lifespan.

Edmund's mother stepped inside, then gestured to the maid. The maid held out a tray that appeared to have a pitcher of water, glasses, bowls, and a pot of something that wafted aromatic steam into the air. "I brought food and water, if you're hungry or thirsty."

"I would appreciate some water." Jalissa did not think she could stomach food just yet, even though it had been over a day since she had managed to eat anything. It had been far longer since Edmund had food.

Edmund's mother poured her a glass of water, then held it out to Jalissa.

Jalissa's fingers trembled as she took the glass, sloshing the water. Thankfully, the glass had only been about half full, so she did not dump any of it on herself.

She managed a few sips, and the water slid down her throat, as cool and soothing as healing magic. She swallowed another sip before she handed the glass back.

Edmund's mother set the glass on the bedside table, adding the pitcher and other glass as well. She said something to the maid in a low voice, and the maid bobbed a curtsy before carrying the tray with the soup out of the room once again.

Turning to Sarya, Edmund's mother gave her a compassionate look. "You should rest. I will stay with them in case they need anything."

Sarya wearily lifted her head enough to glance at Jalissa.

Jalissa waved to Sarya. "Please rest, Sarya. You got us here. Now take the time to regain your strength. You earned it."

Sarya pushed from the chair, bowed to Jalissa, then all but tottered out of the room. Hopefully she would allow herself the rest she desperately needed. She might not have had to keep Edmund alive with a heart bond, but she had expended all her strength and magic to get the two of them to Winstead Palace and safety. No guard could have done more.

Edmund's mother sank into the chair in Sarya's place. "You should rest as well, sena."

Daughter. It had been so long since her own macha had called her that. The word held so much tender love and care that more tears pricked at the corners of Jalissa's eyes.

But she did not want to break down and cry in front of Edmund's mother. She was not ready for something as personal as that just yet.

Instead, she shook her head and propped herself up in a sitting position against the headboard. "Not yet. I am sure General Bloam will be by shortly. I need to report to him as soon as he arrives."

Edmund's mother nodded, then reached into the bag she wore slung over her shoulder and pulled out a piece of embroidery. "Then I will keep you company until he arrives."

"Linshi." Jalissa would need the company to stay

awake. "Julien and Vriska looked like they have been doing...well."

Jalissa was not about to mention the private, near-kiss she had walked into earlier that night. But hopefully the topic would keep Macha talking so that Jalissa would not have to. She did not have the energy for conversation at the moment.

As she picked up her needle, Edmund's mother filled Jalissa in on everything that had happened here in Escarland while they had been gone, ending with, "We have not received word that Essie and Farrendel have had their baby yet."

Jalissa breathed out a sigh of relief. As bad as Edmund being poisoned and having to flee Mongavaria had been, at least it meant that she and Edmund had returned far earlier than planned, meaning that they would be here when word came about their new niece or nephew.

Another knock came from the door, and this time Averett stood in the doorway. His gaze swept over Edmund, then Jalissa. "I just came to check on the two of you. I can't stay long. I can't risk anyone realizing something is up."

Politics. Jalissa was all too familiar with it.

Macha grimaced and bent over her embroidery. "I assume you told them I retired early."

"Yes. Paige is covering for all of us. Julien and Vriska left to chase down Princess Bella." Averett's gaze dropped to Edmund. "How is he, really? And how are you, Jalissa? I've seen the toll a heart bond takes."

"We are fine now, thanks to Nylian." Jalissa squeezed Edmund's hand, thankful that it was finally warm and no longer clammy as it had been.

"I'm thankful your brother agreed to station elven healers here in Aldon. The healers—and the elf warrior checking the food for poison—have proven to be invaluable tonight."

Jalissa found herself smiling, an expression that felt as good as healing magic after everything she had been through. "You know the healers are only here because of Farrendel. With Farrendel's propensity to get hurt, Weylind no longer wants to risk Farrendel being any farther than a few minutes from an elf healer at all times."

Averett laughed and shook his head. "Weylind might start taking the same precautions for you from now on. You and Edmund have been hurt more often than Essie and Farrendel in the past six months."

True. Jalissa shook her head, her hand straying to Edmund's chest again to reassure herself with the steady beating of his heart. "You mean, Edmund has been injured more. Weylind would probably be fine with that, except for the fact that the elishina means that his injuries affect me."

Their mother pressed her mouth into a tighter line, as if she did not find this conversation amusing in the least. Jalissa would not normally find injuries a laughing matter, but her exhaustion seemed to bring out a sense of morbid humor.

Averett tipped his head back and barked a louder laugh than was strictly necessary. Perhaps he, too, found himself dealing with this situation with misplaced humor.

Edmund stirred, groaning, before he cracked his eyes open. "Avie?"

Averett stepped farther into the room and rested a hand on Edmund's shoulder. "Good to see you awake. You look rather awful."

"Feel pretty awful," Edmund mumbled, his eyes cracked to only half-mast. "Better than I was."

Another knock sounded on the door as General Bloam

halted in the doorway. He bowed to the room. "Your Majesties, Your Highnesses. May I intrude?"

"Of course. I should be getting back before anyone notices I'm gone." Averett squeezed Edmund's shoulder, met Jalissa's gaze with a look that said he would make sure the two of them were well taken care of, and exited the room.

Edmund's mother stood, gathering up her embroidery. "I will check on Sarya and make sure she is resting." With that, she left the room, headed down the hallway toward the room Sarya had claimed when they stayed in Buckmore Cottage.

Edmund patted at his shirt, fumbling for the inner pocket, his brows furrowed. "I have...papers..."

Jalissa reached into Edmund's shirt and pulled out the papers from his hidden pocket. She held them out to General Bloam. "These are for you."

General Bloam unfolded them, then quickly scanned them. "Thank you, Prince Edmund, Princess Jalissa. These give me enough proof to order a raid on Lord Farnley's house and all his properties here in Aldon. Is there anything else I should know tonight? Otherwise, I will let you rest."

"Lord Crest..." Edmund slurred the name, as if he was so tired he could not get his tongue to work properly.

Jalissa squeezed his hand and told General Bloam how they had bargained with Lord Crest. Edmund interjected with short sentences, steering the conversation toward the things he seemed to think General Bloam needed to know as soon as possible.

Somehow, even mostly unconscious and still recovering from nearly dying, Edmund's mind worked enough to sort through all the information they'd gathered to pass along the most important bits. They finished with the news about the few outposts the Mongavarians had managed to set up across the border where they had tapped into the telegraph lines and were sending the news back to Mongavaria.

General Bloam nodded. "Thank you. This information is incredibly valuable. You both have done well, Your Highnesses."

Jalissa nodded, something in her relaxing at his words. She had gotten Edmund back to Escarland, kept him alive, and finished the mission by passing the vital information on to General Bloam. "There is more, but Edmund can fill you in on the rest once he fully wakes."

Edmund gave a weak nod, his eyes falling fully closed once again. Through the heart bond, Jalissa could feel him drifting back to sleep.

"Very well." General Bloam bowed once again. "I will leave you to your rest."

As General Bloam left, Edmund's mother returned, taking her seat and resuming her sewing.

By this point, Jalissa was all too ready to curl next to Edmund and let her eyes fall shut, drifting off into the first restful sleep she had enjoyed for days.

THIRTEEN

E dmund woke and blinked up at the ceiling, enjoying the softness of the mattress beneath him. Jalissa curled next to him, warm against his side, her breaths soft and steady in sleep. Outside the windows, the night remained dark, no signs of dawn. Either it was the same night or he'd slept for a full day. Given that weariness still pressed against him, he guessed it was the former.

"Edmund?" His mother's voice drew his gaze to her where she sat next to the bed. She set her embroidery aside and leaned forward. "How are you feeling?"

"A lot better than I was." He drew in a deep breath and let it out slowly, taking stock of how he felt.

A deep weariness filled him, as if his internal organs were tired. A faint ache remained, but it was nothing compared to the clawing agony he had been suffering.

His mother's mouth took on a quirk that said she knew that his words weren't saying much, considering he had been on the verge of death earlier.

At his side, Jalissa stirred, murmuring his name.

His mother pushed to her feet. "I will give the two of you a few moments."

Edmund smiled, then turned to Jalissa, only vaguely noting the click of the door as his mother left.

Jalissa's fingers fisted in his shirt as she blinked sleepily at him. "Edmund."

"I'm awake. I'm fine." He wrapped his arms around her, ignoring the aching tremble that still filled him, and pulled her close.

He had only hazy impressions of a train and his arms over Jalissa's and Sarya's shoulders. His last clear memory was of the night he'd thought about crawling off into the forest to die. He had told Jalissa the information he'd learned in Mongavaria, hadn't he? And they had passed the information to General Bloam, right? Or was that just a part of his fevered dreams?

He shifted his hand and touched his shirt, his heart stopping when he didn't feel the stiff crackle of paper in his inside pocket. Had he lost the papers in his delirium? Had all of this been for nothing?

Jalissa rested her hand over his. "I gave the papers to General Bloam, and we told him the basic information. You were only partially awake, so I'm not sure how much you remember."

Not a dream, then. He relaxed and pressed a kiss into her hair. "You are amazing, you know that? You are so very strong and brave to keep me alive and get me here."

The words felt too small for what she had done. She was truly breathtaking. He had known she could do it, and yet he had underestimated her—and overestimated himself. He had thought he could handle this mission on his own, keeping her out of it as much as possible.

But in the end, they were a team. And they'd found a new depth to their relationship. He was not always the strong one, nor should he ever dismiss her as weak. Sometimes, he was weak. He was flawed. And when he was weak, she was strong for both of them.

He was the human, and she was the elf. He would have to accept that she was the one strong enough to give so totally of herself to keep him alive. Not just in this moment, but for the centuries to come.

"I was not that brave. I just...I just..." Jalissa's voice trailed off in a strangled sound, then she pressed her face into his shirt. "I just could not let you die." The last word ended in a sob.

He held her close as she sobbed. Through the heart bond, he could feel the waves of stress and terror coming from her. All the emotions she'd shoved aside over the past few days so she could keep him alive and get him to safety.

More than the lingering ache of the poison, his heart stabbed with how much these past few days had cost her.

After several more minutes, her sobs shuddered into sniffs, and she scrubbed her face with her sleeve.

"I'm sorry, Jalissa. So sorry. For all of this." He rubbed her back and brushed hair from her face.

"It is not your fault. You did not ask to be poisoned." Jalissa sniffed. "It is Jimson's."

"Still, I drank that brandy, knowing it was poisoned." Edmund could not help the way his arms tightened around her. "I gambled that you could keep me alive with our heart bond. I—"

She pressed a kiss to his cheek. "And you were right. I kept you alive, and we survived. We made it safely to Winstead Palace, and General Bloam and your brothers are rounding up Lord Farnley and Princess Bella as we speak."

"I still gambled with both our lives, and we nearly lost." Edmund could not bring himself to meet her gaze.

"But we did not." Jalissa rested her head on his shoulder. "We always knew going into Mongavaria in the first place was a gamble. Your gamble got us out of there as safely as possible. You found information that will be vital for keeping Escarland, Tarenhiel, and Kostaria safe for years to come. I think we should count this as a victory. Do not spend more time worrying about what could have been and instead celebrate the fact that we are alive and safe. That is all that matters."

He relaxed his hold until he was gently cradling her instead of clutching her to him so desperately. "How did I get so lucky to marry someone as amazing as you?"

How he loved her. He would not have survived that last mission without her at his side. He would never forget that, no matter how long they both lived thanks to their heart bond.

Edmund tilted his head to glance at her. He hadn't dared kiss her back in Mongavaria. But they were safe now, and there was little chance he'd poison her through a kiss now.

Jalissa met his gaze, then grimaced. She placed a finger against his jaw and tilted his head away from her. "No offense, love, but your breath reeks."

Right. He faced the ceiling again so he wasn't breathing on her. The last time he'd brushed his teeth had been back in Mongavaria on the train before they'd ditched their toothbrushes with all nonessentials in the forest. All that vomiting and nearly dying wouldn't have done his breath any favors. There would be no kissing until he had gotten reacquainted with a toothbrush.

Come to think of it, he likely didn't smell all that great right now either.

Edmund tried to subtly tilt his head and sniff at his armpit. Yep. A shower needed to be the first thing on his agenda as soon as he was strong enough to get up. "I'll be fine now, if you'd like to go into another room to get some rest away from my less-than-pleasant smell."

Jalissa stilled, her body tensing as her fingers fisted in his shirt. "I do not want to leave you. Not yet."

There was an edge to her voice, a hint of the desperation of the past few days still tight in her tone.

They'd have to discuss it eventually. But, for now, he'd rather keep their conversation light. Even if that meant mocking his own stench. "Even though I smell terrible at the moment?"

"Worse than terrible." Jalissa relaxed once again, her fingers loosening to smooth over his shirt. "But I have become rather used to it by this point. I do not smell like a flower garden either at the moment."

He chuckled, making sure he kept his face turned away from her so he didn't laugh barf breath on her. "I really am blessed with the most amazing wife who will stick by my side in sickness and in poisonings, in lack of bathing and teeth brushing. Perhaps I should make a few suggestions to update the standard Escarlish marriage vows."

He didn't have to look at her to know she was rolling her eyes as she laughed. Her laugh turned into a yawn.

"You should rest." He peeked down at her, but he could only see the top of her dark hair without tipping his head toward her. All joking aside, the past few days had been rough. She should get all the rest she could.

"So should you," she murmured against his shoulder as her eyes sank closed again.

"I'll sleep soon, don't worry." Edmund patted her hand as she rested it against his chest, as if to reassure herself that his heart remained beating. "But I've been unconscious for the past day. I think I've gotten plenty of rest lately."

She gave another soft, sleepy laugh.

He just held her, gently rubbing her shoulder until her breathing slowed with sleep.

A light knock came from the door, and his mother peeked inside once again. Her gaze flicked from Jalissa to Edmund, and she kept her voice low. "Nylian is here to check on you."

Edmund nodded. "Send him in."

Nylian strode inside, his expression dour as always. He might pretend he disliked being here in Escarland, but Edmund knew the truth. All the elf healers in Escarland had volunteered for the duty, even Nylian.

The elf healer gave a short bow. "May I, Your Highness?"

"Please." Edmund closed his eyes as Nylian rested his hand on his forehead. A soothing sensation spread through him, easing the lingering ache.

Nylian withdrew his hand. "It seems the poison has mostly worked its way through your system. You will still need healings for the next day or so, but the poison will be gone after that."

"Linshi." Edmund hesitated. How did he go about asking this? "What is my long-term prognosis? Will I experience any lingering effects of the poison?"

Nylian stared down his long nose at him. "I do not believe so. It seems the heart bond prevented any deep, unhealable damage to your internal organs."

Edmund breathed out a sigh and nodded. At least that was one worry he probably could set aside. The strength of his heart bond with Jalissa had saved him. The numerous healing potions he'd taken early in his poisoning had likely helped as well. "Linshi."

The door opened again, and this time Averett hurried inside. "Nylian, you're needed at the palace. Vriska has been injured."

Nylian nodded, bowed to Averett, and glided from the room without another word.

"Is she all right?" Edmund started to push himself to an elbow but stopped when Jalissa stirred.

"A bullet to the shoulder, or so I heard. She should be fine, but General Bloam and his men are bringing her and Julien back now." Averett glanced over him, as if to assure himself that Edmund was all right. "They managed to capture Princess Bella before she escaped."

"Good." Edmund sank back onto the bed. "Send General Bloam to me once he gets back. I'd like to talk strategy now that we have Princess Bella as our hostage. Between the information I brought back and our hostage, we should be able to blackmail the new king of Mongavaria into backing off."

Averett's mouth quirked as he clasped Edmund's shoulder. "I'm glad to see you're fine and back to your usual self. I'll send over General Bloam. And a breath mint."

Of course Averett would say something. Their mother had been far too polite to bring it up.

Edmund waved him off. "Go look after Julien and Vriska. I'm fine." Lacking basic hygiene, but not about to die at least.

Averett gave him a look that said he doubted Edmund's claim. As he passed their mother, he said something to her in a low voice. Even though she frowned, she nodded, then entered the room.

She returned to her seat next to the bed.

Edmund gestured toward the door. "You should look after Julien and Vriska. We're fine."

"No, you aren't. Someone needs to stay here in case you need anything." His mother picked up her embroidery, but her fingers weren't as steady as before. "Paige and Averett will look after Julien and Vriska."

Edmund wished there was something he could say to erase the worry lines from his mother's face. It must be terrible, choosing which son to look after when she would rather be at both of their sides right now, impossible as it was. "I'm sure Averett will send word as soon as there's news."

Mother nodded, then returned to her embroidery. "Unless you wish to rest, perhaps you could tell me about your trip to Mongavaria?"

Edmund settled against the pillow. Despite his exhaustion, he was not yet ready for more sleep. Keeping his voice low to avoid waking Jalissa, he told Mother some about the trip to Mongavaria, leaving out some of the classified bits about his sneaking. And the part about him gambling. And some of the evilness of the new King Jimson.

His mother gave him a sharp look several times, as if to make sure that he knew that she knew that he was leaving parts out. But she didn't question him. She had been a queen, a regent, and a queen mother for too long not to know that there were things her sons couldn't tell her.

Just as Edmund was finishing, Julien stepped into the doorway. A bruise on his face appeared to be already healing, probably thanks to Nylian. His clothes were ripped and bloody, but he stood straight, no signs of pain in his stance. Julien glanced between Edmund and Mother. "May I come in?"

Mother glanced over her shoulder, the lines of her face easing. "Please, take my seat. I could use a moment anyway." She stood and walked across the room, halting next to Julien. She rested a hand on his arm. "I'm glad you and Vriska are all right."

Julien shrugged, giving a self-deprecating smile. "Vriska took the brunt of it. I just played the part of helpless prince until it was the right time to fight back."

"Not a role you play often." Edmund kept his tone light, despite his relief at seeing Julien alive and well. If Julien was here, then Vriska must be fine as well. Julien wouldn't leave her side otherwise.

As Edmund wouldn't leave Jalissa if she were the one injured. She still curled against his side, sleeping soundly.

Mother gave Julien a quick hug before she left the room.

Julien settled into the chair she'd vacated. "You're looking better."

"I'm feeling better. Elven healing magic really is remarkable." Edmund couldn't help but glance at Jalissa. Even in sleep, her face had an ethereal beauty, made even more beautiful by the determined, strong woman she was underneath. "She is remarkable. I wouldn't have survived, if not for our heart bond."

Jalissa gave a small sigh in her sleep, shifting, but she didn't wake. Lines of weariness still etched across her face, testament to the toll that keeping him alive had taken on her.

"I'm glad you have her. And that you've formed a heart bond." Julien leaned against the back of his chair, exhausted lines etched around his eyes. He looked like he'd had quite the evening.

Edmund held Jalissa closer, thinking of all the pain Jalissa had suffered because of the heart bond. Even now, she had succumbed to the sleep of exhaustion because of him. "It's different than I thought it would be. I wanted a heart bond and yet...it's painful, knowing that I'm taking so much from her. She's giving me her years willingly, and yet I don't like knowing the extent of the sacrifice she's making for me."

Julien remained silent, just looking at him with that steady gaze of his.

For some reason, Edmund found himself still talking, telling his brother things he hadn't voiced to anyone. Things he'd barely acknowledged even to himself. "Then fleeing across Mongavaria, I saw the way keeping me alive was killing her. There was a moment when she dozed off that I thought about letting go, crawling away before she had a chance to wake, and dying before I hurt her any more. I didn't do it, but I thought about it. It's not a part of the heart bond that Essie and Farrendel talk about."

Edmund snapped his mouth shut. He couldn't believe he was telling Julien this.

But he had to tell someone. Had to process the last few days and what it meant for his and Jalissa's relationship.

"No." Julien rested his elbows on his knees. "But the two of them both know that the years he'll live with Essie will be far longer than however long he would have lived without her. But Jalissa..."

"Jalissa would have lived a long, full life if she'd married an elf instead of me." Edmund stared at the ceiling, unable to face either Julien or Jalissa, even if she was sleeping. This admission hurt. "I knew it, but I wouldn't let myself dwell on it. Until the past few days forced me to face it."

Could he spend the rest of his life taking from Jalissa like this? Stealing her years to live a longer life himself?

How many more times would he ask her to keep him alive because of a crazy gamble he'd made?

"Forming the heart bond was her choice as it was yours. From what I've gathered, you both need to love for it to work." When Edmund glanced at him, Julien was still leaning forward, rubbing a thumb over his palm. "You aren't stealing from her but accepting what she is giving willingly. Feeling guilty would be disrespecting her choice."

It felt like Julien was talking to himself just as much as to Edmund.

Edmund let Julien's words sink into him. He shouldn't feel guilty about the heart bond nor about Jalissa giving him her years. They had talked about it when they started courting. She was doing it perfectly willingly. She had no regrets, so he should have none either.

As for gambling with his life—and thus hers—that was a flaw he'd have to work on in himself. This time, he hadn't had much of a choice. But going forward, he would have a choice. He had a choice to take a step back from the spy world and focus on Jalissa and the family they were building. He didn't know what that would look like yet, but he would have to change, for Jalissa's sake.

"I know." He let himself smile a bit, even if his guilt wasn't entirely gone just yet. "When it's your turn to get married, I don't recommend heading off to an enemy kingdom as part of your honeymoon. Just stick to a nice, calm honeymoon on the beach or wherever your troll wife prefers."

"I think she prefers battles." Julien's grin held every sappy, totally-in-love emotion Edmund had hoped for his brother when he'd headed off to Kostaria.

"Ah, well in that case, I know who to volunteer for the next mission to Mongavaria." Edmund let himself grin, pushing aside his worries for now.

"Thanks, but no thanks." Julien grimaced.

Edmund shared that sentiment. He would be just fine if he never returned to Mongavaria either.

"We should have known the princess was going to make trouble." Edmund shook his head against the pillow, a wry smile tugging at his mouth. He'd just about rolled his eyes when he'd first heard Princess Bella's full name. "Her full name is Princess Bella Gertrude Donna Yenene of the Royal House of Ghentren."

Julien blinked at him, his expression blank. "So?"

"Bella. Donna. Belladonna is a poison. I don't think that was a coincidence." And come to think of it, Jimson was probably named after jimsonweed, which was also a poisonous plant. It seemed being named after poisons was a thing for the Mongavarian royal family. Perhaps Princess Bella would name her firstborn son Ricin, since she liked that particular poison so much.

"Her father named her after a poison?" Now Julien was shaking his head.

"Let's just say I think we're going to need to negotiate for an elf to be permanently stationed here at Winstead Palace to check for poisons. At least, plant-based poisons like ricin or belladonna." Edmund grimaced, just thinking about the full variety of poisons and venoms the Mongavarians could use, if they decided to get creative. "And the Intelligence Office will need to step up our monitoring for Mongavarian interference. But if we play this right, we'll be able to stop any active attacks, at least for a while."

Hopefully Lord Crest held the power he seemed to

think he did. Even Edmund could use a little peace and quiet for a while.

Julien lapsed into silence for a moment, his head bowed. Then he straightened his shoulders, raised his head, and set a tin of mints on the table next to Edmund's side of the bed. "Averett sent this over for you."

Edmund shook his head. Trust Averett to remember the breath mints even with everything else going on.

Julien reached into his pocket again, then set a glass bottle of cologne next to the mints. The same kind of cologne Edmund used whenever he didn't have time to shower after visiting a tavern and needed to quickly cover up the stench of cigar smoke and cheap liquor. "You might find this helpful."

"I feel like you and Averett are trying to tell me something." Edmund would have reached for the cologne, but he doubted even that particular cologne would be strong enough to cut the smell. Not unless he doused himself with so much cologne that the reek would be just as overpowering as his current stench.

Julien crossed his arms, his mouth twitching beneath the stern frown he was attempting to hold in place. "Your hygiene took a turn for the worse while you were in Mongavaria. I'm not sure how your wife is putting up with you at the moment."

She was only putting up with him because she was too terrified to leave him, but Edmund wasn't going to admit that to Julien. Instead, he gestured at Julien's blood-spattered and sweat-stained shirt with his free hand. "You aren't looking all too clean either. You might want to think about a bath before Vriska sees you. You don't want to scare her off before you have a chance to tie the knot."

Julien just grinned and tipped his chair back on two legs in a manner that he'd never dare to do while their mother was in the room. "Vriska likes me a bit bloody and sweaty from battle."

Edmund opened his mouth, then realized he didn't have a comeback for that one. Vriska was a troll. She probably wasn't too turned off by the blood and sweat of a good fight. "In that case, go bother her and let me sleep."

Julien grinned, easing his chair back onto all four legs. "Fine, fine. I'll leave you to rest. Glad you're safe."

"You too." Edmund would have to get the full story of what went down that night out of someone. Once he'd had a good long rest. And a shower. A very long, very hot shower.

After clapping Edmund on the shoulder one last time, Julien strode from the room.

As soon as his brother was gone, Edmund snatched the tin of mints from the table, opened the lid, and popped a mint in his mouth, sighing in relief as the fresh, peppermint taste washed over his tongue.

Barf breath really was no joke.

FOURTEEN

E dmund sprawled in one of the comfortable chairs in the parlor of Buckmore Cottage. It was strangely quiet here without Essie and Farrendel.

Still, he closed his eyes and let the silence soak into him. It had taken some doing to convince Jalissa to leave his side when she was invited to spend time with Paige and Vriska that afternoon.

It was the first time they had been apart since all of this started, and it had been harder than expected. Perhaps they had both suffered more trauma than they realized. She'd only left because he'd told her he'd needed the rest after overextending himself to go to Winstead Palace for breakfast with his family that morning.

A knock came from the outer door a moment before it opened and Julien's voice called down the hall, "Edmund?"

"In here." Edmund didn't bother to get up, staying sprawled where he was.

Julien strode into the room, halting just inside. He shifted, clutching a newspaper in his fist. "I'm not interrupting your rest, am I?"

"I was resting, not sleeping." Edmund gestured to the couch across from him. Julien had a look about him, as if he wanted to discuss something. "Any word from Mongavaria yet? Or Essie and Farrendel?"

"No baby yet. And nothing from Mongavaria yet either. You know better than me that getting word to Lord Crest secretly is going to take a bit of time." Julien curled and uncurled a newspaper in his hand. "That's not what I came to talk about. It's this."

He spread the newspaper on the coffee table between them.

Edmund shoved himself a little more upright, focusing on the newspaper.

The header announced that it was one of the gossip rags, the ones that they usually avoided reading since they were so filled with lies and vitriol.

But he could immediately see why this one had caught Julien's attention. A large, line-drawn cartoon filled a quarter of the front page underneath the heading, "Prince Julien's Troll Bride."

The cartoon depicted a lumpy, rock-like figure wearing a ball gown. She carried a hunk of meat in one hand, a club in the other.

The sight turned Edmund's stomach. "I'm so sorry, Julien. I trust Vriska hasn't seen this yet?"

"No, and there's no way I'm letting her see this if I can help it. Averett is already talking with our lawyers, discussing if we can sue the paper for libel." Julien stared down at the paper, his expression twisting, his eyes both hard and pained. "But they are unsure if going to court would be advisable. Normally the royal family wouldn't respond, but this time if we don't, the newspapers will take that as permission to continue publishing articles like this. Today, it is the gossip rags. Tomorrow, it could be more reputable papers like the *Aldon Times*. If we are going to stop them from continuing to harass Vriska like this, then we need to take a firm stance now and stick to it."

Edmund nodded, his stomach still churning. "It's a prejudicial lie. This isn't who Vriska is. You know it. The family knows it. I'm sure Vriska knows it."

"I'm not sure even suing will be enough." The pain in Julien's eyes deepened, and there was something almost dead inside his gaze when he looked up at Edmund. "You didn't hear the ladies of the court last night. They said such disgusting things, and they didn't care who over-heard them. Vriska was nearly in tears over some of the things said about her last night, and this is Vriska. She rarely cries."

Last night, Julien had remained silent to let Edmund pour out his thoughts. Now it was Edmund's turn to sit there and listen while Julien talked it out.

Julien shook his head and glared at the newspaper. "They're never going to quit harassing her. Vriska is a troll. She isn't traditionally beautiful. She's going to be constantly compared to Jalissa, Essie, and Paige, no matter how unfair and horrible it is to pit them against each other in the press."

Edmund resisted the urge to wince. It wouldn't be fair. Vriska was an amazing woman and so perfect for Julien, but when it came to what the Escarlish press and nobility would consider beauty, she would fall short. Especially compared to Paige—who had years of practice at the regal bearing of a queen—and Jalissa—who was consid-ered exceptionally beautiful even among elves—or Essie

—who had a sense of style and charm that came naturally to her.

The prejudice against trolls was just too strong. It was even in the name *troll*. An insult that the trolls had adopted as their own when they no longer wanted to be called mountain elves.

Perhaps they should re-brand themselves as mountain elves once again, though Edmund couldn't see Rharreth and the trolls doing that. They had formed their own identity so apart from the forest elves that they wouldn't want to go back to claiming that old kinship.

Even calling themselves mountain elves probably wouldn't be enough regardless. This was going to get vicious, and Edmund wasn't sure there was anything that any of them, even Averett, could do to stop it.

It saddened and sickened him, and he could see that same sick disgust twisting Julien's face as he crumpled the paper and tossed it into the fireplace. The low coals of the fire flared to life as they caught the paper, burning it to ash within moments.

He could not imagine the pain Julien was facing, seeing his bride-to-be targeted like this. A physical attack would have been easier to handle. Then Julien could use his strength to defend her. But there would be nothing he could do about this emotional attack.

Edmund leaned forward, waiting until Julien met his gaze. "Whether the lawyers think we should sue or not, the family will stand by you and Vriska."

"I know. And last night, I thought that would be enough." Julien shook his head, then sighed and hung his head. "But now I see that it won't. Vriska could bend over backwards to please them, and it wouldn't be enough. And, yes, we appreciate that the family will stand by us, but enduring this disgusting discrimination will kill Vriska."

Edmund opened his mouth, then slowly closed it. He honestly didn't know what to say. He didn't want to just give a bland reassurance and dismiss Julien's concerns. For they were very real, and Julien had every reason to be worried.

And it wasn't something Edmund had faced. Jalissa was the perfect elven princess, navigating both the elven and Escarlish courts with ease. The only bad things the press had ever been able to say about her was that she seemed cold, she was too perfect, and she was an elf.

Julien heaved a deep breath. "I've come to the decision that Vriska and I need to pull back from royal duties in Escarland as much as possible. We'll show up for full family events, of course. And we want to be there for anything involving Kostaria or the troll community forming in Aldon. But other than that, we can't. I can't. So I'm asking..." Julien's voice cracked and trailed off, as if he was gathering his thoughts through the emotion choking him.

"You're asking that I stop gallivanting all over the place and take one for the family." Edmund let his mouth quirk, trying to lighten the mood a bit. "I owe you after all the times you covered for me over the past few years while I was doing my spy stuff."

"Yes. Exactly." Julien's grin twitched in return, banishing some of the pain in his gaze. His grin faded after just a moment. "So...will you? I know it's a lot to ask. I know you and Jalissa probably want to split your time between Escarland and Tarenhiel, and there's always ambassador duties, and—"

"Yes, we'll take over as much as we can." Edmund's own grin faded, and now he was the one looking away.

"Yes, we'll split our time between our kingdoms, but when we aren't here, Essie might be willing to take on some duties. After this last mission, I was already planning to ask Averett that he never send us on a mission like that again if it can be helped. It just isn't good for Jalissa and me."

He was probably going to tell General Bloam that he needed to quit being a spy entirely. He didn't like the person he became when he was a spy. Jalissa was right that spying made him go morally shady.

Julien held his gaze for a moment, then nodded as if he understood what Edmund wasn't saying, if only a little bit. "Thank you. I know you and Jalissa don't exactly like court functions."

"But we're good at them." Edmund felt his mouth twist with something like a wry grimace. The court functions would be less fun when he and Jalissa were just attending as prince and princess without the hidden agenda of searching out spies or traitors or smugglers as they had been doing over the past six months. But he and Jalissa wouldn't be emotionally wrecked by it the way Vriska would. "And it's only for a decade or two until Bertie and Finn are grown. Once they are of age, and especially once they marry and have kids of their own, the rest of us will matter less. The farther all of us get pushed down the line of succession, the less the court will want us around."

"I'm already counting down the years until then." Julien gave a wry grimace of his own. "It will be nice when Vriska and I can concentrate on building the defenses of the alliance without the pressures of the court hanging over our heads."

Edmund and Jalissa would likely never be entirely free of court life. While they would get pushed out of the

Escarlish line of succession sooner rather than later, Jalissa would remain in the Tarenhieli line of succession for centuries yet, given how unprolific elves tended to be. Right now, with Melantha removed from succession due to being the queen of another kingdom, Jalissa was third in line after Ryfon and Brina.

But that was all right. Edmund and Jalissa could handle being a part of a royal court for centuries to come. Julien and Vriska could not.

Edmund sank against the back of his chair, exhaustion weighing down his limbs once again. He should not be this tired. Sure, he was recovering from being poisoned and nearly dying, but it was still frustrating. All he'd done was walk to breakfast and back, and then he'd napped for hours. After lunch, it had felt like a great feat to walk from his bedroom to the parlor.

Julien pushed to his feet. "I should let you rest. Thanks for being willing to take my place in court. It means a lot."

"We're family. We do what we have to do to help each other survive royal life." Edmund gestured to him, but he let his head sink against the back of his seat. Once Julien left, he might close his eyes for a few minutes.

Just a few minutes.

Edmund didn't hear Julien leave. He must have dozed off because the next thing he knew, Jalissa's gentle fingers traced his cheek.

He tilted his head and kissed her fingers, blinking up at her.

She smiled. "You should be resting."

"I was." He reached for her, tugging her onto his lap. "Until you woke me up."

She laughed, squirming until she found a more

comfortable spot against him. "Somehow, I do not think you minded."

"No, not in the least." He cradled her against him. "How was your afternoon?"

"I am going to enjoy having Vriska for a sister. She is refreshingly blunt. She reminds me of Melantha, in a way." Jalissa rested her head against Edmund's shoulder.

"Well, your sister always was meant to be the queen of the trolls." Edmund leaned his head against the chair once again. "Julien was here earlier. He asked if we could take over most of his royal duties from now on. I told him we would whenever we were in Escarland."

Jalissa's mouth twisted with a hint of a frown, but she nodded against him. "We were covering most of his duties anyway this past summer."

"I'm going to ask Averett that he no longer send us out as ambassadors, except in the direst of circumstances. No more missions like the one we just came from." Edmund forced himself to relax once he realized his arms had tightened around her.

"Good." Jalissa gave a small shudder.

He drew in a deep breath, preparing himself for the next part. "And I'm going to tell General Bloam that I resign from the Intelligence Office."

"What?" Jalissa shoved upright, facing him. "No, you cannot do that."

He stared at her. He'd thought she'd be happy with that, not shocked. "Why not? I thought you would want me to stop spying."

"Yes. And no." Jalissa sighed, then rested her hand against his cheek. "Yes, I am not pleased with some of your decisions as a spy. But I also know you. If you retire from spy work to simply become a prince of the court, you will die of boredom. Do not think I was oblivious to how bored you were at Lethorel."

He chuckled and tilted his head enough to press a light kiss against her fingers before he murmured, "You noticed that, did you?"

"It was hard to miss." Jalissa framed his face with both of her hands and met his gaze, her dark eyes twinkling, before she leaned closer as if imparting a secret. "You, my ispamir, were an absolute pest."

Maybe pestering Weylind hadn't been the most mature way to deal with his boredom.

Perhaps Jalissa had a point. He needed something to keep his mind occupied, otherwise he started playing mind games on what was supposed to be a relaxing family vacation.

"Linshi, my amirah." He tugged Jalissa closer again. "In that case, I'll talk to General Bloam and reiterate that I'd prefer to no longer be sent into the field. What we were doing this past summer was not so bad. Perhaps I could be assigned to counterintelligence rather than active intelligence gathering."

"I enjoyed working at your side for that." Jalissa looped her arms around his neck.

"I would like that." Edmund gathered her into his arms and kissed her.

Two days later, Edmund strolled toward Averett's office, pretending that his legs weren't already aching from the walk from Buckmore Cottage to Winstead Palace.

The door was cracked open, an invitation to enter. He strode inside and promptly sank into his favorite chair facing the desk with his back to the wall.

Averett glanced up from his stack of paperwork, a grin already on his face. At the front of his desk, prominently displayed, was the most grotesque lamp Edmund had ever seen. It was made of twining branches shaped like a screaming human face. It was lit from within by an elven light.

"Where did you get that?" Edmund jabbed a finger at the lamp. He couldn't remember seeing it before—and he certainly would have remembered something like that. It definitely wasn't his brother's usual taste in décor.

"From Weylind." Averett's grin widened. "I lost a wager."

There was something about his grin, the look in his eyes, and the way he said it. What had this wager been about? What would he and Weylind have had a friendly bet over?

Essie and Farrendel's baby. That had to be it. Weylind must have sent word this morning, and Averett was just waiting for the official telegram from Essie and Farrendel before he told anyone else.

Edmund suppressed his own smirk to avoid letting Averett know that he knew. "You sent for me?"

"I received a message from Lord Crest. He is prepared on his end to set up our meeting with King Jimson." Averett's grin dimmed only a little bit as he spoke about Mongavaria. "I just sent off the official message to King Jimson requesting a parley."

"I'm sure he will get back to you quickly. We are holding his daughter hostage, after all." Edmund sprawled in the chair, hoping he looked casual instead of as if he was trying to ease his aching muscles. Recovering from being poisoned was worse than being shot. At least when he'd been shot, only his chest hurt. With the poison, his whole body had a dull ache. Nylian had assured him that the ache would go away in a few days.

"Yes." Averett shrugged, then rested his elbows on his desk. "Julien mentioned that you and Jalissa are going to continue taking over his court duties for the foreseeable future. I think it's a good idea, if you both are up for it."

"We are." Edmund met Averett's gaze. "And I'd rather not get sent on any more ambassador-spy missions if you can help it. I know you didn't have much of a choice to send us to Mongavaria, but I have Jalissa to think of now."

"I understand. Hopefully, no more missions like that will be necessary." Averett shrugged, a twist to his mouth. "Besides, Parliament has been rather unhappy that I've been doing so much of the negotiating with foreign powers lately. I'm sure they'll be happy to take over missions to some of our neighboring kingdoms."

Edmund nodded. Averett had been holding that power close, knowing that as soon as he gave it to Parliament, he would never get it back. It was part of the tug and pull that had been going on for centuries as the Parliament slowly took on more power. Perhaps by the time Edmund was an old man several centuries from now, the Escarlish king would be no more than a figurehead.

Until that day, Averett preferred to keep a balance of powers between Parliament and his throne so that neither of them grew too powerful.

Still, many of the neighboring kingdoms were ruled by oligarchies or an elected senate. They would probably respond better to an emissary sent by Parliament than someone from the royal family.

A knock came from the doorway, and Edmund turned to see a footman standing there. "Your Majesty, Your

Highness. The Queen Mother has received a telegram from Tarenhiel and has requested the presence of both of you in her personal parlor."

"Tell her we'll be right there." Averett pushed to his feet, that broad grin back on his face.

As the footman hurried down the corridor, Edmund eased upright. He tried to pretend he was steady on his feet as he fell into step with Averett. "Do you know something the rest of us don't?"

"Maybe." Averett's grin just about split his face.

Yep, Essie and Farrendel had definitely had their baby.

As soon as they reached their mother's parlor, Edmund sank into a seat on the couch next to Jalissa and took her hand. She was already smiling as well.

Across the way, Paige perched on the edge of her seat, and Averett stood behind her chair, resting his hands lightly on her shoulders Julien and Vriska both stood near the wall, Julien's beard doing little to hide his grin.

They had all likely guessed what this was about. It was the news they had all been waiting for.

Their mother sat in her favorite chair beside the fireplace, a wide smile on her own face and sparkling in her eyes. She held up the telegram. "As you have all guessed, Essie and Farrendel had their baby this morning."

Edmund wrapped his arm around Jalissa's shoulders as everyone else clapped or cheered or burst into questions.

Mother held up her hand for silence, then continued. "They are happy to announce they have a son who they've named Fieran. Both Fieran and Essie are healthy and doing well."

Then Farrendel had gotten his pick of name after all. Fieran meant *Fire hair* in elvish. It seemed Fieran must have inherited Essie's red hair.

Another nephew. Edmund couldn't wait until he could meet him.

Averett glanced around at all of them. "I know everyone probably wants to hop the first train to Tarenhiel to meet our new nephew, but let's give Farrendel, Essie, and Fieran a few days to settle in before all of us descend. If our negotiations with Mongavaria go as planned, we'll be headed north in a few days anyway."

Edmund nodded, squeezing Jalissa's fingers.

She was nodding too, though something in her expression had fallen, as if she had been hoping to leave right away.

He leaned over so he could whisper in her ear. "I know. I'm disappointed too. But Averett is right that we should give Farrendel and Essie time and space."

Jalissa nodded again, her expression easing. "I just cannot wait to see Farrendel as a father."

"Me too." Edmund rubbed his thumb over the back of her hand. As he looked at her, it wasn't his new nephew that he was thinking about.

No, he was thinking about holding his own half-elf, half-human baby and feeling the wonder of being a father fill his chest.

Jalissa was an elf, and elves often struggled to have children. As much as he dreamed of that day, he would more than likely have to be patient. If they had children at all.

No need to borrow troubles. Not yet.

For now, he would simply enjoy having her as his wife.

CHAPTER
FIFTEEN

E dmund sat in his favorite chair in the parlor. He'd pulled the chair up to the desk so that he could fill out his report for the Intelligence Office so that he could give it to General Bloam before leaving for Tarenhiel tomorrow.

In his report, he tried to write down every observation and detail about Mongavaria that he could remember, no matter how small. On another page, he wrote down his conclusions. That way, analysts could go through his notes, come to their own conclusions, then compare theirs with his to make sure their hunches lined up.

With a knock, General Bloam entered the parlor and bowed. "Edmund, may I come in?"

"Of course." Edmund straightened the papers, then shifted his chair to face the room instead of the desk. "I'm still putting together my reports."

"I'd rather you were thorough rather than hurry and miss something." General Bloam took a seat across from him. "I received word from Alvin and James. They have worked their way into positions as planned."

Edmund breathed out a sigh and nodded. Even he hadn't been told where Alvin and James planned to work undercover. But wherever they were, it was good to know that they hadn't been caught by King Jimson.

"As for why I'm here." General Bloam eyed Edmund. "I'd like to talk about your career."

Edmund tensed, his fingers clenching on the armrests. He'd submitted his request to General Bloam yesterday, asking to be permanently assigned to a desk job or to counterintelligence. Surely General Bloam wouldn't ignore his request?

"I received your request." General Bloam leaned back in his seat, studying Edmund with his sharp gaze. "You provided compelling reasons to keep you and Jalissa inside the alliance kingdoms from now on. As you pointed out, you have burned your cover in Mongavaria, at least for a few generations. Given the rumors coming from Mongavaria about your role in their king's death—rumors our ambassadors have been instructed to categorically refute—other kingdoms are going to be wary of having you as an ambassador, even if they don't believe you actually killed the Mongavarian king. While you are very skilled in the field, you are still a prince. We shouldn't risk your safety unless it's absolutely necessary."

"I will be an Escarlish prince in name only in a decade or two." Edmund crossed his arms. He wasn't sure why he was arguing since it sounded like General Bloam intended to give him exactly what he had requested.

"True, but you will still be married to a princess of the elves. Even if you wish to be reckless with your life, your wife's safety remains important for the strength of the alliance." General Bloam's mouth twitched, as if he knew he'd presented an argument Edmund couldn't debate.

He gave a self-deprecating smile and tipped a nod. General Bloam had him there. "So you will acquiesce to my request and assign me to a desk?"

He was hoping it would be in counterintelligence. That would give him the chance to go out in the field occasionally, perhaps with Jalissa at his side, as they had been doing that past summer when they tracked down the remnants of the Mongavarian spy network and sniffed out the Escarlish nobility who had smuggling ties to Mongavaria.

But he would be all right if he was assigned as an analyst for Mongavaria. It would mean more paperwork, which wasn't his favorite thing, but he might be allowed to take some of the less sensitive information with him when he traveled to Tarenhiel to work from there.

"Yes. And no." General Bloam's mouth curved into a bigger smile that held a sharp, cunning edge to it.

Oh, this was going to be good, if General Bloam was giving him that smile. Edmund held his breath, his heart thumping harder. General Bloam had smiled just like that when he'd realized how gifted Edmund was in elvish and decided to send him as a spy into Tarenhiel. That moment had started the greatest adventure of Edmund's life...and brought him Jalissa, the love of his life.

General Bloam rested his elbow on the armrest, relaxing into his seat. "Six months ago, after being given the full report of your exploits in Tarenhiel, King Weylind submitted an official request for the Intelligence Office's help in setting up their own counterintelligence network to prevent infiltration by spies like you or the Mongavarian assassin-spies. I replied that I would give it some consideration since, although Tarenhiel is now our ally, it is a risk to give them this knowledge and training."

Edmund's heart beat harder, hardly daring to hope.

While he would enjoy working in counterintelligence here in Escarland, doing it in Tarenhiel would be a dream come true. A dream he hadn't even dared entertain. He loved Escarland, but Tarenhiel had a special hold on his heart.

It would be tricky, balancing his political duties here in Escarland with training spies in Tarenhiel, but he and Jalissa would make it work. The train and the Alliance Bridge over the Hydalla River made travel between the kingdoms easy enough. Essie and Farrendel were an example of how to make a life in two kingdoms.

"Recently, after the poisoning in Kostaria and the role you played in ending it, we received a similar request for training from King Rharreth." General Bloam's sharp gaze studied Edmund, a twist to his mouth as if he knew how much torture it was for Edmund to stay patient while the general slowly laid this out. "King Rharreth even requested you by name."

"Now that is surprising. I'm glad he no longer wants to bash me over the head for spying on Kostaria." Edmund grinned and forced his fingers to relax on the armrests instead of curling in anticipation. Training spies in both Tarenhiel and Kostaria? Now that sounded... beyond amazing.

"I think it's more that you are the one Escarlish spy he somewhat trusts enough to allow back into his kingdom." General Bloam tapped the armrest with that hint of a smirk still playing around his mouth. "These requests made me contemplate the future of intelligence gathering and sharing in the alliance. Not just now, but in the future. If things continue as they are, we will more than likely go to war with Mongavaria. It might be a few years from now or it might be in a century. Even I can't predict that.

But when that war comes, it will be a war like nothing we have fought before. The alliance will need to be strong. Our armies will need to work together. Our governments will need to cooperate. And our intelligence and counter-intelligence offices will need to work together smoothly."

Edmund nodded. He could see that future playing out as well, one where the war in the shadows would be as important as the war on the ground. While General Bloam might not live to see it, Edmund almost certainly would.

"For that reason, I want to appoint you as the new Liaison of Intelligence." General Bloam's smirk widened, no doubt reading the excitement that Edmund couldn't hide. "You will be responsible not only for training the scouts in Kostaria and Tarenhiel in counterintelligence methods, but you will also be in charge of coordinating the sharing of information between the kingdoms. You will receive copies of everything that comes across my desk, and it will be up to you to determine what to share with Kostaria and Tarenhiel and what to keep classified to Escarland. And you will work to develop relationships with your counterparts in those kingdoms so that they will willingly share whatever intelligence they gather with you, and thus with Escarland."

Edmund sagged in his seat at the weight of the responsibility that General Bloam was proposing. This was so far beyond anything that he had envisioned. It was everything he could wish for his future...and more.

And yet, it was so *much*. Would he be up to this task? Did he have the wisdom to know what to pass along to the other kingdoms of the alliance and what should be kept secret to Escarland? As much as he trusted Rharreth and Weylind, the alliance was still comprised of three separate kingdoms. They would always have secrets from each other, and that was all right.

"Of course I'll do it." Edmund couldn't even pretend to be nonchalant. There was no point. General Bloam could surely read just how thrilled he was about this. His mind was already whirling, planning ways to train the Kostarian and Tarenhieli scouts.

"I knew you would." General Bloam's smirk took on an even more cunning tilt. "But that's not all. Once you've successfully gotten the intelligence networks for Kostaria and Tarenhiel up and running, I would like to also appoint you the Director of Counterintelligence for Escarland. As both Director and Liaison, you will report directly to me."

This was even more than Edmund could absorb. He leaned his elbows on his knees. "Are you sure I'm the right person for the job? As Jalissa reminds me, my moral compass can get a little...shady. I'm not sure my judgment can be trusted to know the difference between protecting Escarland from spies and turning Escarland into a dictator state that spies on its own people."

"The fact that you are worried about it tells me that you are the right person for the job." General Bloam gave a small shrug. "Yes, you will cross a few lines that others wouldn't. You couldn't be a spy if you weren't willing to do some unpleasant things. But you still have lines that you won't cross, and you've never let yourself be fully drawn into the shadows the way some spies do. When you start to go astray, you and I can both trust that Princess Jalissa will steer you right."

True. While he didn't always trust his own moral compass, Jalissa's pointed far more true than his.

"Linshi. I mean, thank you." Edmund hung his head

for a moment before he lifted his head and met General Bloam's gaze. "I am honored by these appointments."

General Bloam waved his hand. "I told you, I'm thinking long-term. Those in charge of the intelligence gathering for Kostaria and Tarenhiel will live for centuries. It only makes sense, for the cohesion of our efforts, that we have someone in place who will also live for centuries. Now you see my brilliance. You will see everything that crosses my desk from now on. Someday in the far distant future when I retire, you will be ready to step into my job and take over as the head of the Intelligence Office."

Now Edmund all but choked as he gaped at General Bloam. He'd just said that he was preparing Edmund to be his successor. That wasn't something General Bloam said or did lightly.

Edmund forced a light smile to hide the weight of everything he'd just been told. "The king has to approve the appointment. Wouldn't my appointment be a form of nepotism?"

General Bloam waved away his concern. "Nepotism is only bad when better, more qualified candidates are passed over for family. But if family happens to be the most qualified, the most trustworthy, and the best individual for the job, then it is simply practicality. And you, Prince Edmund, are the most qualified and skilled person for this job. By the time I retire decades from now, you are going to be even more skilled and experienced than you are now. When the war with Mongavaria comes, the heads of intelligence for Kostaria and Tarenhiel will be the same men or women that you train now. It only makes sense that you face the war as the head of intelligence for Escarland."

Edmund could see the logic in it. It would be difficult

to keep the information flowing freely if Escarland's Intelligence Office kept changing while Kostaria's and Tarenhiel's didn't. Already, the government of Escarland would be entirely different by the time the war came. It ached, just thinking about Averett dead and gone and his son or even grandson sitting on the throne instead.

Edmund hung his head again as he took in the future General Bloam was laying before him. "I appreciate your trust in me."

"It's trust, and perhaps a little pride on my part." General Bloam leaned forward as well, the smirk disappearing for something more somber. "I've never married, and I don't plan to. My legacy will be Escarland's safety, even if no one else knows the battles I've won or lost, and the Intelligence Office I leave behind to face future threats. In a sense, you are my legacy."

This was too much. Edmund cleared his throat, his words coming out a bit thick with the weight of emotion squeezing his chest. "I don't know what to say. I'm beyond honored that you feel that way."

"Don't let it go to your head." The smirk returned to General Bloam's face. "I probably shouldn't even be telling you this, but you probably would have figured out what I was up to eventually. I'd rather be upfront about my intentions. For now, the future will keep. Concentrate on training Kostarian and Tarenhieli spies and improving the communication between our kingdoms when it comes to security matters. The rest will wait until I deem you ready."

Edmund relaxed in his seat. General Bloam was right. By the time he gained the heavier responsibilities, he would have more years of experience and skills to handle them. And he would have Jalissa at his side to help carry them.

Speaking of Jalissa...

"Can I bring Jalissa in to help me as Liaison? She proved to be a great help both in searching out the smugglers in Escarland and while spying in Mongavaria." Edmund held his breath, waiting. He knew there would be times he would have to keep secrets from Jalissa because of his job, but he would rather share as much with her as possible.

"While she is a princess of Escarland through marriage, she technically is still a citizen of Tarenhiel. I can't appoint her to an official position in the Escarlish Intelligence Office." General Bloam shrugged a shoulder. "But I presume you will have pull with the Tarenhieli Intelligence Office once you help set it up. I'm sure it wouldn't be too hard to convince them to appoint her to a position. Perhaps as the Liaison for Intelligence for Tarenhiel, making her your counterpart in their kingdom?"

"Ah, so more blatant nepotism?"

Another dismissive wave. "The best person for the job."

Edmund grinned, the tension inside him easing. Now this was a future he could see himself and Jalissa living. No more undercover missions in foreign kingdoms, but instead using their skills to protect the allied kingdoms and prepare for the coming war.

CHAPTER
SIXTEEN

E dmund gazed in wonder at his newborn nephew
Fieran as he cradled him to his chest. Fieran's
head was covered with the bright red hair he'd
inherited from his mother while his tiny ears were
pointed like his father's. It was too soon to tell exactly
what color his eyes would be, but they held hints of the
bright, light blue like Farrendel's.

What would Edmund's and Jalissa's child look like, if
they should be so blessed? Dark hair like Jalissa's and her
pointed ears? Or perhaps brown hair tinged with red and
slightly curly like his?

Jalissa leaned her head against his shoulder, reaching
out to touch Fieran's tiny fingers. "He is so cute."

"Yes." Edmund grinned down at the baby. Of course,
Fieran was adorable. Anyone could tell he would be
blessed in the looks department with parents like Essie
and Farrendel.

Eventually, Edmund had to pass Fieran along to
Paige. When his arms were empty, Edmund wrapped an
arm around Jalissa's shoulders and leaned against the

wall as he watched as Fieran was passed around the rest of the family. Rheva, Mother, Vriska, Julien, Rharreth, Melantha, and even Weylind claimed a turn before Fieran turned fussy.

As Essie reclaimed Fieran, Averett started hustling everyone out to begin the journey toward the coast where they planned to meet King Jimson to negotiate a peace treaty. Edmund stayed out of the way, not entirely sure what Averett had in mind for him. Most of the discussion on what they planned to do had revolved around Julien, Vriska, the trolls, Farrendel, and Averett.

After giving Edmund a kiss on the cheek, Jalissa joined Essie, Paige, Mother, Rheva, and Melantha, all of them smiling about Melantha's announcement that she and Rharreth were expecting their first child.

Edmund followed his brothers out of Farrendel and Essie's rooms. Outside on the porch, Averett halted and turned to Edmund. "I'd like you to stay here."

Edmund nodded, then hesitated. "Are you sure? I could be helpful in spotting any double dealings on King Jimson's part."

"Perhaps, but I'd rather not confirm to him just yet that you survived." Averett shrugged, a hint of a grin on his face. "I'm not going to go through the trouble of faking your death. That would involve the expense of a state funeral and lying to the Escarlish public, and it's a hassle I don't want to deal with. But while we have denied your involvement with the poisoning to the other kingdoms and let them know that King Jimson poisoned you as well, we haven't directly confirmed your survival to Mongavaria. I'd rather they remain in a state of confusion when it comes to you."

"Too bad. I always thought faking my own death would be fun to try at least once." Edmund smirked, crossing his arms. Then again, he actually had faked his own death when it came to his fake persona of Elidyr, but Averett didn't know all of those details.

Averett rolled his eyes. "Anyway, I'd also feel better knowing you are here, just in case King Jimson decides to lash out, thinking our loved ones will be unguarded while we are at the coast for the diplomatic meeting. If King Jimson learned that the queens of all three of our kingdoms were here in Estyra…"

"It would be bad for us." Edmund nodded. "I'll look after everyone here."

At least Averett was giving him these excuses instead of blaming the fact that Edmund was still recovering from being poisoned as the reason he was being left behind. Sure, Edmund still tired more easily than he used to, but he was no longer aching. It would take him some time to fully regain his strength, but he was well on the road to recovery.

Let King Jimson wonder if Edmund had survived or not. It would itch at him, wondering how he'd done it and what Edmund knew. And when all his efforts to spy on Escarland kept getting countered, he would know who his opponent was in this game of spies and shadows.

Averett gave a final nod, clapped Edmund on the shoulder, then turned to leave.

Weylind glanced back at them, then tilted a nod in Edmund's direction. Edmund had given Weylind an official communication from General Bloam, announcing Edmund's new position as Liaison of Intelligence. Once Weylind returned from the meeting with King Jimson, they would begin the work of setting up an elven Intelligence Office and training the scouts.

As the others left, Edmund turned back to the door. When he peeked inside, he found that Essie had settled onto one of the cushions, a blanket draped over her as she nursed Fieran. Mother, Paige, Jalissa, Rheva, and Melantha sat on nearby cushions, their chatter loud enough to be vaguely heard even outside.

That didn't look like something he should walk into. Let them enjoy their time together.

Edmund sat on the porch and pulled out his notebook. Ever since General Bloam had told him about his plans, Edmund had been making notes on how to create an Intelligence Office for Tarenhiel.

It would look a little bit different than the Escarlish one. After all, the elves would scout along the borders or just on the other side, but they likely weren't going to send in long-term, undercover spies like the Escarlish did. They would rely on the information Edmund passed along from Escarland.

Instead, their Intelligence Office would concentrate more on counterintelligence than active intelligence gathering. They would need a way to weed out humans dressed as elves, and that would involve training those in key positions on what to look out for. They would also need to regularly inspect their food sources for poisons and stuff like that.

The elves could also help Escarland with counterintelligence. While telegraph lines could be tapped easily, the elven root systems could not. If they were cut, the roots shriveled and died, letting the elves know there was a problem.

Perhaps if the important telegraph lines that the Escarlish army outposts used were coated in a layer of root, they could be more secure. Everyone would know if someone had tried to tap into it because the outer root coating would shrivel and turn black.

So many ideas. He didn't realize how long he sat

there, jotting down and refining his ideas, until Jalissa's hand rested on his arm, making him jump.

She sat on the porch next to him and rested her head on his shoulder again. "It is good to see you so happy."

"From spying on Tarenhiel to training Tarenhiel how to effectively spy." Edmund reached over and laced his fingers with hers. "It's a dream come true, using my skills to protect both our kingdoms like this. But are you truly all right with this? It means I'll never leave this life behind entirely. I'll always be a little bit in the shadows."

She squeezed his fingers, resting her free hand on their clasped ones. "I told you. You would not be happy unless you were using your sharp mind for work like this. This new position is a good solution for both of us."

Glancing over his shoulder to ensure they were still alone, he leaned in and kissed her.

After a moment, she pulled away, then rose to her feet, tugging him up along with her. Her expression warmed with a coy twist to her mouth. "Come with me."

He promptly shut his notebook and stuffed it in his pocket. Spying could wait.

JALISSA LED Edmund along the pathways of Estyra, nerves curling in her stomach a bit. This was the first time she had brought Edmund to her rooms in Estyra. Sure, they had been married for a month now, but this was the first time they were together in Estyra since their marriage.

They passed the library, the great hall spreading below them. For the past few years, Estyra's library had become a place of pain as she mourned Elidyr, the elf she thought she had loved.

Now that she knew that Elidyr had been Edmund—

and she had worked through the emotions of being lied to back then—the library was once again a place of good memories that she treasured. As Elidyr, Edmund had gotten her through some tough times, with both Weylind and Farrendel gone fighting the trolls and Melantha becoming increasingly distant.

Edmund would continue to get her through whatever challenges and trials they faced in the future.

But thanks to the recent weeks, she now knew that she was strong enough to get him through those same challenges and trials. When it counted, she had found new depths of determination and courage that she had not known she possessed.

They were stronger together, and their mission in Mongavaria had proven that in a deeper way.

Edmund met her gaze, and her heart rate sped up at the warmth in his eyes.

They reached the broad, royal branch. Weylind's suite of rooms were grown into the tree on the right with his palatial main room first, then smaller rooms branching from there. Melantha's old room was across the way on the left, and she and Rharreth were currently staying there while they were visiting.

Jalissa's room was the next one on the right beside Weylind's set of rooms while the rooms across from her were currently being used as a guest room for Averett and Paige. Julien and Vriska each had guest rooms farther down the branch while Machasheni Leyleira had claimed rooms all the way at the end.

Jalissa tightened her grip on Edmund's hand, sure he could hear and feel the way her pulse was thundering in her chest and hammering in her wrist. "Well, this is it. Our home in Estyra."

Edmund's grin held a mischievous tilt a moment

before he swept her up in his arms.

She laughed, squirming. "Again? You already carried me over the threshold of the cabin where we stayed for our wedding trip."

"But that wasn't our permanent home." Edmund strolled forward with a steady, sure stride, showing no signs of weakness from the poison. "And I missed out on carrying you over the threshold at Buckmore Cottage."

"No, Vriska beat you to that one." Jalissa relaxed in his arms, smiling at the disgruntled frown that crossed his face.

"Ah, yes. Being carried into Buckmore Cottage half-dead was quite the romantic way to start our life together there." Edmund hoisted her a little higher as he juggled her and tried to unlatch her door.

"Half-dead? More like mostly dead." Jalissa reached down and unlatched the door for him.

Grinning, Edmund nudged the door open with his foot. "All right, mostly dead."

He strode inside, then kicked the door shut behind them. Setting her down, Edmund kept a hand on her waist as he looked around, taking in the room.

Jalissa tried to see it as he did. It was a pretty standard elven room, formed of living branches melded together and arching over the windows and doorways. Magical protections over the windows kept out the bugs and could be darkened for privacy. A small section of kitchen cupboards had been grown along one wall, while a seating area had been grown into the other side, including a padded bench along the wall instead of only cushions on the floor. While Farrendel preferred sitting on the floor, Jalissa did not.

On one wall hung a painting of the Kingsley Gardens

that she had purchased from an artist in the Aldon Market. It was the only personal touch in the room.

Most of her personal belongings were in the bedroom, like the book on the Kingsley Gardens Edmund had given her or the photograph portrait that she and Edmund had posed for in a studio in Aldon. They looked far too serious, outlined in black and white and, as instructed, not smiling. But it still made her smile, remembering how long it had taken for them to keep that pose without breaking into laughter.

She glanced toward the nearest window. Through it, she could see the roof of Weylind's main room, even if a screen of broad leaves kept their windows from looking into each other.

A pang shot through her. Farrendel had never lived in his own room here on the royal branch. When Dacha had been killed, Farrendel had still been living in one of the rooms off the king's suite of rooms, the rooms that now belonged to Weylind and his family. When Weylind had moved in, Farrendel had refused a room on the royal wing and instead moved into the farthest set of rooms he could find in all of Ellonahshinel.

Jalissa had been hurt back then, feeling like her brother was pushing her away. And he had, in a way. But now she could better understand how he had needed the space to process and attempt to heal from the trauma. And he had not wanted the rest of them to know how bad his nightmares were.

Even now that things were getting better, he and Essie were perfectly happy where they were. They were not about to move to the royal branch.

Edmund wrapped both arms around her waist, hugging her to his chest. "The royal branch is...cozy."

Jalissa glanced toward the roof of Weylind's rooms

again. Now that she thought about it, his room was uncomfortably...close. The thick leaves and the darkening windows kept the rooms private, but Weylind would be able to see all of her and Edmund's comings and goings. She had never thought about it too much when it came to Weylind and Rheva. They had been married when Jalissa was too little to think anything of it other than be excited that she got to wear a pretty dress and gained a sister. But now that she was the one married...

Maybe Farrendel and Essie had the right idea. A little more space might be nice.

Sure, things would still be on the cozy side in Buckmore Cottage. But at least there, Essie and Farrendel had claimed the turret on the second floor and Edmund and Jalissa had claimed a room on the first floor on the entirely other side of the manor house. They only had to share the parlor and kitchen space.

Cozy, yes. But Farrendel wasn't smotheringly overprotective like Weylind. And who knew how often all of them would be in Escarland at the same time.

"You might have a point." Jalissa turned in Edmund's arms. "I am not too attached to this set of rooms. We can explore Ellonahshinel and pick out new rooms together. If we do not find empty rooms that speak to us, we can always pick an empty branch and have new rooms built. After all, Ryfon and Brina will want to move out of their current rooms to their own suites sooner rather than later. With royalty visiting from other kingdoms more often, having more guest rooms will be appreciated. Averett and Paige, Rharreth and Melantha, could each have permanent rooms here, if they wished. An extra courtesy and symbol of our alliance, perhaps."

She could picture it already. A cozy set of rooms on a

far branch with their own lift like Essie and Farrendel had so they could come and go as they pleased. She would grow that little white orchid into part of the wall, a reminder of what they had survived. Perhaps she would beg a few flowers out of the gardeners at the Kingsley Gardens, and she would have her own mini garden right inside her home.

"Sounds like a good plan to me," Edmund murmured in her ear before he nuzzled her neck. "But I'm thinking maybe we go house-searching tomorrow. For tonight..."

He swept her into his arms again and kissed her.

Jalissa kissed him back, fisting her fingers in the warmth of his loose shirt.

She had loved him as Elidyr, the quiet elf clerk. Then she had loved him as Edmund, the loud Escarlish prince. She had married him as Edmund, the spy prince who had stolen her heart.

Yet somehow their adventures in Mongavaria had tied them together in a new, more intimate way. Perhaps it was the heart bond that made everything between them feel richer, deeper. Or maybe it was the new understanding of each other's strengths and weaknesses. It might even be the fact that she had spent a day and a night never farther than a hand's clasp away from him. She had seen him at his lowest, his weakest.

And they had survived it, coming through it all stronger than ever.

She had not thought it possible, but she loved Edmund even more than she had when she married him a mere four weeks ago.

How much more would their love grow over the years and centuries they had before them?

She was looking forward to finding out.

WEAPONS COLLECTION

This story takes place the morning after chapter 30 of Shield Band *(occurs the morning of chapter 14 of* Peril in Mongavaria).*

Vriska stepped into the private, family dining room in the royal wing of Winstead Palace and drew in a deep breath of the meaty scent of roast sausage, subtle warmth of fried eggs, and the yeasty smell of the array of muffins, rolls, and other items the palace staff had laid out for breakfast.

There were a lot of parts about someday becoming a princess of Escarland that she found daunting—like the balls and social engagements—but having such an abundance of food served up for her enjoyment at every meal was not one of them.

"Vriska, dear, how are you feeling this morning?" Julien's mother was the only one in the room, sitting at the table with a breakfast plate in front of her, and she glanced up as Vriska entered.

"Fine. Just a little sore." Vriska toyed with the edge of the sling that she wore to rest her injured shoulder. At least she'd only have to wear the sling today. Thanks to the elf healer, the bullet wound she'd received the previous evening was well on its way to healing. Not like wounds she'd endured when she didn't have access to elf healers and had to spend weeks healing all on her own.

Elves. They were handy to have around. Sometimes. Though the elf healer Nylian was far snootier than Melantha.

Vriska picked up a plate, transferred it to the hand of her injured arm, then started dishing out her food. Out of the corner of her eye, she could see Julien's mother sink back into her chair, as if she'd been about to jump up to help but had thought better of it.

Good. Vriska didn't need her food served to her like she was some invalid. Sure, her shoulder was aching a bit after she'd had to twist around to get dressed that morning, but it was nothing she couldn't handle.

As Vriska took a seat next to Julien's mother, Paige entered the room with the two boys Bertie and Finn in tow. The ensuing chaos of hungry boys and busy mother thankfully took attention off Vriska.

Vriska concentrated on her food and let the noise flow around her. Blast, but she was hungry. Battles—and getting shot—always gave her such an appetite.

As she started on her second piece of toast, Julien strode into the room, looking no worse for the wear after his near-abduction last night. His gaze landed on her, and a smile creased his beard. He strode across the room, leaned over, and kissed her temple. "Good morning. Your family has returned to their home safe and sound."

While her family had entered the palace last night and spent the rest of the night camped out in her sitting room, they had refused accommodations or the invitation to join Julien's family for breakfast. Instead, Julien had kindly volunteered to see them home. Not that they needed the escort through the streets of Aldon, but Vriska felt better knowing that Julien was looking after her family for her.

"Linsh." She grinned up at him. At least he knew better than to ask after her arm first thing in the morning. "I'm still waiting for my real kiss."

Julien shifted and peeked at his mother before he lowered his voice into that slightly husky one that made Vriska's skin tingle. "Later."

"I'll hold you to that." Vriska tried to put a note of flirtation into her voice, though she wasn't sure she managed it. Flirting wasn't really her thing. But with Julien, she wanted that little thrill that went through her when he gave her that charming grin of his at her attempts.

As he was doing now. After holding her gaze for another moment, he turned and headed for the sideboard laden with the breakfast feast.

And that was another thing she liked about him. He knew when to flirt, but he also knew when food took priority over flirting.

After wrangling Bertie and Finn into their seats and setting plates in front of them, Paige dropped into a seat across from Vriska with her own plate before her. "I'm so glad Princess Bella is gone. Well, I suppose she hasn't left. But it is nice to have a casual family breakfast again."

"Casual, but not relaxed." Julien set his plate on the table, that quirked grin still on his face, and took the seat next to Vriska.

"True." Paige reached over and cut Finn's sausage for him.

"Is Averett still asleep?" Julien's mother pushed aside

her plate, dabbed at her mouth with a napkin, then laid the napkin neatly over her plate.

"No." Paige shook her head and sighed. "He's already up and meeting with Master Wendee, General Bloam, and a few of the senior members of Parliament concerning Princess Bella and Mongavaria."

"Sounds like fun." Julien grimaced and gave an exaggerated shudder.

Vriska resisted the urge to shudder as well. As strange as it was to marry a prince, at least she was marrying someone who, in all likelihood, would stay merely a prince. She'd never have to rule a kingdom at his side. Just protect it, which was how both of them preferred it.

"What sounds like fun?"

Vriska glanced over her shoulder as Edmund strolled into the room, Jalissa tucked close to his side. The gesture looked romantic, but by the way Jalissa kept shooting Edmund a look that was a mix of concern and exasperation, he was likely using Jalissa to steady himself.

"Meeting with Parliament." Julien motioned to Edmund with a forkful of egg. "Should you be out of bed?"

"Yes," Edmund said at the same time as Jalissa gave an emphatic, "No."

Vriska couldn't help but grin a bit at that. She had been so worried about fitting in to this family. And, yes, there were discussions of Parliament and stuff like that over breakfast. But here when it was just the family, they could shed the masks they wore as royalty and just be themselves. And while she didn't exactly like the royalty part, she could fit right in to the normal people behind the masks.

Edmund started toward the sideboard, but Jalissa steered him toward the table, the clench to her jaw more forceful than Vriska had ever seen from the elf princess. "No, sit. I will make a plate for you."

"I am fine." Edmund braced himself against the chair but didn't sit.

Julien's mother pushed her empty plate away and stood. "Both of you sit down. I'll fetch plates for you. You both should be resting after your ordeal."

Jalissa hesitated for another moment before she sank into the seat on Vriska's other side.

Edmund took the seat next to Jalissa, his face a little pale.

Vriska could understand the urge to pretend everything was fine when wounded. After all, she was sitting here with her arm in a sling pretending she couldn't feel the ache of her healing shoulder.

Edmund slouched in his chair, glancing first at Julien, then at Vriska. "So, Julien, have you shown Vriska your weapons collection yet?"

Julien froze. "Uh, no."

Vriska turned to him. "You have a weapons collection?"

And he hadn't shown it to her yet? Or even talked about it? She had a vague memory that he had mentioned something about having a replica weapon or two when they'd been sparring during their morning practices in Kostaria.

But they had been rather busy since arriving in Escarland. The rather punchable princess of Mongavaria had kept them distracted.

Julien shifted in his seat, his face going a hint red. "The weapons collection is"—his voice lowered further —"in my bedchamber."

Edmund rolled his eyes. "The weapons are hanging on the walls of your sitting room, not your actual bedroom."

Julien stirred his eggs on his plate, still not looking at Vriska, as he muttered down at the table. "It still wouldn't be proper."

Vriska snorted. Humans and elves and their overblown sense of properness.

Julien's mother set plates in front of Jalissa and Edmund. "We'll all go right after breakfast. That would be proper enough."

"Mother," Julien gritted out, his face going even more red.

Smiling with a hint of mischief, his mother patted his shoulder as she rounded the table to return to her seat.

Why was Julien so uncomfortable talking about his weapons collection? Was it simply because of his own overblown sense of human propriety? Humans weren't quite as bad as the elves, but they did have different things they were uncomfortable with.

Jalissa finished her bite of eggs and gestured to the sling around Vriska's arm. "How is your shoulder?"

"Healing." Vriska shrugged, stretching the aching muscles. "Elven healing magic is effective."

Jalissa's mouth twitched in one of her serene elven smiles. "Yes, it is. Since meeting Edmund, I have become increasingly thankful for that fact."

"But you love me anyway." Edmund draped one arm across the back of Jalissa's chair.

Jalissa gave a quiet huff, though a smile remained on her face.

Vriska looked away, though the mushy romance stuff didn't bother her as much as it once had. Strange, that.

When they all finished breakfast, Vriska found herself herded down the hallway, surrounded by Julien's family.

Julien halted in front of a door, his face still tinged red. "Um, well, this is my room."

He swung open the door and stepped aside, gesturing for everyone else to enter.

Vriska glanced at Julien before she strode inside. As soon as she stepped into the room, she forgot all about Julien's discomfort, his family's ribbing, or anything else for that matter.

Two of the walls were decorated with rows upon rows of weapons. From poleaxes to halberds to various swords and daggers. They were not of troll design, and she was not familiar enough with Escarlish history to guess what time periods the various weapons might have been from.

One wall held weapons that were tarnished with age. These must be actual historical weapons. The other, larger wall held weapons that appeared shinier and newer.

Vriska turned in a slow circle, taking in all the shiny, gorgeous weapons. So much glinting danger all lined up on the walls.

Vaguely, she heard Edmund and Jalissa quietly talking, though she was too focused on the weapons to pay any attention to what they were saying.

Julien halted next to her. "Well, this is it. My weapons collection."

"It's beautiful." Her voice came out breathy and weak.

"This wall is all actual historical weapons. They aren't actually mine but borrowed from the royal vault." Julien pointed at the wall of slightly tarnished weapons, then at the other wall. "And these are replicas, so they are actually mine. Some were gifts. Like that elven dagger, though that one is real. Farrendel gave it to me. And some I commissioned. The benefit to being a prince with coin is that I can indulge on something like this."

He had a prince's wealth, and he chose to use it to

commission weapons. If she hadn't already been falling in love with Julien, then she definitely was now. Could there be anything more handsome than a man who decorated his walls with gorgeous, shiny, deadly instruments of war?

"Why didn't you want to show it to me?" Vriska tore her gaze away from the weapons long enough to glance at Julien.

He shifted, his gaze going back to the weapons rather than staying on her. "Besides the fact that it is in my room?"

"Besides your human propriety, yes."

"I guess my fascination with historical weapons isn't something I admit to many people." Julien shrugged and crossed his arms as if trying to be more nonchalant than he felt. "Most people in Escarland would find it...odd."

"And you thought I would find it odd?" Vriska crossed her own arms and finally tore her eyes away from the weapons to focus more fully on Julien.

"No." Julien's mouth quirked into a smile briefly before it disappeared. "But the collection is...well, it is a bit personal."

Vriska couldn't help it. She laughed. Of course that was the problem. Julien liked to be in the background, and showing off his weapons collection, even to her, drew too much attention to himself. "I know. It's uncomfortable. That's how I felt the first time I brought you home to my family and you saw where I grew up."

Julien relaxed and took her hand, smiling that charming yet still slightly embarrassed smile of his.

She was still getting used to the feel of his fingers in hers, but she kind of liked it. And she really liked the sight of all those weapons.

She was falling in love with him. She had realized it

last night when she'd chased after the princess and the smugglers to rescue Julien. But even in the light and calm of day, that warmth still remained in her chest.

A knocking sound broke the moment. Vriska turned in that direction and scowled at Julien's brother Edmund. She was going to take back every nice thing she had been thinking about him.

Sometime in the last few minutes, Julien's mother had disappeared. Edmund and Jalissa were now partially out the doorway.

Edmund grinned and grabbed the door handle. "You have five minutes. You can thank me later." With a wink from Edmund—and an eyeroll from Jalissa—the two of them stepped out of the room and closed the door after them.

Never mind. Edmund was officially her favorite future brother-in-law.

When she turned back to Julien, he was scratching the back of his neck, the red look back to his face.

Ugh. Was he going to go all uncomfortable now that they both actually liked each other? They'd been alone together plenty of times in Kostaria, but apparently it was different now that they were in Escarland where being alone together was something to be gossiped about.

She grinned and gestured to the wall. "So when I marry you, what's yours is mine, right?"

Julien laughed, the discomfort bleeding away. "No way. I might consider letting you choose one or two to claim as your own, but these are mine."

All right, that was fair. She wasn't about to go around sharing her weapons either. As Julien had said, weapons were rather personal. "Fine, fine. I understand. The weapons are off-limits."

"But there are two more walls in this room." Julien

gestured. "Plenty of space for you to decorate with your own weapons when…" He trailed off, as if realizing they had strayed into rather personal territory again.

But that was good, right? Healthy. They had spent so long talking about *if* they got married. It was progress to start talking about *when* they got married. And what their life together after the wedding might look like.

It was still an uncomfortable topic, especially since she hadn't exactly admitted to Julien yet that she was falling for him. She would have to do that, and soon.

But until she figured out how she wanted to go about that, their five minutes were wasting. And she didn't want to use the entire five minutes talking, as nice as talking with Julien was.

"I'll hold you to that." Vriska grinned and eased a step closer. "Now, you still owe me that proper kiss."

"Do I?" Julien wrapped his arms around her and tugged her close.

Her knees were already weak from all the beautiful weapons on the wall, and she let herself lean into Julien's strong arms.

He leaned down and gave her a tiny peck on the lips.

She scowled at him. "What was that?"

"A proper kiss." Julien's grin held a teasing edge.

"You know what I meant." Vriska toyed with the collar of his shirt. "I want a real kiss this time."

Then, he kissed her. And if her knees went even more weak, well, it was a really good real kiss.

FAILURES AND FORGIVENESS

This story takes place during Shield Band. *Chapters 1 & 2 happen between chapters 17 & 18 of* Shield Band. *Chapters 3 & 4 take place during* Shield Band's *Epilogue.*

CHAPTER
ONE

Melantha tottered through the passageways of Khagniorth Stronghold, her body aching after a long day of healing.

Laughter came from a nearby room. Since the door had been left partially open, she peeked inside.

Vriska's mother curled on one of the beds, her sleep peaceful despite the noise.

On the other bed, Vriska's younger sister Rikze sat cross-legged, facing the game board that had been set up on top of the quilt. The game was a popular strategy game where players used a variety of pieces as they tried to conquer the entire board.

Two chairs had been placed on either side of the bed. Vriska sat in the one between the two beds, the chair tipped so that she could see the door out of the corner of her eye.

Prince Julien sprawled stiffly in the second chair, his back to the wall, facing the doorway. Bruises still mottled his face from the beating he had suffered a few days ago.

Sitting in that hard chair had to hurt, but he was grinning as he moved a piece on the game board.

Rikze flopped back against her pillows with an overexaggerated groan. "Ugh! Not again! You're supposed to be letting me win!"

Both Vriska's and Julien's gazes flicked to Melantha, but they kept their focus on the game.

Good. That meant everyone was all right in here. No need for Melantha's magic.

Not that she had much magic left to give. But she would find some, if they had needed it.

Quietly, Melantha backed out of the doorway, then tugged it slightly more closed. For a moment, she rested a hand against the wall, gathering her strength. At least there was hope, even with so much death. She had saved some.

The weight of all those she had not been able to save still rested heavy on her shoulders.

After pushing away from the wall, Melantha continued down the passageways until she reached the front doors of the stronghold.

As she opened the doors, the nighttime air brushed against her skin. She drew in a deep breath, relishing the fresh and cool taste of the breeze rather than the stuffy, reeking air of the healing rooms.

Before her in the courtyard, a line of people stretched out of the gates and into the streets beyond. Torches and magical lights brightened the space, casting shadows onto the scared, grim faces of those waiting to find out if their food was safe or poisoned.

Inside the courtyard, the line broke into three as troll warriors directed the people to three tables, where Jalissa and two of the other elves with plant magic tested each sack of grain.

Once the grain was tested, the sack was either handed back to the troll if it was safe or loaded onto one of the carts, pulled by one of the few pack mules they had available. Once the cart was full, a troll led the mule out of the courtyard and began the trek out of the city and up to the plateau that held the ruins of Gror Grar. There, it would be added to the steadily growing pile of tainted grain, where it would be guarded by troll warriors until it could be destroyed.

Rharreth stood next to a table with sacks of grain from Khagniorth's stores. Those who turned in tainted grain were given a sack of safe grain to replace it.

As she strode down the last few steps toward Rharreth, Melantha's legs wobbled with her exhaustion, both physical and the ever-present magical emptiness that she could never rest enough to replenish before she faced another day of healing troll after troll of this disease.

Not a disease. A poison.

She should have seen it. Should have figured it out. Somehow. It didn't matter that she hadn't been trained to look for poisons. If she had not been so focused on looking for a disease. If she had thought to look for a reaction to food. If she had not been so weary and beleaguered that it was all she could do to attempt to keep up with the number of patients, trying to save as many as possible. If…

She paused on the bottom step to swallow back the bitter churn in her stomach. She had been down this road of dwelling on guilt before. Once she had a quiet moment, she would examine what she could have done better, learn from it, and try to let the guilt go before it destroyed her.

Gathering herself, she crossed the courtyard to Rharreth's side.

He half-turned to her and clasped her hand, tugging her close. He could not say anything in front of the people, but Melantha could feel the exhausted pain in his grip on her fingers and in that place deep in her chest.

An elishina, she suspected. It had grown slowly, surely, but it had become more pronounced, deeper, in the struggle of the past few weeks.

Melantha leaned into him, trying to give him whatever measure of strength she had left, even as she plastered on a smile for the next troll in line.

Once Rharreth had handed off the next sack of grain, he took a step back, nodding to Zavni who stepped in to take his place. After tugging Melantha a few more paces away, Rharreth embraced her, holding her tightly as if she was the only thing holding him upright.

She held him, resting her head against his shoulder. For a long moment, they just stood like that, soaking up each other's warmth and strength.

"You need rest." Melantha lifted her head and touched his cheek. His face was far more hollow than it had been a few weeks ago, a testament to the toll this had taken on him.

"Not yet. I need to..." Rharreth trailed off, then gestured back toward the tables. "I cannot leave yet."

"Then I will stay." Even as she said it, she could not help the way she leaned against Rharreth, every muscle and bone aching, her magic so drained she did not dare use what she had left to ease the aches.

Rharreth shook his head, his large hands gently cupping her face. "No. You need rest far more than I do. Get your sister settled. She needs the rest as well."

When Rharreth nodded in Jalissa's direction, Melantha glanced that way.

Jalissa reached for another sack of grain. Her shoulders rose and fell in a breath, and it took a heartbeat longer than it should have for her to call up her magic to test the grain. Weariness carved dark circles beneath her eyes, smudges that had not been there when she had arrived that morning.

Melantha stood on her tiptoes, kissed Rharreth, then forced herself to step out of his arms. Her sister truly appeared in need of a rescue, as much as Melantha would rather linger with Rharreth.

After joining her, Melantha tapped Jalissa's shoulder. "Isciena?"

Jalissa jumped, then looked around, blinking. "What time is it?"

"Late. Come. Let me show you to your room." Melantha gripped Jalissa's elbow and tugged her away from the table.

Jalissa resisted, waving weakly toward the line of trolls stretching across the courtyard. "I should..."

"Your magic is nearly spent. You have done all you can today." Melantha steered Jalissa farther away from the table.

More than enough, really. Jalissa had confirmed the presence of poison, then immediately jumped into searching for it. She had done more than enough for a kingdom that was not even her own.

The troll guards quickly shifted to direct the people into two lines, heading for the tables manned by the elf warriors with plant magic.

More elf warriors should be out shortly to relieve those who had been checking grain for the past few hours. While many of the elf warriors with plant growing magic had been sent out with parties of troll guards to start the process of checking for tainted grain in the rest of the kingdom, ten elf warriors remained here to continue guarding the healers and checking the grain in Osmana.

After another moment of hesitation, Jalissa nodded and fell into step with Melantha as they headed for Khagniorth Stronghold.

As they stepped inside and the huge doors closed behind them with a thunk, Jalissa winced and pressed a hand to her temple.

Melantha fished in the pocket of her dress and pulled out a smooth stone on a loop of leather string. "Here. I made this one to send to Farrendel, but I think you need it more at the moment."

Jalissa took the necklace, looped it over her head, and tucked the stone beneath the bodice of her dress. The tense lines of her face eased. "That is better. Linshi."

They walked in silence through the passageways for a few minutes.

Melantha was not sure what to say to her sister. Last time they had parted, it had been on good terms. And their letters had grown longer and more detailed as their relationship healed.

But that did not mean that she knew what to say to Jalissa, now that she was here in person. When Jalissa had first arrived, it had been easy to talk about Khagniorth Stronghold and give her a small tour.

Now the easy topics had been exhausted, leaving the more personal topics.

Melantha peeked at Jalissa. "Your courtship with Prince Edmund appears to be going well."

A soft smile broke through the weariness on Jalissa's face. "Yes."

"I am sorry that he had to leave right away. I would

have liked more time to get to know him." Melantha turned a corner into another passageway.

The moment Jalissa had confirmed the grain at Vriska's family's home was contaminated with ricin, Prince Edmund had grabbed the bag he had not even unpacked yet, talked Rharreth into sending along Eyvindur, and disappeared into the streets of Osmana to start tracking the smugglers. He intended to follow the trail of troll smugglers—Rharreth would want to know who among his people was willing to sell smuggled grain in a black market—until Edmund discovered the human smuggler supplying the grain.

Eyvindur had been a good choice to go with the Escarlish spy-prince. Eyvindur was the most...discreet of all of Rharreth's shield band. The others—like Zavni and Vriska—were more prone to solve problems with their fists rather than quiet investigation.

Jalissa shrugged, a wry tilt quirking her smile. "This is Edmund. I knew what I was getting into when I started courting him."

Melantha could not help but snort a small laugh. "I cannot believe he is going to be my brother once you marry him. The first time I met him, I knocked him out with my magic."

Jalissa laughed, though the sound still held a hint of her weariness. "I remember. I was still trying to tell myself that I did not love him, but I could not help but be scared when Rharreth threatened him."

"I have never seen someone so unconcerned while being questioned by Rharreth." Melantha shook her head, still smiling. "But he was a gentleman and sat in the front of the dog sled to block the wind on our trip to the border."

"Of course he did." Jalissa's fond smile warmed her

eyes for a moment, before the expression faded back into something tight and weary. "That was the only time he has ever been captured, though he has had other close calls."

Melantha reached out and rested a hand on Jalissa's arm. "I hope it stays that way. Your trip to Mongavaria will be dangerous."

Edmund and Jalissa still planned to travel to Mongavaria, only a week after their upcoming wedding, on a diplomatic mission, despite the recent poisonings here in Kostaria that were most likely linked to Mongavaria.

"The difference is that I will be along, and I plan to do my best to keep him out of trouble." Jalissa's tight mouth twisted into a hint of a wry look once again. "Or I will just join him in the trouble."

"Your spy-prince is a bad influence. I never knew you had this sneaky streak." Melantha gave Jalissa a light nudge with her elbow.

"Of course you did not. I was sneaky about it." Jalissa's smile widened to a grin.

Melantha grinned back, something inside her easing. She had missed this. The light chatter and warmth shared between them as sisters.

This had faded long before Melantha had done the unthinkable and betrayed Farrendel. They had drifted apart during the years Melantha stayed at Estyra to help Weylind and Rheva while Jalissa lived at Lethorel with Dacha and Farrendel. Then they had all shattered more than most of them had realized when Dacha died and Farrendel was tortured. Only now were they—and their familial bonds—healing.

"I know I have already said so before, but I am sorry for what I said a year ago about you having to marry an elf noble." Melantha grimaced, aching all the more at the memories. "I spoke out of my bitterness at my own situation back then. That does not excuse what I said, nor am I trying to defend myself. I—"

Jalissa gave a slight laugh, something that held both humor and a raw edge. "I understand why you said what you said. You were partially right. Likely if I had started courting Edmund right away, the nobles would have been quite put out by it. In the months since, the court has had time to get used to our strengthening alliance with both Kostaria and Escarland. They are far more open to my marriage to a human than they would have been even a year ago."

Melantha searched Jalissa's face as they turned another corner in the maze of the stronghold's passageways. "Still, I know you broke up with Prince Edmund because of it, and my words made your whole relationship with him that much harder."

This time, Jalissa's snort of laughter was genuine, without the edge of pain. "My relationship with Edmund would have been tumultuous even without your words."

Melantha did not know the whole story. All Jalissa had ever told her was that she and Edmund had a complicated history. The complications probably came from Edmund's past work as a spy, though Melantha was not privy to the details. "But you said things are going well?"

Jalissa was, after all, engaged to marry Prince Edmund in a few short months. Things had better be going well.

If they were not, Melantha would need to make an attempt at meddling again and hope it did not turn out as big a mistake as it had been the last time.

"Yes, it is. Edmund loves me, and I love him." Jalissa gave a slight shrug. "The court is getting used to him. It helps that Edmund is so charming. And rather too good at fitting in to elf culture."

There was an undercurrent to those words, a little twist to Jalissa's mouth, as if something she had said was a secret she shared with Edmund.

"Good. I am happy for you, isciena." Melantha halted and gestured at a door on the right. "This is your room. Rharreth and I are next door, if you need anything. Prince Julien is three doors down that way."

The room designated for Prince Edmund was next to Prince Julien's, though he had not needed a room since he had left right away.

"Linshi." Jalissa yawned and reached for the latch. She paused, then turned back to Melantha. "Perhaps we can talk more? In the morning?"

"I would like that." Melantha stifled her own yawn. They were both too tired to linger right now.

But perhaps, here in the far north, Melantha would finally become the sister to Jalissa that she always should have been.

CHAPTER
TWO

Rharreth leaned against the new stone railing that ringed the balcony built into the top of Khagniorth Stronghold. New rock outcroppings now blocked the balcony from Osmana's wall, where his treacherous cousin had once positioned a repeater gun. This balcony provided cover, if it should ever be needed again, and if Melantha's brother Laesornysh ever came to Kostaria, Rharreth would ask for his help in placing a barrier of his magic around this balcony. It would be a simple matter, compared to the wall they had created along Escarland's border with Mongavaria.

Down below, the lights of Osmana spread into the distance, a gleam of yellow sparks in the darkness of night. Above, a sea of stars spread above the silhouettes of the mountains. The distant plateau glowed with blue magic, yet pinpricks of torchlight marked where a band of guards prevented anyone from getting too close to the huge pile of tainted grain.

He had failed. He had failed his people. His kingdom. He had tried to be a better king than his father and brother. Instead, thousands of his people had died on his watch.

They had not died in battle. No, they had died in their homes. In the streets. Women and children and the elderly, poisoned by an enemy, and he couldn't even give the order to fight back without causing even more death.

Was he the weak king his father had told him he would be? That Drurvas and Brathac and others like them had accused him of being?

The cold night breeze stabbed through his thin shirt, but he relished the scraping of the iciness against his skin.

Melantha's soft footsteps padded across the stone before her arms wrapped around him. She leaned her head against his back.

Deep in his chest, he could sense the aching in her heart for their people.

He released a long breath, hanging his head as he slumped even more over the elbows he rested on the railing. "I failed our people. I should have listened to you sooner. If we had gone to the towns on the shore at the very first reports of deaths...or if I reached out to King Weylind to request healers as soon as you said that I should..."

"You were a stubborn troll," Melantha murmured against his back, her arms still tight around him. "Our people are stubborn too. Even if elven healers had arrived sooner, I am not sure their help would have been accepted right away."

Perhaps there was truth in that. But he still should have listened to Melantha's wise counsel far sooner than he had.

But he had been too proud. Too unwilling to beg help from the elf king.

Still had too much of his father's training ingrained in him. Far more than he'd realized.

By the time the elves had arrived, the trolls had been too desperate to protest the help of the healers. And when the poison had been detected, the trolls had eagerly lined up at the collection points to have their grain tested by the elven warriors. Poisonings had quickly dropped off until now, over two months after they had realized the disease was really a poison, they only had a few people left in the healing rooms here in Khagniorth.

Prince Edmund had returned after three weeks of investigation with a list of names of the trolls who had participated in the black market trade. He and Eyvindur had tracked down the bays and inlets the smugglers had been using to offload their cargoes.

Another thing Rharreth had been stubborn about. Persisting in his annoyance with Prince Edmund.

Rharreth had to admit—grudgingly—that the Escarlish spy-prince's skills had proven rather useful.

Not to mention, Edmund was going to be his brother-in-law in a few days when he married Melantha's sister Jalissa. It was time Rharreth let that little spying incident go and simply appreciated that they were all on the same side now.

All on the same side. Like they had been in the Dulraith against Drurvas. As Rharreth, Julien, and Vriska would be when they fought a Dulraith against Brathac tomorrow. Brathac and his cronies would die—Rharreth had no doubts about that—but the taint of their words and actions still echoed in Rharreth's chest.

"Is Brathac right?" Rharreth couldn't find the energy to straighten.

"Of course he is not." Melantha dug her fingers into the fabric of his shirt, her arms tight around his waist.

"Brathac is a prejudicial, hate-filled fool who can not see how much stronger Kostaria is now because the kingdom has you on the throne."

If only he could believe that. After all the deaths he had seen in the past months, he couldn't be so sure.

"If I had never begun trading with the humans, the smugglers would never have had a market here. Our people would have continued to use our traditional sources of food instead of depending on grain from Escarland." Rharreth lifted his gaze to stare down at Osmana, the city filled with so many grieving people.

If he had continued his father's and brother's policy of isolating Kostaria, this never would have happened.

"You cannot know what would have happened." Melantha eased around him until she tucked herself along his side where she could see his face. "I saw the state the people were in when I first married you. The people were starving. Without the grain from Escarland, who knows how many thousands would have starved this past winter? With so many desperate people and no official trade, there would have been even *more* of a market for smuggled grain from Mongavaria. Perhaps more people would have been poisoned."

"Mongavaria only lashed out at us because of our deepening ties with Escarland." Rharreth wasn't sure why he was arguing with Melantha over this. He should take any excuse to let go of this guilt.

But, perhaps, he wanted to wallow in the guilt a while longer. Shouldn't all those deaths deserve him to feel each and every one of them?

"Yes, they did. This time." Melantha shrugged and rested her hand over one of his clenched fists. "But their argument with Escarland began the moment Princess Elspetha married my brother instead of their crown prince. Mongavaria has ambitions, and I doubt those ambitions would have been nullified if we had stayed out of Escarland's affairs. Perhaps, without our new treaties with Escarland and Tarenhiel, they would have seen us as the next logical, easy target for their empire expansion. My point is, Rharreth, that you cannot know what would have happened. Focus on what actually did happen."

He gave a bitter bark of a laugh. "There is still plenty of failure and guilt there."

"I know a bit about guilt." Melantha squeezed his hand, waiting until he finally glanced toward her, meeting her dark brown eyes. "Ask forgiveness of those who need your sincere apologies. Examine your failures and learn from your mistakes. Then you need to move forward. You will not become a better king by wallowing in guilt over things you cannot change."

How did he move forward when so many of his people were dead? Wouldn't it be callous to simply shrug off those deaths?

He was king. Lives were in his hands each and every day.

If he went to war against Mongavaria over this, it would cost lives. If he didn't go to war, it might cost lives if Mongavaria did something like this again. He'd thought he was sparing lives by marrying Melantha, securing peace with Tarenhiel and Escarland, and negotiating for trade in food, but lives had been lost to poison instead of war.

Melantha leaned her head against his shoulder. "You are a good king. A far better king than your father or brother. And you are going to be a better father."

There was something in her voice. This was not the same hypothetical tone she used when dreaming about the possibility of children someday.

No, her voice held a note of certainty this time.

Rharreth froze, then turned to face her, holding her shoulders. "Are you saying…"

Melantha smiled and smoothed a hand over her dress. "I figured out why I have been so tired, even though my healing magic has not been as drained as before. It is early, yet, but I can tell. I am a healer, after all. We are going to be parents."

He was going to be a father. Rharreth sagged against the railing behind him. Yes, he wanted children, and not just because he needed an heir. And he knew that Melantha had been aching for a child of her own, especially recently after Elspeth and Farrendel announced their own happy news.

But Rharreth was still figuring out how to be king. He was still making so many mistakes.

How did he know he wasn't going to be a failure as a father? Yes, he would be a better father than his own had been, but that wasn't a high mountain to get over. He would never raise a hand to Melantha or their child, and that would make him a better father than his father had been.

But that wouldn't make him a *good* father. Just an adequate one.

He wanted to be so much more than merely adequate.

Melantha eased back slightly, her forehead furrowing. "What is wrong? Are you not excited?"

Rharreth shook himself, then pulled Melantha into his arms. She had just told him incredibly good news, and he'd just stood there, frozen. "Yes, I am. Just over-whelmed."

Melantha gave a short laugh against his shirt. "Yes, the timing could have been better. But by the time I am far enough along that we can make the announcement to the kingdom, the people will be ready for happy news."

Rharreth held her close and pressed a kiss to Melantha's hair. As long as he had Melantha at his side, he could weather whatever came. They had already survived turbulent times here in Kostaria. The joy of becoming parents would be something to savor, despite his fears.

"I don't know what I would do without you," Rharreth mumbled into her hair. "I love you."

"I love you too." Melantha snuggled into his arms, then gave a hint of a shiver.

Only then did he feel the cold of the breeze. She wore only her thick, wool dress.

He rubbed her arms, then steered her toward the stairs that led to their bedroom. "You're cold. Let's get inside."

Melantha shook her head on a laugh as she let him steer her toward the stairs. "You are not going to turn all over-protective, are you?"

"I would not dare." Rharreth kept an arm around her waist. He might be tempted to bundle her in layers of protective magic, but Melantha would, rightfully, fight him on that. She was strong, and she was a healer. She would monitor herself, and she would not push herself beyond what she could handle. Even if she had come very close to that line in the past few months.

The past few months had been rough. But, hopefully, better days lay ahead.

He would learn and grow from the mistakes he had made as king. He would learn and grow from any mistakes he made as a parent, too.

CHAPTER
THREE

EIGHT MONTHS LATER...

Melantha stood on her and Rharreth's balcony, bouncing slightly as she rocked her two-week-old son Rhohen in her arms. His tiny mouth puckered in his sleep, and she smiled down at him, her heart so filled it almost hurt.

Rhohen's shock of black hair was the same color as hers while his skin was a far darker gray than her silvery tone, though slightly lighter than Rharreth's. His features were a hint more delicate than Rharreth's, but heavier than hers.

Behind Melantha, a canvas tent covered most of the balcony space. Melantha had checked earlier, and it was well-stocked with furs and wool blankets. Everything Farrendel and Elspetha would need when they stayed here for Julien and Vriska's wedding.

From where Melantha stood, she could watch as the train puffed into sight from between the distant, purple peaks of the mountains. The train halted at the base of the ruins of Gror Grar. A few minutes of nothing, then Farrendel's magic glowed blue and sizzling, the taste of its power tangible even from where she stood a half a mile away.

Melantha held her breath, unable to look away as the magic built. In the streets of Osmana below, the people stopped and stared. Some leaned out of upper story windows or climbed onto the sloped roofs of the homes to better see past the outer walls of Osmana. All of them waited, arrested by the distant sight of Farrendel destroying the pile of poisoned grain so that it could never hurt any of them ever again.

The far-off magic slammed into the ground with a boom that echoed down the valley. The entire Khagniorth Stronghold trembled beneath Melantha's feet.

In her arms, Rhohen squirmed, his eyelids flickering.

Melantha cuddled him close and rocked him. He settled, his breathing smoothing once again. She pressed a light kiss to his forehead. "It is time for you to meet your aunts and uncles."

By the time Melantha strolled through the passage-ways of Khagniorth Stronghold, she arrived in the court-yard only a few minutes ahead of Rharreth as he escorted her family.

Weylind, Rheva, Ryfon, and Brina entered the court-yard first. Ryfon's and Brina's mouths hung open as they stared at everything around them.

Rheva focused on Melantha, stepped forward, and squeezed her shoulders before smiling down at Rhohen. "He is adorable."

Weylind joined Rheva, gave Melantha a shoulder hug squeeze, and stared down at Rhohen. "He looks a great deal like you."

Jalissa eased in next to Rheva. "May I hold him?"

Melantha handed Rhohen over to Jalissa, holding her breath that Rhohen would cooperate. He tended to be a bit temperamental on whether he would put up with being passed around or not. Some days, he would let no one but Melantha hold him, not even Rharreth. Other days, Rhohen was perfectly content to be held by whomever.

Today seemed to be one of his good days. Either that, or Rhohen was too deeply asleep to notice that he had left Melantha's arms.

Melantha stepped back, smiling as she took in the sight of her family cooing over her son.

There were no words to express the almost painful feeling filling her chest. A feeling that was some kind of mix of peace, love, regret, and contentment.

And joy. So much joy. She had not known she could feel this perfectly, joyfully content. With her life. With her family. Inside her own skin.

"He's so cute." Elspetha halted next to Melantha, her red hair in its customary braid.

"Linshi." Melantha shared a smile with Elspetha, then glanced past her to Farrendel.

Fieran, Farrendel and Elspetha's nearly eight-month-old son, squirmed in his arms, making whining noises as if he wanted to get down. Fieran's hair—the same bright red as Elspetha's—was shaggy and long around his ears and over his forehead while his eyes were a bright blue just a shade or two darker and less silver than Farrendel's.

Melantha gestured to Fieran. "He is so big." She had not seen him since shortly after he had been born.

"Yes. And already showing all the signs that he's going to be walking soon." Elspetha sighed and shook her head. "I thought elves aged more slowly than humans."

"They do, though the baby stage is more or less the same. Aging does not slow until the toddler stage." Melantha shrugged, smiling as Fieran wiggled so much that he was nearly hanging over Farrendel's shoulder. "But elves are more athletically inclined, even as children. While Fieran may age slower than a fully human child, he may hit many of the more athletic milestones sooner."

"Great. I'm going to have a toddler who has all the athleticism of a far older child but none of the common sense." Elspetha sighed and glanced at Farrendel. "How do you elves actually live to adulthood? Elven parents deserve a medal for keeping their children alive."

"Safety harnesses." Farrendel let Fieran scramble over his shoulder, but he kept a firm grip on the boy's ankles. "Though elven children rarely need them for long. They have a sense of balance and a head for heights quite young."

Fieran giggled, dangling upside down. He swung himself back and forth, then giggled harder.

"Perhaps elven children do, but Fieran is half-human." Elspetha eyed the way Fieran was hanging upside down, though she did not seem too worried.

Farrendel paused, then gave a short nod. "Yes. Perhaps it would be wise to procure a harness for Fieran as soon as we return to Estyra."

Melantha smiled and gestured to Fieran. "I believe Fieran's propensity to be upside down indicates he inherited a great deal of elven agility."

Farrendel lifted Fieran by his ankles and gently swung him around so that Farrendel was holding the boy in front of him instead of over his back. "He does seem to prefer to be upside down rather than right side up."

"Just like you when you were that age." Melantha wished she could go back in time and savor the time with her little brother more than she had. She had been so bitter, and that bitterness had only grown and festered.

Near the doors into Khagniorth Stronghold, Rharreth, Vriska, and a cluster of guards were beginning to gather.

Melantha nodded to Elspetha and Farrendel before she hurried to join them. As much as she wanted to linger with her family, she needed to be there with the rest of the shield band when they added Julien as their newest member.

THE GREAT HALL echoed with the cacophony of hundreds of celebrating trolls and humans. The human nobles who had traveled all the way to Kostaria to witness the wedding of Prince Julien had been dispersed among the troll guests, the better to facilitate discussions between the trolls and humans. A few of the humans huddled, as if uncomfortable among all the boisterous trolls, but many were just as loud as they threw themselves into the spirit of things.

Melantha winced and forced herself to eat another bite of caribou steak. Even with the moss earplugs, the noise level was barely tolerable, especially after the long day. Between the fighting bouts, then the wedding, and now the wedding feast, she was nearly at her limit for noise.

In her arms, Rhohen was squirming. He was probably only a few minutes away from launching into a scream.

Well, feeding her son was a better excuse than most for bowing out of this party early.

Melantha touched Rharreth's shoulder, then leaned close to speak into his ear. "I am going back to our room."

He nodded, nearly having to shout his reply back. "Do not wait up for me."

As king, he would need to stay until the feast wrapped up well into the early hours of the morning.

Melantha pushed away from the table, cradling Rhohen in one arm. As she eased between the row of chairs and the back wall, she halted behind Farrendel.

He was sitting sword straight, every muscle tensed. One hand fisted around his fork, though he did not appear to be eating anything.

If she had reached her limit, then Farrendel must be far beyond his.

Melantha touched his shoulder, and he jumped.

When he glanced over his shoulder at her, his eyes were slightly wide and wild. Once his gaze fixed on her, a fraction of his tension eased, but not much.

"I am heading to my room. I do not think you would be missed if you wanted to escape." Melantha bounced Rhohen slightly. He was making fussing noises. She only had maybe a minute to get out of here before her surreptitious exit would become far less inconspicuous. Loud as it was, a child's angry scream-cry could probably pierce the noise. And a few eardrums.

Elspetha glanced up from her plate, then she gathered Fieran from her lap and held him out to Farrendel. "Take Fieran back to the room. It's about his bedtime anyway. If you don't mind, I'd like to stay just a little longer."

Farrendel mumbled something that even Melantha could not hear before he grabbed Fieran and shot to his feet.

Together, she and Farrendel—children in their arms—continued their shuffle behind the chairs, heading for the door.

As they passed where Jalissa was sitting next to Edmund, Jalissa leaned close to Edmund, said something into his ear, then glided to her feet, falling into step behind Farrendel.

At the far end of the table, Weylind stared after them with something almost like jealousy, as if wishing that he, too, could make an exit. At one point during the evening, someone had spilled their drink all over Weylind, leaving a clump of his hair sticking to the splotch drooling down his shirt.

But he was the elf king. His early exit would be noticed and remarked upon by the gathered trolls and humans.

Melantha smiled as she took one last glance around the great hall. The obsidian ceiling glittered in the lamplight while, below, trolls and humans and even a few elves packed the tables with a raucous celebration.

At the long table at this end of the room, Rharreth held court with King Averett and Queen Paige of Escarland on one side, along with Essie and Edmund. Weylind sat on his other side, with Rheva, Ryfon, and Brina next to him. While Rheva was quietly taking in everything, Ryfon and Brina had wandered off to talk to groups of young trolls around their ages.

The newlyweds, Julien and Vriska, were wandering hand-in-hand between the tables, occasionally stopping to talk to groups of guests. Each step brought them closer to the far door. Not that Melantha would blame them if they were attempting an early exit of their own.

In Melantha's arms, Rhohen drew in a deep breath, gathering himself for a shrieking cry.

Melantha hurried out the door into the passageway, Farrendel and Jalissa at her heels. All three of them released a breath, almost in unison, as the door closed and blocked the uproar.

The peace and quiet of the passageway lasted for only

one blissful moment. Then Rhohen screwed up his face and wailed at an impossibly piercing octave.

Farrendel flinched. In his arms, Fieran stuffed his favorite stone tree toy in his mouth and chewed it as he regarded his cousin, unfazed by the screaming.

Jalissa shook her head, her mouth twisting with something between a smile and a grimace. "He has quite a healthy set of lungs."

"Yes." Melantha switched Rhohen so that he was propped against her shoulder. She patted his back, but it did not help. Nothing would, until she had a chance to feed him.

His little body swelled with the depth of his gasp—his inhale provided a momentary relief from the crying—before he let loose another wail right next to her ear. Somehow, he managed to hit yet another octave higher.

Melantha quickened her pace to reach her room as soon as possible. Farrendel and Jalissa easily matched her pace.

Fieran squirmed, but when Farrendel did not set him down, Fieran, too, started fussing and whining in between chewing on his tree.

Jalissa glanced between the two children with a slightly bemused look.

Melantha grinned at her sister, raising her voice to be heard above Rhohen's shrieking and Fieran's fussing. "It will be your turn soon enough."

"All in good time." Jalissa smiled with something between warmth and longing.

"Until then, enjoy the peace and quiet." Farrendel adjusted his grip on Fieran as the boy squirmed and wiggled, his whining growing louder.

Thankfully, they reached Melantha's door quickly. Farrendel crossed the space and disappeared up the stairs to the balcony where he, Elspetha, and Fieran were stay-ing. Melantha invited Jalissa in, and the two of them chatted while Melantha fed Rhohen.

Chatting came far easier now than it had even a few months ago. Jalissa and Edmund had visited Kostaria several times over the past few months as Edmund worked with Rharreth to establish Kostaria's Intelligence Office and train those chosen to run it.

Edmund had been so impressed with Eyvindur when they had tracked the grain smugglers together that he had suggested Eyvindur would make a good head of the Kostarian Intelligence Office. Rharreth had wholeheart-edly agreed, and Eyvindur was stepping into his new role quite adeptly.

Edmund and Jalissa were not here in an official capacity on this particular trip. At least, Edmund was not supposed to be working on this visit. None of them would put it past him to use his brother's wedding as some kind of training test for Eyvindur.

Jalissa seemed to be settling into her own role as the Liaison for the Tarenhieli Intelligence Office, though there was only so much she could tell Melantha about her work. But the way her eyes sparkled when she talked about working at her husband's side said it all.

Once Rhohen was fed and burped, Melantha laid him down on his back in his crib. He was already most of the way asleep, and he did not make more than a token fuss when she tiptoed away from the crib.

Crossing the room, she leaned into the stairwell toward the balcony. The door at the top was open, a sign that it was all right to come up. But she called up the stairwell anyway, keeping her voice soft, "Is it all right if we come up?"

"Yes." Farrendel's reply was soft but did not seem tense. Hopefully a good sign.

Melantha shared a glance with Jalissa. Then the two of them tiptoed up the stairs, not wanting to wake up Rhohen or Fieran, if Fieran was sleeping.

At the top, Farrendel lay on his back on a fur rug laid out on the balcony. He tipped his head to glance at them, a hint of a smile replacing the tension of earlier. The few minutes of alone time he had must have helped.

"We do not want to disturb you. Or wake Fieran." Melantha halted at the top of the stairs. Chatting with Jalissa had come easier, but she was still uncertain when it came to Farrendel. He had forgiven her, but there were times that Melantha could still hear the echoes of her own words, the pain of her past actions.

Farrendel gestured toward the tent. "Do not worry. Fieran is asleep, and he stays asleep through almost anything."

"We have put that to the test a few times at Buckmore Cottage." Jalissa shook her head as she pushed past Melantha, then sprawled on the rug next to Farrendel. "Edmund, Julien, and Averett do not know how to laugh quietly. Especially when all three of them are together."

"It is loud. Very loud," Farrendel added, his smile holding a hint of a grimace.

Melantha crept farther onto the balcony, leaving the door to the stairs cracked open so that she could hear if Rhohen woke. "That must be nice. Rhohen wakes at the slightest noise."

As she eased down on the rug on the other side of Farrendel, she caught a glimpse of Fieran past the slightly open flap of the tent, his figure lit by the small, elven light set out of his reach inside the tent. In the wooden crib set up for him, he slept with his face turned toward them and his butt in the air.

"This is nice. I can see why you like this balcony so much." Jalissa gestured upward, toward the star-strewn darkness. The faintest shimmer of green streaked across the sky, reflecting off the peaks of the distant, white-capped mountains. "Even if you almost died here once."

"It is much safer now. Rharreth built walls that prevent an ambush like that again. It is nearly impregnable now that Farrendel added a barrier of his magic around it." Melantha tipped her head to glance at Farrendel instead of the sky. "We appreciate that you took the time to do that earlier today."

Farrendel gave a small shrug, the movement nearly invisible in the darkness. "I needed a few minutes alone after the fighting bouts anyway."

The fighting bouts, where Farrendel had trounced all the trolls he had gone up against. He had finally been able to get out of the ring when he was defeated by Julien, though Melantha was not sure if Farrendel threw that fight on purpose or if his brother-in-law actually managed to get the jump on him.

"So tell me more about these boisterous family gatherings." Melantha tried to relax and simply be in this moment, setting aside the weight of past pain as she stared at the glittering stars and shimmering northern lights.

She was here with her little sister and brother. They were going to stay up late talking far into the night. Laugh as they had not laughed together in a long time, if ever. And she was going to savor the peace, both with her siblings and inside herself.

CHAPTER

FOUR

R harreth rolled out of bed amid Rhohen's cries. He'd thought himself an early riser, until Rhohen had been born. Now he and Melantha were learning how to function on little sleep and a schedule dictated by the tiny bundle currently setting up a wail from his crib.

Melantha gave a groan and rolled onto her back, blinking blearily at the ceiling. "I do not think Jalissa, Farrendel, and I should have stayed up so late talking."

The three of them had still been on the balcony, talking and enjoying the evening, when Rharreth had finally dragged himself into the room once the feast had broken up late in the evening. Well, technically in the wee hours of the morning.

"It was rather late." Rharreth leaned over and gave her a quick kiss.

Even though the crib was set next to the bed within easy reach for Melantha, Rharreth rounded the bed and leaned over the crib, running a gentle hand over the inch of black fuzz that stuck up soft and thick over his son's tiny head.

Rhohen kicked and cried, his little fingers clenching and unclenching.

Carefully, Rharreth picked Rhohen up. His son was so small that he had no problem fitting across Rharreth's large, blunt hands.

As soon as he was lifted from the crib, Rhohen's face twisted, reddened, and he let out a scream of pure *fury*. Not of hunger, though he was hungry. Nope, this was utter rage that Rharreth dared pick him up when all Rhohen wanted was his mother and breakfast. Rhohen kicked and swung his fists, as if he wanted to fight until Rharreth handed him to Melantha.

Or, perhaps, Rharreth was reading more into the baby's expression than was really there, and the two-week-old was simply hungry.

But something—maybe the instincts of a parent—told him that Rhohen had inherited a streak of tempestuous emotions and fighting spirit.

Melantha wiggled into a sitting position against her pillow and the headboard and reached for Rhohen. "Better give him here before he wakes Farrendel, Elspetha, and Fieran."

Rharreth gave a soft laugh and carefully transferred Rhohen to Melantha's arms. "I think it might already be too late for that."

Two doors and a set of stairs lay between them and the balcony, but Rhohen's cries were rather piercing. The two sets of oak would not be nearly enough to block the sound.

While Melantha fed Rhohen, Rharreth dressed, buckled his sword at his side, then stepped around the curtain that had been strung to provide a bit of privacy for the bedroom area.

He opened the door at the bottom of the stairs, climbed the steps, but halted in front of the upper door, knocking instead of opening it.

Strange, to knock to enter his own balcony. But that was the strangeness of having the elf warrior Laesornysh and his family staying on the balcony rather than in a room down the hall.

But such an arrangement had been necessary. Both so that Laesornysh—Farrendel—did not feel so closed in by the stone but also because it was an added layer of security for him and his family. Any troll who was still so angry at Laesornysh that they would try to attack him while he was here would have to go through Rharreth to do it.

After a moment, the door whooshed open, and Farrendel stood there, dressed and wearing his swords on his back. He gripped the door, bouncing on his toes as if it was taking everything in him to stand in one place. His posture remained tight, his face strained.

So much tension, and that balcony would not have nearly enough space, especially with most of it taken up by the tent.

"You need more space." Rharreth was not quite sure how to handle this. Normally, looking after Farrendel fell to King Weylind or one of Elspeth's brothers. Did Farrendel even trust him enough to let him help this morning?

"I will be fine." Farrendel's voice was taut as his expression, that nervous energy shaking the hand he'd clenched on the door handle. "The training arena has too much stone."

Rharreth nodded. It was as he had suspected.

Farrendel had handled the training arena well last night, and the stone infused with Melantha's healing magic would have prevented the headaches.

But after being surrounded by so much stone and people the day before, Farrendel was at his limit.

"May I enter?" Rharreth gestured toward the balcony. Was *enter* the right word? Step outside?

Farrendel nodded, then stepped aside, opening the door wider. "Essie and Fieran are still asleep."

Rharreth nodded, then gently took the door from Farrendel's grip to shut it quietly. "Come. Let's get you some space."

Farrendel glanced toward the tent, then trailed after Rharreth as he crossed the balcony, headed for the opposite corner from the tent.

Rharreth ran his fingers over the seemingly smooth wall of stone until his fingers found the nearly invisible hole that disguised the door latch.

The magic he'd infused into the door recognized him —as it would Melantha—and let him open it. When he'd built this additional wall around the back of the balcony, he'd added this hidden door, one that led into the mountain and a secret passage through the outer wall of Osmana.

Perhaps he was being paranoid, but he wanted an escape route if he and Melantha ever needed it. Again.

Rharreth swung the stone door open, and it made only the faintest of grinding noises. The passage before him was black.

Farrendel halted, his breath hitching.

"Don't worry. There are lights. It's just a short passage through the wall before we'll be outside of Osmana." Rharreth brushed his hand against the wall, sending his magic into the stone to activate the lights.

All along the passage, the white-blue lights flared to life, lighting the stairs down through the mountain and wall.

Farrendel shook his head, then glanced over his shoulder toward the tent. As if he was reluctant to leave his wife and child sleeping and unguarded up here.

"No enemies can cross the barrier wall you created, and the door below is well guarded. Melantha will look after Elspeth if she wakes before we get back." Rharreth waited in the doorway. He suspected that Elspeth wouldn't be so surprised to find Farrendel gone.

Rharreth wouldn't push. Farrendel appeared ready to bolt, and the last thing any of them needed was for a troll guard patrolling the walls of Osmana to get jumpy at the sight of Laesornysh wandering the city or the stronghold alone.

After a moment, Farrendel nodded and inched forward again.

Rharreth led the way into the mountain, closing the door behind them since he would not want to leave the secret passage open.

Only a few stairs down, they passed through the crackling power of Farrendel's barrier, embedded deep into the stone to protect the balcony. Rharreth gave a shiver as the magic crawled over his skin, but this barrier was designed to let him pass.

The stairs were steep and there were far more of them than the short flight to the balcony. When they finally reached the bottom, Rharreth took a moment to press his hand to the wall and send his magic into the stone and out past the wall, checking to make sure the area was deserted.

He didn't sense any footfalls against the ground. It was safe.

This door, too, opened with only the softest grinding of stone on stone.

As soon as the door was open wide enough, Farrendel all but shoved past Rharreth, dashing outside. Once he stepped onto grass growing between the stone and gravel, Farrendel halted and drew in a deep breath. For the first time that morning, a hint of the tension eased in his shoulders.

Rharreth closed the secret door, glanced at the wall top to make sure they weren't seen, then set off along the gully between the mountains that guarded this side of Osmana.

Neither he nor Farrendel spoke as they hiked along the gully until an outcropping of the mountain hid them from view of any guards patrolling Osmana's walls.

Just past the outcropping, the gully opened up in a small meadow, ringed with spruce trees and lush with grass and summer flowers. A small herd of deer jerked their heads up, tails flicking at the interruption to their solitude.

Rharreth gestured to the glade. "I think this is a place an elf would appreciate. Go on, though I would watch out for any bears. Or moose. If you do meet one—"

For the first time that morning, Farrendel grinned. He raised his hand and let a few bolts of his magic play over his fingers. "The moose and bears would do well to avoid me."

Rharreth snorted a laugh at that. "True. In that case, if you do run into any aggressive wildlife, try not to singe them too badly while defending yourself. They make for good eating, and I currently have a stronghold filled with guests to feed."

Farrendel shot him one last grin before he raced across the meadow and disappeared among the trees. The last glimpse Rharreth had of him, he planted a foot on a tree trunk, launched into a flip, then grabbed a lower branch before swinging into the foliage.

Rharreth drew his sword and swept through fighting stances, holding each stance for a moment or two to stretch his muscles. The morning air brushed cool against his skin while the first rays of the rising sun pierced between the mountains, glittering on the drops of dew limning the grass and the trees.

"So this is where you headed off to so early in the morning. I can see why you kept it a secret. You'd have every elf currently in Khagniorth descending on this place."

Rharreth sighed, lowered his sword, and turned to where Edmund leaned against a nearby tree. "I thought you were supposed to be taking a break from skulking."

Edmund shrugged, though he remained casually leaning against the tree as if perfectly content where he was at. "That would be boring. Besides, Eyvindur needs the practice."

"And where is Eyvindur?" Rharreth sheathed his sword and crossed his arms.

"If he's smart, he's figured out I've left my room by now, and he's tracking me here." Edmund gestured toward the gully that led back to Khagniorth Stronghold. "If he hasn't even realized this is all a test then, well, Jalissa and I might have to extend our stay by a few weeks."

Rharreth sighed and shook his head. "You might be the most annoying brother-in-law I have."

Edmund smirked. "Even more annoying than the infamous Laesornysh?"

"Actually, I think he might be the *least* annoying of all of you." Rharreth waved toward the trees, where a brief flash of Farrendel's silver-blond hair was the only glimpse they had of him before he disappeared again. "He politely asks permission before sneaking."

"And Julien?"

"He's now my shield brother. A warrior I greatly respect and trust to watch my back. I only trust you where I can keep a close eye on you."

"Surely I'm at least less annoying than Weylind."

Rharreth paused, thought about that for a moment, then attempted to put a scowl on his face. "Weylind is a good king, and he has been quite fair in our treaty negotiations."

"When you put it that way, I see your point. I'm definitely your most annoying brother-in-law." Edmund smirked. "If I'm already that, then there's no point in trying to be less annoying. I will just have to own my annoying status."

"I'm going to catch you skulking around my kingdom again, aren't I?"

"For one, that time you caught me was an aberration. I don't get caught." Edmund pushed away from the tree. "Two, this is skulking officially sanctioned by both you and Avie."

That did make it a little hard to get riled over Edmund's sneaking when Rharreth was the one who requested Edmund's help in training.

Not that Rharreth was actually riled. No, what he felt right now as he breathed in a deep breath of crisp air tasting of evergreens and stone was peace.

His kingdom was at peace. Both with their traditional enemies—the elves—but also with the human kingdom of Escarland.

More than that, Rharreth was at peace. Within his family. Within himself. After a lifetime of warring with his brother and father, with the guilt of being unable to protect his mother, with what he was ordered to do as a prince of Kostaria, this peace was something to savor.

Hopefully he would have the chance to raise his son in this peace. His son would never know the darkness Rharreth had faced growing up.

Growing up, the only brother he had was Charvod. The only cousin he had was Drurvas. Needless to say, he had never been close with Charvod, and Drurvas had eventually stabbed him in the back.

Now, Rharreth had gained three brothers-in-law, two elves and a human. He was not close to any of them, not yet. But, perhaps, he could grow accustomed to them. Family gatherings would not be onerous.

Then there was his shield band. They had always been more his brothers—and sister—than Charvod ever had. There, too, his family was growing as Vriska married, and Zavni soon would.

Not only would his son never know the darkness Rharreth had, but he would also be surrounded by aunts, uncles, and cousins. He would never lack for family.

Edmund straightened and stepped into the shadows just as Eyvindur jogged into the meadow, his gaze darting about. Before Eyvindur turned to him, Edmund stepped behind him, a small knife appearing in his hand. Edmund lightly touched the flat of the blade to Eyvindur's neck. "You're going to have to be more aware of your surroundings than that if you want to avoid getting assassinated by another spy."

Eyvindur's shoulders slumped. Yet as soon as Edmund started to withdraw the knife, Eyvindur slammed his elbow into Edmund's stomach.

Edmund oofed and stumbled back, gasping for breath.

Eyvindur turned, grinned, and crossed his arms. "I don't need to worry. I'll just pound any spies that try."

Farrendel dropped out of a tree next to Edmund and scowled down at him. "You are making my quiet meadow very loud and crowded."

Edmund had both arms wrapped over his stomach as he wheezed. "My mistake."

Rharreth couldn't help it. He tossed back his head and laughed.

NIGHTMARES AND MONSTERS

CHAPTER
ONE

The scream tore through the night, yanking Essie from sleep. She rolled farther from Farrendel before she pushed onto her elbows, then into a sitting position.

He curled on his side, facing away from her. He cried out again, his arms over his head.

It had been a long while since he'd had a nightmare this bad. But she had been bracing for something like this, knowing the stress of the end of the semester exams might trigger his anxiety.

Essie drew on the magic in the heart bond and placed a shield of crackling magic between herself and Farrendel. Once that was in place, she reached deeper into the heart bond and tugged on Farrendel's magic directly.

His breath caught, his cry cutting off. He stiffened and lay there for a long moment, gathering himself.

Essie dropped the magic, thankful that Farrendel hadn't lashed out this time.

Once she was sure that he was more awake than in the

nightmare, she leaned forward and pressed a kiss to his cheek. "I'm going to check on Fieran, then I'll start the hot chocolate."

Farrendel bolted partially upright, and his forehead would've caught Essie on the chin if she hadn't flinched back just in time. He twisted to face her, his eyes wide and still a bit wild. "Fieran. What if…if he heard…"

"I'll see if he woke up." Essie rolled off the bed, then shrugged into her dressing gown.

Neither of them wanted to voice the fear out loud. It would tear Farrendel apart if his screams had terrified Fieran.

Hopefully Fieran had slept through Farrendel's cries. He'd slept through nightmares before, though those had been milder.

Essie took one of the small elven globe lights and whispered the elvish word to light it. The blue glow lit her way as she navigated across the new bridge that connected their room with Fieran's. When he was older, the bridge would be taken down to give all of them more privacy, but right now it provided a far faster way for Essie or Farrendel to check on Fieran than going down to the main room, then back up to Fieran's room.

The bridge swayed slightly under her feet, but this bridge had been built with lovely handrails so it was secure even in the dark.

When she reached the porch, she brushed past the network of branches that acted like a net to keep Fieran safely contained at night. Elf toddlers were such rambunctious climbers that nothing short of a full enclosure kept them from wandering. They would just climb right over a standard human baby barrier.

Essie wrapped the light in her hand so that only a small glow remained. Then she eased the door open and tiptoed inside. She didn't want to wake him if he was still sound asleep.

She raised the light and let it filter into the room.

Fieran was a lump all bundled in blankets. No, huddled under the blankets. As the light fell on him, he lifted the blanket from over his head and peeked at her with bright blue eyes a shade darker than Farrendel's. "Mama?"

"Fieran." Essie hurried across the room and sank onto the edge of the bed. She set the elven light on the bedside table, then gathered Fieran into her arms. "Are you scared?"

He nodded against her, wrapping his arms around her neck and clutching tight. He mumbled something in his toddler speech that sounded like, "Scary."

"Yes, I'm sure what you just heard was scary." Essie held her son tight, her heart aching. What was she supposed to tell him? She and Farrendel had agreed that they didn't want to lie to their children about Farrendel's past as a warrior. But Fieran was only a toddler. There were plenty of things he wasn't ready to handle and was too young to understand. "Sometimes, dreams can be scary. Have you ever had scary dreams?"

Fieran nodded into her shoulder, still hiding his face as if that could protect him from whatever scary thing his imagination told him was out there.

"And when you have scary dreams, sometimes you scream for me or your dacha to come rescue you, right?" Essie smoothed a hand up and down Fieran's back, hating the way he was still trembling slightly.

Another tentative nod.

"When you do, Dacha or I always come and stay with you until you aren't so scared anymore." Essie pressed a kiss into the long, soft strands of Fieran's bright red hair.

Now how did she go about telling him this next part?

"Sometimes, your dacha has scary dreams too. And sometimes, his dreams are so scary that he cries out in his sleep." Essie held her breath, not sure how Fieran was going to react or how much he'd understand.

Fieran pulled back in her arms and peered up at her, a pucker between his brows. "Dacha scared?"

"Yes, even your dacha gets scared sometimes." Essie waited until she saw the gleam of understanding in Fieran's gaze. "And when he does, I stay with him until he isn't so scared anymore. When I'm scared, your dacha is there for me."

Fieran's face twisted as he pondered this for a long moment. Then he gave a nod and relaxed as if he'd come to some kind of conclusion, though she couldn't guess exactly what he was thinking. At least he didn't seem scared anymore.

"I look after you with lots of hugs." Essie drew Fieran in for another, tight hug. "And kisses." She planted kisses on his bright red hair and gave him a squeezing hug that turned into tickles.

"Mama! Macha!" Fieran squirmed and giggled big belly laughs, his protests coming out in a mix of Escarlish and elvish.

She gave him one more smacking kiss on the cheek before she relaxed her grip to let his giggles die off before he got too wound up and never went back to bed.

Fieran trailed off into a long exhale as he flopped in Essie's lap. After another moment, he partially sat up. "Dacha hugs?"

"Yes, I'll give your dacha lots of hugs and kisses too." Grinning, Essie tapped Fieran's nose.

Fieran scrambled up, as if he was about to climb out of bed. "Dacha hugs."

Essie quickly snagged him before he could go far. "Oh, you want to give Dacha hugs. Not now." Essie kept her tone light, even as a part of her tightened. The last thing Farrendel would want would be for Fieran to see him like this. "You need to go back to sleep. But you can give Dacha a big hug in the morning, all right?"

Fieran cocked his head for a moment, as if considering. Then he nodded.

She set him back on the bed and stood. "All right. Then it's time for you to go back to sleep."

He made a few whining grumbles, but he curled up on the bed and didn't resist as she spread his blankets over him again.

Essie pressed a light kiss to his cheek. "Sleep tight and sweet dreams."

She reached for the elven light, but Fieran pushed to his elbows and made a noise in the back of his throat, his eyes widening. She set the light back onto the table. "I'll leave the light for you, all right?"

Fieran nodded and sank back onto his pillow, closing his eyes.

Essie crossed the room, pausing by the door to glance back one last time at Fieran to make sure he was trying to go back to sleep, before she opened the door and stepped onto the porch.

Instead of heading back to her and Farrendel's room, she tiptoed down the steps to the main room, where the faint glow of a light indicated that Farrendel had already retreated there. Thankfully, she knew the stairs well enough that she could safely navigate them in the dark without the help of the light she'd left behind with Fieran. The handrails—something Farrendel had installed just for her—certainly helped.

Inside the main room, Farrendel sat on the cushions

on the floor, a blanket around his shoulders and his knees drawn up. The heating coil—powered by Farrendel's magic—and the cocoa sat on the kitchen countertop, ready to start making hot chocolate as if Farrendel had started to get it out before he'd retreated to huddle next to the wall.

As she crossed the room, Farrendel glanced up at her, the question burning in his eyes.

Essie sank onto a cushion next to him. A part of her wanted to lie to him and tell him that Fieran had slept right through the nightmares.

But he'd see right through the lie. She would not have taken so long if Fieran had been asleep, and he would have felt her emotions as she talked with Fieran through the heart bond.

Nor should she lie to him, no matter the temptation to spare him. He wasn't so fragile that he needed her to decide for him what he could or couldn't handle, especially when it came to their son.

"Fieran woke up."

Farrendel squeezed his eyes shut and let his head drop against the wall behind him with a faint thump. "He was scared."

"Yes, but we had a good talk about nightmares and how scary they can be." Essie tucked her arm around Farrendel's and leaned her head on his shoulder. "He isn't scared of you. And I think talking about stuff like this might help him grow up knowing he can talk to us about anything."

Farrendel gave a tiny nod, but he didn't open his eyes nor did the tension leave his shoulders.

She wasn't sure he'd fully believe her until he got to hug Fieran in the morning and his thoughts were more clear in the light of day.

This was their reality. Farrendel's nightmares and anxiety would affect their family. There was no getting around that, even though Farrendel had worked hard to get to the place he was at now.

But tonight wasn't the time to talk or make decisions. Right now, she would listen and simply be there. She squeezed Farrendel's hand. "Would you like hot chocolate?"

A pause. "Yes."

"All right." She pushed to her feet and headed for the kitchen to whip up a batch of Farrendel's favorite hot chocolate.

"MACHA!" Fieran's yell held a whine rather than fear.

Essie stifled a yawn as she navigated the bridge to Fieran's room to fetch him for breakfast.

Elves. Even after the late night, both Farrendel and Fieran had woken up far too early.

Farrendel had been up and gone before she'd woken, off exercising in the treetops to work off the last of the tension from the night before. And now Fieran was shouting for her.

She brushed past the tangle of branches, but Fieran wasn't climbing around on the porch just yet. She stepped inside his room, then halted.

The bed was empty. The room was empty.

Where was—

Even as she started to glance up, Fieran's happy squeal came from above her.

"Mama!" Fieran clung to a branch with his feet tucked against the wall and his hands on the ceiling.

Her heart gave a lurch, but she drew in a steadying

breath. This was normal. This wasn't the first time she'd found Fieran dangling from branches far too high up. Elven children apparently went straight from walking to climbing. And by climbing, it wasn't a tame, clamber onto the table or a hot stove. No, it was full-on dangle from the ceiling.

"Macha!" Fieran scrambled partially down the wall, jumped, ricocheted off a table, and flew toward her.

She barely managed to catch him, stumbling at the force of the impact. "Oof! You're getting so big."

Fieran giggled into her shoulder.

Wild elf child. At this rate, Farrendel was going to have to start taking Fieran with him in the mornings to work off excess energy.

Essie bounced Fieran on her hip. "Let's get breakfast."

Fieran gave a happy sound that might have been a word, though it was so garbled she couldn't quite tell what it was.

When they reached the main room, she set Fieran in his chair, then took out fruit from the cold cupboard, cut off the various stems and pits, and placed the fruit on Fieran's plate.

He grabbed one of the strawberries and chomped off a large bite, red juice dripping down his chin and his arm.

Smiling, Essie started the heating coil, then pulled out a loaf of bread and cut it into slices. She placed the first slice in a pan on the coil, toasting it for a few minutes before she flipped it over to toast the other side.

How she loved this heating coil that Farrendel and Lance had invented a few years ago. Without it, they hadn't been able to heat hot chocolate or breakfast in their room since elves avoided open fires inside their rooms.

When the bread had heated, she spread it with the new-fangled peanut butter that was all the rage in

Escarland right now, having been imported from one of the kingdoms to the south. After cutting the bread into pieces, she added it to Fieran's plate.

He grinned and dug in, slathering peanut butter onto his fingers, his face, and somehow into his hair and ears.

Perhaps she shouldn't have given him such a messy meal on a morning when he intended to give Farrendel a hug. Though there weren't many meals that weren't messy for a toddler, and the odds were that Fieran had forgotten all about hugging his dacha first thing in the morning.

Essie started on her own toast. Once it was finished, she spread it with peanut butter and took her seat next to Fieran.

She had just taken her first bite when Farrendel strode into the room, his hair still damp.

"Dacha!" Fieran stood on his chair, then launched himself across the room at Farrendel.

Farrendel stepped forward and caught him, then grimaced. "You are a mess."

Fieran gripped him with fingers made sticky with fruit juice and peanut butter. Grinning, Fieran leaned forward and hugged Farrendel around the neck, then planted an even more sticky kiss on his cheek. "Better?"

Farrendel's nose wrinkled, and for a moment Essie held her breath, wondering if his anxiety at Fieran's messiness would get the best of him.

Then Farrendel smiled and adjusted Fieran in his arms. "Yes. All better. Linshi." He crossed the rest of the room and set Fieran back in his chair. Farrendel glanced from Fieran to himself. "I should not have bothered to wash this morning."

"Probably not. Breakfast turned out to be particularly

messy." Essie licked the peanut butter that had gotten on her own fingers.

"Ah." Farrendel hurried across the room and washed his hands. He claimed his preferred breakfast of bread, cold meat, and cheese rather than bread and peanut butter.

When he slid into his seat across from her, shadows still lingered around his eyes. But a hint of a smile tugged at his mouth.

A rough night, yes. But a good morning. Sometimes, that was all a person could ask for.

CHAPTER

TWO

"Dacha!" The high-pitched scream echoed into the night.

Someone was attacking Fieran.

Farrendel bolted upright and was on his feet before he was fully awake. He already wore a loose shirt and trousers, and he swiped his swords from their place next to the bed here in their turret room of Buckmore Cottage.

In the bed behind him, Essie stirred, then pushed onto an elbow. "What—"

"Stay here." Farrendel gestured to her, knowing he did not have to say more. She would know to use his magic in the heart bond to protect herself and their unborn child if this was some kind of attack.

He did not wait for her to nod before he yanked open the door and dashed into the hallway, even as Fieran screamed for him again.

Only two strides separated their door from Fieran's. Farrendel grabbed for the door, jerked it open, then lunged inside, sword in hand, magic already dancing around his fingertips.

Fieran curled in a ball on his bed, with his back against the wall and his blankets over his head. He peeked out of his blanket pile, wide eyes wet with tears as he blinked at Farrendel. "Dacha?"

No one else was in the room. Fieran was not in danger.

Farrendel released a sigh to ease his tension, leaned his swords against the wall near the door, and tried to convey his relief through the elishina so that Essie would know that there was no danger. After crossing the room, Farrendel sank onto the edge of the bed. "What is wrong, sason?"

Fieran poked his head farther from his protective blankets, then he pointed one tiny finger at the wall. "Monsters."

The bright, silvery beams of the moon cast strange shadows from the bare, winter branches of the tree outside of Fieran's window. A faint breeze must be stirring the branches because the shadows on the wall twitched and waved.

Fieran gave a cry and buried his head under the blankets again.

Farrendel shifted so that he sat cross-legged with his back to the wall next to Fieran. "It is all right. There is nothing to fear. There are no monsters. Those are shadows from the tree outside your window."

Fieran peeked out of his blanket again, forehead puckered as he blinked at the shadows. They shifted, and he squeaked a cry once again. Then he glanced down at the darkness near the floor. "Monsters under bed."

"There are no monsters under the bed either."

Fieran glanced at him with a deep pucker still twisting his face.

Right. Apparently logic was not very comforting to a

toddler.

Farrendel gathered Fieran into his arms and tugged him, blanket and all, onto his lap. "You know I will always protect you, sason."

Fieran shifted so that he leaned his back against Farrendel's chest, though he remained bundled in the blanket. "Uh-huh."

A little better, but perhaps he needed to take more of an Essie approach to this. Logic and sincerity were not enough. Fieran needed something flashier to reassure him.

Farrendel held out a hand in front of Fieran and let a tendril of his magic curl around his fingers. "I will chase any monsters away with my magic."

Fieran reached out and swiped his fingers through the faintly crackling magic.

Farrendel's heart leapt into his throat, but he kept a tight hold on his magic so that it bent around Fieran's skin, not even close to burning him.

Such precautions might not even be necessary. Given that Fieran had likely inherited a similar magic, he would be less susceptible to Farrendel's magic than most. Though, they would not know for sure until decades from now when Fieran came into his magic.

Fieran relaxed in Farrendel's arms, his eyes wide with wonder rather than fear as he played with Farrendel's magic.

Farrendel let the magic twine over Fieran's hands, until Fieran was grinning and giggling at what would feel like a tickling across his skin.

"Someday, you are going to have your own magic." Farrendel released his magic, then waited until Fieran glanced up at him. "It might be scary when you first get it, but I will teach you how to use it."

"And I fight monsters!" Fieran pumped his fists in front of him, making zapping, pewing sounds to go along with whatever magical monster battle he was envisioning. A bit ludicrous, given that monsters did not exist.

But he was excited at the thought of magic—even a magic that would look like Farrendel's. Right now, that was enough. If he wanted to pretend he was fighting monsters with magic, then so be it.

Fieran gave one more jab, complete with sound effect, then grinned. "Monsters all gone."

"Yes, they are. Well done, sason." Farrendel rested his hands in their laps as Fieran sagged against him.

For long moments, Fieran remained silent. Eventually, he grabbed one of Farrendel's hands with his two smaller ones. His fingers lightly traced the faint scars on the back of Farrendel's hand, then the larger, starker scars around his wrist.

Farrendel held his breath, not quite sure what his son would make of the scars or what Farrendel would say if Fieran asked. He certainly was not going to tell his son about the torture and the way the trolls had bound his wrists with stone and magic, causing those scars.

"What this?" Fieran's gaze remained focused on Farrendel's hand and wrist.

"Those are scars." Farrendel struggled to remain relaxed. How could he explain them to a toddler in a way Fieran would understand? "They are..." What was the Escarlish word that Essie often used? "...owies that got better."

Fieran twisted to peer up at Farrendel. "Mama kiss it better?"

His tension disappeared in a whoosh as he released a breath that felt almost like a laugh. "Yes, your macha kissed it all better."

Fieran nodded, as if that made total sense to him. He let go of Farrendel's hand, gripped the blanket again, and yawned.

"It is time to go back to sleep." Farrendel started to gather Fieran up, preparing to set him back onto the bed.

Fieran made a noise and gripped Farrendel's arm, his eyes going wide again. "No!"

Farrendel paused, the fear in Fieran's eyes tugging at him. "All right. I will stay until you fall asleep."

Fieran let go of Farrendel's arm, and he did not protest as Farrendel set him back on the bed. Once he was on the mattress again, Fieran curled into a ball in the blanket with his head on his pillow. His red hair spread in wild abandon, the tip of his pointed ear visible through the strands.

That hair. It was red and long like an elf child's since they had yet to cut it. But it did not behave the way an elf's hair would. It tangled, and Fieran was forever spitting it out of his mouth or shoving it out of his face as if it bothered him.

Fieran might have inherited many elven traits from Farrendel, but his hair was all Essie's.

Across the room, Essie peeked through the partially open doorway, a scrunch to her forehead and a question in her eyes.

Farrendel met her gaze, then pointed down at Fieran, trying to tell Essie through the elishina that he was going to stay with Fieran for a few more minutes.

Essie's smile turned soft, and she nodded, disappearing from the doorway.

Farrendel stretched out on the edge of the bed and listened as Fieran's breathing deepened back into the sleep of a son secure in the knowledge that his dacha would always protect him.

INVENTOR

CHAPTER
ONE

FIFTEEN YEARS BEFORE FIERCE HEART...

Illyna woke to screams. Her body throbbed with pain, especially her left arm and hand. She groaned and tried to lift her arm, but it seemed pinned to her side. When she glanced down, all she could see was a swathe of white bandages soaked in red.

Vague memories of the battle danced across her eyes. Charging into battle with Prince Weylind. The troll warrior swinging his ax. Her shield shattering as he raised the ax again...

She blinked, gasping in another pained breath. She lay on the ground on a blanket with only the spreading branches of the trees far above providing cover. Other elf warriors lay on either side of her, also moaning in pain.

A female elf knelt a few feet away, giving a drink of water to an elf warrior with bandages plastered to his chest.

Another pained scream rang out, and Illyna flinched.

"Who is that?" The warrior next to Illyna caught the nurse's sleeve. "What are they doing in there?"

The nurse paused, glancing toward the healers' tent at the far side of the rows of wounded warriors. "That is the young prince. I heard the trolls filled him with stone to cut him off from his magic."

Illyna shuddered as another cry of pain echoed off the trees. It sounded like even the healing process was torture for the young prince Farrendel.

The nurse gave a smile that was far too stiff and did not reach her eyes. "Do not worry. The healers will be with all of you shortly, once they finish with Farrendel Amir."

"And the king?" Illyna's voice croaked out of a dry throat. Last she remembered, she had seen the king collapsing with an arrow in his back.

The nurse paused, even the forced smile fading from her face. "Our good king Lorsan is dead. Long live King Weylind."

Illyna could only stare, her head whirling and darkness crackling at the edges of her vision.

King Lorsan was dead. Killed in the rescue of his illegitimate son.

Illyna glanced around at the rows and rows of wounded, then at her own bloodstained and bandaged arm.

Was the young prince worth all of this? The loss of so many good warriors. The wounding of many others. The death of their king. Yes, Prince Farrendel was a great warrior. Some said he could be like one of the great elven warriors of old, once he grew older. But he was only one boy, and he was illegitimate. Was his life worth all the death it had taken to save him?

Illyna lay on a cot in the healing shelter at the large, sprawling main camp, waiting for her turn to be shipped back to Estyra to make a full recovery.

Full recovery. Ha.

She lifted her left arm and stared at the stump where her hand had been. A hand taken by the troll's ax.

If she closed her eyes, she was sure she could still feel her hand. She could reach out and grasp her shield like she used to. How could something that was not even there still ache as if it were?

The healers said the ache and sensation might fade with time. Or it might not. Only time would tell. They had done their best to heal the stump of her arm as effectively as possible to prevent such things, but even elven healing magic was not infallible.

Either way, she would live the rest of her life like this. Scarred. Broken. Never whole. Never quite up to the standards of elven beauty and perfection.

The magic, elven lights strung near the ceiling of the shelter were dimmed, and darkness cloaked the sliver of view around the canvas flap that served as a door. Most of the other wounded were resting, though many tossed and turned.

At the far end of the shelter, a curtained-off area marked where the young prince Farrendel recovered from his wounds. Illyna had passed out again long before the healers had finished with him, but she had heard the other warriors discuss how his cries of pain had continued for hours. Thanks to all the stone and troll magic, the healers had struggled to numb his pain while they worked, or so she had heard.

The night deepened, and more of the warriors slept. But Illyna could not.

A cry rang out, startling a few of the others awake. As the cry came again, one of the nurses hesitated, glancing toward the sound.

The young prince…

The cry built into a scream, and the nurse raced from the shelter. Hopefully to fetch a healer. Or the new king.

Either way, someone should go to the prince. He sounded like he needed help. The nurse should have at least checked on him before leaving.

But he was the illegitimate prince. Wielding terrifying magic. None of them wanted to get close.

Illyna glanced around the shelter, but no one made a move to go to the curtained-off section.

Groaning out a sigh, Illyna rolled into a sitting position. Pain flared down her arm and into her left hand—even though her left hand was no longer there. She pressed her arm against her stomach, trying to breathe through the pain. Her head whirled and darkness prickled at the corners of her vision.

The prince's cry built into a scream. She could not leave him like this.

Pushing to her feet, she staggered between the other cots until she reached the far end of the shelter. Her head pounded, her vision swirling. She had lost far too much blood to be up and about, but someone needed to help the prince. With a deep breath, she shoved aside the canvas flap and stepped into the prince's room.

Prince Farrendel curled on the cot, shaking, his eyes squeezed shut. The blanket had fallen to his waist, revealing the bandages wrapped around both of his arms and his thin torso.

So young. Far too young to have already suffered battle and torture.

"Farrendel Amir?" Illyna hesitated, then reached out with her right hand.

No sooner had she touched the prince's shoulder than he flinched away from her. His magic flashed out.

Illyna yelped and fell back onto the floor, the magic stinging her fingers. Her arm gave another throb, sending a dizzy tilt to her head. "Amir?"

The prince's eyes flew open, and he scrambled back, rolling off the far side of the cot.

Illyna peered over the cot, wary about approaching the prince. "Are you all right, amir?"

Wide, silver-blue eyes stared back at her. "Who are you?"

"Illyna. I am..." She was not anything to this prince. But he was staring at her all wild-eyed, and she was not sure how he would react if she did not reassure him. "I am a friend. You were screaming in your sleep."

"Where is Dacha? Weylind?" The prince glanced around, shaking once again as he curled his knees up to his chest.

Illyna opened her mouth but halted. She was not about to tell the prince that his dacha was dead. That was something that should come from his brother.

The flap behind her was thrown aside, and Prince—no, King—Weylind burst inside. He all but shoved Illyna aside as he hurried to his brother. "Shashon. You should rest."

Illyna recognized the moment she should leave. She backed out of the curtained area, staggering a bit as her head swam.

One of the nurses hurried to her side and looped her

arm over her shoulder. "You should rest, warrior. You lost a great deal of blood."

Illyna nodded and let the nurse help her back to bed.

Six Weeks Later...

Illyna drew a deep breath and approached the guards at the foot of the long, winding stairs that led upward into the treetop palace of Ellonahshinel.

The guards' eyes took in her face, then dropped to her left arm. A curl twitched the mouth of the guard on the left.

A sneer. Illyna was getting far too used to the looks since she had returned to Estyra.

It did not matter that she had lost her hand while fighting at the crown prince's side. Nor did it matter that she had helped rescue the younger prince from the clutches of the trolls.

No, all the guards saw was the disfigurement. As if Illyna had been reduced to what she was missing instead of being seen as a person.

She lifted her chin higher and held out the jar of her hair conditioner that she had made. "I brought a gift for Prince Farrendel to comfort him in his mourning."

It was a little thing, but it was all she could do. She could not get the prince's terrified gaze out of her mind, even as she struggled through her own recovery. She had never had any siblings, but the gaze had tugged at her the way a little brother's pain might have.

She hoped the prince did not feel as alone as she had been the past few weeks. He had lost his father and likely lost a piece of himself to the torture he had suffered. Word on the street was that, as soon as his father had been buried, Prince Farrendel had marched into Kostaria and killed the troll king, ending the war. While the citizens of Estyra celebrated the warrior Laesornysh, Illyna could only think about the young boy she had seen, tormented by nightmares and pain.

But Farrendel had his family. Unless they had cast him out as she had been cast out. Due to her injuries, she had been discharged from the army, the only true family she had. Her distant cousins—her only living relatives—would not take her in.

The sneering guard eyed her gift and made no move to take it. The second guard sighed and took the gift from her. "We will see that it is delivered once it has been inspected and deemed safe."

Illyna nodded, then turned back the way she had come. Hopefully the gift would actually reach the prince.

At least she had tried. Perhaps now she could get his pain out of her mind so she could focus on putting her own life back together.

Illyna fumbled with her mortar and pestle, trying to figure out how to steady it with the wooden prosthetic she had been issued.

The wooden hand felt all too clunky and foreign at the end of her arm, heavier than her hand had been. The leather cuff still ached against her still healing stump, even though it was padded with sheepskin. A few roots twined through the sheepskin, providing skin contact with wood as a conduit for her magic.

She was supposed to be able to make the fingers move with her magic, but she lacked the magical strength or practice to make the fingers move in anything other than clumsy twitches. From adolescence, she had trained to take her magic from her chest and wield it through her hands and fingers. It kept throwing her off when she tried to use her magic through the hand her brain still believed was there.

Not to mention, the prosthetic hand was solid wood. It took so much magic and effort to move the fingers when she got it to work as it should. Yet she needed to conserve her limited magic for making her shampoos and conditioners, not using it to make the wooden fingers of her prosthetic move.

She stabbed the pestle into the mortar, blinking at hot tears before they could spill.

She had to make this work. She had nowhere to go and no one to take her in. If she could not turn her hobby into a business, then she would...

She did not even know what she would do. Perhaps she could apply for support from the king, but not everyone found aid that way. Though she had been wounded in Prince Farrendel's rescue. The new king Weylind might be generous.

She would rather make it on her own, as she had always done. Both of her parents had been warriors, and both had given their lives for Tarenhiel when she had been young. She had fended for herself until she, too, joined the army and found a family again.

Now that had been taken away from her too.

A loud tramping sounded on the steps to her home in the upper stories of a tree along the back streets of Estyra a moment before a knock rapped on her door.

After setting down her pestle, she peeked out the window. She froze, her breath catching.

Two royal guards, dressed in their green shirts and

leather vests with the silver tree symbol on the right side of their vest, stood in front of her door.

What did they want? Why were they here? Illyna could not think of anything she might have done that would have brought the guards to her door.

Unless it had something to do with her gift to Prince Farrendel? But it was just a simple gift. She had not poisoned it or anything.

With a deep breath, Illyna opened the door. "Elontiri."

The first guard looked down his long, straight nose at her. "Are you Illyna Tirator?"

"Yes." Illyna glanced between the guards.

"You have been summoned to Ellonahshinel by Farrendel Amir." The guard gestured toward the stairs. "Would you come with us?"

What was going on? The guards were demanding she come right away, but they were at least wording it like a question. They had not clapped her in irons and hauled her off.

Had the prince been offended by her gift? After all, she did not really know him. But small gifts were not an uncommon gesture when a family was in mourning. Surely he had gotten many such small gifts over the past few weeks. His brother King Weylind had undoubtedly been flooded with them.

Illyna strode down the stairs, and the guards fell in around her with one in front and one behind. As they strolled through Estyra, she kept her head down, tugging on her sleeve, though it did not hide her wooden hand. Being marched through Estyra by royal guards was not going to help her fledgling business.

At the base of Ellonahshinel, the guards on duty nodded and let them pass. Illyna tried not to gape as she was led up the winding stairs into the palace itself. The grand hall, library, and other large rooms of the palace were formed of branches decorated with gold and grown in intricate designs.

The guards led her past more and more rooms until Illyna found herself on a far branch of Ellonahshinel. A single set of rooms, far simpler than many of the others, lay before her.

This was not a room on the royal branch. They had passed that several branches back.

Was this the servants' quarters? But why would the guards bring her here? They had said Farrendel Amir had summoned her.

The guards marched her across the final, smaller branch, then one of them knocked on the door.

"Enter."

The voice was harder and colder than she had expected.

One of the guards opened the door but did not step aside. "Illyna Tirator, as you requested."

"She may enter. You may remain outside." Prince Farrendel stood with his back to them, his spine straight as he seemingly stared at the wall with his arms crossed. Unlike the terrified, injured boy she had seen last time, this prince was all hard edges and steel, his swords strapped across his back.

With a nod, the guard stepped out of the way.

Illyna swallowed and stepped into the room. She winced as the guard shut the door behind her, leaving her alone with the prince.

He had not scared her before, but something about this silent figure—boy though he was—sent prickles down her arms.

When he turned, his expression was hard. A scar traced across his cheek while she could now see a few of the scars that wrapped around his wrists.

Yet as he glanced up and met her gaze, his silver-blue eyes held a raw pain that he could not fully disguise behind the hard look.

He held up an empty jar, one that Illyna recognized. "Are you the one who made the conditioner that was gifted me a week ago?"

"Yes." Illyna nodded and dipped into the bow she probably should have given him a few moments earlier. How had the prince managed to go through a whole jar of conditioner in a single week?

"Can you make more? I would pay you, of course." The prince's shoulders hunched a fraction as he lost some of the hard edges, looking once again more the boy than the deadly warrior.

Illyna blinked, then hurriedly nodded. "Yes, of course, amir. I can make more. Is there a particular scent you would prefer?"

She had made his gift a forest and mint scent as it seemed neutral.

Prince Farrendel shook his head, his gaze dropping to the floor rather than focusing on her. "I liked the scent. It is very...clean."

A strange way to phrase it, but she was not about to question her prince's personal choices.

"All right. I can have more for you tomorrow." It was not like she had anything better to do. She had very few orders to fill.

"I would appreciate it." Prince Farrendel seemed to attempt to draw his shoulders straighter, but he only succeeded for a moment before he hunched again. "Could you also make shampoo as well? If it is not too much trouble."

"No, no trouble." Illyna shook her head. "Now that I

have been discharged from the army, I am trying to start a business selling my shampoos and conditioners."

It was the one thing her magic was good for. While her magic was not strong, she could infuse plants with a magic that strengthened the natural properties of the plants and add benefits for hair.

"Trying?" Prince Farrendel lifted his head long enough to glance at her. "Your product is very good."

"Perhaps. But customers are difficult to come by. Especially with this." Illyna grimaced and held out her left arm, the wooden hand heavy against her elbow and shoulder. The healers told her she should take it slow, wearing the hand for longer periods each time, as her body adjusted to the weight and feel of it.

"I understand." Prince Farrendel tugged at his sleeve, as if trying to hide the scars around his wrists.

Now that Illyna thought about it, the prince had not grimaced at her left arm the way most people had. This whole time, his discomfort had been because of himself, not because of her.

It was refreshing, to be treated as a whole person again instead of being labeled by the hand she was missing, without pity or scorn.

For a moment, a comfortable, understanding silence fell between them.

Then the prince peeked up at her again. "You were the one to wake me from the nightmares that first night after my rescue. I do not remember the night clearly, but it was you, was it not?"

Illyna swallowed and nodded. "No one else was stepping forward to help. I..." She was not sure if he would want her sympathy for what had happened to him anymore than she would want his pity.

"You said you were a friend."

Now it was Illyna's turn to wince and focus on the floor. "I am sorry, amir, for being so presumptuous."

"No, I..." The prince cleared his throat and shifted. "I did not mind. I think...I would like a friend."

Illyna froze. How should she respond? It had been presumptuous enough to claim friendship to calm him when he had just woken from a nightmare. But who was she to be friends with a prince of the elves, even an illegitimate one?

But with his scars and pain, she saw the same ache and loneliness that she felt.

"I would like a friend too." She had lost so much when she had lost her hand. She had lost the family she had found in the army. She had lost the customers who now scorned her because of the injury.

But, perhaps, she could find others like her and Prince Farrendel. Those who did not fit the perfectly beautiful mold of most elves. She had already connected with a few others from that night who had been in the same healing hall for an extensive period of time while recovering.

Illyna gestured in the direction of Estyra. "A few of us who were wounded that day"—she did not have to specify which day—"are meeting at a café tomorrow night. Would you like to come?"

The prince's eyes went wide again, and his shoulders hunched, as if he were shrinking into himself. He gave a slight shake of his head, his eyes on his feet.

"We just talk." She was not sure how else to describe their weekly gatherings. Sometimes, it was just talk. Surface level discussions filled with lighthearted laughter. Other times, they *talked*. There was something deeply comforting in commiserating with someone else who had lived the same experience, struggled with the same difficulties, and traveled the same kinds of pathways.

The prince hunched even more in on himself, giving an even more emphatic shake of his head.

She would not push. He needed friends as much as she did, but the thought of venturing out appeared to be more than he could handle.

"Well, it is off of the crossroads of Aspen and Elm if you change your mind." Illyna shifted, reaching for the door behind her. "It has become a weekly thing, so if you do not come this week, perhaps another week?"

Prince Farrendel released a long, shuddering breath, drawing that hard-edged cloak around him once again. "Perhaps."

At the dismissal in that single word, she nodded, opened the door, and left. She was not sure if she had helped Prince Farrendel or not.

But for the first time since she had been wounded, something brighter stirred inside her chest. Something that felt a lot like hope.

TWO

FIVE AND A HALF YEARS AFTER FIERCE HEART...

Illyna gaped at the crowded streets of Aldon. So many humans, packed onto the sidewalks, hustling up and down the streets in carriages, wagons, and on horseback, and bustling between the shops nestled so close together that barely an alley separated the buildings. Everything had a hurried energy that the quiet, serene streets of Estyra did not.

Beside her, Farrendel strolled through the crowd with an ease that spoke of long practice. Though he still kept a wary eye on the crowds that parted for their cordon of guards, led by Farrendel's personal guards, the elf Iyrinder and the human Captain Merrick.

Farrendel wore his swords on his back, along with a small pack. His baby daughter Adriana was tucked into a carrier against his chest. She peered with wide blue eyes at the street while her red-blonde hair flared around her head and over her pointed ears.

Knowing Farrendel as she did, Illyna could picture him going through his checklist that morning.

Swords. Check.

Baby. Check.

Hidden knives. Check.

Bag of every conceivable thing the baby might need in an emergency, including diapers, change of clothes, bottle, snacks, and emergency medical kit. Check. Check. Check.

"Thank you for coming, Illyna." Farrendel made a strange, puckered face down at his daughter, causing her to burst into a shrieking laugh.

"I would not miss it. It is not every day that one of our own graduates from an Escarlish university." Illyna grinned, then made her own funny face at the baby, earning another shrieking laugh.

"Two of us. Iyrinder is graduating as well." Farrendel gestured to the elf guard parting the crowd in front of them.

Iyrinder glanced over his shoulder. "Yes, though I am not the focus of the event. You are the elf prince."

"But you are still graduating." Farrendel shrugged, a movement that wiggled Adriana and sent her into giggles. So Farrendel shrugged again until his daughter was giggling uproariously.

Illyna shook her head, still smiling. After nearly five years of classes, Farrendel and Iyrinder were graduating from Hanford University with their degrees in magical engineering. Iyrinder's mother and sister were coming for the event as well as Farrendel's entire family. King Rharreth and Queen Melantha were even traveling all the way from Kostaria.

This was Farrendel. So of course Illyna had come.

Fingol, Fydella, and many of Farrendel and Essie's other friends in Estyra were also coming, though they had decided to arrive the day of the graduation.

Farrendel deserved all the celebration. He had pushed through a lot to earn this degree.

"We are almost there." Farrendel pointed ahead of them. "That building ahead is Lance's workshop."

Illyna took in the large brick building sprawling ahead of them. Calling this a workshop was a misnomer. Farrendel's small wooden building on the forest floor where he tinkered with magical devices was a workshop. This was huge. And slightly intimidating. What kind of human inventions were built there?

When Farrendel had offered to show her the workshop where he spent his time working in Escarland, she could not refuse. Nor could she refuse this chance to meet this Lance Marion, Farrendel's human friend who had inspired him to pursue a degree in magical engineering in the first place.

The door to the large brick building stood open, and a loud clanging sound came from within.

Farrendel stepped inside without hesitation. "Lance! I brought Adry."

"Adry?" The clanging stopped, though it was followed by a clatter, as if something had been knocked to the floor.

Illyna gaped as she stepped more fully into the building. Piles of junk littered the cavernous space so that she could only see a few yards at a time. It looked like a maze with thin pathways between the towers of metal and gears.

Footsteps pounded between the piles of junk moments before a lanky human man skidded into sight. His dark blond-brown hair fell over the large, tinted goggles that he wore over his eyes, making him look like some kind of mad creature from a nightmare.

The man reached for Adry, then froze, his goggle-covered face swinging toward Illyna.

"And a friend." Farrendel grinned at Illyna while patting Adry's back. "This is Illyna, a friend from Estyra."

Slowly, the man reached up and pulled the goggles up to his forehead. He blinked light brown eyes at Illyna.

Illyna found herself blinking back at him, her heart giving a little flip-flop in her chest. With his goggles off, Lance Marion was the cutest, most befuddled-looking man she had ever met.

She was the most beautiful woman Lance had ever met. Her light blonde hair matched the bright rays of the sun streaming through the upper windows of his workshop. Her sky-blue eyes sparkled in her delicate features. Oh, and her ears were pointed. She was an elf.

Lance could only blink, words utterly failing him.

"I thought we could show Illyna the workshop. She runs her own business making shampoos and conditioners in Estyra." Farrendel started down one of the aisles between the stacks of spare parts, at home in Lance's workshop after spending so much time there over the past five and a half years.

"Oh, right. Of course. Sure, yes, um, if you'd come this way." Lance tripped over the toe of his boot and nearly face-planted into the nearest pile of gears.

Smooth. Real smooth. Why couldn't he just walk and talk like a normal person? Talking to people was always a bit of a challenge. He never knew what to say to them. Except for Princess Essie, who never seemed to mind his awkwardness, and Farrendel, who actually understood his discussions of magic and mechanics.

When it came to magical mechanics, he'd always been too intelligent for his own good and had gone to Hanford University as a child prodigy. It had been good for his career. Less good for his personal life.

As they reached the cleared section at the back where Lance and Farrendel worked, Farrendel started the tour, showing off his neat and tidy desk and his latest project.

Lance winced at the sight of his own desk, piled high with random bits of mechanical detritus and discarded greasy cloths. He hurried to his desk and surreptitiously tried to swipe the grease rags onto the floor and under the desk. He nudged the gears into a pile.

The elf—Illyna—glanced his way. He froze and grinned, trying to lean nonchalantly against the desk.

When she turned back to Farrendel, Lance shoved a few more of the scraps of metal into a semi-neat stack. Oh, there was his nine-sixteenths wrench. He'd been looking for that for a week.

"Now that I am graduating, Lance and I can officially start selling these." Farrendel gestured to the rows and rows of magical power cells holding his magic. A small window of reinforced glass showed the crackling, blue bolts contained in each of the reinforced metal canisters. "Lance has already secured a patent for his design."

Illyna nodded, her eyes wide. "I am sure you will be very successful."

If Lance's calculations were correct, they would be very successful indeed. He already had everyone from train manufacturers to factory owners lining up to purchase the power cells with Farrendel's magic. It would prove to be very lucrative.

Not that Lance nor Farrendel necessarily needed the money. Farrendel was a prince, and Lance already earned enough royalties from previous inventions that he wouldn't have to work another day in his life if he didn't want to.

But the inventions that could be powered with Farrendel's magic...the possibilities were endless. They could single-handedly take Escarland into a golden age of invention. That was the dream Lance had been pursuing from the moment he'd seen Farrendel's magic. He'd done it for the knowledge, the invention, the science of it. The money they would earn was just a bonus.

"How does it work?" Illyna gestured at the hulking mechanical device, which was formed of gears and powered by the large boiler tucked into the far corner of the warehouse. It was shielded behind layers of tempered glass, and Farrendel had even added a layer of his magical protections that would spring from the floor if a major explosion happened. Again.

Lance pushed off from his desk. "Why don't we show you?"

Farrendel nodded and tucked moss earplugs designed for children into Adry's ears. He then snagged a set of small goggles from his desk and eased them over her eyes, despite the baby's squirming. She stopped squirming once the goggles were in place. After all, this wasn't the first time she'd worn them. She simply didn't like the process of getting them on. They yanked on her hair.

Once Adry was adequately protected, Farrendel divested himself of the baby carrier, holding Adry and the carrier out to Illyna.

Illyna shrugged into the carrier, steadying the baby with her left forearm while clipping the carrier into place with her right hand.

Farrendel handed her Lance's spare set of goggles, and Illyna braced the goggles against her face with her forearm, then adjusted the strap with her right hand. She glanced at him, a pink tint creeping into the tips of her ears.

Lance blinked. Illyna was missing her left hand. He hadn't noticed earlier.

His mind spun, ideas and blueprints falling into place. With a few gears, a stainless steel strut there, a bit of wiring here...

"Lance?"

Lance blinked. Wearing his set of tinted goggles, Farrendel was standing behind the tempered glass shield, waiting for him to flip the switches that would start the machine.

Illyna crouched behind the glass shield by Farrendel's desk, hugging Adry to her. The baby was grinning, wide-eyed in the carrier.

Right. They were all waiting on him.

Lance shook himself, then cast a glance over his desk. Where had he left his goggles? He'd been sure he'd had them just a moment ago.

Farrendel smirked and pointed at Lance. "On your forehead."

Ugh. Right. Lance's face burned as he pulled the goggles from his forehead to settle over his eyes, and he couldn't bring himself to glance at Illyna. His absent-minded ways were much less embarrassing when it was just him and Farrendel. What a great impression he must be making.

Oh, well. She was an elf. It wasn't like she would ever

give him a second glance. He was a human inventor while she was an ethereal elf. Such romances worked for a prince and princess like Farrendel and Essie, but not someone like Lance.

Giving himself another shake, he focused on the panel of switches and buttons in front of him. Such a familiar routine, and yet his fingers felt shaky and fumbling as he went through the motions, all too aware of Illyna watching him.

He toggled the switch to fill the pipes with steam pressure and pressed the button to get the machine started. Slowly, the gears spun into motion, filling the room with a chugging hum. He adjusted the dial to low so that the capacitor wouldn't burn out under the force of Farrendel's magic, and double-checked that one of the specially designed power cells was already placed in the machine. One of the other power cells he used for human magicians would simply explode from Farrendel's magic, and it would be just like him to miss that detail with his current distraction.

The last thing he wanted to do was cause an explosion with Illyna watching. That would be beyond embarrassing.

When he had gone through his checklist two times just to be safe, he gave a nod to Farrendel.

Crackling bolts of Farrendel's magic twined around his fingers, deceptively controlled and subdued. He touched the thick wire running over his head, and his magic leapt around it, following the wire over the wall and down into the machine. A pulsing glow filled the space, then centered around the power cell.

Lance kept an eye on the gauge that told him how much magic was stored in the power cell. When it reached the desired level, he nodded and motioned to Farrendel.

Farrendel cut off his magic, but the blue glow remained, coming from the now filled magical power cell.

Lance pushed the button to seal the power cell, then flipped the switches to shut off the machine. Once the whirring stopped, Farrendel stepped around the glass wall and detached the power cell from the machine.

"And that's all there is to it." Lance pushed up his goggles again, turning to face Illyna.

She blinked at Farrendel, then at the power cell. In her arms, Adry bounced and gave her happy squeal, as if she thought the light show was all a game her dada was playing with her.

Illyna turned to Lance. "I am amazed that you were able to find a way to store Farrendel's power."

Lance shrugged, not sure how to respond. He wanted to impress Illyna, but he didn't want to appear boastful either. "It took some trial and error. And a lot of explosions."

Farrendel pushed his own goggles onto his forehead as he strode around the protective walls. He held the power cell where Illyna could see it. "Lance is quite intelligent."

Illyna leaned forward to inspect the magical power cell while still holding Adry. "He must be to have invented a way to contain the magic of the ancient kings. I am impressed."

Lance tugged at his collar, his face heating once again. He swallowed and shifted, not sure how to respond to all this praise.

After a few more minutes, Farrendel glanced at the large, geared clock hanging on the wall. "Looks like we should get moving if we are to meet Essie at the Aldon

Market. She could undoubtedly use the help with Fieran."

Illyna nodded, a smile twitching at her mouth. "Most likely. Fieran inherited your excess of energy."

Fieran was Farrendel and Essie's oldest child, and his abundance of energy made him a handful even on his best days. Farrendel had stopped taking him along to the workshop because it was simply too dangerous to let Fieran run rampant on, around, and over the piles of junk. The last time Fieran had been here in the workshop, he had nearly toppled a half-finished engine onto himself while trying to climb it.

Lance grimaced and added his own nod. He did not even want to imagine the havoc Fieran was creating at the Market.

"Yes." Farrendel grinned and set the magical power cell on his desk. Then he reclaimed Adry from Illyna and strapped the baby back in place.

As they left, Illyna gave Lance one last smile. "Thank you for the tour. It was fascinating to see this place and meet you."

"My pleasure...meet you...to show you too," Lance blurted out, then winced. He gave a belated wave as Farrendel and Illyna disappeared between the stacks of gears and discarded mechanics and inventions.

Releasing a long breath, he sagged against his desk. That could have gone better. Why did his awkwardness have to strike at the most inconvenient of times?

Besides, what was he thinking? It wasn't like the beautiful elf woman would look his way. She was an elf. He was a human.

But that didn't stop the ideas from swirling around his mind. The blueprint unfolding in his mind kept demanding his attention.

Turning to his desk, Lance shoved aside everything he had been working on and spread out a clean roll of paper.

He might not be able to find the words, but he could always invent something that would get her attention. It might be a long shot. It might blow up in his face. But that had never stopped him before.

CHAPTER
THREE

L ance stumbled through the dark streets of Aldon, blinking blearily when he found himself standing on the front step of his townhouse in one of the nicer districts of Aldon with no memory of the walk from his warehouse. His head was still too stuffed with plans and inspiration, even as his gritty eyes and rumbling stomach told him he needed to call it a day despite the lure of the invention he'd left behind on his desk.

He patted his pockets, then sighed when he found them empty. He must have forgotten his key back at his warehouse. Again.

He knocked on the door and waited. After only a minute, footsteps sounded inside. The lock clicked, then the door swung open, revealing his mother standing in the doorway.

She wore a sensible gray dress with a white apron. Even at this time of night, her graying dark blonde hair remained properly pinned back in a bun. "Forgot your key again?"

"Yes. Thanks for waiting up for me, Mama." Lance

stepped inside and hung his coat on the stand by the door while his mama closed the door behind him. He patted his head, but it seemed he had forgotten his hat at the warehouse. Or he'd neglected to wear one in the first place. He couldn't remember.

"The cook left a plate of supper for you, and I've kept it warm." Mama bustled down the hall, headed for the kitchen at the back of the townhouse.

"Thanks." As they reached the kitchen, Lance slid into a seat at the large, worn wooden table in the center of the room.

His mama picked up two towels, opened the oven of the large black range, and pulled out a plate piled high with a beef roast, green beans, and mashed potatoes. She set it on the table in front of him. "Eat up."

It was the same thing she'd been saying to him since he was a little boy. Back then, they had been living in a one-room apartment in one of the rundown tenements. His parents had scrimped and saved so that by the time he was sixteen, they had enough to send him to Hanford University. He'd earned a scholarship which had covered most of his expenses, but he would never have been able to afford the books for studying nor the nicer clothes he'd needed to look the part of a scholar if not for their sacrifices.

As soon as he'd sold his first invention to Escarland's army, he'd moved them to a nicer apartment. He'd moved them again to this townhouse once his royalties had begun to pay off.

Now, his mother acted as his housekeeper, making sure the household ran smoothly while his father did the bookkeeping and oversaw Lance's investments.

Mama took a seat across from Lance. "How was your day?"

Lance pushed some of the mashed potatoes into the gravy with his spoon. As hungry as he was, just the thought of Illyna banished all thoughts but ones about her from his head. "I met a girl today. I think I might like her."

Mama's eyebrows shot up. "I...see."

Lance sighed. "This isn't like last time, Mama. I'm not just infatuated." Well, he kind of was. But he was older and wiser than he'd been the last time he'd thought himself in love at first sight. Seriously, he was now twenty-six years old. Plenty old enough to know the difference between an instant attraction and thinking himself in love. "I'd like to get to know her better."

"Ah." Mama's wary look broke into a relieved smile instead. "Then I hope I will get a chance to meet her. I'm sure she's very special."

"She is." Lance didn't even know that much about Illyna, but he could tell that much. After all, Farrendel didn't let himself get adopted as a friend by just anyone. They had to be special to earn Farrendel's trust. And Essie, for all her friendliness, was careful in picking true friends who she let see past her cheery exterior. "I'm going to invent something for her."

Mama stood and patted his arm as she halted next to him. "Then I'm sure she won't be able to resist."

Lance nodded, thoughts of invention sending his mind spinning once again. He barely noticed as his mama left the room, yawning. Still distracted, he shoveled his food into his mouth, only blinking when his fork clicked against an empty plate.

He supposed he should get to bed. Though he was going to struggle to sleep with this idea consuming his brain.

Illyna sat on the floor of the parlor in Buckmore Cottage, a wooden fort made of blocks constructed in front of her.

Her left pinky finger itched. Which was incredibly annoying since she didn't have a left-hand pinky anymore. But as the itchy feeling verged on burning, she rubbed her right-hand pinky against her leg, trying to trick her mind into thinking that she was scratching the itch.

Fieran, Essie and Farrendel's oldest, sat cross-legged across from her, his face screwed up as he concentrated on placing another block on the top of the tallest tower.

The baby, Adriana, sat a few feet away as she gummed a stone tree. With a shrieking giggle, she waved her arms. The tree dropped from her grasp, and her gaze latched on the fort. In a surprisingly fast movement, Adry dropped onto her hands and knees and crawled to them.

Illyna reached out to stop the baby, but she was not fast enough. Even as she scooped up Adry in her arm, Adry swiped both arms through the tower.

"Adry!" Fieran fisted his hands and jumped to his feet. "Mama! Adry broke my fort!"

Essie glanced up from the pile of toys she had been picking up, sighed, then smiled as she retrieved Adry from Illyna. She sat on the floor with them, holding a squirming Adry and facing Fieran. "Adry shouldn't have broken your fort, but she is too little to know better. She just wants to play with you."

"She still broke my fort." Fieran crossed his arms and glared. "I don't want to play with her."

"Do you want to…play with me?" Without warning, Essie plunked Adry onto Illyna's lap, then lunged across the fort to scoop up Fieran.

Fieran shrieked, then laughed and squirmed as Essie tickled him. "Mama! Macha!"

Illyna smiled at the mix of elvish and Escarlish in Fieran's speech.

A knock sounded on the outer door. Essie started to push to her feet, but Illyna motioned to her to stay where she was. "I will get it."

Illyna set Adry down, and the baby promptly went back to destroying the fort. Since Fieran was too busy trying to avoid his macha's tickles, he did not seem to care.

After rising to her feet, Illyna hurried from the room, down the hall, and opened the door.

Lance Marion stood on the doorstep, his blond-brown hair neatly combed and wearing clean black trousers, a white shirt, and a gray vest complete with a watch chain peeking from the front pocket. He held a rectangular, paperboard box about the size of a quiver of arrows, a bright pink ribbon tied around the middle.

"Elontiri." Illyna smiled, a tightness filling her chest at the sight of him. "I almost did not recognize you without the goggles."

A hint of red crept into his cheeks, and he rocked back on his heels. "I, well, um, I left them at home."

When he did not add anything else, Illyna pointed over her shoulder. "Are you looking for Essie or Farrendel?"

"No, actually..." Lance shifted, glancing from the box in his hands, down to his feet, then finally up at Illyna. "I was looking for you."

For her? Her heart beat a little harder in her chest, a flutter filling her stomach. She had never felt this instant attraction to anyone before. Not like this. It was not love.

She did not even know him. But she wanted to get to know him better.

Did he feel the same? Or did he simply see her as a friend of Essie and Farrendel's and nothing more?

She glanced over her shoulder, but Essie was still in the parlor, playing with her children. Illyna closed the door behind her and stepped onto the front stoop. It was not as private as the back garden might have been, but Illyna did not feel enough at home here at Buckmore Cottage to invite Lance around back.

"I, uh, I made this for you." Lance held out the box, then hesitated, as if not sure what to do.

Heart pounding in her throat, Illyna took the box with her right hand, finding it heavier than it looked. She propped the box on her hip, steadying it with her left forearm, while she untied the ribbon with her hand.

Lance reached out, as if to steady the package for her, before halting and stuffing his hands into his pockets, likely realizing she was just fine. She did not need help.

The ribbon slid free, and she wiggled the lid off the box. For a moment, she held the top before she peeked at Lance and held it out to him rather than just dropping it to the ground.

He just blinked back at her for a heartbeat before he started, yanked a hand out of his pocket, and grabbed the lid.

Her chest tightened, from nerves from his gaze, the uncomfortable and yet filled silence between them, and the anticipation at seeing this mysterious gift.

She pulled back the layer of thin white crepe paper, her fingers brushing cool metal.

The flutters died, a strange disappointment twisting her gut.

Inside, a hand and forearm formed of metal struts and

gears lay inside the box. It was well crafted of such tiny parts. Each finger had multiple joints, and it likely could grip things if needed. A socket and straps sprouted from the end, designed to hold it on her arm.

Illyna swallowed the weight filling her chest and forced a smile onto her face. "Linshi. Uh, thank you."

She should not be so disappointed. It was not as if Lance really knew her. Of course he would make the wrong assumption about what she needed and wanted.

But a part of her had thought that he would be different. Yesterday, he had acted like he did not even notice her missing hand.

It seemed he was no different than anyone else after all.

She took the lid back from him, sticking it under her arm on top of the box without trying to fully put it back on.

The door opened behind her, and Essie appeared, bouncing Adry on her hip. "Lance! Are you looking for Farrendel? He's off somewhere practicing with Captain Merrick, Iyrinder, Julien, and Vriska, but I'm sure they'll be finished up soon."

"No, I...I should be going." Lance glanced at Illyna, his gaze holding a hint of hurt before his expression shuttered closed in a blank look that seemed utterly foreign on his face. His was a face for adorable grins and intense focus, not this pain.

But she was not sure what else she could have done or said. She had done the best she could to hide her disappointment without lying. She could not honestly tell him that she liked his gift, even if she did appreciate some of the thought behind it. She could understand what he was trying to do, even if it had been misguided and ignorant of her true feelings.

Illyna opened her mouth, but she could not think of anything else to say as Lance turned, stuck his hands in his pockets, and trudged down the drive to the gates to the city. While she hated that she had hurt him by not being more enthusiastic about his gift, she would not apologize for her true thoughts and needs.

Essie frowned and glanced from Lance to Illyna, her gaze darting down to the box Illyna still held. "What was that about?"

"Nothing." Illyna was not ready to talk about it with Essie. Still gripping the box with the ugly metal hand, Illyna brushed past her and back into Buckmore Cottage. Hopefully Essie would take the hint and give Illyna a moment alone.

Perhaps it was for the best that Lance had disappointed her. This was just an attraction. It would pass, given time. It was not like Illyna would uproot her entire life to move to Aldon. Nor would Lance wish to move to Estyra, away from all his gears and machines.

A relationship between them would have never worked anyway. Illyna might as well move on now.

Only four more days, then Illyna could go home and put this brief trip to Aldon behind her.

LANCE SLOUCHED as he trudged down the streets of Aldon, not really sure where he was going. He didn't want to go home and face his mama and her questions about how it had gone. Nor did he want to return to his workshop to be taunted by his failure.

What had he done wrong? The mechanical arm had been perfect. Fully reticulated fingers that could grasp firmly enough to hold something in place. Stainless steel struts that were polished to perfection. Fully enclosed bearings so that grease wouldn't smear onto anything she touched.

Was it because the hand was too heavy? He'd made it as light as he possibly could, given the materials he had to work with.

Was there a way he could make it lighter? Maybe he could use aluminum instead of stainless steel? But that would weaken the overall design.

Lance kicked at a pebble, sending it skittering over the bricks of the sidewalk. What was he thinking? Why should he even bother trying again? She was an elf. And he was just the awkward, strange, too-smart-for-his-own-good boy he'd always been.

He might as well give up now. She would be going back to Tarenhiel after Farrendel's graduation in four days. After that, he could put this infatuation behind him and focus on his gears and wires. Mechanics had never let him down. Never made him feel like he was too weird to be their friend. Never left him out when all he wanted to do was play with the others. Mechanics were simple compared to people.

The only people to ever see him as a friend were Essie and Farrendel. Everyone else either saw him as only his brain or as the weird boy to avoid.

Essie, it seemed, had enough social skills to make up for his lack. She was good at that. It was what made her such a good match for Farrendel.

And Farrendel was just as socially impaired as Lance was. He wasn't bothered by Lance's quirks any more than Lance was bothered by his.

Lance halted. What if...

Someone ran into him from behind. A troll brushed

around him, grumbling about how people shouldn't just stop in the middle of the sidewalk without warning.

For a moment, Lance smiled at the troll's back. Nowadays, trolls and elves weren't uncommon sights as they strolled the streets of Aldon. An elf could find a home here and be happy.

Lance would give this one more try, then he would admit defeat. He would ask Essie for advice. She would know what to do.

If that didn't work, then Lance would have to concede that this infatuation was simply not meant to go anywhere.

If there was one thing he'd learned about inventions, there was a time to push through until he found the answer and a time to give up. Sometimes giving up meant giving up forever. Sometimes it simply meant that it wasn't time for a particular invention just yet.

Would he have to give up on the idea of Illyna? Maybe. But he wouldn't know until he'd given this his best try.

CHAPTER FOUR

With a deep breath, Lance knocked on the door to Buckmore Cottage for the second time that day. He'd wandered around Aldon for a few hours, waiting until darkness had fallen.

Hopefully he'd given enough time that Illyna had gone to bed by now. From what he'd observed, elves tended to go to bed early.

He waited, holding his breath. Finally, footsteps sounded inside, then the door opened. Once again Essie stood there, though this time she wasn't carrying a baby on her hip. "Lance? Back again so soon?"

"Uh, yes." Lance rubbed at his elbow, scratching the toe of his boot on the step. Ugh, this was going to be embarrassing to explain.

"Are you looking for Farrendel? Or...Illyna?" Essie hesitated on the last word.

"No, I'm looking for you this time." Lance shifted and scratched at the back of his neck, resisting the urge to pull out his pocket watch and fiddle with that. His hands felt so empty without a mechanical item to keep them busy. "I need some advice. If you have a moment."

Essie blinked at him, then smiled. "Of course. Here, let's step outside and sit on that bench over there."

A bench tucked into a nook at the front of Buckmore Cottage, a place for visitors to wait in the shade of the front landscaping. Currently, it was lit by the gas lamps on either side of the door. While a few bugs flew around the lights, the elven magic Princess Jalissa had placed on Buckmore Cottage kept the space bug-free.

Lance waited for Essie to sit on one end of the bench before he took the other. His legs bounced as he tried to come up with how to phrase his questions. Where could he even start?

Essie waited, staying silent. He'd noticed her doing that more since she'd married Farrendel. Holding back her chatter until the other person told her what was on their mind.

Lance heaved a sigh and stared at his boots. "Earlier today, I gave Illyna a gift. It was a prosthetic hand I'd invented for her. But...I don't think she liked it. And I don't know what I did wrong."

"Did she ask you to make her a prosthetic?" Essie's voice was quiet.

"Uh, no." Lance rubbed at a grease spot stuck in a crease in his palm. "I just wanted to impress Illyna and I thought she might like it."

"Ah." Essie's smile grew as she leaned more comfortably against the back of the bench. "I thought there was something going on between you and Illyna earlier."

Lance's face heated, and he resisted the urge to tug on his collar. When had the evening grown so hot? "It's nothing. She's just...I just...I'd like to get to know her better.

That's all. And I blew it, and I don't even know what I did. Or didn't do."

"I see." Essie gestured toward Buckmore Cottage behind them. "It would have been one thing if she had asked you to invent a prosthetic for her. But she didn't. Instead, you presumed to know what she'd need instead of asking her. By giving her the prosthetic hand, it might have seemed like you were trying to fix her rather than appreciating her for who she is. I know that wasn't your intention, but that's probably how it seemed."

"Oh." That hadn't occurred to him. It had been rather presumptuous. Sure, he'd meant well. But Illyna wouldn't know that. Lance slumped. "She probably never wants to see me again."

"No, you didn't mess up that badly. This wasn't a catastrophic explosion. Just a setback." Essie grinned at him before her grin faded into her rare serious expression. "Maybe try just talking with her. Get to know her. And hold off on inventing anything else for her until you know her a bit better."

Lance winced. Yeah, that sounded like the better option in hindsight.

"Once you get to know her better, you'll find that she doesn't need two hands to make it in the world, but it's the world that needs to adjust and adapt for her one hand." Essie held his gaze, a hint of a smile on her mouth. This was a lesson Essie herself had likely learned by listening to Illyna, Farrendel, and many others. "You'll find other things to invent for her, I'm sure of it."

Maybe. His shoulders slumped even farther. "She's only in Aldon for another few days. I'm not sure I'll have a chance to talk with her before she returns to Estyra."

Essie raised her eyebrows at him, her mouth pressed tight as if she was fighting a smile. "Come back tomorrow. I'm sure I can figure out a way to leave the two of you in the back garden for a while."

Lance straightened. "Really? You'd do that?"

"What are friends for?" Essie grinned back, then the expression turned into a frown just as quickly. "Just… don't hurt Illyna, all right? I like both of you, and I'm happy to set you up if it works out. But I don't want either of you to hold it against me if it doesn't."

"We won't. At least, I won't." Lance appreciated that she was a friend. He had very few people in his life who would be willing to give him advice.

No matter what happened with Illyna, at least Lance had good friends he could rely on in Essie and Farrendel. That was more than he'd had growing up.

ILLYNA SAT by the table in the back garden of Buckmore Cottage. Across from her, Farrendel was trying to convince Fieran to eat another bite of his sandwich before he could run off and play. Essie cut a strawberry into tiny pieces while Adry stuffed them into her mouth and gummed them as fast as Essie sliced them.

Hardly a serene meal, but it was highly entertaining. Especially since Illyna did not have to wrangle either child. She could just sit back and appreciate the hilarity of Farrendel having a stare down with a sassy, red-headed toddler.

"Am I interrupting anything?"

Illyna glanced up and froze, her breath catching in her throat as if she could not decide if she wanted to stay or bolt.

Lance Marion stood there, dressed once again in neat

black trousers and a gray vest over a white shirt. "Essie invited me for lunch today. If that's all right?"

"You are always welcome." Farrendel smiled at him before swinging his gaze back to Fieran, giving his son a frown and holding up two fingers. "You need to eat two more bites."

Fieran crossed his arms and glared at his sandwich, his bottom lip sticking out in an exaggerated fashion.

"Don't worry. I saved a few strawberries for you." Essie gestured to the open seat next to Illyna.

Illyna shifted in her seat. She had wondered who the extra chair and plate were for. But she had not questioned it. Essie and Farrendel always had family wandering over from Winstead Palace and joining their meals.

Illyna forced a smile as Lance dropped into the seat next to her. What was she supposed to say to him after yesterday? He had meant well, and he had put a lot of time and effort into that gift. She knew that. She just...did not know how to talk about what had bothered her. Avoiding him had sounded like the easier option.

Fieran stuffed two more bites into his mouth, his cheeks puffing out. "Done. Can I play now?"

"Yes." Farrendel sounded a bit exhausted.

Fieran leapt off his chair, getting a rather impressive distance before he landed lightly on the ground. He dashed off as fast as he could on his small legs, headed for the forested parkland behind Buckmore Cottage.

"I had better watch him." Farrendel pushed to his feet, nodded to both Lance and Illyna, then he jogged toward the wooded parkland, catching up with Fieran.

With a shout, Fieran started to run faster, but Farrendel caught him, sweeping him up. Fieran scrambled onto Farrendel's back, clinging there and shouting happily as Farrendel ran faster, disappearing between the trees.

Essie pushed to her feet as well, pulling Adry, who was absolutely covered with sticky strawberry juice, out of her high chair. "I'd better get Adry cleaned up. Thanks for stopping by, Lance. Sorry we have to run off."

Essie glanced at Illyna, meeting her gaze as if asking if Illyna would be all right if Essie left.

Illyna suppressed a sigh and gave Essie a nod. She would be fine.

With a more pointed look at Lance, Essie hurried toward the cottage as Adry started wiggling and fussing.

Illyna picked up her last bite of sandwich, though she did not stuff it in her mouth. She could not bring herself to look at Lance. It was too hard trying to sort through the mix of attraction and disappointment that stirred inside her.

"About yesterday..." Lance cleared his throat, and the noise made her glance up. He was looking all adorable again with his darkly blond hair falling over his forehead and his brown eyes going all puppy-dog sad. "I'm sorry. I didn't mean to be presumptuous with my gift. I wasn't trying to fix you or anything like that. I like you as you are. What I mean to say is, I just wanted to help, and I bungled it instead. I should have asked you first what you wanted. I'm sorry."

Illyna drew in a deep breath and stared down at her hand and her stump. "I am sorry too. I should not have reacted—"

She started when Lance reached out, hesitated, then rested a hand on her forearm just above her stump.

When she glanced at him, he met her gaze. "You don't have to apologize for your reaction. You have a right to want others to be considerate of your needs and your feelings."

"I know you were trying to be kind. You were not doing it to be cruel. And you put a lot of effort into it." Illyna knew by now how to recognize someone who was insensitive by accident rather than someone who was purposely hurtful.

Even as she said it, the last of her irritation melted away, replaced with a flutter in the pit of her stomach at having him this close, his hand warm against the skin of her arm.

It took her a moment to gather her thoughts, and she forced herself to meet his gaze. "It has all been forgiven. Can we move past it, do you think?"

"I hope so." Lance swallowed and withdrew his hand from her arm. "I'd like...I'd like to get to know you better. If that'd be all right."

"I would like that." Illyna found herself smiling.

Perhaps the next few days would not be so bad after all.

CHAPTER
FIVE

T he past few days had been some of the best of Lance's life. Even better than being at Hanford University or selling his first invention.

He and Illyna had spent nearly every moment of the day together. With Farrendel's family in town, Essie and Farrendel had been busy with them, leaving Illyna free to spend time with him. And the good part of being his own boss was that he could easily take a few days off once in a while. Sure, he'd have a few projects to catch up on once she returned to Tarenhiel. But it was worth the busyness afterward to spend time with her now.

Now he and Illyna were strolling through Aldon, and his stomach was churning more than it had since he'd graduated Hanford University and been asked to give a speech.

He'd known Illyna for four days. Probably a little soon to bring her home to meet his parents.

But she was leaving tomorrow, after the graduation. He wasn't sure when he'd have another chance.

Really, he had no reason to be nervous. His parents

were amazing, and they would love Illyna. Illyna was lovely and would like his parents.

Still, he couldn't shake the nerves that gripped him.

Strolling next to each other, Lance led the way from the palace gates and through the tree-lined, quiet streets that formed the upscale neighborhoods where the elite of Aldon lived.

He turned down his street, which was lined with stately elm trees, and finally halted before the red brick townhouse with white trim that was nearly identical to the other houses. "This one is mine."

"It looks…grand." Illyna eyed it with the look he was beginning to recognize as her feigned enthusiasm.

He gave her a grin, not offended by her tone. "I know it isn't your taste. I didn't see your home, specifically, the one time I was in Estyra, but I know you elves prefer a lot more space and greenery to cold bricks."

"It is not that. Well, not only that." Illyna matched his grin with a wry one of her own. "It just looks like a place where someone rich would live, and I am not nobility."

"Neither am I." Lance shifted. He had spent money easily on their days together, but he hadn't come right out and said it yet. Not that he was worried about Illyna being a money grubber. Elves weren't like that. But because she wasn't a money grubber, the fact that he was rich might be a hindrance rather than a help. "But…I am…" Ugh, he hated admitting it out loud. "My inventions have done pretty well."

"I see." Illyna drew in a deep breath and faced the townhouse with that tense smile on her face. "You did not seem concerned with money during our excursions."

"It wasn't always like this. I grew up in one of the poorest parts of Aldon." Lance gestured toward his front door. "The cook should have supper ready by now."

Illyna smiled and nodded, falling into step with him as he strode toward his door. He fumbled through his pockets, then sighed. Of course. He didn't have his key. Again. Face burning, he knocked on his own front door.

It whooshed open before he even finished the second rap with his knuckles. His mama flung the door open, her face splitting with a broad smile. She all but knocked him off the top step as she brushed past him and pulled Illyna in for a hug. "It is such a pleasure to meet you, Illyna. I've heard so much about you."

Lance winced, opening his mouth though he couldn't bring himself to say anything. He wasn't sure how to tell his mama that it was considered rude to hug an elf like that without asking first.

But Illyna was still smiling, and she even awkwardly wrapped one of her arms around his mama. "It is a pleasure to meet you too, Mrs. Marion."

Mama released Illyna, then steered her toward the house. "Come, let's sit down, and you can tell us all about yourself."

Lance trailed after them, glad that Illyna seemed to be taking Mama in stride.

Inside, Papa joined them in the parlor. He was a quiet, thoughtful man with thin shoulders and roughened hands from his years working in one of the munitions factories to support Lance and Mama in those early years.

Somehow, Lance found himself next to Illyna on the couch, listening while his mama regaled them with increasingly embarrassing stories from his childhood.

The time he'd disassembled the tenement's door lock to see how it worked, only to reassemble it in such a way that it was permanently locked and no longer worked with their key.

The time he tried to invent a way to raise and lower a

bucket via a pulley system out the window so that he wouldn't have to haul the water up five flights of stairs, only to forget to secure the end of the rope and have the bucket come crashing down on his own head.

The explosion he'd caused in the kitchen when he was ten years old that had gotten them kicked out of that apartment, and they'd lived on the streets for two weeks until they were able to secure new housing in an even more rundown tenement.

The explosion he'd caused when he was twelve that had gotten them kicked out of that building as well. And then there was the time that he…

Lance winced and reached for Illyna's hand, only to halt when he realized he had accidentally ended up on her left side. As it had only been a few days, he had yet to work up the courage to ask how she felt about him touching that left arm. Was she sensitive about it? Or would she like him to act as if there was nothing different about that arm?

So many questions, and he wasn't about to ask them in front of his parents. But he would ask, when he had the chance. In some ways, a relationship wasn't that much different from a particularly complicated invention. It took a lot of work, perseverance, and learning to ask the right questions.

Just when Lance thought every embarrassing story would be spilled in a single evening, the cook stepped into the room. She bobbed a slight curtsy to Lance. "Dinner is served, sir."

"Thank you, Ethel." He'd tried to tell her that she didn't have to curtsy. He wasn't some highfalutin lord. He was the odd little boy she used to babysit while his parents were both working, even though she had her own long hours of mending to see to.

But she couldn't seem to break the habit. Mama had once tried to explain that it had something to do with gratitude, but Lance wasn't sure why Ethel would feel such gratitude to him. Yes, he had hired her as soon as he had enough money to afford it, taking her from the dingy tenement to a nicer home in Aldon. But that was merely a small repayment after all the sacrifices the older woman had made throughout the years so that his parents could earn enough to send him to the university.

Lance hopped to his feet and held out his arm to Illyna. "You'll love Ethel's cooking. She makes the best roast beef and mashed potatoes you've ever eaten."

Illyna smiled and gracefully stood, easing around him so that she could set her right hand on his arm.

Lance hung back, letting his parents lead the way from the parlor toward the formal dining room. Once they were far enough ahead, he leaned closer to Illyna. "Are you sure you don't want to bolt, after hearing all the embarrassing stories of my childhood?"

She smiled in return, the expression lighting up her face and adding dimples to her adorable, petite elven features. "I already knew you were prone to explosions. I have been hearing stories from Essie and Farrendel for years."

Oh, right. That was a trait he had yet to grow out of.

When they reached the dining room, they found it set with the best porcelain tableware, complete with flickering candles set in polished candlesticks and the best white napkins folded into perfect, crisp triangles.

It seemed his parents weren't the only ones excited about him bringing home a girl for the first time ever. Ethel—and probably her grandniece who served as their one maid—had gone to extra lengths tonight.

It looked lovely, but Lance almost wished they hadn't.

Would Illyna think it all too much? Especially since their relationship was all of four days old? He liked her. A lot. And he thought she liked him. After all, she hadn't started trying to avoid him or beg off seeing him or any of the usual ways people found to get out of spending time with him once they realized he was a bit odd. And she was here, meeting his family and smiling as she sat down to supper.

Conversation continued to flow over supper. His mama got Illyna talking about her parents, who had both been killed while serving in the Tarenhieli army, and her own time in the army. She spoke briefly of how she met Farrendel, then how he'd helped her get her business started after she'd been discharged.

She spent more time talking about how she helped Farrendel and Essie with the charity they had started to aid wounded elf warriors. Farrendel and Essie were currently looking at turning the Escarlish estate they had been given along the Hydalla River into a place where both Escarlish soldiers and elven warriors could find jobs and learn skills as they eased into a non-warrior life.

Lance was happy to listen as she talked. Most of this he had already known, either because Essie or Farrendel had told him about it or because he and Illyna had discussed it over the past three days.

Finally, supper was over, and Lance quickly claimed Illyna before his parents could draw her into another conversation. He steered her down the hall past the kitchen. "Would you like to see the back garden? It isn't much, especially not compared to the gardens at the palace. But it is a nice night and..." And he couldn't think of anything else to say, so he just trailed off awkwardly.

"I would love to see it." Illyna fell into step with him.

He would have liked to hold her hand, but he hadn't

worked up the courage to do that yet. It had seemed a little soon for such things. After all, they were only on day three.

But she would be leaving tomorrow for Tarenhiel, and he was serious enough about this relationship that he knew he wanted to keep pursuing it, even if it meant doing it long-distance. Maybe hand-holding wouldn't be so out-of-bounds either.

As they stepped into the garden, Illyna drew in a deep breath. The tense posture of her back and shoulders eased. "This is lovely."

A tiny kitchen garden filled the space on either side of the brick walk. Beyond the kitchen garden, a brick patio formed a small circle that held a metal table and four chairs. Around the patio, rectangular planters filled with tall, blooming flowers separated the patio from the surrounding manicured flower garden that bloomed on the rest of the property. Strings of lights powered by Farrendel's magic winked among the hedges and pathways, providing a low, blue light so they could navigate the paths.

Lance led Illyna down the winding pathways until they reached a bench set in a nook at the far back corner. A small fountain bubbled in front of them, accompanied by crickets in the garden and the background noise of a city at night.

Illyna sat, and Lance took the seat next to her. The bench was small enough that it was cozy, though they weren't close enough that it was awkward.

It was a night for holding hands and enjoying these final moments together before she left.

Lance drew in a deep breath, gathering his courage, and reached for her, stopping short before he touched her. "I'd like to hold your hand, if you would like that? I don't want to take up your only hand or anything or just... never mind."

He squeezed his eyes shut. That hadn't come out right at all.

Her fingers took his hand and squeezed. "I do not mind."

"You don't?" Lance peeked at her.

Her eyes luminescent in the faint glow of the garden lights, Illyna met his gaze briefly. "I was wondering how long it would take you to ask me."

He released a breath in a whoosh. Oh, good. Then he had not misread her.

After another long moment, Illyna sighed and shifted closer to him. "Your family is nice."

"I'm glad they didn't scare you off. Or smother you too much." Lance struggled to find the words he needed to speak. Blueprints and inventing were so much easier than speaking his heart. "I've enjoyed spending time with you these past few days. I like you. A lot."

Illyna's gaze focused on their clasped hands. "I like you too. But...I need to return to Tarenhiel."

"I know." It was far too soon for either of them to think about uprooting and moving for the other. Lance forced a smile onto his face. "But maybe I could visit you in Tarenhiel?"

"You would do that?" Illyna straightened, her gaze searching his face.

"Of course." It wasn't like money was a hindrance. He could easily afford to rent a private train car every month, if he wanted to. That was assuming he didn't manage to catch a ride on the royal train with Essie and Farrendel on one of their trips back and forth. "I'd like to see where this goes."

"I think...yes. Yes, I would." Illyna breathed out a

long exhale. The scent of her hair—something that was a mix of forest and floral—joined the scents of the flower garden and city wafting on the night breeze. "I am not sure when I will be able to visit Escarland again."

"I understand. If I have to come to you in Tarenhiel, I'll do it." Lance grinned, a dizzy feeling making his head swim. She'd actually said yes. She wanted to see him again.

"There is a quaint little inn just down the street from my shop." Illyna's smile bloomed hesitant and adorable for the first time since they'd stepped into the garden. "It is closer than Ellonahshinel, and it would be a lot quieter than staying with Essie and Farrendel."

"Very true." Lance couldn't help but return her smile. Fieran had all of Farrendel's energy with a dash of Essie's loud exuberance. Then there was Adry, who cried every time she was told no.

After a moment, Lance coughed and looked away from Illyna. "Don't take this the wrong way, but you are welcome to stay here, if you are able to visit again. There are plenty of rooms, and my parents live here too. It wouldn't be improper—well, too improper."

"I might take you up on the invitation." Illyna smiled, and for a long moment they sat there in silence. After another moment, she leaned her head on his shoulder.

His breath caught as the weight of her head settled against him. He'd never had anyone trust him like this. But Illyna actually seemed to like him. He couldn't wrap his mind around it.

Illyna gestured with her left forearm. "I actually have a prosthetic arm. It is made of wood, and I can control the fingers with my magic."

"That sounds neat." No wonder she hadn't been thrilled with his gift. Not only was he trying to fix her, he attempted to fix a problem that wasn't even there. Why hadn't it occurred to him that the elves would have their own prosthetics using their plant magic?

Oh, right. Because, like a dolt, he'd just assumed that her missing hand was a problem that needed to be solved.

"Yes, but I do not wear it often." Illyna shrugged against him. "I used to wear it a lot more when I first lost my hand, but now...I am comfortable going into public both with and without it. I might be missing a hand, but this is me. All of me. Besides, my magic is not strong, so it takes a lot of effort for me to control the fingers. Those with stronger magic can move their wooden limbs effort-lessly, but I cannot. To me, the wooden hand is just bulky and uncomfortable, so I prefer not to wear it most of the time when I do not need it for what I am working on."

And that had been his other mistake. He had lumped everyone missing a hand into one group with the same needs and preferences.

But life didn't work that way. Illyna was an individual. She had individual wants and needs, just like everyone else. He couldn't just categorize her and make assumptions based on a physical attribute.

Lance grimaced. "I'm sorry I just assumed—"

Illyna tilted her head to look up at him without lifting her head fully from his shoulder. "You already apolo-gized. And I have already forgiven you. And..." She hesi-tated, glancing from their hands to his face once again. "I think I might try out that prosthetic you made."

"You would? You don't have to, if you don't want to."

"Maybe I will like it better than my wooden hand. I will not know until I try it." Illyna shrugged, then glanced at him. "You will not be too disappointed if I still do not like it?"

"No. You'll give me feedback on what you don't like, and I'll try again. If you want me to. No matter how many times it takes or until you tell me that it just isn't working and you'd rather I stop. Or maybe you'll want me to invent something else entirely." Lance blinked, trying to shove aside the ideas and sketches that begged to take over. Right now, he needed to concentrate on Illyna, not on inventions. "I just want to make it right for you so that you have what you need."

"Linshi." Illyna snuggled slightly closer against him as the crisp night air whispered around them. "How soon do you think you will be able to visit Tarenhiel?"

"A month." Even as he said it, a month sounded far too long. "Three weeks. No, make that two."

They would likely be the longest two weeks of his life.

ILLYNA SAT beside Lance in the rows of benches set up on the grassy, front lawn of Winstead Palace. While it was unusual, Hanford University had agreed to a private graduation ceremony for Farrendel and Iyrinder, once they realized that royalty from three kingdoms would be in attendance and the security concerns would be a night-mare if Farrendel graduated with the rest of his magical engineering class.

Knowing Farrendel, he was likely relieved that he would not have to walk across a stage in front of a bunch of strangers. He probably would not have attended the graduation ceremony if that had been the case.

With Lance holding her hand, Illyna did not pay close attention to the human professors and their pompous ceremony and the long-winded speech on how delighted they were that elves were choosing their university to study magical engineering, thanks to Prince Farrendel's example.

Finally the professor called Iyrinder's name. Iyrinder strode onto the stage, wearing a strange burgundy robe and an odd, square cap perched over his long chestnut hair. The professor handed Iyrinder some kind of official looking, leatherbound item and shook his hand in the human custom.

In the front row, Iyrinder's human wife Patience clapped as best she could while holding her and Iyrinder's son. Captain Merrick gave some type of whistle. Next to them, Iyrinder's mother and sister glanced around, then gave an attempt at a human-style clap.

Iyrinder strode off the stage as if in a hurry, then sat down next to his wife.

Then the professor called Farrendel's name. Illyna grinned as she caught sight of him in the same odd-looking robe and cap. It must be some kind of human ceremonial garb. In addition to the robe, Farrendel also had a medal and a sash hanging over his neck.

Illyna leaned closer to Lance and whispered, "What does the medal and sash thing mean?"

"Farrendel is graduating with honors." Lance kept his voice low in return, though on Illyna's other side, Fingol seemed to be leaning closer as if trying to hear Lance's explanation.

"Do you have a medal and a fancy sash too?" Illyna eyed Lance. Knowing him, he likely did, though he had yet to show them to her.

Lance nodded, looking away and shifting in that way that said he was about to say something that might appear boastful but was simply a fact. "I graduated at the top of my class."

Of course he had. Lance was brilliant. Awkward when it came to people, but highly intelligent.

"You will have to show them to me, the next time I am in Aldon." She told herself that there would be a next time. She was not sure where this thing with Lance was going, but her heart ached with hope.

On the small stage, Farrendel claimed his own leather item, accompanied by exuberant clapping from all of his gathered friends and family. In the front row on the other side from Iyrinder and his family, Essie clapped, grinning, while several of her brothers cheered. Even Adry gave a squeal from her seat on Essie's mother's lap, as if getting in the moment. Fieran just looked confused from where he sat next to his uncle Edmund.

But the loudest cheers came from King Rharreth and Queen Melantha, howling and cheering in the boisterous way of the trolls.

Illyna would have had to let go of Lance's hand to slap her hand on her knee or something like that. And, right now, she was content to simply enjoy her friend's big moment.

Farrendel had come a long way in the years she had known him. He had found a new future balancing life in both Escarland and Tarenhiel. He had grown in confidence with the love of family and friends around him.

Perhaps she, too, could find a future balanced between two kingdoms. She had made her own way since losing her hand in battle, but maybe it was time her life expanded again.

Only time would tell. But as she sat there next to Lance, she could not help but dream about what that future could look like.

CHAPTER
SIX

ONE YEAR LATER...

Illyna gathered her things from the private, first-class compartment as the train pulled into the station in Aldon. There were benefits to having a rich boyfriend. In the beginning, she had protested the expensive train tickets. But the plush seats and the quiet of having a compartment to herself convinced her. She had covered her tickets on the elven train each time, so she supposed that somewhat split the difference.

She wore her favorite of the prosthetics Lance had invented over the past year. This one was mostly made of hollow wood, carved by Fingol and reinforced with his magic. But all the joints were formed of metal ball bearings, with the pieces of wood connected by only slim roots. Unlike her original wooden hand, she did not need to flood the entire hand with magic to make the fingers move. Instead, it only took a small amount of magic through the network of roots to make the fingers move on their smooth metal joints.

She had an entire array of prosthetic hands now, from that first stainless steel prosthetic that Lance had invented, which she found useful when she needed something particularly hardy and indestructible, to her original wooden hand that appeared the most lifelike. She wore that one for formal events when she did not want to be flooded with questions or looks.

But more often than not, she did not wear any of them, and that was just fine too.

The train shuddered to a halt, then let out a piercing whistle to announce its arrival.

After slinging her pack onto her back, Illyna made her way from her compartment, joining the subdued bustle of the Escarlish merchants and nobility as they exited their own first-class compartments and headed for the doors of the train car. A few glanced her way, but most ignored her with that air of genteel snobbery that most nobility —Escarlish or elven—tended to wear.

When it was her turn, she stepped from the train car, down the metal steps, and onto the platform. A velvet rope divided the quieter section of the platform from the bustle of those exiting the passenger cars of cheap seats.

"Illyna!" Lance waved to her from behind another velvet rope, dressed in his customary black trousers, white shirt, and gray vest. A smear of grease smudged his cheek, as if he had made an attempt to clean up but had missed a spot.

She hurried to him, then ducked under the rope rather than go around with the rest of the crowd.

He swept her up in his arms and hugged her, though he refrained from kissing her in public. While she had told him she preferred that he did not, right now she almost wished that he would. It had been a month since she had seen him, and it had been one month too long.

When he released her, Lance gripped her hand, tugging her toward the train station's exit. "Come on. I have something I want to show you."

Illyna laughed and hurried after him. How many times had Lance said that to her over the months they had been courting? Sometimes it was a smaller power cell that he and Farrendel had created. Other times it was the sketch of a magically powered horseless carriage or a flying machine—both things that human inventors seemed to be obsessed with creating. Or it was yet another tweak to a prosthetic that he wanted her to test out before he made the design available to others. Once, he had simply wanted to show off his desk, which he had cleaned and organized for the first time in who knew how long.

It was one thing she loved about him. His excitement for everything. She learned to love his absentmindedness and focus as charming and sweet rather than let it get on her nerves. She was independent enough that she did not need him focused on her every minute. Instead, she appreciated the time for her own pursuits.

Lance led her to his carriage—one with horses, since a horseless carriage still seemed a rather impossible dream at this point—and handed her inside before hopping inside to sit beside her.

As they rattled through the streets, Illyna took in the now familiar sight of Aldon's morning bustle. The occasional elf or troll could be seen among the sea of humans going about their day.

Instead of turning down the street that would take them to Lance's townhouse, the carriage continued into the warehouse district.

Illyna glanced at Lance, but he just gave her an impish

grin in return. He must have quite the surprise planned for her.

As they neared, Illyna thought she caught sight of something winking in the sunlight on the warehouse next to Lance's. She craned her neck, but she could not get a good look at it. Strange. She did not think that was there before.

The carriage halted before Lance's warehouse. The double doors were actually closed. Odd, for him. Perhaps he was actually growing security conscious. Or Farrendel had finally convinced him that they were inventing things that should not be stolen.

Lance hopped down, and she followed him, landing lightly on the cobblestones. He paused next to the double doors, then glanced at her with that same, excited grin. "Welcome back to my warehouse."

He tugged on the latch, but the doors did not budge. He gave another tug, a slight flush creeping up his neck, before he halted and patted his pockets.

Illyna laughed, reached into a pocket, and pulled out the ring of keys he had given her a few months ago.

"Thanks." He took the keys, found the right one, and unlocked the doors. He immediately handed the keys back to her, and she stuffed them back into her pocket for the next time he locked himself out of his warehouse or townhouse.

"Let's try this again." He flung the doors open and stepped inside with a flourish. "Welcome to my new and improved warehouse."

Illyna gaped and stepped into the expansive space. She always knew the warehouse was huge, but it was usually filled with so much junk that one could not see more than a few yards at a time.

Now, all the piles of junk and discarded inventions

had been cleaned out, leaving the space clear all the way to the back corner where the workshop section remained set up as before. A few gears and belts hung from the ceiling, as if something large and mechanical was in the process of being installed.

"I did not think I would ever see your warehouse so empty." Illyna turned to take in the entire space. "Let me guess, Farrendel finally had enough of the mess and decided it had to get cleaned up. But where did it all go?"

Besides a few racks holding both empty and full magical power cells, she did not see anything that looked like storage. Certainly not enough for all the junk that had been here.

Lance shifted, his grin quirking a tad lopsided. "Yes, well, there was that. Farrendel has been on my case for years to clean this place up. So when I purchased the warehouse next door, he was more than eager to help organize everything once it was moved there for storage."

"You bought the warehouse next door?" And he had not mentioned it to her in his letters? It seemed like a large thing not to mention, especially since he was this excited about it.

Lance nodded, then motioned to her as he started for a set of doors built into the left wall that she had never seen before. Though, that did not mean anything since they could have been hidden behind stacks of stuff. "Yes. Now that Farrendel has joined my business as a silent partner, we desperately need more space for experiments. And it will be much easier to integrate the magical power cells into inventions and test the effectiveness with a large space to conduct experiments."

When they reached the doors, Lance flung them open. Sunlight poured in, and they stepped into what had once been the alley between the two warehouses. Now, both ends of the alley had been walled off with locked gates. A ceiling made of metal and glass panels—much like the skylights in the roof of the Aldon Market—arched overhead, providing shelter from the rain.

On one side of the alley, a black metal table with two chairs sat in a sheltered nook surrounded by potted plants.

Lance gestured to the quaint setup. "I know it isn't as green and growing as you're used to in Tarenhiel, but I thought this might be a pleasant place to eat lunches when you come for a visit."

"If I can pry you away from your work long enough for lunch." Illyna slid onto one of the chairs and gazed up at the skylight. It was a lovely space away from the prying eyes of the city. Illyna could picture herself and Lance sitting here as the rain drummed on the glass and ran down in rivulets.

If she could get him to sit down and eat. She had eaten many a lunch with Lance distracted by some invention running around in his head.

"True." Lance shifted. His hand strayed to his pocket, something in his expression turning white and tense.

"Is something wrong?" Illyna half-turned in the chair. It was odd, how quickly he had gone from excited to this strange nervousness she had only seen from him those first few days of their courtship when they did not know each other well.

"I..." Lance cleared his throat and pulled something out of his pocket. He knelt on one knee before her and presented something glittering and shiny to her. A silver ring with diamonds and emeralds embedded into the band. "I know a ring is a human custom and you might not want to wear it. But I wanted to get you one and..."

He swallowed again, and his brown eyes lifted to meet her gaze.

Something in his expression made her heart beat faster, even as her mind was spinning. This was a human custom she should recognize. Had Essie or Farrendel told her about it at one point?

Lance's eyes softened. "Illyna, will you marry me?"

"What?" Illyna stared at him, then the ring.

She had known this was coming, but still. This moment was here, and it was big, and the moment she said yes, her life would change.

But she was going to say yes. Over the past year, the human inventor kneeling before her had become precious to her.

"Is that a yes?" Lance started to lower the ring, his voice hesitant.

"Yes!" Illyna wrapped her arms around his neck and hugged him. Somehow, the hug turned into a kiss, and Illyna found herself sagging against him, his hands gentle against her cheek and in her hair.

When they finally broke apart, Lance hesitated, then slid the ring onto a finger of her right hand. It winked there, a band of silver and emeralds that reminded her of her home in Tarenhiel.

A home she would be giving up to move here to marry Lance. She had known that. While Lance enjoyed his visits to Tarenhiel, he was a man of mechanics and machines. He did not fit in the quiet, serene life of Estyra.

Besides, most of Illyna's customers were humans here in Estyra. While it would be difficult figuring out a place to grow the plants she would need, she would save a great deal on shipping costs and trade tariffs if she relocated here.

There was much she would miss about Estyra. She

would miss her friends there and the community. She would miss all the trees and the quiet.

But she would have Lance, and they could still visit Estyra when they had a chance. She would at least have Essie and Farrendel, whenever they were in Escarland, so she would not be entirely friendless here.

Lance just held her hand for another moment, grinning from ear to ear in an expression she had only ever seen on him after a breakthrough in his latest invention.

Then, he sprang to his feet and tugged on her hand. "Now that you've said yes, I have something else to show you."

Illyna laughed and let him tug her toward the set of double doors into the second warehouse on the other side of the alley. This was why life with Lance would be worth it. Instead of the quiet, staid life in Estyra, every day with Lance would be filled with twists and turns, surprises and adventure.

When Lance opened one of the doors and they stepped inside, Illyna found herself in a vast space filled with racks upon racks of mechanical parts and gears. She did not know enough about mechanics to know what it all was, but it seemed to be organized rather systematically. It was far better than the jumble of before.

A clanging came from around the nearest set of shelves before a tall, gray-skinned young troll strode into sight. He was lanky, not yet come into the bulk of adulthood.

Lance gestured to the troll. "Illyna, this is Voron. He's working for me and Farrendel to save up to study magical engineering at Hanford University. He's been a great help with the move and organizing. Voron, this is Illyna. My fiancée."

Voron grinned, first at Lance, then at Illyna. "I'm so

glad you said yes. Mr. Marion has been telling Farrendel and me all about his plans for the past month. After all the work we—" He cut off, his gaze focused on Lance.

When Illyna glanced at Lance, he was still gesturing wildly, mouthing something to Voron. At her glance, he straightened and snapped his mouth shut.

"Oh, right. That's still a surprise." Voron waved to Illyna. "I hope you like it."

"I am sure I will." Illyna grinned back at Voron. He was a nice young troll, and he seemed to fit right in with Lance. "It has been a pleasure to meet you. Thank you for all your help organizing this mess. It looks lovely, and Lance certainly needed the help."

Voron just grinned before he hefted the stack of gears he was carrying. "I should get back to work. Enjoy your surprise."

With that, Voron hurried off down another aisle.

"Now I understand how you managed to clean up so much in the past three months since I saw this place last."

"Voron has been invaluable. I don't know what we'd do without him. He works harder than anyone I know." Lance shrugged, then tugged on her hand again, heading to their right.

Ahead, a metal, cage-like lift tucked against the wall, headed for a dark, upper space that must lead to the roof. Beside the lift, the entire corner of the brick warehouse had been walled off with wood, carvings of elven design tracing over the wooden boards and the arched doorway into the space.

Lance gestured. "Um, well, this is for you. I would have put it in the other warehouse, but that warehouse will have a lot of noise and machinery and the occasional explosion. I thought you might appreciate someplace quieter."

Illyna squeezed his hand as she took in the walled corner before her.

He had built her a new place to continue to make her shampoo and conditioner. Even before knowing if she would say yes.

This gesture was not like the prosthetic hand he had invented for her when they first met. This time, he knew her. He had listened. He had known, through their chats on where to live once they married, that she would miss her home in Estyra even though she was willing to give it up.

Her throat too choked to say anything, she let go of his hand and stepped forward, running her fingers over the carvings on the door before she pushed it open.

Inside, high windows set into the brick and skylights in the roof beamed sunlight into the space, making it far brighter than the dingy, dark interior of the rest of the warehouse. Wooden countertops ran along two walls, providing plenty of workspace, while the other two walls held cupboards and shelves for far more storage than she had back in Estyra. A large, wooden table provided even more workspace, should she need it.

She could hardly take it in. Her heart had been aching at the thought of packing up her shop in Estyra. And, yes, that ache still remained.

But a new thrill also filled her at the anticipation of filling these shelves and working here instead. Spending quiet mornings working here, meeting Lance in the sunlit alley for lunch where they could talk about their progress. Walking with him in the evenings back to *their* home.

As Lance entered behind her, Illyna circled the space, running her fingers over the countertops and cupboards. So much space. So much thoughtfulness to build it out of

TARA GRAYCE

wood instead of metal. So much of Lance's personality in the way it was laid out.

At the corner of one countertop where it met the wall of cupboards, a strange device sat on the countertop. Four metal brackets stood upright, set within grooves carved into the wooden countertop and with a piece of leather on the inside of each of them. Below the countertop, the space was open instead of filled with cupboards, while another strange device sat on the floor.

"What is this?" Illyna gestured at it. She was not sure what to make of it.

"It's a bowl clamp." After stepping to her side, Lance opened the cupboard next to her and pulled out a stainless steel bowl. He set in on the counter in the center of the four metal pieces. "You set a bowl here. It fits everything from three inches in diameter to twenty inches. Then you press on the foot pedal down here until it clicks, and the hydraulics clamp the bowl in place."

He stepped on the device on the floor, and the four metal pieces moved along the grooves, pressing tight around the bowl he had set there.

"When you're done, you step on this other lever here, and it will release." Lance stepped on another part of the device beneath the countertop. With a click, the clamp released, and the metal brackets eased back along their grooves.

Illyna blinked, a heat prickling at the corners of her eyes. This time, instead of trying to fix her, he had fixed the space around her. With this device, her bowls would remain steady, leaving her hand free for stirring and adding ingredients.

"Do...do you like it?" Lance shifted, turning to her with that vulnerable look once again.

Illyna could not find the words to express everything

542

filling her chest. Instead, she flung her arms around his neck and buried her face against his shoulder, holding tight.

Lance staggered back a step before he steadied himself against the countertop. His voice held a hint of a husky laugh as he wrapped his arms around her in return. "I got more reaction out of this than I did proposing."

The ring was pretty and sparkling, but this invention meant far more. Lance showed his heart through inventions like this to help those he cared about.

"Linshi," Illyna mumbled against his shirt. After another moment, she straightened, swiping at her eyes before the tears could leak out. "Linshi. This is just all...so much."

Lance took her hand, rubbing his thumb over her new ring in a way that made it spin on her finger. He held her gaze, his brown eyes warm. "When we talked, I know you said you would be all right with moving here. But I want you to not just live here but feel at home. I will do everything I can to provide that home for you. Because I love you."

And there was that squeezing emotion in her chest again. All she could murmur was, "I love you too."

Lance grinned, and he adjusted his grip on her hand. "Come on. I have one more thing to show you."

"More?" Illyna stumbled after Lance, still in too much shock to fully process everything.

He led her back out of her new workshop and to the lift. While she braced herself against the brass lattice-work of the lift's cage, he turned the center crank. The lift raised from the floor and ascended upward until they reached a small space surrounded by brick walls with only a single door in front of them.

Securing the lift in place, Lance opened the door. Sunlight flooded inside.

Blinking against the brightness, Illyna stepped into the late morning sunlight. Instead of the hard brick or wood that she had been expecting for the roof, her foot sank a little on something softer.

Dirt.

As her eyes adjusted, she found herself standing on a rooftop covered in earth and loam. To her right, the glass roof of her workshop sparkled in the sunlight while another glass structure stood on the roof beyond it.

While they were still surrounded by the buildings of Aldon, they were level with the roofs of the surrounding ones and only a few buildings near the city center stood taller. The air still tasted of smoke and the general dirty city smell, but the breeze wafting this high up, not blocked by other buildings, kept the air far more fresh than down in the streets and alleys below.

"I've heard of how the ogres in the south grow plants on the roofs of their homes, and I thought it might be possible to do something similar here." Lance gestured at the roof around them. "It took a team of troll engineers to reinforce the building enough to hold the added weight as well as ensure the roof would remain watertight. But this should provide you with plenty of space to grow the plants you need. Assuming they will grow here in Aldon. And there's a greenhouse over there so that you can have fresh plants all year. We can build more greenhouses, if you'd like. I wasn't sure how much space you would need."

He had done so much to prepare this place to be her home. It was so overwhelming that for a moment all she could do was stand there, trying to absorb it.

This would be home. For the first time, she could truly

feel it—taste it—in a way she had not been able to when she and Lance had talked about the possibility of her moving to Aldon.

She could be happy here. Not just happy but thriving.

It turned out that her home was always meant to be here in the bustling capital city of the human kingdom of Escarland with her adorable, absentminded inventor.

FREE BOOK!

Thanks so much for reading *Heart Bond*! I hope you enjoyed reading what is essentially an extended, extraneous epilogue to the Elven Alliance series. I had so much fun exploring the romances for several side characters! If you loved the book, please consider leaving a review. Reviews help your fellow readers find books that they will love.

A downloadable map and a downloadable list of characters and elvish are available on the Extras page of my website.

If you ever find typos in my books, feel free to message me on social media or send me an email through the Contact Me page of my website.

If you want to learn about all my upcoming releases, get great book recommendations, and see a behind-the-scenes glimpse into the writing process, follow my blog at www.taragrayce.com.

Did you know that if you sign up for my newsletter, you'll receive lots of free goodies? You will receive the free novella *Steal a Swordmaiden's Heart*, which is set in the same world as *Stolen Midsummer Bride* and *Bluebeard and the Outlaw*! This novella is a prequel to *Stolen Midsummer Bride*, and tells the story of how King Theseus of the Court of Knowledge won the hand of Hippolyta, Queen of the Swordmaidens.

You will also receive the free novellas *The Wild Fae Primrose* (prequel to *Forest of Scarlet*) and *Torn Curtains*, a fantasy Regency Beauty and the Beast retelling.

Sign up for my newsletter now

DON'T MISS THE NEXT ADVENTURE

ELF KING

This is the story of the elf kings of Tarenhiel.

Iron Heart
It all started with an arranged marriage.

When Ellarin, heir to the King of Tarenhiel, finds out that he is dying, his father forces him into an arranged marriage with Lady Leyleira. Will the pressure of the king and the court draw them closer or pull them apart? Will they fall in love before it is too late?

Elf King
This elf king was not always so grumpy.

When Prince Weylind of the elves falls in love with a simple healer's daughter, life seems peaceful and perfect. But a troll attack and an unexpected younger brother change everything, placing more and more burdens on Weylind's shoulders. Will Weylind find his way back to the person he used to be? Or will he be too late to fix the damage to his own family?

Follow four generations of kings as they shape Tarenhiel into the kingdom it is during the *Elven Alliance* series.

Releasing June 2! Preorder Now.

IN THE MOOD FOR FAE FANTASY ROMANCE?

FOREST OF SCARLET

The fae snatch humans as playthings to torment. The Primrose steals them back.

Vowing that no other family would endure the same fear and pain she felt when her older sister was snatched by the fae, Brigid puts on an empty-headed façade while she rescues humans in the shadowy guise of the Primrose, hero to humans, bane to the fae. Her only regret is that she can't tell the truth to Munch, the young man in the human realm who she's trying very hard not to fall in love with.

Munch has a horrible nickname, an even more terrible full name, and the shadow of his heroic sister and five older brothers to overcome. It's rough being the little brother of the notorious Robin Hood and her merry band. The highlights of his life are the brief visits by Brigid, the messenger girl for the dashing fae hero the Primrose.

When an entire village of humans is snatched by the fae in a single night, Munch jumps at the chance to go to the Fae Realm, pass a message to Brigid and through her to the Primrose, and finally get his chance to be a hero just like all his older siblings.

But the Fae Realm is a dangerous place, especially for

a human unbound to a fae or court like Munch. One wrong decision could spell disaster for Munch, Brigid, and the Primrose.

Will this stolen bride's sister and Robin Hood's brother reveal the truth of their hearts before the Fae Realm snatches hope away from them forever?

Loosely inspired by *The Scarlet Pimpernel*, *Forest of Scarlet* is book one in a new fantasy romance / fantasy romantic comedy series of standalones featuring magic libraries, a whimsical and deadly fae realm, and crazy fae hijinks by bestselling author Tara Grayce!

Find the Book on Amazon Today!

ACKNOWLEDGMENTS

Thank you to everyone who makes these books possible! Thank you to my dad and mom for always encouraging me to pursue my dream of writing. For my brothers Ethan, Josh, and Andy for being even more amazing than Essie's fictional brothers. To Alyssa, Abby, and Meghan for proving that sisters-in-law make the best sisters. To my nephews for being the inspiration for Bertie and Finn. To my nieces, who I hope don't mind that I stole their names once they are old enough to read these books. To my friends Jill, Paula, and Bri for celebrating every writing milestone with me! To my writer friends, especially Molly, Morgan, Addy (with a special thanks to Addy for asking to see the dares play out in the Family Vacation short story), Savannah, and Sierra for all your fangirling and encouragement and support. To Deborah, for all your patience with me sending this book to you at the last minute, and to Mindy for pushing through a busy time of the year to find the time to proofread this book! And a very special thanks to Kim, disability-visability-cheerleader, who stepped up to read over the novella *Inventor* to double-check the portrayal of Illyna's limb difference.

Thanks once again to all of you, the readers, who pick up these books and have stuck with this series as it has continued to grow! *Elf King* is going to be the last book! For sure this time!

ALSO BY TARA GRAYCE

ELVEN ALLIANCE

Fierce Heart

War Bound

Death Wind

Troll Queen

Pretense

Shield Band

Elf Prince

Heart Bond

Elf King

Peril: Elven Alliance Collected Stories Volume One

Inventor: Elven Alliance Collected Stories Volume Two

COURT OF MIDSUMMER MAYHEM

Stolen Midsummer Bride (Prequel)

Forest of Scarlet

Night of Secrets

A VILLAIN'S EVER AFTER

Bluebeard and the Outlaw

PRINCESS BY NIGHT

Lost in Averell

Printed in the USA
CPSIA information can be obtained
at www.ICGtesting.com
LVHW051513110923
757848LV00026B/311/J